GALATEA: UNDER SHATTERED STARS

Jorge Sanchez

ISBN 979-8-9917366-0-2

First Edition

Chapter 1

City of Daalamas, Kliinat

Tau Ceti System

June 6, 2681

Maalek sat on the coarse, gritty floor of a ruined warehouse, resting his head against the back wall. He stretched his legs and tapped his left with his finger in time with the distant explosions. The air turned thick with the sharp tang of metal as a pressure wave reached him. It was heralded by a thunderous blast—a dead giveaway of an orbital strike. Around him, his squad wasted no time ripping open their packs and diving into their ration bars. Maalek closed his eyes, willing away the dull, irritating throb from the shrapnel in his right leg. The fragments had been a nuisance for six months now, an unwelcome memento from a fragmentation grenade. And every so often, a careless movement would trigger a sharp twinge.

The wound healed before he could extract it, so there it stayed.

He rubbed the spot with his finger to nudge it to a more comfortable position, then took a drink from his canteen. He poured a cupful of water on his head and ran a hand over his scalp, savoring the relief. His hair had grown long; he would shave when—if—they returned to base. Light streaming through two large holes in the ceiling illuminated dancing dust particles, revealing his squad mates' worn and tired expressions.

Beside him, Andaeer cleaned his battle rifle with the same precision he had once applied to his lectures at Daalamas University. He'd suffered so many wounds they'd stopped keeping count, and he hadn't slowed down. A few steps away, Tyreen scribbled in her journal, enduring Ammaalise's colorful—and unwelcome—commentary. The two young women were more than skilled with thermal knives; they were lethal, moving silently through enemy lines with equal parts grace and ferocity. Maalek couldn't deny the edge these girls— no, these young soldiers—gave his squad, but their presence stirred a growing unease. Year by year, as the resistance ground on, younger faces kept joining their ranks. Watching them, he couldn't help but think of his own daughters—a thought that left a bitter taste in his mouth.

He shut his eyes, savoring a swig from his canteen. The cool spring water soothed his parched throat, a slight relief from the relentless heat and dust. Maalek reflected on how his life had changed, how something once so ordinary had become such a precious resource. Those easy comforts from his old life felt like a distant dream now—nothing like the constant scramble to keep his crew in the trenches for another day of fighting.

Maalek handed his canteen to Andaeer, who coaxed the last drops from his own with a grimace. "Did I not tell you to fill up in the spring?" he asked.

Andaeer took a quick drink and winced. "I did. But eating these rations is like trying to swallow the desert."

Another explosion shook bullet-scarred walls that already looked ready to crumble at the mere whisper of a breeze. Maalek questioned their choice of a resting spot—if the mountain pass hadn't held them up, he might have searched for something better. He shrugged off the thought and took a hearty bite of his dry ration bar.

What could the humans be bombarding now? He wondered.

They controlled every major city in the region—and the ones they didn't, they had bombed to rubble. If someone had told him two years earlier that alien abductions and sightings of strange flying objects were real, he would have laughed and reported them to the authorities. If they'd also told him that those same aliens, the humans from the Earth Union, would invade his planet, he might have locked them up himself.

Maalek rolled his shoulders, stretching out the kinks, and caught the morning light washing over his arms. The usual deep gray of his skin looked faded—probably due to his recent diet with more air than food. He crammed the last of the ration bar into his mouth. Andaeer was right; it had the grainy texture of sand and was just as flavorless. He knew he shouldn't complain—divisions in the dry south resorted to boiling desert weeds to stave off hunger. That might be his fate soon if their insurgency campaign continued to face setbacks. He pushed the thought aside and focused on the here and now. They needed to stay mobile to avoid roving patrols, and they'd spent too much time at the warehouse for his liking. Maalek checked his rifle and reloaded the magazine with armor-piercing slugs. The auxiliary magazine still had two explosive rounds left. That would have to do.

The walls shook under another explosion, this time closer. A pressure wave rolled through, carrying the sharp scent of burnt vegetation. Maalek recognized the telltale signs of a recent orbital strike. Wisps of acrid smoke drifted through the shattered walls, stinging his eyes and throat.

Andaeer stood and picked up his rifle. He sniffed the air and locked eyes with Maalek.

"I am not sure if you noticed, but something is burning," he said, his lips twisting into a wry smile.

"Your ability to state the obvious remains unparalleled," Maalek said, the corner of his mouth twitching up. His expression sobered as he motioned to a ladder on the far wall. "Head to the roof and scout ahead. Maybe it's nothing of concern. Maybe it is."

A distant mechanical growl snagged Maalek's attention. He thought it must be one of the Union drop-ships patrolling the area. That was the last thing they needed. It had been months since he used their last surface-to-air portable missile. Maybe they could try throwing rocks at it.

Maalek sighed—wishful thinking wouldn't keep them alive, but four hours of hard marching might. Their temporary shelter lay on the outskirts of Daalamas, a gritty trek on foot to the nearest Union garrison. Best to move before that drop-ship got any closer.

He slung his rifle across his back with practiced ease and tightened the straps to keep it snug. His pack followed, swung over his shoulder with a thud. A swift snap ensured his thermal knife was secured at his side, ready to slice through the cold or an enemy. He bent to pick up his canteen when the whistle of a bullet sang close—too close—behind him. Reflexes honed by countless near misses sent him crashing to the dirt.

Andaeer made a hasty descent from the ladder. "Maalek," he said, gasping and hitting the ground running, "a Union squad is taking positions around the building. You will not believe this, but explosions are lighting up the sky." He stared at Maalek, who still lay prone on the floor, then spotted the fresh bullet hole in the wall. "The Goddess surely blessed you. That bullet had your name on it."

Maalek stood up and dusted himself. "The day is not over yet; we will see how blessed we are. We make our stand here."

Andaeer was already moving, diving for the nearest window as the first echoes of gunfire tore through the walls. Maalek gave his rifle a quick once-over, then joined Andaeer at the building's edge. The sounds of battle grew as Maalek's squad opened up with their own rifles. Bullet impacts tore up pieces of concrete, covering the fighters in dust and grime.

A sudden, choked cry cut through the discordant sounds of battle, pulling Maalek's attention to the side. He saw Tyreen lying on the floor, clutching her abdomen as violet blood seeped through her fingers. Her eyes met his in a fleeting look of pain and resignation before rolling back, her body going still.

Ammaalise dropped next to her, hands trembling as they reached out, then pulled back. "Tyreen, no," she said. Her words strained against the continuous roar around them. She turned to Maalek, her eyes brimming with tears that had no place in the dry dust of the battlefield. "She is gone."

Ammaalise said nothing else as she picked up her rifle, but Maalek noticed the quiver in her lips. The girls had been as sisters.

Maalek's chest tightened as memories flashed through his mind—Tyreen's laughter echoing in their makeshift camp, her fierce determination in battle, the way she'd lift their spirits even in the darkest moments. Now, her absence left a void that seemed to swallow the air around them. Another bright flame extinguished, another name to be whispered in remembrance when this was all over.

"We will see her again, Lissee, but not today," he said.

Ammaalise nodded, wiping her face with a dusty sleeve before resuming her position by the window. She peered out, shoulders squared and jaw set firm, rifle in hand. At that moment, the war delivered two wounds: one mortal, one that might as well be. Her determined silhouette against the backdrop of loss spoke louder than words.

Maalek would mourn Tyreen later, but they still had a battle to fight. He rolled out of cover and fired. His shot struck a soldier square in the chest, but the bullet skidded off the heavy armor. He ducked as return fire blasted the surrounding walls. A bead of sweat trickled down his forehead. Curse these humans. Not only had they taken over his planet, but they were excellent soldiers, too.

Kliinat's military fought against the invaders for three brutal months before being reduced to isolated pockets of resistance.

Now, half of Kliinat lived under occupation, but surrender was a word that died in the throats of many Klii. They couldn't match Union warships or their advanced technology, but for two long years, his people gave them a fight anyway.

A week ago, Maalek attended a briefing where he pored over the latest intelligence on the standoff at Neskfaat—an island fortress in the Sea of Tranquility. Its citizens, a warrior caste born and bred, had held off the invaders with their formidable anti-air defenses and a heavy dose of stubbornness. But now, reports spoke of a gathering storm—a significant force amassing for a frontal assault. The term "bloodbath" hung unspoken.

In the waning days of the invasion, what remained of the Klii Armed Forces formed a resistance in Mount Tendra on the icy northern mountains. The rough terrain and frigid weather slowed the Union advance. Maalek's heart sank when the briefing officer revealed that an orbital strike had turned that last bastion into rubble and ash.

"Maalek, a squad of their light mechs dropped in. They are covering the exits," Ammaalise said as she took cover to reload.

"We chose a great resting spot, Maalek," Andaeer said, each word punctuated by the kickback from his rifle.

"I recall asking for your counsel and receiving none, old friend. I think we stumbled upon one of their search-and-destroy teams," Maalek said.

Andaeer harrumphed.

Maalek ran a hand slick with sweat down the leg of his trousers, casting a glance Andaeer's way. "Remember, their armor is weak at the neck joints." Despite his outward calm, a knot formed in his stomach as he noted the overwhelming number of Union soldiers. The air thickened with the acrid tang of smoke and the fine, omnipresent dust of inevitability. He coughed to relieve the grittiness that had settled in his throat, then aimed his rifle. The weapon kicked back against his shoulder with each pull of the trigger.

A soldier fell—Maalek's round had gone straight through his visor.

Andaeer pinned a squad inside a metal shack on their left flank, but Maalek's ears caught the telltale dip in fire from Ammaalise's direction.

"Lissee," he asked, not daring to divert his gaze from the iron sights. "Are you injured?" He squeezed the dual trigger, and an explosive shell decapitated one mech in a fiery spectacle.

Her reply came between gasps. "Only... if you consider... a gunshot wound an... injury," she said.

He looked at her. She remained determined, rifle bucking as she fired, even though her right hand was bloody, marred, and missing two fingers. Those fingers would regenerate, given time they didn't have. Her uniform was painted with blood and torn by shrapnel.

A chunk of the wall above the window disintegrated from a high-caliber bullet. Maalek chuckled in that throaty way of the Klii. Today, he'd cross the Great Sea to join his family.

"Maalek, I have one round left," Andaeer said.

"Then make it count."

Andaeer's bullet hit the shoulder joint of a soldier trying to flank them. Two shots later, Maalek's rifle clicked empty, and he hurled the useless weapon to the ground with a curse. His fingers found comfort in the handle of his trusty blade, accepting—welcoming—the inevitable. He'd been wrong to tell Ammaalise they wouldn't see Tyreen today. Though he'd fight with his last reserve of strength, he hoped the end came quickly for Andaeer and Ammaalise; they deserved a soldier's death. A prickle of dread crawled down his spine, but he shoved it aside as strange sounds from above caught his attention.

Unfamiliar silhouettes streaked across the sky through a gaping hole in the shattered roof. Maalek furrowed his brow in confusion—these weren't Klii planes or Union transports. With a deafening roar, the ships unleashed hellfire.

What in the Goddess? Why did they open fire? More aircraft followed, flying in pairs. Their rockets slammed into Union positions, turning the battle with overwhelming firepower.

Maalek went from perplexed to stunned—the Klii military had no planes left, and he'd never seen their like. He walked outside. Stepping over smoldering debris, he glanced skyward at the sight of a second wave of ships soaring toward the garrison in Daalamas.

The acrid stench of burnt explosives and melted circuitry assaulted his nostrils, making his eyes water. Maalek's body buzzed with adrenaline as he surveyed the aftermath, a ghostly glow cast by flames and smoke. Not a soldier survived, and only the flaming wreckage of their drop-ships remained.

Two ships hovered nearby—machines of war, no doubt. Unlike the sleek, smooth Union drop-ships, these looked angular and angry, like birds of prey on the hunt. Scorch marks marred the dull green paint, drawing his gaze to dents in the fuselage. Maalek could tell where it had received quick repairs. He guessed it must have seen many battles, ferried warriors to many more.

One settled onto the street with a soft hiss. The ramp unfolded the moment its skids touched the ground. Maalek took a tentative step forward, a gray, four-fingered hand outstretched in the Klii sign of peace. He gasped.

Ten human soldiers dashed out, setting up a tight perimeter in moments. Dust clouds billowed under their boots as they took strategic positions with military precision. More soldiers poured from the second ship, fanning to cover the flanks. Their movements were purposeful and coordinated. From hidden compartments in the ships, half a dozen drones buzzed into the air. The tense atmosphere filled with the mechanical whir of their propellers.

Andaeer and Ammaalise joined Maalek, wearing cautious expressions. Andaeer narrowed his eyes, studying the scene before him with a thoughtful gaze.

"And what is this now?" Andaeer asked, scrutinizing the advancing soldiers with a raised brow and skeptical head tilt.

The soldiers moved forward, weapons ready, scanning for trouble. Their rifles weren't pointed at him. Yet. Not that they needed to—their war beasts swung lethal guns back and forth while drones hovered overhead, ready to rain fire from the sky.

One man removed his battle-scarred helmet, wearing armor was weathered as the ship behind him. He spoke in the invaders' tongue, piquing Maalek's curiosity. Despite earnest attempts, his words remained incomprehensible.

"What do you think he is saying, Andaeer?" Maalek asked.

"I do not know. His words are foreign, and his intent is unclear," Andaeer said, his eyes never leaving the slowly approaching soldiers.

The man's effort to bridge the language gap was apparent, but Maalek couldn't make sense of the words.

"Do you have your blades?" Maalek asked his companions.

"Always," Andaeer said, his hand resting on the hilt of his weapon.

"It never leaves my side," Ammaalise said, tightening her grip on her blade while her eyes scanned the horizon.

Maalek's gaze locked onto the man, taking in every detail of his posture and body language. "His actions speak of peace, or at least truce," he said to Andaeer and Ammaalise. "They are avoiding direct threats and staying aware of their surroundings. This man must be their leader."

Tension radiated from his companions—after years of conflict, their distrust was inevitable. Yet Maalek saw an opportunity—a desperate gamble that might shift the tide in their favor.

"Andaeer, let us see if they understand us." Maalek turned to face the human, standing tall with his shoulders squared, ensuring his voice carried clearly over the ambient noise. "I am Maalek, Fourth Scouts, Third Mountain Division of the Free Army of Kliinat."

The man stared back at him with a puzzled expression. He talked with his soldiers for a while, then touched his index finger to his ear, engaging in a hushed conversation that Maalek couldn't hear. A few nods, a furrowed brow, and after a tense couple of minutes, he spoke again, his words now clear.

"My name is Carson. Your ally. We will help you fight the Union. Free Kliinat," he said.

The pronunciation sounded rough, but it sparked an ember of hope. All Maalek had wanted since the war started was a fighting chance, a way to strike back at their aggressor, and now he had it. The Goddess had indeed blessed him. The soldiers raised their rifles as Maalek stepped forward, but the man in charge motioned for them to lower their weapons. Another encouraging sign.

"What fresh hell is this?" Andaeer said, his jaw tight as his narrowed eyes swept the scene.

Maalek's lips pulled into a slow, confident grin. His chest tightened, not with dread, but with something unfamiliar: the stirring of hope. "No, Andaeer," he murmured, the words slipping out as if the realization hit him. "This... this is how we take   back   our   planet."

Chapter 2

Launch Bay, CCV Galatea

In Transit to Tau Ceti

June 6, 2681

Lieutenant Matt 'Skip' Carson settled into his seat aboard the Griffin, the Colonial Navy's reliable workhorse for ground attack and troop transport. Carson's stomach lurched as the shuttle rotated within the launch tube that would catapult him and his team into battle. Vibrations from the deck buzzed up his boots, sending a tingle up his spine. This wasn't a garden-variety drop from orbit, and it made him restless. He hoped his brittle smile wouldn't betray the tension behind it. Any moment now, the fleet would storm into the Tau Ceti system, guns hot, set to break the Union's iron grip suffocating the locals. His home ship, the Colonial Strike Carrier CCV Galatea, flagship of the Fourth Fleet, would lead the charge with full might—fangs bared and claws unsheathed.

As soon as they jumped into the system, Galatea—Gally to her crew—would launch the Griffins into Tau Ceti E, or Kliinat, and hurl every one of her Dauntless fighters at the unsuspecting fleet. The two other Strike Carriers would engage planetary defenses and orbital stations. It was a bold strategy, banking on the element of surprise to overcome the system's formidable defenses. And formidable they were—the Union Navy had poured resources into fortifying the system and boasted the best anti-ship missiles and mass driver coil guns in the galaxy. He did not want to face down the barrel of a Union coil gun again—at least, not after last time.

Frankie Rodriguez, the squad's top sharpshooter and demolitions expert, sat across from him. "Rodriguez, how about a few rounds in the gym after this milk run? I'll go easy on you," Carson said.

"You looking for a punching bag, ell-tee?" Rodriguez said.

"That one time was an accident, you know that. Sometimes I forget my own strength."

Rodriguez snorted, clearly unconvinced. Carson couldn't blame his skepticism. What he'd called an accident had actually been a lucky hit. Rodriguez had slipped on a wet spot, and Carson landed a haymaker at the base of his neural implant, making it glitch and reboot every few minutes. That had caused quite a stir with the muckety-mucks at Navy HQ in Athens, leading to a system-wide firmware update.

Williams snickered. "Ha, a stiff breeze could've knocked his sorry ass down, ell-tee."

Carson assumed she said it in jest; Rodriguez stood a

towering six-foot-five and packed 250 pounds of muscle. In Marine combat armor, he looked like a hover tank.

Carson glanced at Lizzy Williams, the platoon's newest member. She carried herself like a seasoned veteran, and her squad mates had taken an instant liking to her. Williams wore her easy grin and sharp wit like armor, belying her prowess as a Marine who painted death with a scoped M45 battle rifle like an artist with a brush and canvas. Carson imagined what her close-cropped strawberry blond hair would look like if she let it grow, letting his mind wander down a road best left untraveled. Dangerous territory, that.

Carson fiddled with his harness again as the straps bit into his armor and dug into his shoulders. He had dozens of combat drops under his belt, but they never got easier. He expected he'd log dozens more as the front lines shifted. The Colonial Navy had just kicked the Union out of Teegarden when the Quick Reaction Fleet shattered their blockade around the Antares mining colonies in a daring strike.

But their victory was short-lived—the Third Fleet's attempt to establish a beachhead in Proxima Centauri ended in crushing defeat. They limped to Athens after tangling with the Union's Combined Fleet and a Task Force of Dreadnoughts that had jumped in hours before the battle, to the surprise of pretty much everyone. A classic stalemate that neither side managed to break. But maybe today, things will change.

Carson's own platoon showed the wear and tear of continuous combat, and the shuttles had taken a beating. Carson forced himself to relax. He was overreacting to the usual pre-drop jitters. Yeah, that was it. An old wound, courtesy of a 5 mm round that had carved a too-intimate path along his leg, throbbed in protest. Carson's fingers found their way to the spot again, dancing around the edge where his armor rubbed against it.

Gunny Reisman's voice crackled on his private channel: "They'll be fine, Sir. The platoon's ready. And stop poking at it," she said. "You're going to make it worse."

Carson couldn't help but smile. To say he was lucky to have Gunnery Sergeant Evangeline Reisman on his platoon would be akin to saying that the ocean was somewhat wet. You couldn't find a better Marine in either the Union or Colonial Navy. An Arcturian Imperial Nightguard might give her a challenge, maybe. She was the living, breathing, occasionally swearing embodiment of what it meant to be a veteran of the Corps: battle-hardened, tough as hull plating, and ready to lead a charge into the trenches—or into a bar.

The shuttle's ambiance shifted as the lights flickered to a deep amber, casting soft, shifting shadows in the cramped space. Carson squared his shoulders. He spoke into the platoon-wide channel.

"Second Platoon, gear up. It's time to punch the Union in the face. Call it in."

His Marines hustled, checking their armor integrity, weapon systems, and the charge in their backup batteries. The squads, spread in two shuttles, signaled the go-ahead—green across the board. Funny, he didn't feel antsy anymore.

The lights danced to red for an incoming fleet-wide announcement over the One Main Circuit, or 1MC—the ship-wide channel.

"Fourth Fleet, this is Captain Mori of Galatea—I'm going to

keep this short. We're jumping into battle in sixty with our guns locked and loaded. The people of Tau Ceti E have been fighting to wrench the Union's boot off their necks, and that makes them our brethren. Their struggle is our struggle. Their fight is our fight. We're about to lend them our fists and kick the Union's ass all the way back to Earth. Oorah."

Cheers and oorahs erupted around him. Captain Mori's rapid rise to command a Strike Carrier was no fluke—she stood out as one of the brightest officers in the fleet. According to scuttlebutt, she'd be the next Admiral by year's end. Her mauling of the UNSS Illustrious carrier group with her aging cruiser and two escort destroyers became the stuff of legend at the academy. Carson and Mori attended the Naval Academy together, and he'd carried a torch for her ever since.

Carson briefly wondered if she'd throw him out an airlock if he asked her out for coffee. It might be worth a shot, he mused.

The 1MC snapped back to life with a message from Galatea's executive officer: "General Quarters, General Quarters. All hands to battle stations. Jump in three, two, one. Jump."

The moment the jump kicked in, a familiar blend of déjà vu and vertigo flipped Carson's stomach. Sailors called it the FTL jitters, and they always made him queasy. He'd never get used to slicing through a hole in the fabric of space-time created by a technology powered by tritium—the same chemical that made his watch glow in the dark. FTL jumps could last anywhere from a mere blink to a drawn-out eternity. This jump stretched twenty seconds, each filled with reality-bending queasiness. His stomach settled, and after an agonizing five-minute wait where his squad went over their ammo load-out and mission brief again to keep the nerves at bay, the shuttle gave a telltale shudder.

The deck vibrated with deep, ominous thrums. Carson braced himself. The Griffins were on the move. Oorah.

Then came the unmistakable voice of Flight Lieutenant Tammy "Missy" Jones, their shuttle's pilot, ringing clear in Carson's neural. She'd worked as a pilot for a heavy freighter in Delphi before the war and still flew like it. "Thank you for flying with Missy Air Services. If you glance out the starboard window—well, you'll see the starboard window. Wake up, Jarheads, we're up next. I peeked at Galatea's feed, and let's just say, you better find something sturdy to cling to. Strap on tight and enjoy the ride, tally-ho!"

As amplified music filled the shuttle, Jones' usual mix of 20th-century Earth's rock, Carson found himself nodding to the beat. He hoped they wouldn't explode in space, only into it.

Carson braced as the shuttle burst out of the launch tube. The sensation of weightlessness, followed by the gut-wrenching acceleration, left his stomach in knots. He linked into BattleNet, figuring he might as well do something useful before his brains scrambled inside his helmet.

Carson saw the entire wing of Griffins lighting up the grid while Galatea rained destruction on the nearest battleships. She took some licks herself but shrugged them off like a brawler. Colonial Strike Carriers took as much punishment as they dished out, and they dished out a hell of a lot.

Orbital defense platforms came to life and knocked out two Griffins. Carson cursed. In space, the Griffins were balloons in a needle factory, lacking any real countermeasures until they hit the atmosphere and could start dodging death with a bit more grace. Then, a destroyer shifted its attention from the battle and tagged another Griffin with a Taipan missile. Ten more Marines, plus three flight crew, would have their names added to the ever-growing monument at the Navy Memorial in Persephone.

CCV Artemis and her strike group jumped into the system and hammered two orbital stations in an unrelenting assault. The battle started well, with the Strike Carriers catching the Union fleet with their breeches down. It was a refreshing change of pace not to be on the receiving end of an ass-kicking.

The Colonial Navy couldn't bring as much iron to bear in battle as Union fleets, but the winds were shifting, and the Strike Carriers had tilted the playing field. If this battle signaled things to come, he'd be home with his sister Gianna in time for Christmas. He could almost see himself sitting at the kitchen table with a slice of her famous sour cream and raisin pie.

The shuttle rattled and sang an eerie tune of strained Tritanium when they entered the atmosphere. Carson had once described the experience of an orbital drop on a Griffin as being stuck in a cosmic blender. This drop put all others to shame. If not for the inertial compensators in their armor, they'd need to be scraped off the bulkheads with a spatula.

After ten wild minutes where the Griffin fought against the turbulence and atmosphere of Kliinat, Lieutenant Jones announced their arrival over the surreal purple grasslands near Daalamas. Carson reviewed his mission parameters: link up with the Third Battalion for a full-scale assault on the Union stronghold in Daalamas, with Colonel Martinez taking the lead; engage targets of opportunity with beneficial mission outcomes; extract and secure critical intelligence and resources.

The chess pieces were moving, and it was time to play.

Carson let a curse slip under his breath as the Griffin took a hard swing to starboard in an evasive maneuver. Concussive blasts from AA batteries rattled the bulkheads—the tight bank probably saved their skins. He opened a channel to Jones.

"Jones, how about a heads-up before any more corkscrews? One of my teeth came loose."

Jones's reply was no-nonsense. "Griffin One-Seven engaged offensive, Lieutenant. Right two, three clicks low. Dropping flares and chaff now. ETA to LZ five mikes."

"Roger." He switched to the platoon channel: "Look alive, Marines. We'll be landing soon. Let's show the Union what the business end of an M45 looks like."

The answer was a chorus of oorahs.

"Lieutenant Carson, this is Jones. Griffin One-Eight relayed a sitrep: they've spotted a skirmish east of our primary LZ. It involves a small unit of local Klii forces engaged with Union soldiers. The Klii are outnumbered. One-Eight is maintaining visual but staying out of engagement range. Your call on how we proceed."

"How many Klii are in the crossfire?" Carson asked.

"Three showing up on scanners. Another Recon platoon is approaching northeast by east."

"Jones, reroute us to the skirmish east of our LZ. Initiate air support to even the odds for those Klii forces. Once we stabilize their situation, find us a safe spot to set down. I want boots on the ground ASAP. We're the cavalry now, tally-ho."

"Roger that, ell-tee."

When they reached the skirmish site, Jones and the second Griffin neutralized the Union squad with their Vulcan Gatling guns. Thanks to a pair of Ballista missiles, the Union Dart shuttles turned into flaming wreckage. Jones reduced speed and touched down. Carson clicked the harness release, and his Marines prepped for contact. They looked good, damn good—the way warriors ought to look. The whirring sound of gears and whine of servos reached Carson when the rear door yawned open. Thirty seconds later, Second Platoon set up a perimeter around their shuttles and the perplexed locals. Carson studied the readout on the virtual screen projected by his neural.

Atmospheric pressure: 0.96 Earth normal.

Air composition: 22% oxygen, 75% nitrogen, 2% water vapor, 1% other.

Twenty-six green dots blinked in the lower left corner of his heads-up display, showing friendlies. Three orange dots that flashed ever closer represented the people he'd come to save.

The inhabitants of Kliinat called themselves Klii. Three of them stood before him, stoic, walking the line between humanoid and something out of a galactic heavyweight gym. Carson might have mistaken them for some off-the-books branch of Marines if he hadn't been briefed otherwise. The leader raised a hand with four fingers—a greeting or a warning, Carson couldn't tell. Hopefully a greeting. The Klii sported a splash of rank on the sleeve of his purple tunic—meaning they were military.

Carson couldn't help but marvel at the vibrant colors and the distant, majestic, snow-capped mountains of Kliinat. If you ignored the rubble from bombed-out structures, the planet looked gorgeous. He popped his helmet off, breathing in air rich with the tang of recent combat and the perfume of Kliinat's flora.

"Whoa, what're you doing, ell-tee? The air could be toxic," Rodriguez said, stepping back and looking around as if the very atmosphere might bite.

Gunny turned to Rodriguez, her brows knitted together. "You numbnuts, didn't you read the brief or the sensors in your visor? I swear you make me—"

"Lieutenant Carson, Echo Company," Carson said, facing the Klii, helmet tucked under one arm.

The three Klii stared at Carson, eyes unblinking. He tried again. The two Klii soldiers only muttered with each other, but their stance—tense and battle-ready—made Carson nervous. His attempt at diplomacy hit a snag when his translator glitched, leaving him grasping at the random crackle and hiss of static.

"Anyone else's translator acting up?" He asked.

A chorus of affirmatives and one hand raise from Muller. "I'm getting nothing but static, sir."

Perfect. Because it was too much to ask for a mission to go as planned for once.

"Gunny, how's your Klii?" Carson asked.

"'Bout as good as my eye-talian, sir. Bon-gior-no."

Rodriguez piped up. "Let me talk to them, ell-tee. I speak a little Spanish."

Before Carson could reply, Gunny's hand made a sharp

acquaintance with Rodriguez's helmet. "Didn't I tell you to be quiet?"

"Lieutenant? I don't like how they're looking at me," Williams said.

Carson raised a hand. "Okay, quiet, all of you. Give me a moment." But Carson was out of moments.

It took him all of two seconds to kick it upstairs. He keyed his neural to Battalion. "Battalion actual, this is Echo Three-Seven."

"Go ahead, Echo Three-Seven." Colonel Patel's voice betrayed no sign of the intense battle he was orchestrating, coordinating the ground assault on Daalamas while under fire himself.

"Colonel, we ran into locals engaged with Union troops and offered assistance. We need help communicating. They don't speak English, and the universal translator is Fubar."

"Call Galatea and have one of their translators sort you out. Next time, check your equipment before a mission, Lieutenant. Battalion actual out." Patel must have been in a good mood, Carson thought. He wasn't known for being this friendly.

Carson called Galatea and, with the help of one of their translators, managed to break the ice. He took his time with each word, paying close attention to the shifts in tonality and even the glottal stops. It worked.

The tallest Klii stepped forward and mumbled something that could've been a greeting or a recipe for Marine stew, hard to tell. The Marines introduced their rifles to the conversation when the Klii took another step forward, but Carson waved them down. After an awkward pause, the Klii cracked what passed for a smile and slapped Carson on the shoulder.

Jorge Sanchez

That could have been smoother as far as first contacts went,
but   he'd   take   it.

Chapter 3

CIC, CCV Galatea

Tau Ceti System

June 6, 2681

Captain Tomoe Mori flicked the tethered microphone off, letting her fingers linger on its cool surface. She could have opened a channel to the fleet through her neural implant, but Naval traditions die hard. Using the microphone made the connection to her crew feel more tangible, more genuine. Though the Admiral often delivered fleet-wide messages, he had passed her the mic with a nod and a knowing smile.

"I hope that wasn't too bad," she said, glancing at Admiral Antonov.

Antonov grinned and gave a thumbs-up. "That was better than anything I could've said. Well done."

Jorge Sanchez

After sharing a smile with the Admiral, Mori handed the mic to her XO, Captain Norman Carrigan. "Your turn, XO. Battle Stations."

"Yes, Captain." Carrigan's response was crisp. As Mori studied him, she took in the rugged map of experiences etched across his face. All those years hadn't stopped Carrigan from turning into a cantankerous old man, though. He wore his bitterness like a shield and was unhappy at being outranked by someone with fewer years and scars. He and Mori had struck a truce, and she considered it a win that she hadn't thrown him in the brig for insubordination—yet. He was a prick, yes, but he was their prick. The man was a hell of an officer who knew how to run a ship, even if his management style involved more cursing than was strictly necessary.

Mori's gaze swept over the Command Information Center, the heart of the bridge. Her crew—her responsibility—surrounded the holographic nerve center of Galatea. The soft glow of the display illuminated their faces, revealing subtle shifts in expression as they readied the ship for battle. They looked alert, prepared.

Mori undid her top button. Each face in the CIC belonged to someone under her command. Someone she was about to take into battle. She took a sip of water. How many would still be there tomorrow?"

Carrigan placed the mic back in its cradle. All eyes turned to Mori as an expectant hush fell over the bridge. The moment had come to take Galatea to war.

Here we go.

Mori leaned forward, her gaze locked on the main display.

She drew a breath, held it for a heartbeat, and began.

"All right, let's light this candle. Astrogator."

"Go."

"Engineering."

"Board is green. Go."

"Tactical."

"Tactical is Go."

"Very well. XO, Galatea is Go for FTL jump."

Mori exchanged a knowing glance with Admiral Antonov, who sat near the helm. She knew he enjoyed being close to the forward viewport and seeing things up close. Of course, calling it a viewport was a stretch. The CIC lay deep inside Galatea, nestled in a triple layer of ablative armor and redundant shield generators. Antonov had his own flag bridge, complete with actual windows. Still, Mori knew it would take a hydraulic wrench to drag him away from the action on her bridge.

This moment was the culmination of years of nightmares and hard training for Mori, ever since she first set foot in the academy. She was ready to dive headfirst into Tau Ceti, weapons hot, missile batteries bucking for action. This was personal—a chance to exact payback for everything she'd suffered at the hands of the Union. Her ship had carved a bloody swath across the frontiers of colonial space, leaving a trail of shattered Union hulls in its wake. Yet for Mori, it wasn't enough. The Union's debt to her ran deep, etched with scars that time couldn't fade. And she wouldn't rest, couldn't rest until the Colonies crushed the Union once and for all—until she could lay her ghosts to rest.

Mori's fingers tapped a restless rhythm against her leg as the FTL drive hummed to life. This jump would make history—a leap that had the brass back home holding their breath. Fenris to Tau Ceti in one go, leapfrogging all the jump points. After decades of dead ends, some brilliant minds had cracked the barrier that had stumped engineers for generations.

Galatea surged forward, and Mori felt the familiar lurch in her gut. Her eyes locked on the tactical display, watching Artemis and Cassiopeia hold formation beside her. At least they weren't diving into this alone.

Then came the disorienting pull—that sensation of being stretched across space itself. The displays went dark, and for a heart-stopping moment, Mori wondered if they'd miscalculated.

But the screens flickered back to life, and she leaned in, searching for their target. If the calculations were correct, they'd be mere light-seconds from the planet. If not... well, that was a problem she'd deal with when it came.

As the static cleared, the Klii home world materialized on screen in all its tragic beauty. Dark-blue oceans stirred memories of Gaia, Mori's distant home. But it was the scars that drew her eye—craters and ruin marred a landscape that spoke of the heavy orbital bombardment. The scars on Kliinat mirrored Gaia's wounds. Two hundred years ago, Union battleships had devastated her home world with orbital strikes just like these. Hundreds of thousands had perished, many of her family among them.

As the tactical map lit up with the flurry of ships caught off guard by their arrival, a cold resolve settled over Mori.

"Lieutenant Bell, get me a firing solution for the Hades batteries. XO, scramble the fighters," Mori said.

The Hades, named after the god of the underworld, were Galatea's pride—colossal Gauss guns capable of launching high-density tungsten sabot rounds at incredible velocities. These rounds penetrated the toughest armor and were encased in a lighter material that peeled away after firing, allowing the dense core to strike with devastating power.

The Colonial Navy didn't knock on doors—it kicked them down. The Carriers unleashed swarms of fighters, bombers, and interceptors, flooding space with a lethal storm of Colonial might.

Mori couldn't hear the Hades roar to life from her position on the bridge, but she didn't need to. She knew the scene well— the subtle glow from the barrels as they fired supercharged rounds with the ferocity of unleashed lightning. Each deadly tungsten core tore through shields and shredded armor. The tactical screen captured each hit in vivid detail—a brilliant flash and a cloud of debris marking the death of a warship under the full force of Galatea's firepower.

A Union cruiser, caught in the crosshairs, buckled under Galatea's assault. Hydra ship-killer missiles streaked through space, finding their mark on a frigate and reducing it to debris. Fighters swarmed a destroyer, overwhelming its defenses with precision strikes.

A subtle tension eased from Mori's jaw as she watched their tactical display. Galatea and her sister ships easily outmatched anything the Union threw at them, raining down destruction with each burst of their guns.

Jorge Sanchez

As Mori assessed the battle's progress, Galatea's comms officer cut in with an update that wrinkled her brow. "Admiral Antonov, sir. Calliope and Thalia report damage and request cover. The Griffins made planetfall but suffered casualties," she said.

Antonov, ever stoic, nodded. "Thank you, Lieutenant. Tell the cruisers help is on the way."

"Hold one, sir, incoming message from the Corvus. The FTL drive on Gladius malfunctioned, and the squadron displaced back into Fenris. Captain Vogel says it'll be another hour for them to spin the—"

Before the comms officer could finish her report, Galatea got a rude surprise—a missile strike that slipped through her layered defenses. Mori shifted her stance slightly, but inside, the gears were turning. Someone on the bridge would get an ass-chewing later for letting that one slide. Her jaw tightened; her eyes narrowed. No one hit her ship. No one.

"Mr. Bell, make that cruiser regret waking up this morning." She keyed her comm to engineering. "Damage report, STAT."

"Hull breach on deck three, ma'am. Casualties still counting. MedBay is prepped and waiting."

Another hit made the bridge lights flicker, and the tang of burnt circuits filled the bridge.

"Goddamn it," Mori said under her breath.

A jolt rocked the ship. This time, engineering reported before Mori could ask.

"Captain, engine nacelles took a hit. Shields absorbed most of it—nothing critical," the engineering officer said, perhaps with a splash of optimism.

"Keep me posted," Mori said dryly.

"Yes, Captain."

The battle raged on, fierce but tilting in their favor. Artemis and her bombers hammered the Union's orbital defenses. Victory came at a cost, though. Artemis carrier group had weathered a furious counterattack. The strike carrier now bore angry scars, venting air from multiple hull breaches. Her escorts limped alongside, battered and bruised.

A Union missile found its mark, turning a screening destroyer into a blinding fireball. Mori spared a thought for the fallen—war is hell, after all. But they were close. Just a little longer until the cavalry arrived, and they'd clean house.

That's when the Gods decided to punish her hubris. New blips appeared on the tactical display, bringing a new level of "interesting" to the party. Lieutenant Grant, Galatea's tactical officer, had his work cut out for him. His fingers danced over the holoscreen, updating displays and recalculating odds. He tracked something big, something that didn't bode well for Artemis and her battered group.

"Holy—" Grant caught himself as Mori's eyes flashed with a warning that needed no words.

"Mr. Grant, let's keep the colorful metaphors to ourselves, shall we?" Mori chided, half-amused.

"Yes, Captain." Grant's fingers flew over his console. "Sensor contacts, coming in fast, bearing zero-eight-nine degrees by zero-four-three degrees, starboard bow," he rattled off, all business.

Mori glanced at her own display, noting the identification of the newcomers. The sensor readings matched UNS Furious, UNS Audacious, UNSL Fearless, UNSL Triumphant, and UNS Centurion. Two cruisers, two carriers, and a Dreadnought. This wasn't a mere skirmish; it was an invitation to a brawl. The squadrons of destroyers were almost an afterthought.

The CIC became quiet, save for Galatea's systems' persistent beeps and warnings.

"How the hell did they get here so fast?" The XO said, his scowl deepening. "That's half of the Third Expeditionary Fleet, which was supposed to be in Eridani. Intelligence screwed up. Again."

Mori tapped her console with a distracted finger. "Their base is next to a jump point in Cancri, but a jump to Tau is right at their limit, which means they're at high readiness fleet-wide," Mori speculated, her mind racing through the implications. The intelligence lapse was irritating, but there'd be time for finger-pointing later.

But why did they have their drives spooled? she wondered.

"Say what you will about the Union, but by God, they make good-looking ships," Antonov said, admiring the view even as it threatened to obliterate them.

"Yeah, pity we'll have to mess up that pretty face," Mori quipped back. The Colonial fleet might not win any beauty contests, but they knew how to throw a punch.

Like the rest of the fleet, Galatea was built like a spaceborne tank—angular, bristling with weapons, and graceful as a sledgehammer. Functional, yes, but nobody was hanging posters of them in their bunks. The Union ships, though, had style, like UNS Centurion, gliding through space with the sleek menace of a shark. Beautiful, but deadly.

"Admiral," the comms officer said, turning to look at Antonov. "Artemis is asking for orders, sir."

"Tell Captain Biyombo to hit them hard. Captain Mori, you're on Centurion detail. Make it count. I'll be in the flag bridge."

"Yes, sir," Mori said, her mind racing through tactics. "Helm, make your course nine-oh degrees by mark four-five degrees, emergency flank speed on my override authority."

Always the voice of reason, the XO furrowed his eyebrows and leaned in. "If you're trying to blow the engines to hell, going flank that long ought to do it."

"Your objection is noted, but I'll remind you that the new Pegasus Mark V engines can operate at sustained maximum thrust for twenty minutes." She turned back to tactical, done with the discussion.

"I put little stock in what the manual says. The inertial compensators can't handle that acceleration. If they fail, there won't be enough left of us to spread on toast."

Mori let it slide. Now wasn't the time for a debate. They had a job to do. "Your concern is, again, noted, XO," she said.

"Hmph."

She looked past him and addressed the Chief of the Air Group. "CAG, vector the 99th interceptor squadron on those carriers, let them know what it's like to be in the crosshairs of the finest pilots in the Colonial Navy. Weapons, prep the Gorgon batteries."

"Gorgon batteries standing by."

Mori watched on the tactical display as the Gorgon torpedoes launched, each splitting into eight projectiles as they closed on their targets. Centurion's point defenses would be getting a workout.

With the torpedoes away, Mori shifted her focus to her ship's formidable heavy guns. "Status on the Hades guns?"

"Gun number four has a casualty in the traverse mechanism, sir. Chief Engineer is on it."

Perfect. One Hades gun down as they charged headlong into the jaws of the Union fleet. Facing a Dreadnought would be dicey enough, even with all her weapons systems intact. Now, they'd have to survive with depleted missile stores and one of her Hades guns out of commission. Mori pushed aside the tingling sensation in her spine. This was going to be close.

"That'll have to do."

As they closed in, Grant shot up in his seat. "Skipper, incoming! Scimitars, but they're picking up speed—no, wait, they're—"

Whatever they were, they hit hard. The bridge rocked, consoles sparked, and smoke filled the bridge. Mori grabbed her console to steady herself, cursing under her breath. The backup comms station crackled with sparks and jets of flame. Grant walked over and doused it with a fire suppressant.

"Damage report," she coughed out as the scent of burnt electronics bit at her throat.

The list was long—engines down, launch tubes gone, hull breaches, and casualties. Galatea was wounded but not out.

Beside her, the XO picked himself up, shaking his head as he regained his footing. He gritted his teeth. "They faked us out. Had to be Broadside torps."

Mori heard Grant's urgent report rise over the crew's rapid communications and the din of alarms. "Captain, we've got more incoming, and two squadrons of Space Hornets made it past the CAP."

A new wave of torpedoes screamed towards Galatea. The Vulcan Gatling CIWS spun up, laying a wall of lead that shredded most of the incoming threats—but one got through, rocking Galatea. The warhead tore a jagged hole through the ship's superstructure, shaking the bridge and everyone in it.

The UNS Furious wasn't about to let up and sent another broadside their way. But this time, Galatea's point-defense systems were up to the task. The missiles never had a chance once the AI had recalibrated.

Someone yelled from their seat at the tactical display. "Captain, incoming coil gun salvo from Centurion."

Alarms screamed in Mori's mind. Union coil guns. Every captain's nightmare. "Hard to port!" Mori said, voice rising into a shout. "Throw everything we've got at those discs. And I mean everything!" Her left hand silenced the proximity alarm. The finger lingered there, unsteady

Time slowed. Each incoming round, each countermeasure tracking across the display meant life or death. One hit was all it would take. Despite their efforts, one of the rounds hammered home, sending shockwaves through Galatea that buckled knees and threw bodies. Mori herself went down. The deck rushed up to meet her in an intimate embrace that left her seeing stars. A warm, sticky liquid trickled down her forehead, and she wiped it away with the back of her sleeve. The fabric came away red. "Ma'am, are you okay?" The XO's voice reached her through the ringing in her ears. Did she just hear genuine concern?

"Yeah," Mori managed, the word strained as she pushed herself up, ignoring the pain and the blood. "I'm fine." She braced herself on unsteady legs and surveyed her bridge. Two of her crew lay motionless on the deck, while the rest appeared shaken and bruised. Bell, the weapons officer, stared up at the ceiling with vacant eyes, his neck twisted at an unnatural angle.

She keyed her neural. "Orderlies to the bridge. I need crew transported to MedBay, STAT."

"XO, go to the MedBay," Mori said, noting the unnatural angle of his arm.

The XO steadied himself on the console, pain flickering in his eyes before a scowl masked it. "I'll see the doc as soon as we kick their ass," he grunted.

Around them, medical teams rushed to tend to the injured crew. Mori watched the XO, noting his clenched jaw and white-knuckled grip. That damn stubbornness—both an asset and a liability. She admired his toughness, but now wasn't the time for old habits.

Her voice brooked no argument. "MedBay. Now. That's an order."

He nodded. "Yes, Captain."

After the XO left the bridge, Mori's attention shifted back as the comms officer hailed her. "Ma'am, I have a message from

Admiral Antonov. Help is on the way, and we're to assist Artemis."

Mori's eyes flickered as a vague plan took shape. To save Artemis, she needed a miracle, and in the depths of space, miracles were something you made for yourself. "Get Artemis on the horn." Galatea still had her claws, and they were sharp.

A minute later, Mori had Artemis's Captain on comms. "Barry, what's your status?"

"We're bleeding from a bunch of holes. I have a hundred casualties and counting, and two of my engines are offline. The repair parties can't keep up with the pounding. That Centurion is a monster."

"Is your powder dry?" she asked.

"Hell yeah."

"I have an idea to take her out." She knew Galatea could match Centurion blow for blow and still come out ahead, but it would come at a cost to her ship and her crew. Her mind raced with the details of her plan. "I want to link your weapons systems to Galatea. All the fighters, too."

Biyombo's response was as immediate as it was incredulous. "Did you wake up with a hole in your head? If we overload the AI for even a millisecond, we'll be nothing but floating targets. I will not risk my ship."

Mori wasn't in the habit of backing down. "Galatea's AI can handle it. We need to kick Centurion in the teeth, now."

Biyombo's reply was half threat, half resigned agreement. "If anyone else had asked me, I'd have already put a missile up their ass."

"But it's not anyone else, Barry," Mori said, a silent plea lacing her words. "It's me."

A pause, and then Biyombo sighed. "This better work."

"Thank you," she said, quiet enough that it might have been a whisper, then cut the connection. She bit her lip, a flood of what-ifs racing through her mind. This wasn't just about her crew anymore; she'd placed the lives of everyone on Artemis in jeopardy, too.

It's going to work. It has to work.

She positioned Galatea to trap Centurion between them and Artemis. The gap between the ships might as well have been a dark alley on Gaia for all the intimacy of their impending clash.

She entered the instructions into her console, her fingers moving faster than she could remember. She planned to bury Centurion under an avalanche of fire from both capital ships and their squadrons in a tidal wave of destruction. If she nailed the timing, their rail guns would punch through Centurion's defenses like a sledgehammer through glass. Eddie, the ship's AI, would earn his pay by running the nanosecond-accurate calculations.

"Captain." Eddie's voice came over her private channel. "I have a firing solution. Should I proceed?"

Mori leaned forward, every muscle tense "Hell, yes. Fire."

Her gaze fixed on the holoscreen as the missile salvo streaked toward Centurion, showcasing the strike carriers' raw power. She brushed aside hair stuck to her damp forehead. The recycled air of the bridge grew stifling, and she shrugged off her jacket.

Centurion weathered the initial wave, venting atmosphere from numerous hull breaches, then retaliated.

Mori's fist tightened. That first barrage had hit hard, but she knew it wasn't enough to put the beast down. They needed another round, and they needed it now.

But the battle had other plans. Over the bridge's cacophony of alerts and tactical calls, Grant's next words snapped Mori's attention to him. "Skipper, Artemis's weapons are down."

Without her guns, Artemis would be exposed and vulnerable. Mori didn't hesitate. "Shield her. Put us between her and that monster. Fire the Hades when ready."

"Aye, Captain."

As Galatea slid into position to protect Artemis, Mori sensed the ship's subtle shift more than felt it. A deep, rising hum vibrated through the hull—the Hades guns' massive capacitor banks charging for the devastating salvo.

Mori's eyes tracked Centurion through the long-range feed. The electromagnetic discharge hummed through the console under her hands. Waiting. Ready.

The volley unleashed—a deadly barrage of Hydra missiles and sabot rounds aimed at Centurion's heart. For a heartbeat, the Dreadnought seemed indomitable, weathering the storm. Then, a well-placed slug found its mark, striking an aft engine. The hit triggered a catastrophic chain reaction, spelling Centurion's doom.

Even in her death throes, the wounded beast lashed out. A final, defiant salvo of coilgun fire and missiles streaked towards Galatea. But it was too late; Galatea's defenses held firm. Her

Vulcans blazed to life and parried what might have been killing blows.

"We're taking hits from a cruiser, Skipper," Grant said.

"Launch the Vindicator interceptors to reinforce the CAP," Mori said. She sensed a presence on her right and turned. The XO stood at attention, snapping a crisp salute despite his bandaged left arm hanging in a sling.

"Permission to resume my post, Captain."

"Will that be a problem?" she asked, eyeing the bandaged left arm that hung from a sling.

"No, ma'am."

She nodded, her gaze softening slightly. The XO was tough, no doubt about it, and his steady presence had a way of balancing out her sharper edges.

"Permission granted. We've got pods to collect and a lot of people to bring home. Let's get to work."

"Yes, Captain," the XO said and turned to the CAG. "Launch rescue Griffins and send medical teams to the hangar."

Galatea's final salvo found its mark. Centurion came apart in a series of brilliant detonations, marking the definitive end of the battle. Blinking lights filled the tactical display as escape pods jettisoned from the shattered Dreadnought. In the CIC, the atmosphere lightened. Officers exchanged brief smiles. Grant shot up from his seat, pumping his fist in the air. "There she goes!"

She raised her hand, quieting the room as she spoke, "Solid work, everyone, but stay sharp. The battle isn't over yet," she reminded them. This was not the time to get lax.

Another report from Grant soon redirected her attention away from the holoscreen. "Skipper, new contacts on the port beam, bearing two-seven-zero by one-nine-eight. They're ours—colonial transponders. It's the Dreadnoughts—Gladius, Xiphos, and Corvus."

"About time," the XO said. He leaned over to look at the display, wincing as his injured arm knocked against the console.

"Castor, Hephaestus, and Hestia are preparing to leave Corinth," Antonov said, walking into the CIC. "Along with their escorts. They should arrive in three days."

The XO turned to Antonov. "Three heavy cruisers from Home Fleet? That's a ballsy move." He gestured with his head at Mori. "I can see where she gets it."

Grant turned in his chair. "Skipper, their carriers are steaming toward the jump point. The other ships are striking their colors."

"Too bad. We had them right where we wanted them, didn't we, XO?" she said.

The XO nodded. "Damn right."

Turning to face Antonov, Mori stood tall and braced at attention. "Admiral, welcome to Kliinat. Mind the mess."

Chapter 4

Launch Tube, CCV Galatea

Tau Ceti System

June 6, 2681

Lieutenant Commander Derek "Jammer" Kodai completed pre-flight checks aboard his FA6 Dauntless, lined up with the rest of VF-19, Saber Squadron. He flicked through menus and status updates, checking his load-out: a full complement of Ballista missiles and enough ammo for the Vulcans to build a literal wall of lead.

A rising hum filled the launch tube as the catapult charged, ready to unleash the fighters into battle. Harsh orange hangar lights cast long shadows across his cockpit. Time to fly.

His neural link chimed with a message from flight ops. "Saber Leader, Galatea Control. Interval check."

Even through gloved hands, he could feel the smooth, well-worn surface of the stick as his grip tightened around it. The familiar sensation grounded him, as if the fighter became an extension of himself.

Vibrations hummed through his seat as the catapult powered up. He gave a thumbs-up to the shooter, bracing for launch. "Galatea Control, Saber Leader two-two-one. All green. Thrust positive."

"You're go for launch, good hunting."

"Galatea Control, Saber Leader acknowledges."

The console's dizzying array of lights danced across his visor, bright against the dark backdrop of space. The rumble of bay activity and the deep growl of his engines reached him even through his helmet. Pinpricks of starlight stretched into brilliant streaks as the catapult slammed him back, hurling him into space.

The launch tube's roar cut to silence. Just him and the stars now. He vectored away from the launch tube but became momentarily transfixed at the sight of the ship's massive Hades batteries traversing portside. Few things were as awe-inspiring as a Colonial Strike Carrier firing her guns in anger.

"Begin combat air patrol," Jammer said once Saber Squadron flew in formation. Quick affirmatives echoed through the comm.

"Rust Devils, you know the drill. Keep to your vectors, monitor your fuel, and don't go chasing kills." He paused for a beat. "Got that, Two Bit?"

The voice of his wingman, Sue "Two Bit" Hercut, crackled

over the comm. "Hey, Jammer, there's some putz who sounds just like you on the squadron channel."

Jammer grinned. "Just wait till I knock you off the leaderboard."

"Keep dreaming. Try to keep up if you can!"

Two Bit's words carried their usual playful edge, but Jammer knew better. Behind that banter lurked a competitive fire that had propelled her to the top of the ace board. Two Bit always brought out his best flying. Had to, to keep up with her. And lately... well, beating her on the scoreboard wasn't the only thing that mattered.

As Galatea's entire wing of Dauntless fighters and Devastator bombers entered the fray, Jammer maintained his position on her starboard flank. A lot of good pilots, good friends, would not be coming back, but that was the life of a fighter jockey, wasn't it? You strapped on tight and hoped that on any given day, you were better than the other poor sucker.

After a quiet twenty minutes, his holoscreen lit up at the sudden arrival of a Union battle group. There were suddenly monsters in these here waters.

"Shit, that's a big one." Jammer's throat tightened as he transmitted. "Stay alert, Rust Devils. Fan out for maximum cover."

His grip tightened on the stick almost of its own accord. The Dreadnought filled his viewscreen, its massive silhouette blotting out the stars behind it. Its gun batteries swiveled, zeroing in on the carriers.

"Jesus, that Dreadnought is massive. Artemis is in for a

fight," Two Bit said.

"Time to go big-game hunting," Jammer said through a clenched jaw. "Hold one, Two Bit, I'm switching to squad-wide."

"Copy." The word was clipped, Two Bit's usual playfulness giving way to laser focus.

"Saber Squadron, this is Saber Leader," Jammer said. "Message from the CAG: Gally is going full blower at the Dreadnought, and so are we. Keep an eye on your tritium levels."

His scanner lit up as a wave of Scimitars fired by the Dreadnought headed for Galatea. The sensor warnings echoed the alarms blaring in his head as the missiles picked up speed.

Jammer's hands flew over the controls, banking his fighter hard to intercept. His pulse quickened as he opened the comm, "Those aren't Scimitars! Saber Squadron, take down those rockets! We can't let them hit Gally."

The squadron's Vulcans lit up, shredding the first wave of missiles into exploding debris. Three made it past the gauntlet, streaking toward Galatea despite the squadron's best efforts and the frantic barrage from the ship's Argus Laser Turrets and Vulcan CIWS.

The detonations filled Jammer's field of vision with blinding light. One of Galatea's engines left a glowing trail of plasma, and jagged rents in her Plasteel and Tritanium hull vented atmosphere into space. The massive shockwave sent two Dauntless fighters from VF-22 careening into each other, erupting in a spectacular fireball.

Two Bit pinged him again. "That was Hotdog and Digger. Did you see them eject?" She asked.

"Negative."

"Shit."

Galatea shook under another brutal missile salvo. "Dammit, she's taking a beating," Jammer said, watching the damage reports flicker on his holoscreen. "Rust Devils, tighten up and cover her flanks. Run head-on at those Scimitars if you have to."

Jammer had to fight the stick as he wrenched his fighter hard to starboard. The inertial dampeners strained against the stress of the maneuver and the immense G-forces that pushed against his chest. His Vulcans whirred to life, shredding the approaching missile into a brilliant cascade of fiery debris.

Then, a sudden surge of alarms jolted Jammer as his scanner erupted with a swarm of incoming bandits—each one a spear aimed at Galatea's heart. He activated the comm. "Saber Squadron, this is Saber Leader. Bogeys headed to Gally. Brace and switch to attack formation. Beaker, Alphabet, hold back and intercept any leakers. Guns free." The ominous drone of his Vulcan cannons spooling up reverberated through the hull, sending a buzz up his spine.

Bolts from the Rust Devils' guns tore through space, slamming into the enemy fighters. Two Hornets broke apart as their shields failed, ejecting a cascade of flaming wreckage. Another pair careened out of formation, shields flickering and venting plasma. Then, without warning, the harsh reality of combat hit home as a Dauntless from VF-20 split apart in a white-hot flash when a Stinger round struck the reactor. As the blinding light of the explosion faded, a deafening silence filled

Jammer's cockpit, punctuated only by the faint, static-laden buzz of the comm. The holo-screen displayed the disintegration of another friendly Dauntless, its signal ceasing, blinking into nothingness.

More friendly signals winked out on his display. Not just blips—pilots. Friends. He had to focus. Keep Galatea safe. That was the mission.

He jammed the stick to the left, squeezing every drop of juice out of his engines to get a Hornet in his crosshairs. The harness strained against his chest as the Dauntless sent a ripple of vibrations that traveled from his boots to his shoulders. His stick thrummed in sync with the drum of his guns as he let loose a salvo. The Hornet made a sharp, evasive maneuver, but Jammer painted it with his radar as the inertial dampeners kept him from turning into jam. The tone of his targeting system quickened, its pitch rising until it merged into a single, solid note—lock confirmed.

He spoke into the squadron channel. "Saber Leader, Fox one."

His missile struck the Hornet, sending it tumbling. He pointed the nose at another Hornet, maxing out his starboard maneuvering thrusters, keeping the guns on target even as his fighter banked hard to port.

"Saber Leader, guns, guns, guns!"

The Vulcan's firestorm turned the Hornet into twisted Tritanium.

"Alpha Mike Foxtrot! Nice shooting, Jammer," Two Bit said over the squadron channel.

"Thanks, Two Bit." Jammer said. A warmth spread through him that had nothing to do with the battle.

The conversation ended when his shield readout blinked red as an enemy fighter stitched him with its guns. A cascade of sparks danced across his visor as his shields flickered under the relentless hail of the Stinger gun. A flashing orange light bathed the cockpit, signaling a hull breach. Thank God for his helmet.

"Jammer, you've got a bandit on your six. Break, break, break!"

Jammer banked hard. He wrestled with the stick as the controls fought back under the mounting G-forces. Sweat beaded on his brow as the cockpit temperature spiked, life support systems diverting power to the shields. The right wing sported a neat pattern of holes, and a fuel line warning flashed—compromised but not yet critical.

His shields flickered as the Hornet hunted his Dauntless. Bullet impacts resonated like discordant drumbeats inside his helmet. Jammer swerved into the charred remains of a destroyer, escaping the firestorm of tungsten rounds. Collision alarms screamed as the fighter jinked through the dense debris field. Sharp turns sent vibrations through the hull, metallic groans of grazing scrap overwhelming his erratic afterburners.

Glimpses of bodies floating in space flashed past, forcing Jammer to shove aside thoughts of the battle's toll and concentrate on surviving. His heart sank as his console beeped with the dire alarm of a missile lock.

"This is Saber Leader. I've been painted. I'm going evasive," he said over the channel.

Jammer released a doppelgänger—a drone with a Dauntless

transponder—along with a chaff canister. The chaff sputtered into space, failing to deploy and disperse. He barreled his fighter left and right, but the beeping turned into a solid, ominous tone—the missile was right on his tail. Having run out of options, he pulled on the eject handle.

A red, blinking warning light appeared on his visor: Eject Failed.

Seconds left. His trembling hand found the front pocket of his flight suit, feeling the outline of his twin sister's picture. She'd been a Navy pilot too, his best friend in the world, until childbirth took her away—leaving behind the most beautiful baby niece in the galaxy.

He closed his eyes. Time slowed. Each beep of the missile lock might be his last. His sister's picture pressed against his chest through the flight suit. The steady missile lock tone seemed to grow louder, drowning out everything else—

Then silence.

Jammer's eyes snapped open. Still alive. His neural crackled to life with Two Bit's voice.

"Splash one. Yippee Ki Yay, asshole! You owe me a pint, Jammer."

"A pint? I owe you a goddamn steak dinner!" he said, heart still pounding in his chest.

"It's a date. No Union puke is taking out my wingman on my watch."

"Thanks for having my back, Sue."

Sue. Her name had just slipped out. Best not to think about why. He pulled out his sister's photo, letting himself look at her smile for just a moment.

Despite the dampeners, his body took a beating, and his back ached. His right forearm throbbed from the white-knuckled hold on his stick.

Two Bit chimed in over the comm. "Jammer, can you still fly with all that damage? Your afterburners are cutting out."

Jammer checked his systems, rerouting power and bypassing damaged lines. "It's the fuel line, I'm syncing it with the Reaction Control System. It's a Band-Aid, but it'll hold."

"Yep, afterburners have a sweet glow now," Two Bit said.

His holoscreen flickered, and for a second, the stick became unresponsive. "Dammit," Jammer said, slapping the side of his console as if the physical act could steady it. He ran a quick systems check—the power distributor linking the reactor to the ship's systems had taken damage. The cockpit had very few physical switches, one of which activated backup power. He flicked it, and the backup batteries kicked in, reviving the Dauntless. A few hours of flight time—more than enough to get the job done.

As Jammer maneuvered to rejoin the formation, his gaze swept across the battlefield.

Centurion smacked Galatea with two uppercuts from her rail guns. Sure, the Colonies didn't build the prettiest ships, but he'd be damned if Colonial Strike Carriers didn't have an iron jaw.

A priority call from the CAG sliced into the squadron's comm channel.

"All squadrons, Galatea's AI will take over your missile

systems to target Centurion. All fighters disengage. Stand by."

The squadron channel was filled with incredulous chatter and choice words from the pilots.

"This is nuts! We're gonna let some machine take over our birds?" Two Bit said.

"Let's hope the AI's aim is better than yours," came the reply from Sam "Beaker" Goldman.

"Shut up, Beaker. You couldn't hit the ground if it wasn't for gravity," she said.

The chatter didn't let up, so Lieutenant Mandy "Lunchbox" Saetang, an experienced and well-respected pilot with golden hands, tried to inject some sense into them. "You all need to calm your tits. The Captain doesn't do anything half-cocked."

"Cut it." Jammer's voice snapped across the comms, shutting down the chatter. "We're Colonial Navy aviators, and we're gonna act like it. If the Captain wants us to shoot finger guns at the Union, that's what we're gonna do, and we're gonna do it with a smile. Clear?"

The squadron channel crackled with muttered 'copies.'

After a few seconds wait, the Missile Armed message flashed on his holoscreen. "Rust Devils, the AI has the keys," he relayed, bracing as his Dauntless locked onto the target and changed attitude. "Here we go."

Hundreds of missiles launched in a synchronized wave, visible as brilliant streaks of light that accelerated toward the Dreadnought.

Jammer opened a Squadron-wide channel when the AI returned control to the pilots. "Stay in formation. We keep

Gally safe while the heavy hitters do their job. Keep those fingers on the trigger."

He glided back into position and glanced at the Dauntless slotted on his starboard side. He noted the scorched streaks from Stinger rounds and the slight, subtle wobble of the port engine. The nose sported a gash that looked like a claw mark from some mythical beast. She'd pulled his ass from the fire, and he looked forward to returning the favor. He smiled when Two Bit turned to look at him and flipped him the bird.

As the battle raged, the space around Galatea filled with debris and electromagnetic noise from the destroyed ships, creating patches of interference that scrambled sensors. The steady beat of radar pings became a buzz of static and dissonant electronic chatter.

Jammer boosted sensors and routed signals, multiplexing the primary and secondary scanners to clear the clutter on his displays. "Rust Devils, eyes up," he broadcast, quieting the comm chatter. "We've got a lot of debris skewing the sensors. Keep tight and cover Gally." His gaze remained locked on the menacing silhouette of the Dreadnought, advancing ever closer. He looked at Galatea, seeing the myriad scorch marks and hull breaches. That was his ship, his home. "No one breaks through," he said.

Within moments, his warning proved prescient as a squadron of Tornado Interceptors from a light carrier raced to Galatea.

"I don't want a single scratch on the boat. Vector to head off those Tornadoes," Jammer said to his squadron.

The Rust Devils cut down the nimble interceptors before they even got within weapons range of Galatea. Jammer sensed the hum of his guns resonating through the frame as he sheared the wing off a Tornado. Two Bit delivered the coup de grâce with her Ballista missile, reducing the interceptor to smoldering wreckage.

"Hey! That was my kill," Jammer said over a private channel.

"I'll let you share it, but only because I'm feeling generous," Two Bit said.

That was their last real threat, especially as Galatea hammered Centurion and her escorts.

Alphabet's urgent report burst over the squadron channel. "Jammer, I took a round from a Tornado and lost compression in the engines. All I've got is the RCS. Request permission to disengage."

"Copy. Beat feet to Mom. See you at chow."

"Roger. I'll keep the lights on."

A few minutes later, Jammer pumped a fist as his holoscreen showed him the fiery destruction of the Dreadnought. Back in Antares, it had taken almost two hours for Third Fleet to take down the Dreadnought Monarch. They'd just done the same to Centurion in forty minutes with two Strike Carriers.

His console beeped, new green dots appearing on his scanner—a squadron of Vindicator interceptors from Galatea reinforcing the CAP.

"Is the CAG really gonna trust interceptor pukes with keeping Gally safe?" Classic Lunchbox—never met a Vindicator pilot she respected.

"Hey, I flew Vindicators before I joined you aces," Jammer

said. He sat a little straighter in his seat, but his mind wandered to those first few combat missions on the old Warhawks. Different machine, same butterflies.

Two Bit's sarcasm cut clear through the comms. "Aw, look at you, taking the training wheels off."

"Hey, those Vindicators can buck you real good if you're not paying attention." Great, now he sounded like a defensive rookie.

"Can't be that hard if you can do it." Two Bit's laughter rang clear through the comm.

Jammer chuckled. The easy banter washed away some of the battle's tension until his scanner pinged again. New ships arrived—the Colonial Dreadnoughts. His shoulders sagged as he exhaled his fourth or fifth sigh of relief.

His back screamed with each movement, muscles protesting the beating they'd taken. He rolled his shoulders. Too close today. Way too close.

A knot formed in his chest as his thoughts drifted to the pilots who'd have their lockers cleaned out by their squad mates. His gaze lingered on a piece of debris that used to be a fighter—Union or Colonial, he couldn't tell. In the end, it didn't matter—war was hell, and it was time to get back to work. He put his Dauntless on a gentle arc toward Galatea just as his neural buzzed with a message from the CAG.

"Saber Squadron, attaboy from the Captain. Come home to Mom."

Jammer lined up for approach on the starboard bay. Those Hornet kills would look real nice on the leaderboard. Two Bit was   going   to   hate   that.

Chapter 5

Earth Union Navy Headquarters

Mars Naval Shipyards, Deimos

June 20, 2681

Admiral Thomas Stevens tuned out the Secretary General's ongoing diatribe. Liam McIntire's voice had long since faded into background noise, blending with the Martian vista beyond the window. Stevens' fingers traced the brass on his uniform—for a brief second, he half-expected to see blood on his hands.

How many careers had he crushed? How many bodies piled up to reach the top? As McIntire droned on, Stevens' mind drifted to a particular memory—the day he ordered the bombardment of Ganymede. The screams of civilians, muffled through the comms, still echoed in his nightmares. He'd justified it as a necessary evil then, but now...

The memory of those decisions pressed down on him. Each brass button beneath his fingertips seemed to represent a life altered or ended by his choices. When did duty become so damn heavy? Stevens wondered. It was almost laughable—the master strategist, blindsided by his own conscience. The game board had shifted, and for once, he wasn't sure of his next move.

He couldn't help but grasp the full irony of the situation—facing the end of his career in disgrace rather than glory. With luck, he'd only be locked away in a colonial cell, but he'd probably just suffocate to death from a Hasha terraformer. Remorse and honor, once abstract concepts, clung to his mind like a creeping fog, forcing him to face what he'd long buried. A faint smile crept onto his face. Well, what do you know, he thought. Turns out I've got a conscience after all.

"Stevens, are you even listening?"

Stevens snapped back to reality. He regarded his peers when he shifted his focus back to the viewscreen. They avoided his gaze, apparently lacking conviction—and a spine. Only General Kaneda, a steadfast friend and mentor, returned his gaze with a determined stare.

The contrast couldn't be more evident—McIntire, luxuriating in the opulence of a resort in Alpha Centauri while his officers grappled with the realities of war. Stevens' jaw clenched as he observed McIntire's plush surroundings. The Secretary General's manicured nails and soft hands had never known the grit of Martian dust or the acrid smell of burning hull plating.

How could someone so detached make decisions that cost

lives? It was a clear example of the gulf between those who command and those who execute.

Stevens sipped his juice, letting the tangy flavor distract him from the weight on his shoulders, if only for a moment. The Martian light cast long shadows across the conference room's metallic walls. Even the hum of the air systems seemed muted, as if the tension had thickened the air.

"Sorry, can you repeat that?" Stevens asked, setting his glass down with enough force to send ripples across the surface of his drink.

McIntire leaned forward, already on edge. His impatience manifested as a finger jab toward the tactical map. "What do we do now that we've lost Kliinat and the Hasha keep advancing on the outlying systems?"

Stevens rubbed his eyes, feeling a headache coming on. He let out a slow breath before speaking. "Look, I wish I had a simple answer here. We've been reallocating our forces, thinning our presence along the borders. We can't keep shuffling our defenses forever because someone is bound to notice. It's time we come clean and go public, because while we debate who's at fault for what, our people are out there, dying as they try to hold back the Hasha."

"Are you out of your goddamn mind? You go public with this, and we'll all rot in a cell. Do you think the Union Parliament cares about a few lost systems when they get wind of what we were really after? I'm not throwing my life away for some moral crusade.

"The words "come clean" left a bitter taste in Stevens' mouth. It meant admitting to years of deception, but as he looked at the tactical map, with its blinking red warnings, he realized the truth might be the only weapon they had left. No, it wasn't a moral crusade; it was the only way they could save the Union. He fixed his gaze on McIntire.

Stevens leaned forward, his hands gripping the edge of the table. His knuckles whitened as he spoke, each word deliberate. "We have no choice. We underestimated the Hasha, and Athens caught us off-guard with their new FTL drives. They can strike us here now."

"That's preposterous. They don't have the balls. Jumping a fleet to Sol is suicide." McIntire said, aligning another empty glass alongside its fellows on the table.

Stevens' temper flared up. "The Colonial Senate might not, but Antonov does. He'll fight for every millimeter of space, and now he has the ships to do it. We're too stretched to fight on multiple fronts."

Kaneda, running a hand through his close-cropped hair, weighed in. "Tom's right. The new Colonial Strike Carriers are monsters, and Athens is ramping up production across the board."

McIntire dismissed the concerns with a flick of his hand. "Typical overreaction."

Stevens sighed, weary. "It's not an overreaction. The intelligence is solid. Hell, a colonial carrier group alone has the firepower to turn the Expeditionary Fleets to scrap. We need a truce with Athens."

McIntire smirked. "Careful, Tom. You go public with this, and you might find yourself explaining why Kliinat wasn't just about resources or Athens."

"It was for the good of the Union," Stevens said, eyes narrowing.

"Yeah. Good for our pockets, too. Let's not kid ourselves." McIntire reached for another glass and gulped it down. "Besides, I'm starting to question the reliability of your so-called 'solid intelligence.'"

"Screw you, Liam." The words escaped through Stevens' gritted teeth, his knuckles white as he gripped the edge of the table.

"We're not just talking about military mistakes. If the colonies dig deep enough... well, let's just say the gold in Kliinat won't stay buried forever," Kaneda said. He tapped a steady beat on the table. "But we can still salvage this. Our counterattacks against the Hasha are too slow off the mark because of our outdated jump tech. Tom, imagine if we could leverage the colonial FTL drives?"

Stevens perked up, feeling a glimmer of hope for the first time in days. He leaned in, curiosity getting the better of him. "Okay, I'm listening."

"Acquiring their FTL technology could let us reinforce positions before the Hasha fortify theirs."

"That's a colossal 'if,' but it might level the playing field. We still don't know how they're wiping out entire battle groups, but it's a start," Stevens said.

McIntire leaned in, finger stabbing at the tactical map like he could push his point into reality. "And how do you propose we lay our hands on this tech? Our forces are pinned down in Kliinat, with the Colonial Fourth Fleet standing guard—a fleet that, need I remind you, swept us out of the system in less than an hour."

Stevens met McIntire's gaze, the words he'd been wrestling with for days coming to the surface. "We sue for peace, swallow our pride, and ask the colonies for help. That's how."

Stevens felt a strange mix of defeat and hope as he uttered the words. It was an admission of failure, but also a chance at redemption. For the first time in years, he was doing the right thing, not just the necessary thing.

"There's another avenue. We could reach out to our new friends," Kaneda said, letting the suggestion linger.

Stevens' eyebrows rose slightly. Now that was an angle he hadn't considered.

"Interesting," he said, a spark rekindling in his eyes. "You might be onto something there. Athens probably hasn't shown them all their cards, and yet..." He leaned forward, his earlier weariness fading. "We'll need to be cautious, but this... this could open up some unexpected opportunities."

"Agreed. They're eager for change and might have the motivation to do some digging for us," Kaneda said. "It's time they return the favor. We'll mobilize our assets in the fleet, too."

Stevens leaned back, considering the possibilities. "This could pay off. They've standardized systems on their front-line ships. That's a thread we can tug."

McIntire finished his drink, a smirk spreading across his face. "And if that doesn't work, we can always just take what we need."

Stevens' stomach churned, but McIntire wasn't wrong. If their plan failed, they'd have no choice but to seize what they needed, consequences be damned.

Chapter 6

Forward Operating Base Charlie, Daalamas

Kliinat, Tau Ceti System

June 22, 2681

Maalek stepped out of his quarters at Forward Operating Base Charlie as midday approached. Today wasn't just about the looming recon mission; he needed to pay respects to Kaalahera, the Goddess of Hunters, hoping to find a sliver of peace.

He walked at a steady pace toward the main gate, timing it so he'd be neither too early nor too late. As he got closer, a convoy of colonial transports rumbled in, bringing fresh Colonial Marines, supplies, and construction equipment. This base, once the heart of Klii military power known as Eastern Bastion Daalamas-Kaarja, had seen its share of rulers. The Union had claimed it first, draping it in their colors. Now, the colonies held it, promising to return it to the Klii as soon as possible. Maalek, ever the optimist, believed he'd see that day.

Maalek's thoughts drifted to the morning's briefings as he continued towards the temple. He frowned, remembering the vague answers that had left him with more questions than before. The colonial officers had been frustratingly noncommittal, tossing around phrases like "We're exploring all options" when pressed about plans to push back Union forces. Talks about returning occupied cities to civilian control had gone in circles, with fuzzy timelines and mentions of "phased withdrawals" that sounded more like stalling tactics. And the touchy subject of Union POWs had only gotten them uncomfortable glances and mumbled promises of "humane treatment."

His recent serendipitous encounter with Lieutenant Carson presaged good fortune, but it had become a double-edged sword. Maalek found himself too close to the political machine, rubbing shoulders with the type of politicians and bureaucrats who had flourished under Union rule. He'd seen their true colors, and it was a palette he didn't care for.

Maalek's attention shifted when he spotted four Klii scouts looking lost. They snapped to attention as he walked over.

"May I help you?" Maalek asked, keeping his tone friendly.

"Sir," the senior scout said, his eyes darting between Maalek and his companions. He shifted his weight from one foot to the other. "We need to report to the Mess Hall, but we're not sure where—or what—that is."

Maalek nodded, his expression softening. "Ah, I see. The Mess Hall is just a fancy name for the dining room. Head down this road to the intersection, then take a right, third building on your left."

"Thank you, sir."

Watching the scouts blend into the base's activity, Maalek's mind wandered to recent events. The Colonies had reinvigorated the resistance, helping reclaim two key Klii cities from the Union. While colonial Marines had led the offensive, it was the critical intel from scouts like these that tipped the balance. Among the liberated areas was Daalamas—Maalek's homeland, where his family had sacrificed everything so others could live free. A spark of hope kindled in him that perhaps his world was on the brink of reclaiming its lost future.

He replayed the memory of the day the sky fell, as vivid as a nightmare. He had been on the commuter train, the city sprawling below, when the first signs of invasion tore through his world. Chaos ensued; the train derailed in a tumultuous, surreal crash. He emerged with minor injuries, driven by an urgent need to get home. Seeing Sanya safe, her embrace, and the scent of her hair that day was a cherished memory.

"Maalek. Oh, Maalek, thank the Goddess, you are safe."

"I came as quickly as I could. It is madness out there. Are you alright? What about the girls?"

"We are all safe, but I cannot reach Mother. The news says armored soldiers have taken the capital, and spaceships are bombarding all council buildings. What... what is happening?"

"Pack food and water. We will head for the library shelter."

"What about Mother? I cannot leave her alone!"

"We must. There is no time, my love. Once we are safe, I will find her. I promise."

The decision to leave, to put their children's safety over everything else, had been agonizing.

Aliens. The word turned bitter on his tongue, a concept relegated to fiction and street prophets. Yet, it was their reality now, their city reduced to rubble, their lives upended by an unimaginable force. In the shelter's dim light, they had endured among strangers who became family, clinging to the hope that the radio's silence was temporary. But when he found Sanya's mother, it was too late. The devastation was complete, the invasion absolute.

Maalek pulled a small gold bracelet from his pocket, and suddenly, he was back at the temple of Seeha, Goddess of Nature and Oceans. Before Sanya, religion was just a curiosity to him. But she made it real, becoming his moral compass and emotional rock. That trip for Solee's coming-of-age was burned into his memory.

The trek to the ancient temple on Mount Tendra had been an adventure. Sanya, patient as ever, fielded the girls' non-stop questions about the Goddess as they joined other pilgrims on a two-day hike through stunning landscapes to the spot where, legend said, the Goddess planted the first flower.

They'd hiked through lush valleys, along bubbling creeks, and over waterfalls. They spent a night by a calm lagoon, where Maalek taught his girls to fish, as his father had taught him. They huddled around crackling fires, swapping stories of princesses and queens. The temple itself was a sight to behold— tucked among old stones, fed by the Raal River, bathed in soft orange light that filtered through the trees.

During their stay, they dove into the old ways—tending gardens, poring over ancient scrolls, and meditating, which helped Maalek tune into nature. He made flower crowns for his daughters and picked up spiritual practices from the temple keepers—prayers, blessings, songs. They lived off the land, enjoying fresh fruit and herbal teas. A storm on their last night had the girls dancing in the rain, laughing—a memory that Maalek could pull up anytime.

Two days after returning home to Daalamas, orbital strikes ripped their world apart. Now, catching a scent of mountain flowers reminded him of everything he'd lost. Rain always took him back to those peaceful days.

Maalek tucked the bracelet away, a memento of good times, but also a reminder of his planet's exploitation. The gold and uranium that the Union wanted lay under the land he loved. The uranium was the dark lure, one the Council of 64 had deemed too dangerous to touch. Now, human greed was tearing through his homeland.

For a moment, Maalek mulled over divine intervention. He'd seen Marines pray and wondered if some higher power was tipping the scales. It was a tricky concept for someone who preferred hard evidence, but recent events had him wondering if they might not be alone in this fight after all.

Maalek fiddled with the universal translator on his ear, colonial tech adapted for Klii biology. Its light blinked green and red, showing its active status. He looked up, half-expecting to spot a battleship in orbit, even knowing they were too far to see. A light streaked across the sky, and for a second, Maalek dreamed of far-off travels—about as likely as seeing a Kaava fly upside down, he thought with a chuckle.

Maalek secured the translator and headed toward the front gate, ready to lend a hand. The area bustled with activity as Marines and Klii worked together to unload supplies. Just then, he overheard Lieutenant Carson arguing with another Marine. Carson had become a familiar face in the base, someone Maalek respected, though they had never had time for formalities.

The other Marine, whom Maalek recognized by his lower rank insignia, carried a stack of datapads.

"I need those grenade launchers if we encounter a mobile armored division. Union hammerheads will get nothing but an itch from our M45s. I won't take chances because our supply officer sent the stupid requisition form too late," Carson said, his voice rising with each word.

"I didn't send the form late, ell-tee. Command earmarked those launchers for Hell Divers. I've been hounding the armory, but I called in a favor and put you in for the next delivery. They'll be here in two weeks."

"Two weeks? Two weeks? We're skids up in three days! I need those launchers, Lieutenant."

"Yes, sir. As soon as I drop these off with Bravo company, I'll see the logistics officer."

"Don't come back empty-handed, or the next conversation won't be this friendly. Dismissed."

Some things were universal, Maalek guessed. He had many similar conversations with his own supply officers.

Carson turned around and almost ran into him.

"Excuse me. Oh, hey, Maalek ur Jeet. How are you?"

"I am well, Lieutenant Carson. And yourself?"

Carson shook his head. "Same shit, different planet. Call me Skip, by the way."

Maalek nodded. "Very well. You also do not have to address me as Maalek ur Jeet. We reserve the ur honorific for formal greetings or introductions."

"Roger that."

"Skip, it has been a fortnight since you came to our aid, and I am embarrassed that I have not yet thanked you properly. Your timely and fortunate aid saved us from an uncertain fate. I dare not think what would have happened had we fallen prisoner. Death is preferable in such circumstances."

"Don't sweat it; it's been a hectic few days. You're rolling out with Kilo for recon tonight, right?"

"Yes, we will depart this evening. There is a briefing soon. I wanted to go to prayers first, but I saw the convoy arrive and thought I would make myself available." Glancing toward the busy entrance, Maalek reconsidered. "It seems they have enough hands without me."

"Yeah, I wouldn't worry too much about it."

"In that case, I will go to the temple." An impulse struck Maalek; without thinking it all the way through, he invited Carson. "Would you care to join me? If your duties do not press you, it is customary for us to make an offering on behalf of one who has done a significant favor, as you did for me." The invitation lingered in the air, and Maalek immediately second-guessed it.

"I would be honored, but I would hate to intrude," Carson said.

The tension left Maalek's back. "It is no imposition."

"After you, then. I'm not religious, but having more help on our side wouldn't hurt."

They made their way across a parade ground still bearing the scars of the heavy colonial assault. Stepping around craters and hopping over rubble, they exchanged salutes with Colonial Army engineers busy putting the base back together.

"Skip, may I ask you something?" Maalek broached a subject that had been on his mind. "Please tell me if it is out of line. As I understand it, your people believe in a single god. Am I correct?"

Carson seemed to consider for a moment. "Well, it's complicated. Back home and in the colonies, beliefs vary. Some follow monotheistic religions, others polytheistic, and then there are those who don't subscribe to any religious belief."

"And these different practices are all accepted?" Maalek asked. It was an encouraging sign that he'd already noticed similarities between the Klii and their new allies.

"Sure, personal freedom is a big deal for us," Carson said.

"It is not so different here. While some honor Athaam, the All-Father, most pray to the Daia, our twelve guardian Goddesses. Here, follow my lead," Maalek said as they approached the temple.

At the far end of the base stood a simple, modest prefab temple. The emblem of the Daia—twelve concentric circles in vibrant purple—adorned its exterior. Inside, the air felt different—calmer, somehow. The twelve stone effigies of the goddesses seemed to watch over the space, each with her own story etched in the lines of her face. The familiar scent of incense tickled Maalek's nose, a comforting reminder of the countless prayers he'd offered here before.

Maalek and Carson slipped off their shoes at the entrance. Maalek placed his palms together and lowered his head in a gesture of reverence. Carson mirrored the action, though his movements were a bit less fluid.

"Before we pray, we cleanse," Maalek said, guiding Carson to a washroom to perform the ritual washing.

"No trouble at all," Carson said.

After drying off, they returned to the sanctum, where Maalek fetched fresh prayer mats and handed one to Carson. They positioned themselves before a statue of a goddess with a spear. Her robes flowed to her feet, and her hand rested on the fur of a mythical beast.

Two Klii priests sidled over as they settled, handing Maalek and Carson delicate candles. Maalek lit them and placed them before the statue. He knelt, as so many times before. Carson echoed his movements with a bit less grace.

Maalek pulled a well-worn book from his tunic, its pages creased from use, and read aloud: "Kaalahera, Goddess of Hunters, grant me the endurance to carry my spear through the endless hunt, the clarity to strike true. I shall be loyal to my friends and deadly to my foes."

He then prayed for Lieutenant Carson: "May his resolve be steadfast and his spirit resilient," Maalek said, sprinkling water from a stone basin as a gesture of purification.

The room fell quiet, giving Maalek space for his thoughts to wander to his family—Solee's gold bracelet, his daughters' laughter, Sanya's radiant smile. The silence stretched on until Carson stirred, pulling Maalek back to the present. He extinguished the candle with a snuffer.

"Sorry to disturb you, Skip. It is customary to put out the candles after a prayer."

"No problem at all. Thanks for letting me be here. Quiet moments are rare on the ship, and I miss them."

"My wife introduced me to meditation," Maalek said as they prepared to leave the temple. "She cherished the peace of our garden during the colder months, savoring the wind. I try to find time for it when possible, though today I may have stayed longer than usual. Should we head back to base? We need to prepare for tonight's mission."

"Sure, let's go back," Carson said.

They put away the prayer mats, laced their boots, and bowed one last time. As they made their way back across the parade ground, Maalek felt a sense of peace he hadn't realized he'd been missing. The demands of command, the looming mission, the ever-present threat of the Union—it all seemed a little more manageable now. He glanced at Carson, wondering if he felt it, too. There was something to be said for shared moments of quiet, even in the middle of a war.

"Thanks again for inviting me, Maalek," Carson said, breaking the silence.

"You're welcome to join me anytime. The temple is always

open if you need a quiet moment."

"I might take you up on that. The chapel on the base can get pretty crowded. Thanks also for letting me be a part of the ceremony. Is it always like this?"

"Yes, but we do tailor prayers to each Goddess. Many of our Scouts pray to Liraa, Goddess of Wisdom and Perseverance. Kaalahera is the Goddess of Hunters; I have pledged my sword to her. She guides my hand as we fight to reclaim our home."

"Well, put in a good word for me, too."

"I already have," Maalek said.

Three days later, Maalek settled at a table in the rec room—a space designed for Marines and Klii resistance members to relax and socialize. He had seen little mingling between species, but the occasional shared story or meal suggested that attitudes were slowly warming.

He powered up his datapad, a marvel of colonial tech. The Klii had technology—wireless communications, portable computers, and planet-wide networks. But none of it matched the raw power of a colonial datapad. It was so light he'd double-check his pockets to make sure it was still there. The breadth of information amazed him. The datapad he received had a program that translated any page he found into Klii, and it improved with each translation. It didn't take long for Maalek to forget he was reading in a foreign tongue.

He pulled up a bookmarked page with links to colonial radio broadcasts. Though his mastery of Galactic Standard English remained rudimentary, he knew that the sooner he accustomed his ear to the sounds of his ally's language, the better. He even picked up words from context and tried to converse a few times without his translator. Results had been... mixed. He was thumbing through broadcasts when Carson plopped down opposite him.

"Hey, Maalek. One of your Scouts said I'd find you here. Got a couple of seconds?"

Maalek set the datapad aside. "Of course, Skip, how may I help you?"

Carson leaned in, all business. "Can I buy you dinner? I want to pick your brain about the terrain around Maatan. The briefing was short on details, and I want to get a feel for the hills around the city. We're dropping in to support Third Battalion, and I don't like going in blind. Well, not blind per se, but I'm a little foggy about where to set up the launchers. Care to join me in the officer's mess?"

Maalek had trouble keeping up with Carson's colloquialisms, but he appreciated the opportunity to help in whatever capacity he could.

"I would be glad to help. My wife's kin are from Kaal Eena, a short Vaal's hop from Maatan. Means' Hunter's Gathering' in your tongue. I know the area very well."

"Hot damn, it's a date then. Come on; dinner's on me. And I just received a care package from my sister. She sent me Athenian chocolate. I think you're going to love it."

Chapter 7

Captain's Quarters, CCV Galatea

Kliinat, Tau Ceti System

June 23, 2681

The nightmare that had long tormented her haunted Mori again. It had been a while since its last visit, and she had almost convinced herself it was gone for good. Yet, it returned, as vivid as ever, unfolding just as it always did.

There she was again, a younger Mori. She lay sprawled on her bunk in the cramped family quarters, feeling the cold bulkhead against her back. Datapad in hand, she lost herself in the rhythm blasting through her earbuds. The faint glow of the screen cast shades of blue across her face, creating a ghostly contrast in the dim cabin.

They were en route to Appia, heading towards a name that

promised a fresh start on the frontiers of known space. Two weeks down, two to go, and the biggest excitement had been avoiding cabin fever. Rumors of pirate raids and eerie tales of vanished ships could make her heart skip a beat, but these moments only highlighted the overwhelming monotony. She glanced at the time, remembering the one thing that broke through the tedium.

She yanked out her earbuds with a dramatic flourish, hoping to catch her dad's eye. He was buried in his work, probably crunching numbers for their new home. She coughed, exaggerating it for effect. Once, twice. On the third try, her dad's gaze lifted from his papers. This whole move, this massive upheaval—it had all been his idea, dragging them away from everything familiar just shy of her fourteenth birthday. And he hadn't even bothered to check with her first. The initial sting had faded, replaced by a grudging understanding of his reasons, but it sure hadn't gone down quietly.

Her dad's smile was warm and familiar, like an olive branch between them. "Go on," he said. "I'll let Mom know. Where is she, anyway?"

Mori responded with a hug and a peck on the cheek. "MedBay. She's covering a shift."

"I'll bring dinner to Mom," Mori promised, then dashed through the ship's corridors. She treated the pathways like her personal racetrack as she headed toward the command center.

She slowed her pace, not wanting to burst in like a comet. When she entered the bridge, it was alive with the dance of holoscreens and the focused energy of its crew. From the central viewport, space stretched out infinitely, a vast canvas of black.

"Permission to enter the bridge," Mori said.

"Granted. You made it just in time. I'm about to order the jump. Come, sit next to me."

Mori took the empty seat beside Adams, her hands gripping the armrests in anticipation. She watched the woman's steady hands move across the controls with practiced confidence, reflecting years of experience. "Thank you, Engineer Adams," Mori said, a tremor of excitement in her voice. In a few moments, the stars would swirl in front of her as the ship's FTL drive folded space, and she couldn't wait.

"Want to press the button?" Adams asked.

Mori's eyes widened. "I... yes."

"Hit this big green button on the holoscreen. On my signal, okay?"

"Okay." Despite her heart pounding, Mori remained still, eyes fixed on the viewscreen.

"Valorous Hope is go for FTL in three, two, one, jump." Adams said, then whispered with a conspiratorial edge, "Now, Tomoe."

Reality warped when Mori pressed the button, and her heart soared with the ship.

But the serene approach to Soor-Kech shattered in an instant. "Welcome to Soor-Kech. All systems are nominal... huh, this is strange."

That "huh" was the first pebble. The officer's next words triggered the avalanche. "Ma'am, I'm picking up three ships on an intercept vector, one two zero degrees by zero one three degrees starboard bow. Signatures don't match colonial ships. Marking them as hostile and putting their image on the main holoscreen."

Adams frowned. "The reports said the Navy cleared this system of pirates. Sound general quarters and turn on afterburners. Third-rate scavengers on dressed-up freighters won't keep up with an Athenian colony ship," Adams said, but her assurance faltered as she studied the display. "These don't look like any pirates I've seen before."

Curious, Mori looked at the holoscreen. The ships were bizarre amalgamations of metal and tentacles, unlike anything she'd ever seen. A chill crept up her spine. These couldn't be ordinary raiders.

"The scanners picked up shields and active warheads, ma'am. Those are warships," the bridge officer said.

Adams's next order hit Mori like a cold splash of reality. "Tomoe, back to your cabin."

But before Mori could move, the situation plummeted. "Contacts! Missiles inbound."

Adams's eyes widened before she steeled herself. She leaned over the console, her fingers flying across the controls. "Transmit a mayday and tell whoever's on the other end that we're under Union attack. Send the order to evacuate the ship," Adams said.

Mori dashed out of the bridge in a rush of panic. She chose the ladder over the elevator. Gravity betrayed her; a sudden jolt sent her crashing down. The metal deck greeted her with a painful blow. Blood trickled from her brow. Dizziness overwhelmed her. Despite the ship being rocked by more explosions, she pushed herself up and ran faster through the wave of confusion.

Anxious murmurs turned into loud, panicked screams. Another violent shudder, then explosions rang in her ears. Cries escalated into wails of terror. She reached her deck and frantically searched for her parents among the crowd rushing toward the lifeboats. Many were still in their nightclothes.

She made it to her cabin and into her mother's arms. For a split second, Mori felt a wave of relief wash over her. It felt so warm, so safe. "Oh, baby, thank God. Thank God," her mother said. Wrapped in that hug, Mori could almost forget about the madness all around them.

"This way, to the lifeboats!" her father yelled, dragging them through smoke, fire, and despair. He shoved people aside as the ship groaned with every shudder.

An explosion rocked the ship, and a section of the corridor just... disappeared. One second it was there, the next it was gone, sucking people into space.

Mori's father acted in an instant. He looked at them, and Mori saw... everything. All his love, right there in his eyes. Then, before she could blink, he hurled them through a nearby hatch with a strength born of desperation. The last thing Mori saw was her father's smile as he slammed the door shut, forever etching that final image into her memory.

"Dad!" Mori's scream tore from her throat, raw and primal. Her mother's grip, firm but shaking, pulled her away from the door that now separated them from her father forever.

"The galley's this way. Hold tight," her mother said, eyes

shiny with tears. She guided Mori through the chaos that had engulfed the Valorous Hope. They shoved past a crowd frozen in fear and shock. The air reeked of fried electronics and fuel, making their eyes water as they ducked under falling debris.

Mori's whole world had just gone to pieces. Every step away from that sealed hatch felt like a betrayal, but survival instinct kept them moving through this nightmare their home had turned into.

They picked up the pace, weaving through panicked crowds and colliding with those too disoriented to move. Propelled by her mother's sheer force of will, they reached the lifeboats. A bleak reality confronted them: lifeboats were already taking off, doors locked tight. They raced from one to another, her mother's grip tight.

"No, wait!" her mother yelled as they reached a lifeboat about to shut its doors.

A sailor answered, face smudged with soot, uniform torn and scorched. "The boat's full, lady. Take the next one."

Her mother's eyes darted around, looking for options. In the end, there wasn't going to be a next for both of them. She shoved Mori towards the lifeboat. "Please, take her. Please."

Their separation, as cold and unforgiving as space, was cemented with one final act of love.

"Mom, no!" Mori tried to yell, but she was already being stuffed inside. The world outside receded as someone strapped her in, the harness cold and hard compared to her mother's warmth. Through the small window, she saw her mother's lips move: "I love you."

The lifeboat shot off without warning, flinging Mori into space just the Valorous Hope exploded in a blinding flash. The shockwave tossed the lifeboats around like leaves in a storm. The last thing Mori saw, burned into her memory forever, was her mother's face—set and determined—waving goodbye.

Mori bolted upright, gasping. The nightmare was fading, but her heart was still pounding. She wiped her eyes, finding them wet with tears. Fumbling in the dark, she found the water dispenser. The cool drink didn't do much to settle her nerves or quiet her mind.

The clock blinked 2:30 a.m. Galatea was quiet at this hour. The ship had become home since... well, since that day. Mori flopped back onto her bed, knowing sleep was a lost cause now. Her brain was stuck halfway between memory lane and reality.

She tried to ground herself in the present. The tug of artificial gravity and the hum of life support anchored her. She was safe now. But her bed felt just as tight as that damned lifeboat that had carried her through space.

Those first days after the attack were a blur of tears and numbness. She'd curled up in a corner of the lifeboat, her mom's screams playing on repeat in her head. Time lost meaning as the boat became its own little world—filled with festering wounds, foul air, and constant hunger. She remembered when a fight broke out over a stolen water bottle. The last bits of civility, gone just like that.

Lost in her own pain, Mori had stared out at the stars. She'd imagined her parents out there somewhere. And she'd wondered—was there another girl like her, who'd lost it all, looking up at those same stars?

Guilt weighed on her. She knew her curiosity had played a part in what happened to her parents, and that knowledge only made her hate the Union more.

She made herself a promise: she'd hunt down every Union ship, captain her own vessel, and make them wish they'd never heard of her. That white-hot anger kept her going when others gave up.

The lifeboat just drifted. Weeks crawled by, days melting into one big blur of pain and emptiness. Some hearts just gave out. Others took matters into their own hands. Most just faded away. The ones left tossed and turned, their whole world shrunk down to this metal prison floating through space.

On the twenty-eighth day, they saw it: a Dragon-class destroyer against the backdrop of space. Mori's knees buckled and she swayed on her feet as relief flooded through her. First Lieutenant Barry Biyombo popped the hatch. When he reached out to steady her, Mori grabbed on like a lifeline— the world felt real again. Clinging to him, she felt a tiny flicker of hope. She could start over. She could still keep that promise, to fulfill her   vow   of   vengeance.

Chapter 8

Forward Operating Base Charlie, Daalamas

Kliinat, Tau Ceti System

July 10, 2681

Under the heavy, cloud-laden sky of Kliinat, Carson rallied his band of misfits, the Echo Company Purple People Eaters, on a makeshift breakball field in the old parade ground. Dark clouds loomed above, threatening to unleash a downpour at any moment. They trailed by three points against the Kilo Company Try Babies in a rough-and-tumble game. With the ball in their half and time running out, their prospects looked... dire. It was a stroke of luck that Muller had twisted his ankle, paving the way for Jammer to jump in. While Muller was no slouch, there was a reason Jammer had been the starting Breaker at the academy. He'd wrecked the Try Babies' right wing and even scored a half-try after snatching a fumble.

Bent over, hands on knees, and trying not to keel over, Carson gathered his team. "Who remembers the end of the game between the Dragons and Spartans in the Origin Cup two years ago?" he asked, trying to mask his exhaustion, and failing.

Rodriguez nodded. "You mean how Bruiser Kolisi scored that last try after barreling down the middle?"

"That's the one." Carson pointed with the authority of a man with a plan—or at least the semblance of one. "Williams, Sousa, Jammer, and Rodriguez. Blast me open a hole, and I can nail the center goal before time runs out."

Williams shook her head. "That's nuts, ell-tee. You do remember Dozer, right? The guy's been flattening us all game. Assuming we can keep him off you, and assuming he won't steamroll our defensive line, you still have to make a throw from the boonies."

"Trust me," Carson said, "Dozer and I go way back, I know his favorite moves." He neglected to mention that one of those moves ended with Carson full of bruises under a pile of players. Of course, he couldn't let his team know that. "Get me to the thirty, and I'll do the rest."

Williams half-smiled, skeptical. "Sure thing, ell-tee. I'll just need an address to send the condolence letter to your sister."

"Hand it to me, Williams. I'll give it to her when I bring back what's left of him in a shoebox," Jammer said. Sweat dripped from his brow, and his breath came in heavy gasps.

Carson threw his hand in for the team huddle, mouth guard back in place. "On three," he said, the team's hands stacking over his.

"One, two, three—Echo!" they shouted, breaking the huddle with renewed energy—sprinkled with a dash of nerves.

Gunny blew her whistle, followed by the eager eyes of human and Klii spectators. Sweating and determined, Carson scanned the field behind the scrum line and exchanged a knowing grin with Maalek from across the pitch.

Rodriguez rolled the ball back, starting a heart-pounding nine-second countdown. Williams and Sousa charged like hover tanks, sending the Try Babies' fullbacks reeling with impressive tackles. Carson darted after Rodriguez, slipping through gaps in the defensive line, ball tucked under his arm, lungs burning. Seven seconds. Jammer brought down a fullback who'd locked onto Carson. A feint here, a pivot there, and just as he broke free, he saw Dozer lining up to stop him. Five gut-wrenching seconds.

In a move that defied gravity, Carson vaulted over Dozer's diving tackle. Three seconds. With the grace of a man running on nothing but adrenaline and sheer panic, he stiff-armed another defender into yesterday, planting his feet to make a throw from the 35-meter line. He launched the ball like a missile spiraling through the air. It soared over the defenders and straight into the center net for a try. Six points. Game over.

Cheers, whoops, and the Klii's imitation of human applause erupted from the crowd. Gunny's whistle blew again to declare the Purple People Eaters the victors in a match that would surely be talked about for... well, at least until next week.

As the dust settled, Carson extended a hand to help Dozer up.

Dozer accepted, chuckling. "Thought I had you. That was

quite the move."

"Thanks. If I hadn't seen you make that tackle against Olympia Tech, you'd be scraping me off the field."

"Next week, then? Rematch?" Dozer asked, the corner of his mouth twitching as he fought back a grin. Made Carson wonder if Dozer was plotting revenge.

"It's a date," Carson said.

The players mingled post-game, exchanging a flurry of handshakes and back slaps, filling the air with the thick smells of victory and the less pleasant scent of defeat.

Carson was in a sea of high-fives as he basked in the afterglow of victory. They'd played their best game yet, and with some luck and a lot of sweat, that battalion trophy might just end up in their hands this year. The thought of rubbing it in Lieutenant Akitani's face after last year's shellacking by Alpha Company was too sweet. As the crowd dispersed, a few Klii tried their hand at breakball. Their enthusiasm was evident despite their awkward attempts. Riding high on the victory, Carson shared some tips and caught up with Maalek after a less-than-perfect pass.

"Hey, Maalek. Want some pointers?" Carson said, approaching him on the field.

Maalek's eyes lit up. "I would welcome them," he said, already adjusting his stance.

Carson taught him how to grip and throw the ball, launching it in a smooth arc. Maalek's next throw showed noticeable improvement, the ball sailing just wide of the target. "It's all about the follow-through," Carson said, proud of his impromptu coaching skills.

Maalek's next throw looked better and even hit the frame around the net. "Thank you, Skip. What an exciting game, this breakball. There is more strategy involved than I had first realized," Maalek said.

"Yeah, I love it. Some teams get really fancy with plays, formations, and such. We didn't run all our plays, though. I'm saving those for the battalion championship."

"You seem very well-versed. As I understand it, you played at a high level?"

Carson flushed and rubbed his head with his left hand. Whenever someone complimented him, his natural response was awkwardness. "I played a lot growing up and had a few opportunities, but life took me in a different direction. How about in Kliinat? Do you have any popular sports?"

"Yes, we do. Most are contests of strength and endurance, but a popular sport is called Baak. It involves two teams of six on either side of a line drawn on the ground. We bounce a soft ball back and forth, using only elbows, hips, and knees. It is exhilarating."

"Well, maybe once things settle down, you guys can resume playing," Carson said.

"That would go a long way into making life feel normal again."

Their sports talk led to a spontaneous breakball session. Laughter and shouts filled the air as the Klii got a quick lesson on Carson's favorite pastime. The scrimmage wrapped up with the Klii showing promising potential, leaving Carson impressed and a bit wary of the competition he'd just created.

As they headed off the field, Carson offered Maalek the ball. "Keep practicing," he said.

"Thank you, Skip."

"I'm going to chow with the rest of the team. Care to join me?"

"If it is alright with you, I don't want to disrupt your celebration," Maalek said.

"Not at all. Come and help me drink some beer."

They walked side by side through the parade grounds, past marching Marines and crews training on Centaur Tanks and Trident Infantry Fighting Vehicles. The sound of marching feet and the clang of equipment made Carson feel at home.

"I haven't seen you for a few days. What have you been up to?" Carson asked.

Maalek clicked his tongue, a Klii gesture of distaste that Carson had come to recognize. "I have received requests to attend meetings between the governor of Daalamas and colonial officers. I cannot think of a greater waste of time than hearing politicians debating. Their very existence is an affront to decency."

"Tell me how you really feel about them," Carson said.

"I believe I just did."

Carson laughed. "You would have gotten along with my dad."

"I am honored by the compliment, thank you. Is your father also a Marine?" Maalek asked.

"He was. My father died during the last war."

"Forgive me, Skip. I didn't mean to touch on a sensitive topic."

Carson dismissed the concern with a smile. "No need to apologize. My dad died a hero, and I'm proud of what he did." He paused, reflecting how his father's sacrifice had reshaped his life, replacing his childhood games with responsibilities. "Life changed after that. I had to grow up fast, helping at home instead of playing like the other kids."

"How did it happen, if I may ask?"

"During the Battle of Platea. His platoon held their ground to cover the battalion's retreat, twenty years ago now. That battalion played a key role in repelling the main attack on Athens two days later."

"A brave warrior. I can see how you have become one yourself," Maalek said.

"Thank you. I don't know if I can fill Dad's shoes, though. The name Samuel Carson carries a lot of weight back home. There's even a school named after him."

"Skip, your Rodriguez Marine mentioned that your regiment has old ties to your ancestral planet. Is that true?"

Carson welcomed the lighter turn in the conversation. Too many people had told him they saw much of his father in him. They told him they expected great things of the son of Sam Carson. Something told him they'd all be disappointed. "Yeah, sure is. There's a fun anecdote about that, too. Want the quick version?"

"Yes, please."

"Okay, let's see... the Colonial Marine Core is modeled after Marines from Earth. They came from a country called the United States of America. Like your Wars Between the Cities, Earth had its own major conflicts," Carson shared, his voice mingling with the distant thuds of Griffin shuttles touching down.

Maalek nodded. "That was a dark time in our history."

"This was the first major war, and people called this one the war to end all wars. Spoiler alert: it wasn't. We went back for seconds... and thirds," Carson quipped, a rueful twist to his smile.

Maalek shook his head in disbelief. "Madness."

"Tell me about it. There was World War Two, and then we had the Resource Wars because, apparently, we humans aren't good at sharing. Follow that with the Colony Wars, where Earth's nations decided they hadn't messed up their own backyard enough and took the fight to space," Carson said, shaking his head. "Anyway, back to the story... In this first war, when the Marines from the Two-Five received the order to retreat, Major Williams exclaimed, 'Retreat? Hell, we just got here!' And that's how we got our motto."

Maalek laughed. "I like this officer. Is there any relation between him and your Williams Marine?"

"Lizzy? Now, that's a thought. She's got the same 'never back down' vibe. Our regiment, 5th Marines, originated when Marines from America, the Two-Five, provided security on the colony ships. Seems like we've been safeguarding the galaxy—or at least keeping it lively—ever since. And there's even a Union counterpart still active back on Earth." He shrugged. "Who knows? Maybe we'll meet them on some distant planet someday. That would be quite the story to tell."

They neared the mess hall, tantalized by the aroma of pizza straight from the oven, but Carson's neural device buzzed with an urgent message before they could enter. Marines dispersed in a flurry of activity. Carson checked the incoming alert as he stepped aside to let them pass.

He turned to Maalek. "We have a situation about fifty kilometers west. Union forces tagged a Griffin Heavy with MANPADS. We're rolling out in ten to secure the spot for the rescue shuttles. Guess the war isn't taking a break. Rain check on beers?"

"That means a postponement because of unforeseen circumstances, yes? Good hunting, Skip. Stay safe," Maalek said.

"Thanks, Maal. Okay, see you later," Carson said, running after his Marines.

Chapter 9

The sky over Kliinat roiled with angry clouds, spitting rain that pelted the idling Trident IFVs in relentless sheets. The armored vehicles' massive tires sunk deep in the mud, but the mag-suspension compensated, shifting and adjusting to keep them level. Their engines thrummed with pent-up energy, ready to spring into action. Nature unleashed her fury, but the Colonies' finest tech shrugged it off.

These steel beasts were designed to carry eight Marines, including the driver. They offered protection from the harsh elements outside and a stout defense against the more tangible threats of stray bullets and things that went "boom."

Carson paced the line of vehicles, his gaze sweeping over their hulking forms. Talos auto turrets crowned each Trident, their quad-barreled chain guns glinting under sporadic flashes of lightning. Each automated sweep promised swift, mechanical doom.

"Alright, Marines," Carson said, shouting to be heard over the storm's uproar. "Our Griffin Heavy is down in the forest bordering Kaarja, right in the Union's backyard. It's as dense and welcoming as a wet cat, and that's where we're going. We've got people trapped and Hell Divers down—we're not leaving anyone behind. Oorah."

As he rallied the troops, the wind intensified, driving sheets of rain across the landscape. It lashed their faces, fogged their visors, and drenched their gear.

Gunny stalked along the line, her gaze sharp and piercing beneath the shadow of her helmet. "We need to secure the zone for the rescue birds," she said. "Keep your heads down, stay sharp, and stick to the plan."

Carson nodded, then turned to the logistics officer supervising the Trident CARGO. "Everything loaded up, Lieutenant?" he asked.

The officer wiped rain from his face before responding. "Yes, sir. FORTs, portable barriers, AutoDocs, and quick-deploy tarps are all secured. We've got the Hermes machine guns, too—a nice bit of extra firepower."

"Good work," Carson said, clapping the officer on the shoulder. "What about ammo for the Talos turrets?"

"Absolutely, sir," the lieutenant said, his chest puffing slightly. "Each vehicle's loaded with more than enough to chew through whatever the Union might throw at us."

"I love those turrets," Gunny chimed in. "Nothing beats manual control when I can get up close and personal. There's something satisfying about the kick of those 25 mm rounds going downrange."

Carson watched Gunny crane her neck up at the Talos, using her tablet to cycle through the turret's rotation sequences. "Try not to have too much fun up there, Gunny."

"No promises, sir," Gunny said with a smirk.

Carson turned back to the logistics officer. "Make sure everything's strapped in tight. Word is the ride's gonna be bumpy."

"Yes, sir."

Carson then caught sight of the sergeant overseeing the medical team by the door of the Trident MEDI. "Sergeant, is your team ready to move out?"

"Almost, sir." the medic said, signaling his team as they loaded the last medical supplies. "Just securing the final AutoDocs."

"We're Oscar Mike in five minutes. That means on the move—hustle up," Carson said.

He then pointed to an Auto Loader hauling a skid toward the Trident CARGO. He shot a glance at the logistics officer. "Paint me a picture," he said.

"We're loading up the last of the ammo canisters now, sir," the officer said, gesturing toward the incoming skid. "Hermes and Talos rounds—should be done in a tick, but we can use some extra hands to speed things up."

"Marines!" Carson said, his voice booming even louder. "Lend a hand with those canisters. Snap to it!"

As Marines hustled to unload the skid, Carson caught Gunny checking inventory on her tablet. "Gunny, did we pack the heavy hitters?"

Gunny's jaw worked. "Two Ballista Launchers, sir. Two." She jabbed at her tablet. "Manifest says four."

Carson let out a half-grin, shaking his head as if he'd just heard the day's least surprising news. "You know what I've always said about smooth operations, Gunny."

"That they're for drills, sir."

"Exactly. We'll just have to charm our way through, as usual."

Gunny smirked. "Right, sir. I'll be sure to pack my dancing shoes next time. Maybe we can waltz past the Union defenses."

Carson's grin widened. "Save me a dance, Gunny. But for now..." He glanced at the time on his neural, then surveyed the rain-drenched assembly of Marines and machines. With a wry smile, he raised his hand. "Alright, people. Mount up!"

Boots scraped against armor plate. Weapons clicked into vehicle mounts. Someone swore as a helmet banged the hatch rim. Gear rattled as Marines wedged themselves between ammo crates. Screens lit up one by one. Blue sensor readings crawled across displays. Orange threat indicators pulsed in corners.

"Corporal, hold up," Carson said to Sousa, torso sticking out the passenger door. "Maalek?" he said, squinting through the rain.

"Command thought you could use a guide," Maalek said, shouting over the howl of the wind.

"Well, I'll be damned. Couldn't have timed it better," he said, waving Maalek over. "Get in here. You're with me."

The Marines shuffled to make room as Maalek climbed aboard. Carson secured the door and buckled in. "Corporal Sousa, let's stretch that long-range antenna. I want to see what fun awaits us out there."

"Roger that, sir." Sousa's fingers danced over the controls. With a low hum, the antenna began to extend, pushing through the hatch and rising into the stormy air above.

As the antenna reached its full height, Gunny swept her gaze over the team, then fixed her eyes on Muller. "Link up the turrets. I want them on their toes." Her voice hardened. "Anything that moves and is wearing Union blue, I want it perforated."

Muller nodded, tapping commands into the console. The Talos turrets obliged, their barrels rotating in a smooth, sweeping 360-degree arc, vigilant over every conceivable angle as the seven-vehicle convoy trudged through the soaked terrain.

The convoy crawled along, stopping often to maneuver around fallen trees and test the path.

Carson's gaze jumped from monitors to Marines and back. Shadows flickered across the screens. Inside the Trident, only the click of weapon checks and the soft brush of armor against seats broke the quiet. Muller's fingers drummed against his weapon. Williams kept adjusting her armor straps. Business as usual.

The convoy slowed at the river's edge. The suspension whirred, lifting the chassis higher. Warning indicators flashed across Carson's display—depth readings, current speed, and entry angle. His eyes were glued to the monitor, watching the churning water.

"Corporal Sousa," he said, "keep a close eye on those water levels for me."

The Trident's nose dipped. Water surged over the hood, slapped against the windscreen. The current shoved them sideways—the suspension whined, then compensated. Carson's grip tightened on his harness as they fought their way across.

Further down the road, the lead vehicle braked hard. Carson's harness bit into his shoulders. His tablet clattered to the floor. A wall of fallen trees and rock, with branches tangled like razor wire was visible on the monitor. "Looks like we've hit a snag," Carson said over the comms. "Sit tight while we figure this out."

The lead driver called him over comms and said the road was impassable. It would take a couple of hours to clear the jam. He turned to Maalek with a wry grin. "Unless you've got a giant can opener hidden in your uniform, we might need to rethink our route. Any local shortcuts that don't involve us having to swim?"

Maalek's finger traced paths on the map display, stopped, backtracked, and traced again. He tapped a spot on the screen. "There might be a way around. See this old logging trail? It will be difficult terrain, but it should see us through."

"Alright, let's give it a shot," Carson nodded, relaying the new plan to the convoy. The Tridents' engines roared to life as they veered off the main road, digging their massive tires into the muddy earth.

Lightning flashes illuminated their path, offering glimpses of the dense forest closing in around them. Maalek pointed out a faint glow weaving through the underbrush.

"Those glowing vines," Maalek said, his voice taking on a reverent tone, "on Kliinat, they are more than part of the landscape. We see them as guardians, a sign of the planet's spirit. They even shield us from Union scanners." He paused, his chest swelling slightly as he spoke. "It's Kliinat's way of looking after her own." His eyes narrowed as he spotted something else. "See those little streaks? Those are Leereks—insects that feed on the vine sap, but their bite can be quite painful."

The neglected trail turned the ride from uncomfortable to downright brutal. Every bump and jolt tested the Marines' resolve—and their stomachs. Carson gripped his seat, wondering if the Trident's suspension had been secretly swapped for tritanium bricks.

Rodriguez braced himself as the vehicle bucked and heaved. He clutched his stomach, grimacing. "This ride's rough enough to toss my lunch," he said.

Williams braced against the next bump, still checking her weapon. "Better than losing your lunch every time you catch your reflection," she teased.

"Shut up," Rodriguez grumbled back, tightening the grip on his midsection.

"How about you both shut up?" Gunny said. "I swear, if you had dynamite for brains, you wouldn't have enough to blow your noses."

Their lighthearted exchange was interrupted by sudden movement on the exterior monitors. Bright, reflective eyes flashed in and out of view, scattered among the dense undergrowth.

"Hey, did you see that?" one of the Marines asked, leaning in for a closer look.

Maalek nodded, recognizing the creatures. "Those are Haali," he said, "also known as glimmerclaws. Local legends say the goddesses sent them to guide lost wanderers in the forest."

The Marines leaned closer to the monitors, shoulders relaxing.

"Hey, check this out," Rodriguez whispered, tapping the screen. "Never seen anything like it."

The creatures' eyes flickered in the headlights, appearing for a heartbeat before fading into the dark.

Murmured conversations replaced the tight-lipped silence. Carson became aware of their immediate surroundings. The air inside the vehicles was thick with the scents of wet gear and damp earth. The raw smell of the forest clung to their uniforms despite the scrubbers doing their best to clean the air.

The Trident's frame shuddered over the logging trail. The suspension groaned against rocks, bottomed out in ruts. Inside Marines braced against the walls, grabbed handholds, and cursed as gear clattered loose. Muller's knuckles went white on the grab rail. Gunny planted her boots wider, knees flexing with each jolt.

The moment they swung back onto their original route, shoulders loosened. Rodriguez unclenched his grip on the seat. Williams rolled her neck, letting out a long breath. The terrain smoothed out, giving them a much-needed break from all that shaking and rattling.

"Alright, Marines," Carson said, eyes sweeping across the cabin. "Time for a gear check. We're about to be center stage, so let's make sure we're ready." He paused for effect. "Our mission's simple: get in there, plant our flag, and bring our people home. Nothing to it."

The Griffin Heavy's hulking form became visible through the dense foliage, its outline hazy in the green tangle. "There she is," Carson said, his eyes flicking between the scene and the scanner readouts. "Survivors confirmed. Let's get to work."

The convoy ground to a halt at the clearing's edge. Marines poured out, forming a perimeter as rain cascaded down their armor. Carson was right behind them, boots squelching in the mud. "Corpsmen, attend to the wounded, STAT. Get those vehicles into cover, and let's hustle with those tarps. Clock's ticking."

The shuttle was a mess. Sheared metal gaped where the hull should have been. Wiring dangled like exposed nerves, sparking in the rain. The port nacelle had carved its own trench through the mud before coming to rest thirty meters from the main wreckage.

Carson's nose wrinkled at a scent that burned the back of his throat. His visor's hazard indicator flashed yellow. He traced it to a shimmering puddle nearby—leaked tritium fuel from the downed shuttle. A hiss cut through the rain's patter: pressure bleeding from the shuttle's fractured hull. Dying electronics crackled and popped.

Near the cockpit, a cluster of bodies shifted, breath misting. One propped against twisted metal, a hand raised weakly as

Carson approached. A pilot cradled his injured gunner. The gunner's breath came in sharp gasps, fingers clawing at mud. Another crewman had rigged an IV bag to a makeshift stand of branches, dripping its lifeline into a Hell Diver's arm. The diver's fingers twitched with each drip. Improvised stretchers of shuttle debris held other wounded. Their moans mingled with the relentless drum of rain.

Corpsmen splashed through the mud, scanners up, calling vitals.

"Multiple fractures here!"

"Need a stabilizer!"

"Got a bleeder—pressure pad, now!"

Their lights painted urgent patterns across broken metal and still forms. Medics planted AutoDocs in the mud. Walking wounded passed pressure bandages down a line, sorted stims into piles. Shattered Hell Diver armor plates stuck up from the ground like broken teeth, marking a trail to the tree line.

Carson's boots squelched in the sludge as he surveyed the perimeter. He switched to a direct comm link. "Gunny, tighten this perimeter till it starts holding its breath. Set up crossfires, get those portable barriers in place, and roll out the Hermes guns. We're not here to hand out free shots."

"Aye, sir," Gunny said. She orchestrated the Tridents' placement and directed the deployment of barriers. "Marines, mount those Hermes and keep 'em manned. Williams, Rodriguez, I want eyes everywhere—drones up, STAT. And stay sharp; this mud's slicker than a greased eel. Keep those Talos turrets ready, or we're doing this the old-fashioned way." She barked her orders, making even the rain seem like it was hustling to get out of her way. Marines moved faster.

Williams lay prone behind her Hermes machine gun, tweaking the manual controls. She squinted through rain-smeared optics, swiveling the barrel. Her foot rested on a canister of 15 mm caseless sabot rounds. "Roger that, Gunny. Looks like it's squid frying season," she said. Her lips curled as she sighted down the Hermes, finger ghosting over the trigger.

As the Marines secured the perimeter, Carson spotted a familiar face. Corporal Jensen, a Griffin gunner, leaned against the crashed shuttle's hull, his uniform torn and caked with mud, a nasty bruise blooming on his cheek. Carson clapped him on the shoulder. "Jensen, you've got a knack for scenic pit stops. From Teegarden to here, your travel diary's becoming a series of cautionary tales."

Jensen's laugh caught in his throat. He doubled over coughing, one hand pressed against his ribs. "Figured I'd collect enough frequent flier points for a free trip back to the barracks. I just hope the next time is more 'smooth flying' and less' crash-landing.' Didn't expect to see you here, ell-tee."

"We owe you one for hitting those Tritium tanks back in Teegarden; kept the S3 commandos off our back," Carson said.

Jensen flashed a grin. "Is this a bad time to mention I was aiming for that YETI mech?"

"Well, now you'll have to hitch your own ride home," Carson said, patting him again before turning his attention back to the crash site.

He tracked the rescue operation, marking each Marine's position, each gap in their coverage. They weren't out of the woods yet—literally or figuratively. But Gunny's defenses were taking shape around them at a good clip.

The Tridents' engines growled. Water cascaded from leaves as they moved. Tires churned furrows in the mud—one vehicle to the north, two east, two west. Their bulk cast deep shadows over the crash site. Talos turrets swung through their arcs, targeting systems painting invisible lines through the rain.

Marines locked portable barriers together, mud sucking at their boots. A gesture from Gunny—three steps left. Another— two right. Hermes guns clicked into place at each gap, barrels crossing to create lethal interlocking fields.

Maalek approached with one of his scouts in tow. Maalek gestured from the glowing plants to the moss patches, to the dense canopy above, marking each detail for Carson. "Skip, remember those? They're suitable positions to conceal heavy weapons," he said, then pointed to a stretch of land. "And see that blue moss in those dips over there? Perfect camouflage for mines."

Carson nodded, the corner of his mouth lifting. "Good eye, Maalek. Any more of those in your scout bag of tricks?"

Maalek pointed to a lush area nearby. "The sap from those plants is highly flammable. Could be useful for a firebreak or a quick distraction if we find ourselves cornered."

"Let's plant some surprises there, too. Coordinate with Muller on setting up those positions," Carson said, giving Maalek a firm pat on the shoulder.

He ducked under the Trident's shelter where Rodriguez hunched over his display. "Rodriguez, what's the word on those drones? We need eyes through this soup."

Jorge Sanchez

The drone feed flickered, pixelated, died. Came back as a blurred green haze, then died again. Rodriguez swore, cycling through channels that showed nothing but static and shadows.

"This freaky weather's scrambling the feed," Rodriguez said. "I've got them skimming low for better coverage."

Shadows deepened between the trees. Mud sprayed—a Marine caught himself against a barrier, water sheeting off his armor. His boots left deep craters in the muck.

"Lieutenant, our long-range sensors are draining the batteries fast. We might go dark if we keep this up."

"Keep them on. The early warning's worth a few drained cells. Get the spares lined up."

"Yes, sir."

Carson switched to a secure channel to Cassiopeia, their orbiting command vessel. "Cassiopeia, Echo Two-One. Requesting immediate medevac for multiple criticals."

The response crackled through, distorted but clear enough. "Echo Two-One, Cassiopeia copies. Medevac en route, ETA five mikes. Maintain position and stabilize casualties."

"Echo Two-One copies."

Carson wove through the makeshift triage area. Medics worked quickly under jury-rigged shelters, focused despite the mud that clung to their equipment. He approached a sergeant tending to a pilot's arm.

"Let's keep everyone in one piece until that evac lands, alright?" He said, smiling.

The medic's hands never stopped moving, applying pressure

bandages as he spoke. "Solid copy, ell-tee. I've got them all glued together. They're not going anywhere on my watch."

The rescue shuttles' running lights smeared into dim halos through the downpour. Carson had to lean within arm's length of Williams before her outline became clear. Marines lifted their boots high with each step, mud sucking them back down. Proximity alerts buzzed through crackling comms. Carson's armor chirped—temperature regulator cycling, cycling again. His undersuit clung cold against his skin.

Water ran in rivulets down armor plates. Marines huddled behind portable barriers, hands steady on their Hermes guns, shoulders hunched against the endless rain. They swept the weapons in slow arcs, covering every approach. A branch cracked in the darkness. Three Hermes guns swiveled as one.

Maalek leaned in, zipping up his jacket. "We call this rain Viizul, or 'the weeping sky' in the local dialect. It scrambles Union systems, too. It has been to our advantage more than once."

A storm that messes with tech. Because regular rain just wasn't exciting enough. At least it was screwing with the Union too.

His comm crackled. Rodriguez's voice cut through the rain's drumbeat, distorted by static and the unmistakable roar of approaching armor. "Ell-tee, we've got movement on the sensors! Visibility's shot, but they're right on top of us—Union forces!"

"Everyone, cover! Incoming!" Carson dropped behind the nearest barrier, tracking the Lynx ATVs as they emerged from the tree line.

Jorge Sanchez

Rain streaked his visor. Gray shapes wavered, solidified into Union infantry, dissolved again. Carson counted Union infantry shapes through the rain. One. Three. Seven. He let out a slow breath. Always during a medevac.

He ducked behind a chunk of the downed Griffin as the sudden crack of gunfire drowned out the rain's patter. A Lynx's turret chewed up the ground around him, sparks flying as rounds pinged off his makeshift barricade. Carson pressed his shoulder against the metal, counted the spaces between bursts. Let's see how much they enjoy this Viizul, he thought, then popped out of cover and returned fire.

Chapter 10

Shuttle Crash Site, Kaarja

Kliinat, Tau Ceti System

July 10, 2681

Wind gusts blew over the battlefield, indifferent to the unfolding drama. Marines scrambled for cover—behind smoldering wreckage, Trident hulls, and portable barriers that did little against the downpour.

Carson toggled his comm, raising his voice over the drumming on his helmet. "Cassiopeia, this is Echo Two-One. Abort medevac approach. I repeat, abort medevac. Hostiles engaged, LZ is compromised. Over."

A burst of feedback made Carson wince. After a beat of crackling static, Cassiopeia's reply cut through. "Echo Two-One, Cassiopeia confirms. Medevac aborted. Maintain position.

Over and out."

Gunfire became constant, tracers sketching green lines through the rain.

Carson opened a channel to Sousa. "Corporal, get crew and wounded in the shuttle's cargo hold, now."

"Sir," came the crisp reply.

As Williams let loose with her Hermes, the ground grew treacherous. A Marine, shifting cover, slipped in the mud. He silhouetted against the dark sky—a perfect, if accidental, target.

A sharp crack split the air. The high-caliber round struck the Marine's helmet, scattering shards as his head snapped back. He crumpled, sprawling motionless on the ground.

Before Carson could move, Muller was charging through the slop. Another shot rang out. Muller flinched as a bullet redecorated his shoulder armor, leaving a gash as it skimmed off the reinforced plates. "Oh, c'mon!" he grumbled, his words muffled by the pounding rain. "It's Sanada!" he yelled.

Muller grabbed the drag handle on Sanada's armor, pulling him back to the relative safety of a Trident.

Carson was there in seconds, taking in the scene—the ugly reality of mud and blood mixing in the rain. "Hang tight, Sanada," he said, administering a ReGen shot to the Marine's neck. The medic scrambled over, slipping in the mud, her kit clutched to her chest.

Carson glanced at Muller, eyeing the gouge in his armor. "You good?"

"Just a scratch, ell-tee. Might leave a mark, though," Muller said, gaze fixed on Sanada.

The battle's edge exploded into action. Maalek and his team flanked the Union troops, using glowing plants for cover. Incendiary rounds ripped through the air, kicking up dirt and debris.

The battlefield pulsed with the thunder of heavy guns and the whine of energy weapons. A mine blew, swallowing a Union squad in flames and scattering debris. Lightning revealed Marines darting across the field, casting quick shadows as they pushed forward.

"Reinforce the right, Gunny!" Carson's order rose above the rumble of IFVs and comm chatter. "They're trying to flank us."

"Copy that. Squad three, plug that gap with the Hermes. Move it!"

Wind howled and bullets sliced the air. Carson shouted into the comm, "Hold the line, Second Platoon! Push them back!"

His Marines answered with a volley of gunfire. A Lynx ATV burst from the foliage, guns blazing, tires flinging mud. Marines ducked, returning fire in sharp bursts. One grenade later, the Lynx was a smoking wreck, crumpled and aflame.

Carson squinted as his helmet's optics struggled to cut through the blur. "Sousa, keep that squad off the shuttle's left. Get the Talos on them," he said, slogging to better cover in his mud-caked armor.

Drones buzzed overhead, fighting the gusts. The enemy advanced through the rain. He keyed his comm. "Rodriguez, set drones to full assault. Now."

Static filled the line. Carson's eyes swept the tree line, Lynx closing fast.

Rodriguez's voice burst through the static. "Copy, el-tee. Switching to—" A sharp cry cut him off.

Carson's grip tightened on his rifle. "Rodriguez! Status?" he said into the comm.

The reply came after a beat. "Took a hit, but I'm up. Drones going hot. Might need a ReGen shot, or two," Rodriguez grunted.

Seconds later, drones dove, hammering Union positions. Blasts rocked the field, stalling the enemy's advance.

Caught between the Marines' barrage and Maalek's flanking, the Union troops fell back. Burning vehicles lit their retreat, casting long shadows. They hauled their wounded, peppering cover fire as they withdrew. The sharp tang of gunpowder and scorched metal mixed with the sizzle of rain on hot barrels.

The firefight died down to scattered shots. Marines moved fast, tending wounds. ReGen shots hissed, DermaGel smeared, bandages wrapped. Some swiped at grime-caked visors. Others, nerves still jittery, fumbled with ration packs, wolfing down bites between ragged breaths.

Carson steadied his breath and activated the comm. "Cassiopeia, Echo Two-One. We've secured the LZ. Requesting ETA on evac."

The reply crackled back, distorted by the storm. "Echo Two-One, Cassiopeia acknowledges. Rescue shuttles ETA twenty minutes. Maintain defensive posture. Out."

Carson removed his helmet, dragging his sleeve across a sweat-streaked face. His dry mouth had a subtle acridity lingering from the fight. He wrestled open an energy gel with quivering hands. The sweet, tangy notes of the gel were refreshing, displacing the bitterness that had settled during combat.

Taking advantage of the lull, Carson checked his rifle. His movements were fluid despite the cold numbing his fingers. Satisfied that his weapon was ready, he glanced around the camp. His eyes landed on Gunny, who slotted a magazine into her M45 with a satisfying click.

"God, I love these Hermes," she said, glancing back at Carson with a grin. "I might have to adopt one, name it, and take it on walks." She slung her rifle and flipped up her visor. After taking a drink of water, she added, "The line held, sir."

"It did, Gunny," Carson said. "But let's stay sharp. Get with Corporal Sousa and plug any holes in case this was just the appetizer."

"You got it, sir."

Rain whipped through the air, mixing with battle's remnants. The Marines sought refuge under the shattered shuttle, beside their Tridents, and behind barricades. Their breath merged with the cold, becoming visible in the chilly air. Carson seized the fleeting moment of peace to keep things moving, but a heated argument between Sousa and Gunny caught his attention. The strain of the recent battle lingered, and a discussion on defensive preparations escalated into a fierce debate.

"Gunny, the east flank's been hammered; I'm saying we shift two Hermes from the west to bulk it up. That extra firepower could make the difference if they come at us again," Sousa said, hands on hips, her gaze locked onto Gunny's.

Gunny shook her head, and then her expression hardened. "Stripping our sides is asking for trouble; they'll just flank us. We need a tight perimeter, cover all bases—that's Defense 101, corporal."

Carson weighed the options. Sousa was onto something with her aggressive pushback strategy, but Gunny's play-it-safe tactics had kept them breathing up till now. Really, both ideas had merit.

He made a call. "Gunny, Corporal Sousa's right. They'd be stretching themselves thin if they try to flank us on both sides. It's not just about defense—it's about hitting them hard if there's a second round, so there won't be a third. We shift the Hermes. And let's give everyone a breather, then lock this place down tight."

Gunny agreed with a grudging nod. "Alright, sir. Corporal, take point on the shuffle. But keep everyone in the loop. If they switch tactics, we switch faster."

"Aye, Gunny," Sousa said. Her smile was small but victorious as she spun on her heel to set things in motion.

With the immediate decision settled, Carson trudged away, watching his footing in the sodden earth. The distant thud of artillery was a relentless drumbeat that might have been echoing inside his skull for all he knew. Twenty minutes in open ground stretched like an eternity, but it was also a precious pause to regroup, to reflect. He leaned against a damaged barricade, his gaze drifting to the horizon. His thoughts wandered to his childhood—another storm that demanded quick decisions.

The memory took him back to their farm in Alexandria,

when he was just eight years old. He could almost feel the dirt under his feet and see the sky turning that ominous shade of gray.

"Matt!" His dad's voice cut through the howling wind. "Dust storm's coming! We've got minutes—help me with the tarps!"

They bolted across the fields, clothes snapping like flags in the gale. Two crops stretched before them: rows of delicate white asparagus they'd nursed all season—their cash cow—and patches of tough, dependable cabbage.

His dad's voice fought against the rising roar. "The asparagus is out of reach, Matt! We gotta save what we can actually get to!"

"But Dad!" Carson hollered back, his words snatched away by the gusts. "The asparagus is worth way more!"

His father's response came between huffs as they started laying tarps over the cabbage. "Sometimes, son, the right choice is what's right in front of you. We can save this cabbage. The asparagus is just wishful thinking now."

They had just secured the tarp when the first real gusts hit, sending them scrambling for the house. From the window, Carson watched the tarp over the cabbage strain and flap but hold firm. The asparagus field, though—that just... vanished under a cloud of swirling dust.

His dad's hand landed on his shoulder. "We did what we could, Matt. Not what we wished we could. That's what leadership is—making the tough calls fast and living with the results."

The memory faded, and Carson found himself back on the

battlefield. Debris scattered like his old farm fields; his Marines battered but hanging on like that hardy cabbage. His call to shift the Hermes echoed his dad's pragmatism. Protect what you can reach, what you can defend.

Just like shielding that cabbage all those years ago, he'd redirected their firepower to where his Marines were most exposed. It wasn't about holding every inch—it was about making sure they'd live to fight another day.

Aware that every second counted, Carson pushed himself up and walked to the triage area. He needed to make sure everything was in order.

The medics bustled inside a FORT—Field Operational Reinforced Tent. Next to Sanada, tubes, lines, and monitors snaked from a compact AutoDoc, keeping him in medical stasis. The low hum of the life support systems blended with the buzz of preparations outside.

Carson approached a medic hunched over a portable monitor. "How's he holding up, Sergeant?"

The medic didn't pull any punches. "It's not great, sir. His helmet took most of the hit, but we're looking at a depressed skull fracture. There's significant brain trauma—a cerebral contusion and a developing subdural hematoma."

"Mind breaking that down for me, Sergeant?"

"His brain's badly bruised, sir, and there's bleeding under the skull. It's putting pressure on his brain. He needs surgery, and soon, to relieve that pressure and fix the fracture."

"Can we move him?" Carson asked, his eyes flicking to Sanada's still form.

"He's as stable as we can make him here, but the clock's ticking. He needs to be on that first shuttle out," the medic said.

Carson nodded. "Make it happen. Keep me in the loop."

"Affirmative, sir. He's ready to move; we go the second those skids hit the ground."

Carson left the medical team to their critical work and headed toward the shuttle debris. On the way, he spotted Rodriguez perched on a fallen log, lost in the methodical task of patching up his battle-worn armor. Shrapnel glinted in the mud around him like deadly confetti.

"Holding up okay there, Frankie?" Carson asked, sidestepping a puddle only to sink into muck.

Rodriguez looked up, a smile on his face. "Just some scratches, sir. Takes more than a bit of flying metal to put me down."

"No doubt," Carson chuckled. "Next time, I'm using you as my personal shrapnel shield."

"Better keep up then, ell-tee," Rodriguez said, grinning. "I move quick."

Carson returned the smile. "Get some rest, alright? Could be a long day."

As he approached the shuttle, Carson saw the pilot examining a datapad under a makeshift shelter. Rain dripped off the tarp, adding another layer to the sodden landscape's rhythm.

"So, how did our impromptu bunker hold up?" Carson asked, nodding toward the battered cargo hold.

The pilot glanced up, brushing rain from his brow. "Better than we had any right to expect. Took a beating but kept us mostly in one piece."

"Where were you headed before all this went down?" Carson asked, ducking under the tarp to escape the persistent drizzle.

"Neskfaat," the pilot said, flicking through the cargo manifest. "We were supposed to drop off medical supplies and a team of Hell Divers for drills. This storm threw us way off course."

Carson leaned against the shuttle's hull, brows furrowed. "Neskfaat, huh? Always wondered why the Union didn't just crater that place from orbit."

The pilot chuckled, shaking his head. "You didn't get the memo? It turns out Neskfaat is sitting on a goldmine of rhodium and iridium. Their Prime, Adaara, is in talks with us for mining rights now that the Union's backed off."

Carson's eyes widened. "You're kidding. They were living on top of that the whole time?"

"Yep. Had no clue they were perched on a mountain of creds," the pilot said.

Carson let out a low whistle. "Well, no wonder they didn't glass the place. Must've been planning to swoop in and take it all along."

"Exactly," the pilot nodded, tapping the manifest. "We were even supposed to bring back some samples. So much for that plan."

Carson pushed off from the hull. "Anyway, I'll let you get back to it. Give me or Gunny a shout if anything comes up," he said, giving the pilot a quick fist bump.

Satisfied with the shuttle crew's status, Carson turned his attention to the rest of the camp. He spotted Muller hunched over a Talos turret that stuttered and jerked as it traversed back and forth.

"Muller," Carson said as he approached, "please tell me you can get that thing back in fighting shape."

Muller looked up, a confident grin spreading across his face. "This old girl? She'll purr like a kitten when I'm done with her, sir."

Carson's eyes traced the sprawl of components around Muller. "Sensors giving you trouble?"

"Yeah, this storm's thrown the IR for a loop," Muller said, his hands never stopping their work. "I'm boosting the power to cut through all this interference. Pulling some juice from the barrel cooler gizmo—figure this rain's doing plenty to keep 'em cool anyway."

Carson watched as the turret's jerky movements evened out. He nodded, impressed. "Smart thinking. Think you can do the same for the other turrets?"

"Already on it, sir," Muller said, reaching for another tool. "I'll have our whole perimeter seeing clear as day."

Leaving Muller to his work, Carson spotted Williams on an upturned crate under a tarp. She was cleaning her Hermes, its barrel now gleaming in contrast to the mud-caked body. As Carson approached, she looked up with a weary smile. "Barrel's done, sir, but these triggers are mud magnets."

Carson chuckled, shaking his head. "Maybe we should

commission a double-barreled Hermes for you. Double the firepower, double the fun."

Her laughter rang out, brightening her eyes. "I would so love to see the Union's faces when that thing comes at 'em."

Carson nodded at the weapon. "Keep it clean, Williams. We need every round to count if they come back for seconds."

Her smile was alarmingly enthusiastic. "Oh, I'm more than ready, sir. If they want another go, I've got a whole menu of lead to serve 'em."

"Alright, chef," Carson said with a grin as he moved on. "Keep that kitchen hot."

Seeking a moment's peace, Carson stepped to the edge of their improvised base, where the alien landscape stretched before him. The rain lent a silvery sheen to the purple flora, making the bioluminescent plants glow. It was the kind of scene that could almost make a guy forget about the evening's firefight.

Maalek hadn't moved an inch, muscles coiled like he expected the enemy to materialize from the rain itself. That kind of intensity couldn't last. "Maalek," Carson said, raising his voice over the intensifying rain, "Take a break and reset. I need you sharp, not burnt out."

Maalek managed a grin, swiping a grimy hand across his brow. "Stillness is a bullet's friend, Skip. I want to soak in the moment, fleeting as it might be." His eyes scanned the slick terrain. "It was a fierce battle," he said.

"Yeah, hell of a day," Carson said. "Keep your team sharp, okay?"

Time to check the perimeter. But his comm burst to life. "Echo Actual, this is Cassiopeia. Rescue shuttles two mikes out. Over."

"Copy that, Cassiopeia," Carson said, then switched the comm to broad mode. "Listen up, Marines. Shuttles inbound in two. Lock down those defenses and prep for extraction."

The camp erupted into action, fatigue forgotten as Marines scrambled to their positions. Carson made his way to Gunny and Sousa, who were knee-deep in the grind of coordination.

"Corporal, double-check the shuttle crew; make sure they're set to move," Carson said. "Gunny, I want eyes on those tree lines."

"Yes, sir!" they chimed in unison, diving back into their tasks.

Carson then headed for the medical tent to check on Sanada and the other wounded. The medic gave him a reassuring nod as he approached. "Sanada's stable, sir. We're good to move."

"Get him on the bird the moment those skids touch the ground," Carson said as he stepped back into the intensifying rain.

The distant whine of engines grew louder, drawing everyone's attention skyward as the shuttles broke through the cloud cover. Their lights pierced the gloom, prompting someone in the camp to shout, "Here they come!"

The Griffins descended, engines roaring against the storm. Marines slogged through the thick mud toward the waiting shuttles, determined despite their heavy loads, while medics hurried alongside them with IV bags swinging with each step. Wounded soldiers leaned on their comrades, struggling toward safety. Jensen, propped up by a jury-rigged crutch, yelled over the din, "Thanks, ell-tee! You've racked up another one on my tab!"

Carson shot a quick grin at him. "Don't worry, I'll be collecting on that soon enough!" he called back.

The moment of levity shattered as the comms snapped to life with Rodriguez's urgent voice. "Incoming, fast movers, heavy armor on approach!" The brief respite gave way to the immediate, pressing reality of steel and gunpowder barreling down on them.

The Marines dashed back to their positions with renewed focus. Carson's eyes darted to the monitors, spotting the Puma IFVs rolling forward with guns primed. "Ground contact is imminent—back to defensive positions, now!" he barked into the comm over the rising wind. The Marines braced themselves to face the Union's counterstrike.

As a Griffin shuttle strained against gravity and wind, catastrophe struck. A Puma's Mamba missile found its mark, causing the shuttle to tremble and spew a tail of smoke and sparks as it fought to stay airborne. By some miracle, and likely a heavy dose of skill, the pilot wrestled the crippled craft out of its slow, clockwise descent. He coaxed the battered shuttle to claw its way back into the sky and limp off into cloud cover, trailing smoke and flickering flames.

The Marines dug in, reinforcing their positions while Stinger fire lit up the night. Above, evac shuttles roared through the stormy skies with engines growling. Sparks flew from bullet impacts, and the sharp clang of metal rang out as rounds pelted the armored hulls. The Griffins weaved and dodged, taking fire from all sides but powering through, carving a path through enemy fire.

Behind the solid Tridents and the debris of their makeshift camp, the Marines' rifles cracked in steady bursts, followed by the wet thuds of incoming rounds embedding in the mud. Grenades tossed into the storm exploded, sending Union troops scrambling as dirt and debris turned into deadly shrapnel.

Carson lined up his shot as the steady drizzle muffled the battlefield din. Despite the armor's protection, the chill seeped through, mingling with the surge of adrenaline. He breathed a steady rhythm, focusing through the streaked lens of his scope.

A grenade landed two meters from him. The blast slammed him against a metal barrier. The impact reverberated throughout his body as shrapnel embedded in his armor. Dark fragments glinted in the gray light. His visor cracked with web-like fissures that obscured his vision while a persistent buzzing filled his helmet. The explosion knocked the air from his lungs and sent a sharp pain through his shoulder and jaw.

Gunny rushed to his side. Her brows drew together, and her lips pressed into a thin line as she surveyed his condition. The ringing inside his helmet muffled her voice, but he could just make out her words: "Are you okay, sir?"

Carson gasped for breath, brushing off the debris and adjusting his cracked visor. His shoulder throbbed. "That sucked," he winced, more to himself than to Gunny. "Yeah, Gunny, I'm okay. Still in the fight."

With Gunny's help, Carson steadied himself. He checked the magazine in his rifle and snapped it back into place with a click.

He rolled his shoulder to ease the ache. A grimace crossed his face as the persistent humming refused to clear. Spots danced before his eyes. He crouched behind the battered barricade and scanned the shifting battlefield.

The final rescue shuttle battled against the adverse weather and enemy fire. Its ascent was highlighted by a burst of bright exhaust as the pilot maxed out the afterburners.

The shuttle vanished into the clouds, but down here the battle ground on. Distress signals kept coming through the comms. More Marines down. More blood in the mud. The Marines might be dead tired, but muscle memory took over. Reload, aim, fire, move. Tale as old as time.

This position wouldn't hold much longer. One breach, that's all it would take. He activated his comm.

"This is Echo Two-One to Cassiopeia, requesting immediate Close Air Support. We have armored units advancing from multiple directions; marking specific targets is not feasible. We're activating IR beacons to mark friendlies."

"Copy that, Echo Two-One. Air support is coordinating for a wide engagement area. IR beacons acknowledged. Keep your heads down. ETA ten minutes. Out."

"Ten minutes?" Gunny shouted from behind a wrecked shuttle. "Those big bastards'll turn us into Swiss cheese before then!"

Gunny was right. They needed something now. "Rodriguez, get those drones in the air! Focus on the heavies!"

"On it, ell-tee," Rodriguez's voice rang back. Seconds later, the drones shot into the turbulent sky.

The drones dove through the rain, lighting up the night with bursts of fire. But the Pumas' armor shrugged off impacts with infuriating indifference. Some drones, thrown off by the wild weather, spiraled off target, their payloads exploding midair and raining shrapnel onto the Union infantry.

Rodriguez didn't give up. He tweaked the drone controls, aiming for pinpoint strikes. Two drones hit a Puma back-to-back, turning it into a blazing wreck.

From his vantage point, Carson noted Gunny's strategic maneuvering. She repositioned herself. "Keep them coming, Rodriguez!" she said, firing another round into the disorganized enemy troops.

"Sorry, Gunny. That was the last one." For a moment, only the howl of wind and rain filled the comms.

Then, two Marines with Portable Ballista Launchers stepped up. They took aim, steadied themselves, and fired. Missiles streaked across the dark sky, leaving fiery trails in their wake. They hit home, turning a Puma and a Lynx into spectacular fireballs, scattering deadly shrapnel across the clearing.

A deafening crack erupted behind Carson. It was followed by a dull boom as one of their Talos took a hit. Sparks and smoke outlined the damaged Trident, shuddering under a hail of impacts. "El-tee! Left flank's wide open!" Sousa shouted.

The ground shook before Carson could bark a new order as a massive YETI mech came crashing through the tree line. Its sensors, blinking red in the gloom, zeroed in on the gap in their defenses. The mech's arm-mounted Gatling gun whirred to life with a high-pitched whine that made Carson's teeth ache.

The gun erupted, its rapid bursts merging into one long,

terrifying rip. Bullets tore through the air, striking earth and barriers. They churned up the muddy ground, sending dirt and debris flying. Marines hugged the ground, feeling the vibrations and hearing the zip and hiss of rounds passing close enough to ruffle their hair.

Carson shouted, "Light that mech up! Now!"

Two Talos swiveled atop their Tridents. They opened up, spitting deadly streams of 25 mm rounds. Their tracers painted eerie trails through the rain-soaked night. The rounds slammed into the mech's frontal armor with a fury that rang like a demonic bell.

"Thing's built like a bunker," a Marine shouted over the din as the shots from his M45 pinged off the armor.

The mech staggered as the barrage hammered its frame. Smoke spiraled up from its battered armor. But its Gatling gun kept droning, pouring bullets into the colonial lines. A torrent peppered a Trident, shredding its armor. Hydraulic fluid spurted out, mixing with rainwater. Marines scrambled to keep their footing around the damaged vehicle, cursing as they slipped in the treacherous mix.

Carson scanned the battlefield. He snapped his gaze back to the mech as its arm swung in another devastating arc. "Williams!" he barked. "Get that Hermes on the mech! Target the sensors!"

"Roger, ell-tee, on it," Williams shouted back. She swung her machine gun around, painting a line of fire from the mech's center mass up to the cluster of sensors on its dome.

The YETI, suddenly blind and confused, sprayed bullets in a frenzied arc across the field. The Talos turrets seized the moment, hammering the behemoth with a furious barrage that tore through armor and limbs. The mech lurched, its Gatling gun sputtering a last volley before falling silent. With a thunderous crash, the massive machine face-planted into the mud.

Carson hugged the ground behind a portable barrier, calling to Sousa. "Corporal, plug that hole, now! Lock down the perimeter." He paused to catch his breath. "And get medics over here ASAP. We've got Marines down."

Carson surveyed the battlefield as Sousa sprinted off. The YETI was down, but that wouldn't buy them much time. Already the Union forces were regrouping. Another push coming, and soon.

Williams hadn't let up once during the YETI assault. Now that the immediate threat was down, she could focus on the remaining forces. If anyone could keep the Union off their backs while they fixed the defenses, it was Williams.

As if on cue, Williams pounced on her Hermes, matching the ferocity of the lightning crackling around her. "Choke on this, you friggin' squids! Wooo, twelve... thirteen!" she roared. Her voice battled the thunderous growl of her gun, each word drowned in the din. Steaming trails sliced through the rain with each burst.

Suddenly, the gun's thunder cut out, replaced by the angry beep of a thermal shutdown. "Oh, c'mon!" Williams snarled, smacking the gun's side as if sheer force of will could get it working. She had turned a Lynx into a blazing heap, but now, with her primary weapon down, she had only her rifle.

Without missing a beat, she snatched up her M45. "Ell-tee,

Hermes is overheated. We'll do it the old-fashioned way," she gritted out. She squeezed the trigger, and the rifle kicked against her shoulder as she switched targets rapid-fire.

"Twenty... and counting!" she said, whooping over the sharp cracks of gunfire. Each round found its mark with deadly precision. Then, a reassuring beep from the Hermes signaled the gun was ready. "Hermes back up, ell-tee! Time to bring the pain!" Williams said, swinging the big gun around. It roared back to life, spitting lead like it had a score to settle.

The comm crackled. "Cassiopeia to Echo Two-One, reinforcements en route, ETA 2 mikes. Maintain position."

"Roger, Cassiopeia," Carson shot back. "We have wounded marines that need evac." He switched to the squad channel. "Brace up, Marines, Cass is sending the cavalry. Hold your ground."

Carson took a breath, scanning the battlefield. His Marines clung to their positions, using every bit of cover they could find. Sweat-streaked faces showed the strain, but their jaws were set with that stubborn Marine grit.

A flash of movement caught his eye—a Union soldier taking aim at one of their Tridents. The rocket was already streaking across the field before he could open his mouth.

The battered Trident didn't stand a chance. Its engine erupted in a fireball, lighting up the gloomy sky for one spectacular moment. Debris rained down, some pieces whistling past Carson's makeshift bunker—a patchwork of shuttle scraps that suddenly seemed a lot less sturdy.

Carson knew they needed air support, fast. He tapped his comm. "Cassiopeia, Echo Two-One. Marking targets for air support. Sending coordinates now." He wanted to make damn sure Cassiopeia's Griffins knew where to rain hell and where not to.

He ducked behind a nearby Trident's hull, as close to safety as he was gonna get out here. "All units, light up your IR beacons," he said into his comm. His visor lit up with a constellation of friendly signals. He leaned back against the cold, wet metal, as the dampness seeped through his armor. His breath fogged up his visor. Just him and his thoughts for a moment. Hell of a time for reflection.

The steady swell of engines cut from the distance, announcing their aerial backup, Griffin Attack Shuttles. "Echo Two-One, this is Griffin Lead. I spot your beacons. Engaging now," the pilot's voice pierced through the comm static.

"Roger that, Griffin Lead," Carson said, his eyes locked on the shuttles hovering like birds of prey. "Give 'em hell!"

The night sky erupted as the Griffins' Vulcan cannons lit up, raining fire with an intensity that felt almost personal.

But the Union wasn't about to roll over. A missile streaked toward one of the Griffins. The pilot veered hard as the Vulcans spun up, unleashing a torrent of metal that shredded the missile into a fiery wreck.

For a heartbeat, everything seemed to pause. Then, as if personally offended by the attack, the Griffin struck back with a vengeance. It unleashed a barrage of missiles, one after another, each tracing a fiery path to its target. Vulcans hammered the enemy positions without mercy.

It was like watching the wrath of some ancient god unfold in real time.

The other Griffins joined the fray, raining hellfire on Union positions. Lynx ATVs scattered, their drivers swerving and zigzagging in search of cover. One Puma IFV swung its turret around, bringing its Stinger to bear on the shuttles.

The air filled with a deafening buzz as the rotary cannon spat out a torrent of rounds, forcing one of the Griffins to break off its attack run. Another Griffin swooped in, guns blazing. The Puma erupted in a fireball, lighting up the battlefield like daybreak.

Union infantry scrambled, popping smoke grenades that billowed across the field. But the Griffins stitched lines of fire through the haze. Return fire came in sporadic bursts— desperate potshots from the few Union positions still standing. A rocket streaked up from somewhere in the mix, missing a Griffin by mere meters. The shuttle banked hard, then dove, unleashing a barrage that silenced the launcher for good.

As the enemy fire started to fizzle out, Carson jumped on the chance to speed up the extraction. "Medics, get our people loaded now," he said into the platoon channel. "Keep those beacons lit until we're clear of this mess." Above them, the Griffin shuttles wrestled with nasty gusts. One swooped down, its lights cutting through the gloom, guiding the medics as they hauled in the wounded.

Combat faded to background noise, just rain tapping on his helmet now. Like nature trying to wash away what they'd done here. He took in the battlefield—a junkyard of twisted metal and scorched earth. Vehicles sat abandoned, half-swallowed by fresh craters now doubling as muddy pools. The Griffins' blue lights cast an otherworldly glow, making the aftermath feel almost peaceful. Almost.

Gunny slogged over, her face a map of pure exhaustion. "We did it, sir. Held 'em off. Critical cases are out, and we've got Griffin cover for the exit."

Despite their exhaustion, the Marines snapped to. Some locked down the perimeter, prepping for a quick getaway, while others gathered their fallen. They handled the stretchers with the care of seasoned warriors looking after their own.

Griffin shuttles hovered overhead, their engines thrumming as the rain tapered off. Amazing how quiet a battlefield could get. Just comm chatter now, and boots in mud. The calm after the storm—until the next one.

Carson sidled up to Maalek, eyeing the Klii's uniform—once a vibrant purple, now a sorry shade of mud. "How you holding up, Maalek?"

Maalek was crouched by a patch of bioluminescent plants, their glow contrasting with the sodden, dark, and dreary earth. He stroked a leaf, lost in thought. "In Kliinat, we say rain washes away lies. Today, it only shows the ugly truth of this war." He stood, scanning the horizon. "But I live to fight another day. And you, Skip?"

Carson's eyes swept over the battered clearing. "I'm in one piece, mostly, which is more than I can say for some."

He raised a finger, spinning it in a circle—the universal 'let's move' signal. "Alright, let's get a move on," he said.

The Marines sprang into action—securing gear, grabbing supplies, prepping the wounded for evac. They moved with the smooth efficiency that only comes from combat and hard-earned experience.

Williams was scrubbing at the caked mud on her helmet, her grimace morphing into a wry grin. "Nothing says 'spa day' like a good mud bath," she quipped, hefting her Hermes with a grunt. "Really makes the armor sparkle, you know?"

Gunny's voice cut through the bustle, "Eyes sharp, everyone. The last thing we need is a surprise from some Union straggler."

As they loaded the last of their gear and piled into the Tridents, Carson took a final look over the hellscape. The night rolled in as if trying to hide the day's carnage. They'd slugged it out and won. Now, it was time to get the hell out.

He slapped Maalek on the back, grinning. "Let's head home. I owe you a beer."

Maalek nodded, managing a tired smile. "That sounds rather appealing, but first, I may rest. Perhaps on our way back."

Carson chuckled, giving Maalek a light tap on the chest. "Good luck with that. Williams is driving, and she thinks speed limits are just suggestions."

With a final glance back at the battlefield, Carson hauled himself aboard. The thought of a meal and a bunk was all the motivation he needed right now. Tomorrow's problems could wait   their   damn   turn.

Chapter 11

Conference Room, CCV Galatea

Kliinat, Tau Ceti System

July 30, 2681

Maalek pressed closer to the viewport, counting ships until his breath fogged the glass. He had expected the colonial fleet to be impressive, but the scale and activity surpassed his imagination. Drones darted around the bustling space dock with surprising agility, reminding him of Leereks at the start of spring. The formidable Vindicator interceptors patrolling the area were as awe-inspiring as Kaavas, Kliinat's apex predator.

Stepping into Galatea's hangar—large enough to house the grandest parks of Daalamas with room to spare—Maalek found himself in the middle of organized chaos.

The Klii council of 64 had called upon Athens for a decisive blow against the lingering Union forces. This request had sparked a flurry of activity aboard Galatea. Even through this maelstrom, Captain Mori had orchestrated a welcome for the Prime Consul that was both grand and slightly surreal, given the backdrop of frantic preparations.

The welcome for the Klii delegation was dignified and organized with impeccable detail. Colonial Marines, dressed in crisp gray uniforms, stood in perfect rows, their salutes in unison, showcasing colonial military precision. Captain Mori and Navy Prime Lord Antonov stood at the other end of the ceremonial carpet. Antonov presented a ceremonial sword to the Prime Consul—a gesture that stirred Maalek's memories of a martial tradition now relegated to the annals of Klii history.

As they moved past rows of colonial officers, Maalek stepped forward to meet Mori. He'd drilled with Carson to master the ship's greeting protocols. With this knowledge, he was ready to make a favorable first impression.

He executed a turn to his right with the fluidity of a seasoned warrior and saluted. His boots clicked together while his fist struck his chest with a thud that was felt more than heard. Facing Mori once more, he repeated the salute. "Permission to come aboard, ma'am."

Mori responded with a smile that could thaw the peaks of the Heavenly Mountains. "Permission granted," she said.

Rejoining the line, Maalek found himself under the frosty gaze of the Prime Consul, whose eyes shone with a virulent glare. The Prime leaned in, his breath hot on Maalek's ear, words hissing out low and sharp. "Remember, we are allies of convenience. Your advisory seat hangs by a thread, ready to snap at the flick of my pen."

Maalek wasn't one to be rattled by threats, veiled or otherwise, least of all from a jumped-up bureaucrat. "As easily as a vote can usher in a new Prime," he countered, his voice level. "Remind me, what was your role during the occupation? Appointed overseer of Izaaba by the Union, correct? One wonders if coercion was the only reason."

The Prime Consul's jaw clenched tight, but he did not continue the argument.

Maalek glanced around and caught Carson's eye across from him in the briefing room. They shared a quick nod and a smile—nothing big, but enough to show their growing camaraderie. As he took in the room, he noticed the colonial officers sitting steady and calm while Lord General Graal ranted on. The Klii delegates kept their composure, but Maalek could see their recent history etched into every tense muscle. But he wasn't interested in dwelling on the past. He saw something different here, something worth building. Where others saw danger, he saw opportunity.

Lord General Graal's voice boomed across the conference room, his hand coming down on the table with enough force to make the water glasses tremble. "We shall not, under any circumstance, swap one tyrant for another. You might think us provincial, easily impressed by your powerful ships, but we are not cowed by shiny trinkets. What you're suggesting is nothing short of repugnant, at best, and at worst, an act of war."

The Prime Consul remained serene, his finger tracing slow circles on the rim of his goblet, too precise to be casual.

Antonov's hand rose in a deliberate, calming gesture, a clear attempt to steer the conversation back to diplomacy. His brow furrowed, lips pursed as he gathered his thoughts. He scanned the room before speaking. "I don't understand why you're dusting off an old argument when we are so close to what even you described as a momentous event," Antonov said, his fingers drumming against the table, voice tighter than before.

"What you suggest is pillaging the resources and birthright of future generations of Klii, sir," Graal said. "Your honeyed tongue might have plied the civilian leadership, but as the steward of our patrimony, I will not be so swayed. My sworn duty is to protect my people from all threats, whether they come wrapped in fine silks or shot from a cannon."

Antonov's jaw tightened, his words could have etched glass. "We have an old saying in my family: 'Don't piss on my leg and tell me it's raining.' So, enlighten me, what further concessions would appease you, Lord General?"

Maalek's nails clicked against his chair's arm once, then stilled.. This was diplomacy walking a tightrope, and Antonov had just given it a nudge.

"Very well. Let us be forthright," the Lord General said, his shoulders squaring. "For access to the Great Glowing Lakes, a squadron of destroyers. For mining rights to Teela, a battleship with a complement of fighters. And for the excavation rights in the Heavenly Mountains, an open treasury to refurbish our infrastructure and military."

Maalek studied the Prime Consul, trying to pick apart the political game unfolding before him. The Lord General's demands reeked of a smokescreen, a trick to let the Prime voice his wishes without getting his hands dirty. If successful, the

Prime would be in a stronger position in the Council, and with a fatter wallet.

The Prime had stumbled into his role almost by chance after the invasion wiped out most of the Council's leadership. Now, with an election looming and the formidable Prime of Neskfaat breathing down his neck, his grip on power was shaky at best. This push for colonial concessions had the feel of a desperate play. Turn the colonials into unwitting allies, shore up his support, and maybe hang onto that seat of power. Politics as usual, Maalek thought, but with the stakes higher than ever.

The colonial powers had extended an olive branch of military support and reconstruction assistance—a generous offer that the Klii leadership seemed intent on squandering. Maalek sent a prayer to Kaalahera, hoping these "leaders" wouldn't manage to break what even the Earth Union had left intact.

Antonov's eyes flicked to the Chancellor, and that look said it all. This was serious business. The Chancellor gave a slight nod, and Antonov pushed to his feet.

"No," he said, letting the word hang in the air, a full stop to the escalating demands. His gaze locked onto the Lord General, unwavering. "You seem to have forgotten the price we paid—over two thousand colonial lives lost defending a planet not their own. We're not here to barter lives for resources; we seek a fair exchange, a partnership. We offered you an alliance, a path to formal acceptance as a colony, and all the benefits that entail. We extend a friendly hand, and you clench your fist. You're pushing the limits of our tolerance, sir."

Maalek found himself nodding in agreement with Antonov. No amount of riches could compensate for the colonial blood spilled on Kliinat's soil. The colonials weren't after the tritium or the gold out of greed, but for mutual benefit—a chance for Kliinat to flourish alongside the colonies. The tritium in the Great Glowing Lakes could power the entire Colonial Navy many times over, yet it was decades away from being of any use to Kliinat. As for the gold, the Heavenly Mountains were rich in it, and the banks of the Raal River glittered with deposits. Yet here they were, negotiating as if with the ever-shifting sands of the Eastern Deserts—no promise of solid ground in sight.

The Lord General's sudden movement sent a carafe toppling, shattering the tense silence. "No, Admiral, it is you who—"

Antonov's response was swift and decisive. His hand struck the table, sending ripples through another carafe—a fitting metaphor for the crumbling talks. "Enough!" His voice thundered through the room, making Maalek's ears ring. "Our patience wears thin, Lord General. This ends now." He dismissed the Klii delegation with a finality that brooked no argument, signaling the end of both the talks and the colonial presence in Kliinat. "The Fourth Fleet will make all preparations to depart Klii space. You may keep the tritium and the gold. But we claim Teela by Right of Conquest. Please give my regards to Admiral Stevens when he returns with the Union's Sixth Fleet. Tell him I owe him an ass-kicking and a bottle of Ice Brandy."

As Antonov's declaration echoed through the room, Colonial Marines materialized behind the Klii dignitaries. A Navy steward, the very picture of protocol and polish, approached the Prime Consul and the Lord General with a courteous nod. "This way, if you please, your Excellency, your Primeship." His tone was respectful, but the message couldn't have been more explicit: the exit is that way.

Maalek grasped the full implications of invoking the Right of Conquest. This tactic, once common among the ancient Klii city-states, epitomized the principle of 'might makes right' that had dominated his homeland during the Wars of Unification. It was a bold move, and although on the losing side, Maalek couldn't help but respect the thoroughness of their preparation. Whoever Antonov had put in charge of researching Klii culture deserved a promotion. Whoever put the Prime Consul in charge deserved to be thrown off the nearest cliff.

Determined not to stay silent against what he viewed as the ultimate betrayal, Maalek strode toward the Lord General as tension filled the room. After all his sacrifices, silence was no longer an option. "May you see a thousand seasons and never cross the Great Sea, Lord General." The words hung between them.

The Lord General's face cycled through shock and outrage. His throat worked silently before words burst out. "How dare you... you... you are nobody to say such a thing to me."

But Maalek stood his ground, close enough to count the sweat beads on the General's brow. "You have finished the job the Union started, but this is not the end. My Scouts and I will continue to fight the enemies of Kliinat. Every last one of them." His words weren't just a declaration but a vow etched in stone.

The Chancellor raised his voice to restore order, perhaps sensing escalating tensions. Maalek, distracted by the effort to maintain decorum, found the Lord General and the Prime Consul huddled with their entourage, the General's finger jabbing the air toward him like a missile locked on target.

The Chancellor stepped in, positioning himself between the clashing parties. His call for calm was as much a diplomatic effort as a desperate attempt to avoid escalation.

"My friends," he began, his voice a soothing balm to the room's nerves. "Our leaders are passionate, a reflection of their deep commitment to their people. Surely, we can all see the benefits of signing the agreement already ratified by the Council of 64 and our own Senate." His words hung in the air, a gentle reminder of the political realities at play.

"Let us not delay cementing this great alliance," he urged, his tone growing more serious, "lest we face Union battleships when we're most vulnerable." The sudden chill in the room had nothing to do with the environmental controls.

"I propose we pause for refreshments, allow tempers to cool, and approach this with clearer minds." The Chancellor's suggestion was delivered with a smile, but Maalek could see the steel behind it. It was a strategic move, offering an olive branch while reminding every one of the high stakes.

As the tension in the room began to dissipate, Maalek wondered if the brief break would be enough to bridge the chasm between their positions, or if it was merely delaying the inevitable.

Chapter 12

Carson sidled up to Maalek, undoing the top button of his jacket. "Maal, you look like a man who needs a drink. Beers are on me."

Maalek started to reply but caught another glare from the Lord General. He chose to ignore it. "Thank you. I am glad to see you here, Skip. I thought you said you would not be attending?"

"Yeah, the skipper pulled rank on me. When she summons, you don't just send your regrets. How'd you find your first trip among the stars?"

Maalek thought for a moment. 'In Daal, we have 'Qaaneh'—

it's like longing for a place you've never been. That was me with the stars. But after today, that yearning is gone.' "

Carson chuckled. "I don't think you realize how much sense that makes."

They headed for the Wardroom, where a mix of human and Klii dishes were on display—a tasty bit of diplomacy. Maalek stumbled, and Carson steadied him with a firm grip. The ship's tricky gravity was still giving Maalek trouble.

Maalek watched in wonder as the humans navigated through the shifting gravity fields. His own skin tingled, and he struggled to keep his balance. "How do you get used to this?" he asked, his eyes wide with a mix of fascination and frustration at mastering such an alien sensation.

"I'm more accustomed to solid footing. The sensation here is... disorienting," Maalek said with a touch of embarrassment.

"Yeah, the grav generators are first-rate, but it still takes some getting used to it. Be glad we're not on a frigate. Those little ships have generators that make it feel like you're walking on a sponge."

Maalek grimaced. "That does not sound particularly appealing."

"Actually, it's kind of fun."

Maalek couldn't help but overhear the Lord General and Antonov still sparring in the Wardroom. He felt torn. He was loyal to Kliinat but found himself siding with the colonials. They'd come all this way, given up so much to free his people. And now Kliinat's leaders were squabbling over the leftovers like petty thieves. Maalek wondered if he'd been focused on the wrong enemy all along.

The dining hall was a feast for the senses, laden with exotic fruits, synthetic meats, and various pastries. Among the spread, Maalek spotted an intriguing golden-brown snack.

"Those," Carson said, following Maalek's gaze, "are Cream Cheese Habanero Poppers. Pretty popular at these things."

Seeing another officer grab a couple without batting an eye, Maalek figured he'd give it a try. Big mistake. The moment the popper hit his tongue, Maalek's eyes went wide. Maalek's claws scraped the table, searching for napkins, water, escape routes—anything to save his melting tongue. In his panic, he ended up spitting it out, and the half-chewed popper made a less-than-graceful landing on the deck.

"Quick, try this," Carson said, grinning, thrusting a glass of cooling green liquid toward him. The drink was a lifesaver, quenching the fire and leaving a pleasant melody of sweet and tart on his healed palate. "It's apple-granate juice, one of my favorites."

As Maalek caught his breath, he found himself grinning. Sure, the pepper had melted his taste buds, but sharing this meal—and near-death experience—with friends from across the galaxy felt special. Even with all the heated talks and disagreements, they could still bond over something as simple as the fiery kick of a Habanero Popper.

The lingering burn made Maalek wonder about the sanity of anyone who enjoyed such heat for fun. "Feels like swallowing a burning log," he said, incredulous.

Carson chuckled, playing his part as the culinary guide. "Oh, it's more than just a pepper; it's a tradition. It's a special pepper brought over on the very first colony ship. We call it the Lava Reaper Habanero. Our farmers, and a couple of psychopaths who want to see the world burn, have been messing with it ever since." Handing over an Olympian Lager with a flourish, he said, "This here is the antidote to any fire, real or metaphorical—Olympian Lager, the best beer in the known universe, and I'll fight any man who says otherwise. You've earned it."

Maalek took a swig of the lager, and his eyes lit up. The cool brew swept away the pepper's burn, leaving him with a clean slate and a new appreciation for human drinks. "This beer is excellent," he said, his tongue flicking to catch the remaining foam off his upper lip.

Carson handed him another and clinked his glass in a drinking ceremony familiar to Maalek.

"Cheers, Maal, to new friends, old friends, and fallen friends."

"To our brothers and sisters."

Still curious (and hoping to cool down his burning mouth), Maalek headed for a bowl of what Carson called 'shrimp.' He paused, running a finger over the curled, orange things nestled in ice. They looked a lot like the pincer fish he used to catch with his father.

Maalek tracked Carson's technique—grab, dip, eat—before reaching for his own. The shrimp's texture was chewier than what he remembered of pincer fish, yet the flavor bridged him back to his childhood. Before he knew it, Maalek was grabbing handfuls, each bite zapping him back to those lazy summer days by the lake.

"Hey, Maal, the ocean called. It wants all its shrimp back,"

Carson said.

Maalek apologized, but with a mouthful of "shrimp," his reply became a mumbled mess.

"See, this is why I like you, Maal. Deadpan delivery," Carson said, squeezing Maalek's shoulder.

With a swift move, Carson grabbed the bowl of shrimp and the tray of Habanero Poppers, guiding Maalek to a more secluded spot in the Wardroom. As they settled into their chairs, away from the heated discussions, Carson filled his plate and pondered the outcome of the negotiations.

"What do you think, Maal? Is the Generalissimo going to let the grown-ups finish the deal?" Carson asked as he loaded his plate.

Maalek's nostrils flared, and he clicked his tongue. "I believe so, but only after they extract even more concessions from your government. It is a transparent ploy by the Lord General and Prime Consul to solidify their positions."

Carson chuckled. "Well, they'll have to try harder if they go another round against the Old Man. Did you know Antonov once stared down an Arcturian heavy battle group with nothing but a rusty frigate and a bucket of fried chicken? Man's got a pair of cast iron balls. I wouldn't be surprised if he earns naming rights to the General's firstborn by the end of this shindig.

"He could not. The General named his firstborn Reela. She is an excellent pilot."

Carson shook his head, a smile playing on his lips. "Anyway, do you know where that Arcturian battle group is now?"

"No, I did not see that information in the morning briefing."

Carson raised his glass and arched an eyebrow. "That battle group is attached to Fifth Fleet as an auxiliary, and the Arcturians are hunting for a seat at the colonial table." He took a draught of the beer. "True story."

While they enjoyed their meal, Carson became distracted. Following his gaze, Maalek saw Captain Mori in deep conversation with the Chancellor. Even to Maalek, who was new to these interactions, it was evident that Mori had a commanding presence, a quality he knew was respected across cultures.

Their eyes met, and they acknowledged each other with a nod. After conversing with the Chancellor and the Captain of Artemis, she walked toward them. Maalek tracked her approach with keen interest, sensing her aura of authority.

Maalek looked at his friend, whose hand froze halfway to his glass. "Skip, are you all right?"

"Yeah, I... I just... uh..."

Maalek, drawing on the wisdom of Daalamas, mused, "A ship veers off course when one oar is out of sync. If you wish to court the Captain, we can chat again later."

Maalek pushed his chair back to stand up, but Carson whispered through gritted teeth. "Sit down, Maal. And for Christ's sake, don't say things like 'court' about the Captain unless you want us both to get spaced," Carson said.

"Spaced?"

"Yes, spaced. Remember, in space, no one can hear you scream, and if the Captain shoots us out of an airlock, there'll be plenty of screaming."

As Mori approached, the two men stood, Maalek offering a bow that blended Klii tradition with the moment's significance. "Captain Mori, it is an honor. Your ship is a beacon of hope," he said, perhaps a bit too grandiosely.

"Maalek ur Aal ur Jheet vas Daalamas. It is a pleasure to meet you officially. Hey, Skip. Is this seat taken?" she asked.

Maalek's eyes brightened at her flawless pronunciation of his full title and name. Her unexpected fluency was a welcome surprise.

"Gawd, if that man pinches my elbow or calls me sweetheart again, I swear I'm going to have the Master at Arms shoot him out a torpedo tube," Mori said.

Carson looked at Maalek with an expression best described as "I told you."

"Oh, Habanero Poppers, I love these. Any more beer in that pitcher, Skip?" she said.

"Yes, Ma'am," Carson said, filling her glass.

"So, Maalek, how do you like outer space?" Mori asked.

"Space, much like your Galatea, is a realm of untold beauty and mystery, Captain. Both command my deepest respect."

"Thank you, Maalek. I love compliments about my ship." She flicked her eyes toward Carson. "I understand you two are good friends?" she asked Maalek.

"Lieutenant Carson is more than a friend. He is a brother."

"I love hearing that. We need more people like you two. I have some ideas I want to run by Admiral Antonov and Colonel

Patel about that. Assuming this deal ever gets done, we're going to be allies. I want to take that all the way."

"Captain ur Mori vas Galatea..."

"Captain alone is fine, Maalek."

Maalek nodded. "Captain, do you have a mate?"

Carson's eyebrows shot up, and he kicked Maalek under the table. Maalek kicked him back.

Mori's water glass paused halfway to her lips. "Excuse me?"

Maalek paused, wondering if he'd crossed a line. Klii were direct in conversation, but he'd learned that colonials danced around topics. He trusted his instincts and forged ahead. "In Kliinat, a necklace signifies a life bond. When I glimpsed your necklace, I wondered whether you have a comparable tradition. Please accept my sincere apologies if I am being presumptuous in asking."

Mori touched the pendant that hung around her neck under her uniform jacket. "This is a picture of my parents. They died in a Union attack years ago. I always carry it with me." She opened the small golden pendant and showed Maalek the picture. Her expression softened. A soft smile graced her lips as her finger traced over the image.

Maalek reached into the inner pocket of his tunic and pulled out a thin sheet of plastic, a picture of his wife and daughters.

"They're... beautiful," Mori said.

Maalek dipped his head. "Thank you. They died within the first few days of the invasion. Now, they wait for me beyond the Great Sea. I will see them again one day."

Mori and Maalek exchanged family stories and soon laughed like old friends. Carson relaxed and fetched "shrimp" and beer at Mori's gentle prodding.

Maalek found himself fascinated by the dance between Carson and Mori. Carson would avoid Mori's eyes, then sneak peeks when he thought she wasn't looking. The captain, to Maalek's amusement, was doing the same. When they reached for the same glass and their fingers touched, Carson recoiled so quickly Maalek half-expected to see smoke rising from his hand.

"Skip, you realize I have a ship to run?" Mori said when Carson refilled her glass.

"Oh, sorry, Captain."

"I'm just kidding. Give it here," she said.

Maalek tracked the dance: Carson studying his glass when Mori looked his way, Mori suddenly fascinated by her plate whenever Carson glanced up. He pondered if their exchanges were mere military decorum or hints of...something else. "Captain, do you know Skip from before the war?"

"Oh, yeah. We went to the academy together. I was, what, three years ahead?"

"Two," Carson said.

"Right. You should have seen Skip on the Breakball court, Maalek. We beat Army for three straight years. The first and only time that's ever been done. I am still trying to figure out how he could be so good on the field yet so clumsy. Skip, remember that time you spilled applesauce all over my jacket? I had a report due that day, too, and I didn't have time to change it. I went to class smelling like an apple tree threw up on me."

Carson cringed and changed the subject. "Maalek, how are Andaeer and—"

The Chancellor interrupted their friendly banter. "Ladies and Gentlemen, let us return to the conference room. We have a full agenda, and the day wanes. Captain Mori?"

Mori rolled her eyes and pushed her plate away. Carson, ever the gentleman, leaped up to pull her chair out. But in his rush, he knocked the shrimp bowl, sending sauce arcing across the table. Mori sprang back, sauce droplets splattering the edge of her uniform as she dodged the seafood tsunami.

"Skip, what the..."

Carson froze. His napkin twisted into rope between his fingers. The shrimp bowl mockingly dripped sauce onto the deck. All eyes fixed on him. Maalek stepped back, taking it all in—Mori's poised coolness, the Chancellor's smooth exit, Carrigan's not-so-veiled frustration. He caught the XO muttering about Carson's ancestry and his brain being somewhere south of where it should be. Maalek made a mental note to ask Carson later if this was some sort of human medical condition.

Mori dabbed her sleeve with a napkin, her movements unhurried as if sauce-dodging was part of her daily routine. "Thank you, Lieutenant," she said with a nod and a smile. "See you back in the wardroom." She stood and walked away at an easy pace, exchanging pleasantries with the Chancellor and Prime Consul before heading for the door.

People filed out of the room with no apparent concern about the mishap. Maalek breathed out, feeling the weight lift off his shoulders. He suspected any punishment would have already been dealt.

"Skip, let us join the meeting," he said.

Carson found something fascinating about the bulkhead's rivets, his shoulders parade-ground straight. He nodded and blinked twice, then put the crumbled napkin on the table. He fastened the top button of his jacket. "Right. Okay, Maal, lead the way."

They exited the room, but the XO intercepted them at the door. He nodded to Maalek but addressed Carson with hard, narrowed eyes, like a Kaava's hind claws.

"Now you've done it, twinkle toes. My office. Tomorrow. 0600."

"Yes, sir," Carson managed, throwing up a salute that was more reflex than respect. The XO walked away.

Maalek leaned in close to Carson. "Will you be okay?" he asked.

"Yeah, it's not my first scorcher with the XO. The Captain's the one I'm worried about."

They entered the conference room, the doors closing behind them, and they split paths to their seats. Tension crackled through the air like static electricity. Around them, voices dropped to whispers, eyes darting from face to face.

Adaara, Neskfaat's Prime, glided in with her delegation, every bit as regal as the legendary Warrior Queen. It was no cosmic accident that Neskfaat had weathered the occupation with its sovereignty intact. Adaara chose the seat beside him. He dipped his head, doing his best to hide his surprise.

"Prime Adaara, blessings and good fortune."

"And to you. What do you make of these two idiots, Maalek?" she asked.

He had no interest in mincing words. "Imbeciles. They pose a threat to Kliinat, which is equal to the Union. Perhaps greater if they mishandle this. That recklessness has not been seen since the last War of Unification. I fear what lies ahead if they remain in a position of power."

She flashed him a wry smirk. "Me too. What do you think we should do about them?"

"What can we do? The Council may come to their senses and vote them out. Or we could send them gift-wrapped back to the Union. There are worrisome rumors about the Prime's dealings with the territorial governor during the occupation."

Adaara gave a nod that could have meant anything. "I have heard them as well. But without proof, they shall remain rumors. But something tells me fortune may yet smile upon us," Adaara said.

"Fortune owes us a great debt. She has paid us back somewhat with the timely arrival of the colonies, but she has now burdened us with these two."

The meeting resumed, and they listened in silence as the Lord General argued his case again, tension drumming a beat in the background. Still, Maalek noticed that the Marine escort had stayed in their posts.

A colonial comms officer arrived and spoke with Antonov. He walked over to the Klii delegation and handed Adaara a document. He distributed copies to the Chancellor, the Lord

General, and the Prime Consul. Adaara's touch on his thigh nearly sent him through the ceiling. Her smile suggested that was exactly the reaction she'd expected.

She smiled at his discomfort. "Now we are going to see something interesting, I think," she said, rising from her seat. "Admiral Antonov, Chancellor Coloccini, I fear this meeting has tarnished your opinion of Klii leadership. Let me assure you, here and now, this charade is over. The Council of 64 held an emergency session to expedite the stabilization of the planet. Much work is to be done; much work is to be expected. And we need help." She turned to the Lord General. "As the new Prime of Kliinat, I would like to thank you for your candor, dedication to our people, and tireless devotion. I grant you the title of Noble of the Robe, with all the lands and stipends befitting your station."

Adaara is the new Prime?

Chairs creaked. Datapads clattered. A thousand whispered calculations of new allegiances filled the air. Making someone a Noble of the Robe marked the end of their career, a forced retirement intended to avoid public embarrassment. It was best done behind closed doors, not in the middle of negotiations with an interstellar species. The Lord General sunk into his seat. The Prime—the former Prime—went pale.

"Now, before we bring this meeting to a close," Adaara said, "I fear we have not heard the words of those brave soldiers who have fought against the invaders, those whose blood has stained the lands of our home world. Their voices carry as much weight with me as I trust they do with you, Chancellor."

The Chancellor nodded. "Of course, Prime Adaara."

"Maalek ur Aal ur Jheet vas Daalamas, rise and offer us counsel on this matter of an alliance."

Maalek's throat constricted, his words stuck somewhere between his chest and mouth. His stomach churned, but not as much as his left hand trembled. He looked across the room for help, any help. Carson gave him a thumbs-up. Mori offered him an encouraging smile. A mixture of duty and a dash of dread propelled Maalek to his feet.

He took a deep, steadying breath. "We owe a blood debt to the colonies," he said, surprised at how steady his voice sounded despite the jitters in his stomach. "Ten thousand suns will rise, and this obligation will remain unpaid. I am prepared to shed my blood—nay, I look forward to it —if it brings the scales closer to balance. If we can mitigate this great inequity with our gold and tritium, the ancient code of honor demands we see it done. To do otherwise is unforgivable. It is immoral." Maalek saluted Captain Mori before resuming his seat.

"I could not have spoken truer words, Maalek," Adaara said. "As my first official act, I approve the Agreement of Friendship and Cooperation between the sovereign world of Kliinat and the colonies, to be signed without delay. I intend to call an extraordinary senate session, as is my right under Article 7, Paragraph 2 of the agreement, to request the formal introduction of Kliinat and planets under our jurisdiction as the 23rd Colony."

As Adaara spoke, Maalek couldn't help but marvel at how quickly things had changed. One minute, they were arguing over scraps; the next, they were talking about becoming the 23rd Colony. He blinked at each new declaration, trying to map the political battlefield that had just shifted like desert sands.

Adaara swept her hand over the Klii delegation. "I understand we have much to prove yet, and the process is long and arduous, but let us begin the journey with this first step."

Chapter 13

Command Deck, CCV Galatea

Tau Ceti System

August 14, 2681

Captain Mori stepped out of the elevator into the heart of Galatea. The hum of clanging tools and the crackle of welders swept over her, a far cry from the quiet ready room she'd just left. Each sound and vibration was one step closer to getting her ship battle-ready. As she turned into the corridor leading to her cabin's solitude, she heard someone call her name.

"Captain," the XO said, flanked by a figure of undeniable martial bearing. "This is Sentar Talyn, he's been assigned as our new weapons officer."

Talyn stepped forward, his amethyst eyes meeting Mori's steady gaze. His black uniform, adorned with medals and ceremonial threads, stood out against his vibrant sky-blue skin, emphasizing his imposing presence.

Mori studied the intricate decorations on Talyn's crests, a tangible representation of the Arcturian warrior culture she'd only read about until now. A thin scar running across his right cheek from ear to chin gave him a touch of daring. He performed the Arcturian blade salute, drawing his dagger in a smooth arc, pointing the tip down as he bowed.

"Legatar Mori," Talyn said, straightening. "Your command, my blade."

"Welcome aboard Galatea, Sentar," Mori said, her tone balancing warmth with authority. "I have a busy day ahead. Would you walk with me?"

"As you command, Legatar," Talyn said, falling into step beside her as they navigated the corridor's temporary clutter. Mori noted the curious glances from crew members hurrying past.

"I expect you're familiar with the weapons systems of colonial strike carriers," Mori said. "We remain on high alert and may jump into combat at any moment."

"Yes, Legatar," Talyn replied, his voice steady. "Before this, I served as weapons officer aboard the Longbow-class carrier Longstrike. Arcturian Longbow Carriers share many of the same colonial systems."

Mori raised an eyebrow, impressed. "Longstrike? I heard she held her own against the Union's Fifth Fleet in Isendar."

Talyn's crests flared, and his lips curved into a subtle smile. "A fierce battle. Longstrike proved her mettle, as did her crew."

They ducked under a set of loose cables as they reached her cabin. "Galatea is a formidable warship to survive such a battle. You honor me with this distinction," Talyn said, taking in the chaotic scene.

Once at her cabin, Mori activated the door with a touch, stepping through as Talyn followed.

She accepted the datapad from the XO and reviewed the official orders before signing. "Here, we value swift action and sound judgment, Sentar; it keeps us ahead in battle," she said, handing back the pad.

"Speak command and see it done, Legatar," Talyn said, who stood at rigid attention, arms behind his back.

Mori's expression softened. "While aboard, you may address me as Captain. And I understand 'Sentar' is equivalent to our rank of Commander, correct?" She glanced at the XO for confirmation.

"Affirmative, Captain," the XO said.

Talyn gave a respectful nod. "Understood. The title of 'Sentar' or simply 'Talyn' would be proper."

"Then, Talyn, how soon can you assume a watch?"

"I stand ready to serve, Legatar—apologies, *Captain*."`

"Then again, welcome aboard. Carry on, Talyn."

Talyn bowed, pivoted, and exited. Once the door slid closed, she addressed the XO. "Keep him close; I want to know how he handles the watches. We need him fully integrated, but I'm counting on your judgment here."

The XO nodded. "I'll make sure he's ready."

"Very good," Mori said. "Keep me updated. Carry on."

The XO saluted. "Good morning, Captain."

Once alone, she poured herself a steaming mug of coffee, the aroma mixing with the sterile air of the ship. Settling into her command throne—less regal, more practical—she powered up the holoscreen. The warm light greeted her as she began her routine of managing requisitions and transfers—and one in particular she had been looking forward to: a Daal Butter Fruit. Its rich flavor was a delightful fusion of strawberries and peaches, and the governor of Daalamas had gifted her two cases.

She set her coffee aside, cracked a knuckle like a soloist prepping for a concert, and dove into her inbox. She sorted through a hundred "urgent" messages, many criticizing Captain Carrigan. The XO had turned the repair crews into his personal marathon runners, minus the running and plus the marathon. She and the XO were of one mind when it came to Galatea, and if the crew had issues with his style, they'd find her to be a nightmare in a uniform. She tackled the messages, her fingers tapping a measured cadence on the keyboard.

Ten minutes later, thirteen new messages flooded her inbox—Mori's shoulders sagged. Galatea demanded her attention, pulling her between showcasing the ship for dignitaries and preparing for the looming encounter with the Union. The Colonial Fourth Fleet played a cosmic chess game, with destroyers and cruisers guarding jump points and Dreadnoughts looming at strategic positions, ready to unleash their firepower. Artemis was licking her wounds—Centurion gave her a thrashing, after all—but Cassiopeia tagged in, orbiting above Kliinat's capital city, Naadan, coordinating infantry operations. In her opinion, every credit spent on Kliinat struck the Union Navy like a bullet, a worthy investment.

Then, a ping from Clara cut through the routine. Mori's face softened at the familiar chime. Clara, more sister than friend, was a welcome reminder of life beyond the command deck. They'd been inseparable since childhood, their bond only strengthening through the years. After Mori's harrowing space ordeal, it was Clara who'd helped her find her footing again, piece by piece. Mori grinned as her image appeared on the screen.

"Tomoe, you're alive! It's been eons since you snagged the reins of that shiny strike carrier. Thought you forgot all about me."

"Guilty. I'm swamped, but what about dinner at the Seven Swans next shore leave? My treat. Call it my way of making up."

Clara's gaze wandered, a mock sternness in her eyes. "Might do the trick. But only just. Hey, did Sophia's masterpiece make it to you?"

Sophia was like a miniature Clara, from her rich chocolate hair to her petite frame. To Mori, she was more than a goddaughter—she was the child Mori never had, but loved as her own. Mori's eyes rested on the drawing, given a place of honor by her bed. Every time Mori saw Sophia's drawings, her heart warmed. "I framed it and put it on my nightstand. You know, Sophie looks just like you."

Clara's laughter chimed through the comm. "Let's keep that our little secret, shall we? Harry's under the adorable delusion that she's his carbon copy."

"He wishes."

"You still coming over for Christmas? I'm baking your favorite sour cream and raisin cake."

Mori leaned back, her relaxed posture contrasting with the pensive frown creasing her forehead. "I don't know. It all depends on how things shape up here."

Clara leaned into the screen with a sternness that Mori knew all too well. "Tomoe Mori, don't make me jump my ship to Kliinat and drag you here 'cause you know I will."

"Alright, I give up, but you also better make those little potato-filled pastries."

"Deal." Clara agreed with a grin, waving off-screen. "Duty calls. Love you, sis."

"Back atcha. Safe flying." Mori's salute was more familial than formal as the call ended. Before Mori could return to her work, Eddie interrupted her. "Captain, apologies for disturbing you; Prime Adaara has arrived for your meeting."

Mori's smile lingered as her growing rapport with Adaara came to mind. She shut the holoscreen down and pushed away from her desk. "Ask her to come in, Eddie, and can you ask the steward to bring refreshments?"

At that moment, a steward entered carrying a tray filled with sweet bread, a carafe of coffee, and fresh fruit. The aroma of sweet bread coaxed a broader smile from Mori.

"Did you say refreshments, Captain? I cut some of the Butter Fruit you're fond of."

"Thank you. You have impeccable timing."

"It is my pleasure, ma'am. I prepped your dress uniform for tonight's dinner; it's in your quarters. Do ring if you require anything else."

Adaara opened the door, and the mixed escort—Klii scouts with their ceremonial knives, Marines with their parade-ground posture—flanked the door. "Your Primeship," the steward said, "I recall you enjoyed Olympian sweets on your last visit. I asked the mess to prepare traditional bread and treats from my hometown. I hope you will forgive the intrusion."

Adaara's smile was a sunrise. "That smells wonderful, thank you. What is it you humans like to say? You read my thoughts? No, you read my mind. You are very kind."

"You are most welcome, your Primeship." The steward bowed and left.

After the steward excused himself, Adaara sank into the sofa, her clothes rich with cultural significance and a subtle statement of diplomacy. Her hairstyle was more than a fashion statement—it was a crown of Klii heritage.

Mori's utilitarian uniform left her feeling like a spacer on a junker next to Adaara's finery. She couldn't help but drink in Adaara's radiance, aware of how the long hours in recycled air had taken their toll on her own appearance while Adaara shimmered like she'd been dusted with starlight. Mori caught herself standing with her arms crossed and felt her cheeks warm. Some host she was, looking like a stern drill instructor. She straightened up, reminding herself she was a strike carrier captain. Time to act like it and set a welcoming tone.

"Coffee? Sweets? Tomoe, why do I feel you're buttering me

up? Did I get that right?" Adaara said.

Mori smiled as she prepared her charm offensive. "Why, Adaara, I don't know what you're talking about. I know how much you love coffee, and you're my honored guest. Here, have another bombolone."

Adaara chuckled, a lag in her laughter suggesting a brief delay in the translation. She gestured for Mori to continue. "I knew it. Out with it."

Mori raised her arms in mock surrender. "Okay, you got me. Have you considered my proposal of a combined company of Klii Scouts and Colonial Marines?"

Adaara sipped her coffee, closed her eyes, and savored the bitter brew. "I have thought about it," she said, placing her cup down and marrying a bombolone to the brew in a dunking ceremony that Mori noted had become a Klii favorite. They fell in love with coffee, and the few cafés that sold it in the big cities made a fortune.

Adaara took a bite of the pastry, her eyes narrowing as she considered her next words. She sipped her coffee again, and with a grin that could light up the darkest of space, said, "I agree. As you put it last time, I had to twist a couple of arms. Klii generals are the most stubborn creatures, and my office faces some roadblocks."

Mori felt a twinge of sympathy. Nothing's ever easy, she thought, giving a slow nod. "I'm sorry to hear that. Let me know if I can help."

"Yes, me too. But do not worry; the generals will fall in line. Some are still loyal to the former Prime, working behind the scenes to undermine our efforts, but we will root them all out in time.

"Let me know if I can help," Mori said. "We're all set to go on our side. The admiral signed off, and I have the perfect candidates lined up. The Arcturians are also very interested, but the Emperor wants to see how this works before committing troops." She topped off both cups with a practiced pour, the rich aroma of the coffee filling the air. Mori picked up her cup with both hands and took a slow sip.

"I would love to meet an Arcturian. I've heard so much about them," Adaara said, curiosity lighting up her eyes.

"We extended an invitation for them to evaluate the new company, assuming it gets off the ground," Mori said, pausing as she set her cup down with a soft clink that was sharper than intended. "But the red tape has been more tangled than usual." She bit back a comment about it being stifling even by Arcturian standards. No need to let her frustration seep into the conversation.

"Then let us get it off the ground. When should we begin?" Adaara asked, leaning forward.

"As soon as possible. Also, I was hoping you'd stay for dinner?"

Adaara's response came with a smile that had all the warmth of a sunny day. "As long as you keep the coffee coming."

⋈⋈⋈

Mori worked through her inbox, halving the unread messages—a minor win in her book. She stopped to massage her tired eyes and glanced at her wristwatch, a keepsake from her great-grandfather's time in the Navy, which showed 15:50.

Its steady ticking was a comforting sound. Her thumb traced the worn leather strap, decades of Naval history in every crack. She stood up to stretch and ease the day's accumulated tension from her muscles. "Eddie, what else is on my schedule today? And please message Adaara that I will swing by her cabin a little earlier. I want to run my speech for the signing ceremony by her. Also, I need a speech."

Eddie's voice came through her neural link, the AI's presence as familiar as it was efficient. "Message sent. I have placed a speech in your inbox. Please let me know if there's anything you wish to change. You have one last meeting today, Captain, with Lieutenant Carson."

"Right, at what time?"

"Ten minutes ago. Lieutenant Carson has been standing at attention outside your door for the past fifteen minutes."

Mori's great-grandfather's watch ticked an accusation from her wrist. "Send him in, Eddie," she said, straightening her uniform. A moment later, Carson walked in, saluted, and stood at attention. "Captain, you wished to see me?" he asked.

Mori smiled and walked around the desk to face Carson. "At ease, Marine. Skip, I'll keep this short. Typically, this would fall to your commanding officer, and I am technically outside your chain of command. However, we haven't tried this before, so we're winging it, and the brass is all on board."

"Ma'am?" Carson knitted his brows together.

"First, the bad news," Mori said, her shoulders sagging slightly. "You're losing Second Platoon. Something to do with... what does it say here?" She pulled out her datapad, scrolling through a couple of screens. "Right... Colonel Patel thinks it's time for a change, and I'm sorry to say HQ agrees." She sighed, rubbing the back of her neck. "They believe your leadership skills are needed elsewhere."

Carson's gaze dropped, a flurry of emotions passing across his face. His shoulders slumped, and his brows knitted together in a frown. "I... I'm not exactly on Colonel Patel's Christmas list this year, but I..." He paused for a moment, then straightened his back. "I understand, Ma'am. May I ask who my replacement will be?"

Mori allowed a small smile to play at the corners of her mouth. "Well, this is where things get interesting." She pulled out a small black box from her pocket and opened it, revealing the silver bars of a Marine Captain. The glimmering insignia caught the light, drawing her eyes to them.

"That's going to be up to you. Two weeks ago, Colonel Patel put you in for a battlefield promotion for your actions during the liberation of Daalamas. Your platoon destroyed three enemy missile batteries and captured twenty prisoners. Besides securing the crash site for that downed shuttle, Major Hong says the Hell Divers owe you one, and let's leave your rescue of Maalek's unit out. Adaara has something special planned for you, by the way. Admiral Antonov signed the paperwork weeks ago; we were just waiting for the confirmation from HQ. Congrats, Captain Carson."

Mori stepped closer and pinned the bars on his collar. "I gotta say, they don't look half bad on you."

Carson's shoulders squared, silver bars gleaming on his collar. "I don't know what to say, Captain, other than thank you."

"Don't go thanking me just yet. We're assembling a mixed company with Colonial Marines and Klii Scouts, Echo Company. You're going to lead it, and because it's my idea, I get to oversee it."

"Echo what now?" Carson blinked like a man introduced to gravity for the first time.

"Okay, let me spell it out for you. We're putting you in charge of Echo Company, the first-ever mixed Marine company. Colonel Patel will fill in the details tomorrow, but we expect to have the company roster completed in two weeks. It's your prerogative to choose from the list of Klii volunteers. The approval for this new company came from the very top, so I will be the liaison with Klii leadership and ultimately responsible for its success and failure. Hence, why you're standing in my office... with that terrified look."

"Permission to speak freely," Carson said.

"Granted."

"Okay, uh, that's a lot to process. Where are we going to train the new recruits? Should we have a boot camp? Do we need to wear translators? Are the Klii going to be okay taking orders from us? I'll have more questions once I can, um, think straight."

Mori's lips twitched with a suppressed smile. "Klii high command knows we're running this show; I'm confident they won't give you any trouble. As for your other questions, Eddie has sent all the details to your datapad, but I expect we'll figure out much of it on the go."

Carson nodded once. "I can do that. Figuring it out on the go got me through many late nights at the academy."

"I remember. I'm also sending you the list of Klii volunteers I received from Adaara. You'll see some familiar names there, but you have the latitude to pick your team."

"Thank you, ma'am," Carson said.

"A lot is riding on this. If you have any reservations, now's the time."

Carson pulled his shoulders back. "No, ma'am. And, again, thank you, I'll try not to let you down... too much."

"Okay, Skip. Dismissed. I'll be following up in the next few days."

"I look forward to it, Captain." He smiled, and their eyes locked.

Mori tucked her hair behind her ear, the room's temperature suddenly not cool enough. A tingling sensation reached her stomach. They looked at each other for only a few heartbeats, but the silence that lingered made it feel like minutes.

"I mean... not like, overly looking forward to it," Carson said.

She looked at him with a cocked head, her brows knitted together in curiosity.

"Not that I won't be looking forward to it at all; it's more like the right amount of looking forward one does for normal, everyday follow-ups," he said, stumbling over the words.

Carson closed his eyes for a moment. He offered Mori a crisp salute. "I should probably get up to speed with Colonel Patel. By your leave, Captain."

"Carry on, Captain," Mori said, returning the salute.

Once alone, Mori felt a lingering warmth from his visit. She caught herself wondering why the room's temperature spiked when he walked in. And why did he have to look like the picture-perfect Marine officer, complete with boyish good looks, magnetic charm, and disarming smile? He obviously felt something too, or he wouldn't—no, goddamn it, she didn't have time for that. She should be plotting courses, not heartbeats.

"Captain?" Eddie's voice interrupted, its tone shifting to something that sounded almost like concern.

"Yes, Eddie."

"Your heart rate is elevated, and I'm detecting a change in your breathing pattern. I would say you're having a cardiac episode, except there's a spike in your levels of dopamine and norepinephrine consistent with opposite-sex attraction. Are you alright?"

"Shut up and let me work." The AI fell silent. Tomoe Mori, Captain of Galatea, shook her head. Of all the challenges she'd faced, this was one battlefield she'd never expected to navigate.

Chapter 14

Forward Operating Base Charlie, Daalamas

Kliinat, Tau Ceti System

September 15, 2681

Kliinat's sun was merciless, much like the grueling obstacle course Gunny had prepared. Carson and his Marines navigated the course, trudging through thick mud that weighed down their boots and sapped their strength. Carson vaulted over wooden barricades, gasping for air as he raced to the next challenge. He ducked under razor wire, collecting nicks, scratches, and tears in his t-shirt, then rappelled down the ropes, the roughness against his palms taking him back to his early days of training. He tapped into his reserve strength, pushed through the last stretch, shrugged off the sharp pain in his side, and raced to the end. Gunny stood at the finish line with a stopwatch.

"Five-twenty. Excellent time, sir."

"Still got it, Gunny." Sweat trickled down his forehead, and his lungs burned from the exertion.

"Never doubted it, sir," Gunny said.

Gasping for air, Carson joined Williams, Rodriguez, and a Klii scout at the cooler for a drink of water. He finished fifth out of sixty, not too shabby, considering his throbbing knee. He'd been delaying the suggested knee replacement in favor of simple ice bags.

Three minutes later, after the last Marine finished, Gunny called them together. "Look at this soup sandwich of a performance. Now square yourselves away and apologize to Captain Carson for dirtying his air after that goat rope of a run." She singled out two chattering Klii recruits. "You two, lock it up, or I will put my foot up your ass and wear you like flip-flops. The rest of you, take a drink of water, then we'll do it again, go, go, go."

Carson walked up to Gunny, wiping mud from his neck. They'd been hammering Echo Company with all the finesse of an anvil. What took twelve weeks at boot camp back home, they compressed into six here. It was down to him and Gunny to mold these Marines, and they were almost there.

"Have you seen Maalek? It's not like him to miss a training exercise," he asked her, taking a sip of water—a welcome relief that eased the dryness of his throat.

When Carson received Mori's list of Klii volunteers, he was thrilled to find Maalek's application. He immediately approved it, promoted him to Lieutenant, and tasked him with selecting other Klii scouts. Maalek picked hard-nosed, fearless warriors who followed orders to the letter.

"He, um, had an important meeting with the, um, yeah... brass," Gunny said.

"Really? That's weird. I don't remember seeing any messages about that."

"Sir, that's all I know. I'm sure he'll turn up sooner than later."

Gunny was already on her way, barking at a Marine who'd become a little too acquainted with the mud. Carson's gaze drifted to the horizon. Kliinat's sun draped everything in an otherworldly orange glow, making the sky look like it was on fire. The alien landscape, with its vibrant purple vegetation against a brilliant cerulean sky, was striking. In the distance, Faanu birds darted between the blooms, their presence considered sacred by the locals. Maalek had mentioned they were keepers of the forest, spirits blessed by the deities.

Gunny started the stopwatch and blew her whistle, "Start running, petunias."

The Marines started the run with a will, bumping into each other as they jostled for position. Sousa twisted her ankle and hobbled to the first obstacle: long planks on stilts.

Gunny gave her a little encouragement. "That ankle ain't broken, is it, Corporal? No? Then let's see some motivation, move it!"

"The beatings will continue until morale improves, right, Gunny?" Carson said, tossing her a bottle of water.

She removed the cap and took a long pull. "Yes, Sir. Nothing beats a nice muddy run while under bombardment to boost morale. Oh, that reminds me." She tapped her ear and opened a neural channel. "Anti-Aircraft Aether Battery, you're clear to fire."

Carson looked at her with a cocked eyebrow. "Do I want to know what this is about?"

"You'll find out in a tick, sir."

On cue, the sky screeched a tune of incoming faux-doom. The first explosion ripped through the middle of the course, causing a couple of newbies to drop to the ground. Even Carson flinched a smidge.

"Fireworks and fanfare, sir. It's like a spa treatment but with more adrenaline and less lavender," Gunny said, a wicked gleam in her eyes.

Explosions sent clods of earth flying, coating the runners, with the Klii recruits catching the worst of Daalamas' finest mud. If nothing else, it was an instant lesson in the art of duck and cover. Two Klii stood dazed, perhaps contemplating the merits of mud as a facial.

"Aw, what's the matter? Do you need a glass of suck it up? The finish line is that way. Get moving."

The training exceeded Carson's expectations, with Klii recruits fitting in well. With Gunny by his side, they'd have the company ready lickety-split.

"Gunny, give them a break after this run, then four more laps. After that, send them to the showers and chow. We're going to the range with live ammo this afternoon. I want them sharp."

"Yes, sir."

"I've got a fever, Gunny, and the only prescription is more shells. Let's make the next run really spicy."

"It will be my pleasure," Gunny said.

Carson noted the budding camaraderie. The Klii were more than keeping pace—they were setting it. The new platoons were gelling much quicker than he'd expected. His Marines were battle-hardened, well-trained, and familiar with the life of a Colonial Marine. Still, he needed to figure out how the Klii would fit in. Turned out he needn't have worried. Klii excelled in training and were eager to absorb everything their instructors had to teach them.

He left Gunny to her circus of motivation and trudged to his quarters. After a refreshing shower and changing into fresh threads, he plunged into the core duties of running Echo Company. Sorting applications and crafting progress reports were standard fare, but today, he had a special task: requisitioning Klii knives to use as bayonets. After seeing the knives in action, the idea had hit him like a rail gun slug, and he was itching to get them for the company. Who wouldn't want a sweet thermal blade on the end of their rifle?

Carson's neural flicked to Alexandria's time zone without conscious thought—just in time to catch the nightly ritual of his nephews fighting bedtime with the determination of tiny lawyers pleading their case. He opened a Q-entanglement channel from his holoscreen and waited for the call to connect. Gianna picked up after three rings.

"Matty! What's up?" she asked.

She stood in the kitchen, picking up dirty plates from the table. A tuft of blond hair darted behind her, following the wagging tail of their family dog as one of his nephews gave chase. Gianna adjusted the datapad to keep it upright.

"Kinda late for dinner, isn't it?" he asked.

Gianna put the stack of plates on the washer and wiped her hands with a towel. She approached the screen, drew closer, and settled into a chair. "Emily had to work late, so we waited for her. Oh, she says hi."

Carson waved. "Hi, Emmy." Emily was Gianna's wife, and Carson couldn't imagine a more perfect couple than the two of them. They raised two kids, held jobs, volunteered at their kids' school, and helped his mother run the family farm.

"How's your new company coming along, or is it top secret?" Gianna asked.

"You know I can't talk about that," Carson said with a smile, though a shadow flickered across his face as he spoke. "I just wanted to say hi and make sure you guys are okay."

Gianna's eyes narrowed. "Spill it, Matty. You've got that 'carrying the world' look again."

He scratched his chin, managing a half-smile. "That obvious, huh?" He paused, his gaze drifting off-screen. "It's just... I'm not sure I'm the right man for this job, if I'm being honest."

Gianna tilted her head, her eyebrows raising in a silent prompt. "And what makes you say that?"

Carson rubbed the back of his neck. "Tell me to charge a tank to disable the turret, and I'll be the one running in front. What if I can't be the one to give the order?"

Gianna's expression softened. "I know what you're thinking. Dad gave those orders, sure. But being a leader is more than charging ahead or giving orders, Matty."

Carson's eyes flicked away for a moment, focusing on something off-screen that only he could see. "It's easy to lead from the front. It's harder to send others into the grinder, knowing I'm responsible if they don't come back." The words came out quieter than he'd intended, like confessing a secret he'd been keeping even from himself.

She leaned toward the camera, bridging the distance between them. "But that's exactly what makes you the right person. You care. Dad cared too, but his way was... different." A gentle smile formed on her lips. "Your empathy, your hesitation—that's your strength. It makes you think; it puts all those lives in perspective."

"And if that hesitation costs us?" Carson fidgeted with the edge of the tablet.

Gianna's finger wagged at the holoscreen with the authority of a mom who'd just found crayon art on the living room wall. "What if it saves us? Leadership isn't about having no doubts, Matty. It's about what you do despite having them. You're not Dad, and that's okay. You have a way of bringing people together, making them better. Don't lose sight of that."

Carson nodded, the corners of his mouth twitching into a tentative smile. "Thanks, Gi." He smiled the same sheepish smile she'd seen a thousand times, from scraped knees to graduation day. "I know I have to stop trying to fill his giant clown shoes, but it's hard sometimes."

Giana sat with a mock stern expression, hand on her hip. "Listen, and listen good, Matthew Carson. I'm not saying this because you're my little brother, and I love you. They put you in charge because they believe in you. You should start believing in yourself, too. Oh, Emily says you're being a turd."

"Tell her I love her too." The laughter bubbled up unexpectedly, genuine and warm. Trust Gianna to know exactly how to pull him out of his head.

"She's rolling her eyes, but she'll take it," Gianna said, chuckling, then whipped her head to the side. "Sam! If you trip over that dog, I swear I'll—"

"Looks like you have your hands full with the kids. I'll let you go. Call you next week?" Carson said, smiling.

"You better. Mom wants to know if you'll be home for Christmas. I told her I'd ask."

"I don't think so—" he saw the familiar disappointment flash across her face "—but I have liberty in a few weeks. If the stars align, I can swing a visit. Maybe catch one of Sam's infamous tea parties this time."

Her eyes brightened. "We would love that. Be safe; love you tons."

"I love you, too," Carson said.

The call ended, and Carson leaned back in his chair, taking a moment to reflect. Christmas was a no-go, but a quick detour home? He added it to his mental list of promises he hoped he could keep.

✳✳✳

After lunch, Carson wandered the base, half-lost in thought. He meandered to the front gate and peered toward the horizon. Naadan's cityscape was stitching itself back together, thanks to Klii resilience and some good old colonial elbow grease.

Jorge Sanchez

His neural pinged—a summons from Eddie, Galatea's AI. "Captain Carson, you are requested in building 1A for a meeting with Prime Adaara and Captain Mori. At your convenience."

"Thanks, Eddie, on my way," he said. What the hell was going on? When did the Captain and Prime arrive at the base? He knew what at your convenience meant and walked to the building with all haste.

Once there, the receptionist directed him to the base commander's office. As he reached the office, the sight that met his eyes surprised him—Maalek and Andaeer engaged in a lively conversation with Mori and Adaara. Maalek wore a rather mischievous grin. A Navy photographer was setting up a tripod and camera drone.

Mori approached him.

"Skip, remember the little surprise I told you about?"

"No, Captain, I can't say that I do."

Mori's eyes held that familiar glint that always made Carson forget about rank and protocol for a dangerous moment. Some habits were harder to break than others, even after all these years of carefully maintained professional distance. "Well, you know what they say about pictures and words."

Carson found himself sandwiched between Prime Adaara and a lineup of Klii dignitaries, all beneath a banner that might as well have read "Smile or Else." Adaara, armed with a wooden box and a ceremonial air, faced him, and Carson could almost hear the drumroll.

"Captain Carson," Adaara said, "for your timely assistance to one of our units during the operation to liberate our planet, it is my pleasure to bestow upon you the Council Medal of Valor."

He stood ramrod straight as Adaara placed the medal around his neck, suddenly very aware of every muscle in his face trying to form an appropriate expression. He wasn't made for spotlights; he was more a "shadowy nook" kind of guy.

Adaara gave him two ceremonial pecks, then an official handed her another box. She eased it open and removed a braided, purple cord. "It is also my great honor to award the Fifth Colonial Marine Regiment the Distinguished Order of Lilac, given to those who display exemplary bravery in battle," she said. "It is the oldest award in our military, dating back to the days of the Wars Between the Cities. It represents the ligatures of the armor worn by the ancient knights. Wear it with pride, knowing that you have the thanks of an entire people."

The Order of Lilac made the Council Medal look like a participation ribbon. Adaara, with a flourish, bestowed the purple cord upon him. Applause erupted as if on cue, and Maalek swooped in for a bear hug that almost cracked a rib. Carson shielded his face from the sudden flurry of camera flashes. When he faced Maalek, dark spots filled his vision.

"Let us take the field in many battles, my friend," Maalek said.

Carson's reply was warm and sincere. "It would be an honor, Maal."

Mori offered a handshake that was equal parts congratulatory and consoling. "We wanted to do a whole thing, but with the ongoing operations and the rebuilding effort, we could never synchronize our watches. I hope this is okay."

"It's more than okay, Captain. I don't know what to say."

Mori smiled. "You don't have to say anything."

A thought clicked in Carson's mind. "Can we take a few snapshots? My sister's gonna want proof I didn't make this up."

"Great idea," Mori said.

For the next ten minutes, Carson posed for photographs with the attendees and Mori. His arms dangled as if trying to decide whether to conduct an orchestra or start a campfire. He dreaded looking at the result.

Once the pomp faded, Carson escaped, only to be wrangled by Mori's arm barrier. "Not so fast. Seeing you out of your element is too much fun. Let's get some air."

Squinting into the sunlight, he saw his company cheering and waving their lilac cords. The sight warmed his heart, even as it made him want to crawl into a hole. Mori nudged him forward with a playful push, guiding him towards a nearby building.

"Just a little further, Skip," Mori said with a grin that suggested she knew something Carson didn't.

As they approached the officer's mess, Carson heard the muffled sounds of music and laughter. Mori opened the door, and suddenly, Carson found himself at the center of an impromptu party balloons bobbing overhead and a laden buffet table. He fought the urge to retreat back through the doorway as faces turned toward him, smiling.

After a blur of handshakes, toasts, and a speech that slipped from his memory as soon as he'd given it, Carson found himself nursing a plate heaped with local treats. As the crowd thinned and conversations softened to murmurs, Carson's shoulders finally dropped from their ceremonial height. Though he still couldn't shake the feeling that someone would realize they'd given the medal to the wrong Carson.

Adaara offered a parting cheek kiss, turning his face crimson. Mori sidled up to him as the crowd thinned, her brow knit in concern. "Why do I feel something's eating at you?"

Carson paused. His chest tightened the way it did before combat drops, except this time the enemy was a room full of people wanting to celebrate him. He rubbed his eyebrow with his right index finger, ensuring they were out of earshot. "It's not that I'm not grateful, I am, but this... I've done nothing, Captain. Every day, we lose good people out there. No medals, no parties. Just names on a wall back home. Those are the real heroes, you know?"

Mori's face went tender. "Skip, you're standing here because you did what few could. That medal isn't just yours. It's a token of solace for Kliinat, a tip of the hat from Athens, and a salute to the brave we've lost. If you don't think we celebrate their sacrifice every day in my Navy, you haven't been paying attention."

"You're right, Captain. I didn't mean to sound ungrateful. It's just... I'm not very good at this."

"Me either. Want some advice?" she asked.

"I would love some, actually," Carson said.

"Enjoy the moment, get to work, and wear that medal with pride. You and your Marines earned it with blood, tears, and hella guts. See you in a couple of weeks."

Jorge Sanchez

Carson snapped a crisp salute. "Good afternoon, ma'am."

He returned to the celebration and rolled up his sleeves to help with clean-up. They had daylight left, and those targets at the range weren't going to shoot themselves.

Chapter 15

Forward Operating Base Charlie, Daalamas

Kliinat, Tau Ceti System

September 15, 2681

Maalek found a quiet corner to watch the late afternoon gathering. The sun was setting, casting a warm glow over everything. Carson, sporting his new medal, had become the center of attention. He was drawing in Klii and human guests alike, who were celebrating his achievements with plenty of enthusiasm and camera flashes. Maalek watched the mingling crowd, noting how easily the Klii and humans moved between conversations, their laughter bridging old divides.

Carson, modest as always, still caught the eye of a journalist from the Olympia Daily. The reporter seemed eager to capture Carson's every interaction. As things quieted, Maalek considered joining Mori and Carson's conversation but decided to stay back. "Three wheels can tip the cart when one is loose," he thought. When Adaara tapped his arm, he knew it was time to go.

"Ready for a quieter walk?" Adaara asked with a smile that promised some peace.

Maalek inclined his head, the tension in his shoulders easing. "I can't think of a better way to end the day."

They slipped away from the celebration, walking along quiet paths as twilight set in. They managed to avoid groups of officials trying to catch Adaara's attention. Maalek realized he'd come to look forward to these walks through Daalamas. As the formal gathering faded behind them, the evening air felt different somehow, full of possibility.

"Maalek, I would love to see the new garden you mentioned. If you have time," Adaara said.

"Of course, but I must resume training soon. Are you not currently pressed by your duties?"

"Nothing that cannot wait for a couple of hours."

"In that case, I would be delighted."

As they walked together, Maalek noticed how they stood out against the base's activity. Their footsteps found a shared rhythm, out of step with the base's usual tempo. Passing soldiers and humming vehicles faded to background noise, as if the evening had carved out a space just for them.

Adaara stopped and waved off her bodyguards. "I doubt I will be in danger here, surrounded as we are by our finest soldiers. Wait for me by the entrance," she said.

"As you wish, your Primeship," her guards said, retreating to a respectful distance.

She turned to Maalek. "This is better. Now we can have some privacy."

Maalek glanced around at the open, bustling parade ground, raising an eyebrow. "Privacy isn't something we get much of here."

Her laughter cut through the base's busy noise, bright and clear. "Oh, do not be so obtuse. You know what I mean."

They walked along a familiar path, arm in arm, until they reached a quiet spot in the garden. Adaara glanced at Maalek, looking more vulnerable than usual. "These gardens are much like our city-states—beautiful but requiring careful, constant tending. Since becoming Prime, the careful balance, the push and pull... it is like nurturing these plants."

Maalek kept his attention on her as she spoke. It hit home that behind all the political maneuvering, there were personal sacrifices and moments of doubt. Seeing Adaara looking so unfazed, but at the same time so vulnerable, reminded him of when he first took command of a unit, where every decision felt like walking a tightrope.

"A fitting metaphor. I sense this nurturing weighs heavily upon you."

Her gaze drifted to the horizon. "Those vast deposits of Iridium and Rhodium under Neskfaat are like a Kaepyr's tail: two sides, each as distinct as day from night. Now, as Prime, I face the delicate task of negotiating mining rights. It's not just Neskfaat anymore; every city-state believes they deserve a share of what's beneath us," Adaara said.

He recognized that look—the same one he'd seen in his own reflection during those first months of command, when every decision felt like it could shatter worlds. "Such wealth can tempt some to elevate their status, perhaps even to wield more power," he said.

"Yes. I would be lying if I said this thought has not robbed me of sleep. Will I bind our people closer or fracture what unity we have? And through it all, I must remain impartial and ensure that Kliinat's future does not tilt into greed or strife."

Maalek wanted to help, to take some of that burden from her, but all he could do was lend an ear. "Yet, here you are, finding time to share a quiet moment, to walk through gardens," he said.

Adaara smiled, tired but genuine. "We find strength in quiet moments. It reminds us of why we fight. It's more than minerals and politics. It's about creating a Kliinat where our children can walk through gardens without fear, without the shadows of greed and oppression darkening the path."

"Then, for now, let us enjoy the scent of flowers and freshly cut grass and give you a moment of rest," Maalek said. They strolled down a path lined with fragrant Winter Blooms, then sat on a bench to soak in the peace. The garden was a sanctuary of colors and scents, a world away from the demands waiting for them outside. Here, time seemed to slow down, letting them savor each moment.

As they sat, leaves swayed in the soft breeze, and Faanu called in the distance, filling the quiet between them.

He found himself cataloging small details—the way her freckles crinkled when she smiled, how her hands moved when she spoke—things he'd trained himself to overlook since Sanya. Each smile of Adaara's brought Sanya's memory closer, not dimmer. The familiar ache of loss tangled with something unexpected—a warmth he'd forgotten how to name.

"I know your heart is heavy with sorrow, and if you allowed me, I would shoulder some of that burden with you," Adaara said. "I do not want to replace Sanya, nor could I, but the Goddess Amunkeera has opened a door for us. Let us walk through it, together. Tomorrow is never guaranteed, and the present is fleeting, Maalek."

"I do not know how to open that door anymore. I thought I had locked it forever until you walked into my life," Maalek said.

"Perhaps all we need to do is crack it open a little and then a little more. What if we start with dinner next time you have liberty? Something casual, just the two of us. You can tell me more about the trips you took with your daughters. I have gotten to know them through you, and it would not be too presumptuous to say that I feel a strong kinship with them."

"I have a forty-eight-hour pass in two weeks, and I would be a fool to decline such an invitation." The words came easier than he'd expected. His mouth curved upward before he could catch himself.

"I have heard it said that I'm a decent cook. And this was before I became Prime and compliments became obligatory. Tell me your favorite dish, and I will make it."

That was an easy one. "Pincer fish stew with root vegetables."

"Ah, the famous Daal dish. I know it well. My mother would make it for Father, using the traditional recipe of Neskfaat."

"What, the one that uses Ack Root? Was she trying to poison him?"

Adaara's response was tender, her lips brushing his cheek with a kiss. "He is handsome and has a sense of humor. I am a lucky one indeed." She stood, her eyes suggesting a future he had never dared to imagine. "See you in two weeks. Now, let me see your ribbon."

As Adaara's convoy disappeared down the road, Maalek ran a finger over the ribbon pinned to his epaulet. He smiled, his fingers drifting to where her lips had brushed his cheek. He traced the ribbon, savoring the lingering warmth of the evening. Above, stars were beginning to pierce the darkening sky, each one a distant point of light in the vast silence of space.

Chapter 16

Bridge, UNS Trent

Dalton System, Edge of Earth Union Space

September 23, 2681

Only one thought ran through Captain Domingo Alvarez's mind as the timer ticked down: inevitability. The countdown to destruction had begun, and there was no escaping it.

He strode onto the bridge of UNS Trent, buttoning his jacket. He'd been out of bed and mostly dressed within two minutes of the urgent call from his XO. There'd been time to splash water on his face, but not to shave. That could wait for later. If there was a later.

"Have they made contact yet?" he asked, fastening the last button and accepting a lukewarm cup of coffee from his XO. The question wasn't directed at anyone in particular, but the comms officer spoke up. He was a young man paying his dues on the fringes of Union space aboard a Navy ship so old her maintenance logs predated half the crew's birth certificates.

"No response, sir. Just dead space where communication should be."

"Keep trying."

Captain Alvarez took a sip, the coffee's bitterness and oily film registering only as an afterthought. "How long before they reach Colombo?"

"At their current speed, fifty-six minutes."

Fifty-six minutes to figure out how to stop an unstoppable enemy. The cruisers UNS Trent, UNS Albion, UNS Vanguard, and six destroyers patrolled the Dalton sector on the frontier of Union space as part of the Second Expeditionary Fleet. These nine ships were all that stood between the frontier colony outpost of Colombo—with its 2 million inhabitants—and an enemy fleet that jumped in without warning. Another breach, another fight they hadn't seen coming.

Seven systems and three Naval outposts had already fallen in the last year. The Union warships that came to the aid of the planets, always too late, found terraforming machines before being turned back by overwhelming firepower—when they weren't also destroyed. What they never found were survivors.

"Open a q-channel to HQ."

"We can't, sir. We've lost the quantum channel. It's like they're jamming us."

A sigh. "Then use the laser to tell the colony to evacuate. Now."

"Yes, sir."

The XO tapped on his terminal. "Sir, we have a couple of drones at the jump point. I can program them to jump to Icarus; maybe they can send reinforcements."

"They wouldn't get here in time, but…program them to jump in two hours, and start telemetry recordings. We'll either be dead by then, or not, but Command needs to see this."

"Yes, sir. And if the fleet goes down before that?"

"Then they jump immediately."

"Aye, sir. On it."

The comms officer turned around. "Message from Albion and Vanguard, sir. They're asking for instructions."

"Put them on the vid screen."

Moments later, the two captains were conferenced in. Their faces on the vid screen matched his own state of mid-sleep interruption—uniforms hastily donned, clutching the same regulation mugs of bad coffee that passed for normalcy.

"Hey Hank, Sandra," he greeted them.

"Any reply yet?" asked Henry Carnes, Albion's gruff skipper, a Navy lifer well past middle age, running out the clock until retirement.

"Nothing but crickets, Hank."

"Shit. That's what I was afraid of."

"We count three capital ships and a dozen destroyers," said Sandra Torbani, Vanguard's captain, young and ambitious, eager to prove herself. "What's the plan? We can't just sit here."

Alvarez sipped his coffee before answering. "Here's how I see it: We can call for reinforcements, but the closest fleet is at Icarus. That's half a dozen jumps...puts them here three days from now. Two, we can steam to the jump point, discretion being the better part of valor and all that, or three, we can see how this plays out."

"If we jump out, it's an automatic court martial. We'd be running in the face of an enemy," Carnes said.

"And if we stay, we're likely all dead in an hour," Sandra said.

They were outgunned, outclassed, and out of options, but they had to try because they swore an oath, and in Domingo Alvarez' Navy, that still meant something. "We have a duty to stay and protect our people. So that's what we're gonna do," he said. The two captains met his gaze through the vid screen, their faces carrying the same grim acceptance he felt. They'd all read this story before; they just hadn't expected to be in it.

As they discussed strategy, Trent's tactical officer interrupted. "Sir, new sensor contacts. Heading two-eight-one, mark three-one-one, port."

"Ours?"

"No, sir. Sensor signatures match Hasha warships."

"How many?" Alvarez asked.

"Four capital ships, six troop transports, and a dozen frigates and destroyers."

Alvarez's mouth went dry as the tactical display filled with new contacts. Numbers that spelled out their obituary in cold, clean data. "Battle stations. All ships, form up on Trent."

The call ended, and Alvarez stood, taking in his bridge—not

the consoles or flashing warnings, but the mean and women who'd made this old ship home. His crew moved through their stations with the brittle efficiency of people trying not to think about their odds. They'd hold. They'd stand their ground, and Domingo was proud of them. These men and women served in a rust bucket on the edge of space, day in and day out, without complaint. If this was how he went out, he couldn't ask for better company.

"Sir," the XO said. "They're accelerating. New estimate has them reaching Colombo in twenty-eight minutes."

Carnes cursed. "At that speed they can damn near outrun our torpedoes."

The next twenty minutes crawled by—the bridge hummed with charging weapons and half-whispered prayers—some to God, some to luck, some to the Union engineers who'd built their aging shields. The Union ships formed up, nine against twenty-two. The math was simple, final.

The tactical officer broke the silence. "Sir, energy readings from their capital ships just went off the scale."

Alvarez moved to the console, watching energy readings climb past any threshold he'd seen in twenty years of service. "That's... strange. Reinforce forward shields."

Suddenly, Trent went dark. Every system—shields, engines, weapons—shut down in an instant. The bridge plunged into darkness, grav generators went offline. Crew members grasped wildly for handholds, their training warring with the primal fear of floating untethered in a dying ship.

"What the hell was that?" Alvarez asked.

"I—I think we were hit with an EMP, sir!"

"But the shields were..."

"Backup systems are initializing...sensors are up, but weapons and engines are offline." The XO stiffened. "Sir! Seventy-two projectiles inbound! Ten seconds to impact!"

"Brace!" Alvarez's warning was lost in the thunderous roar of the first impact. Each hit sent vibrations through the hull that felt wrong—not the familiar shudder of normal combat damage, but the deep groans of a ship being torn apart. The force flung Alvarez from his chair, slamming him against the deck as the ship buckled. Around him, crew members crashed into consoles and bulkheads. Sparks showered from ruptured panels, and the sickening screech of tearing metal filled the air.

He heard Carnes' voice through the static-filled comms: "...taking heavy fire! Shields failing! We're—" The transmission cut off in a burst of static.

Torbani's voice came next, punctuated by explosions: "...lost an engine! Venting atmosphere! Launching escape pods! We can't—"

Alvarez watched in horror as Albion tumbled past on the viewscreen, her hull shredded and venting atmosphere. Vanguard limped behind, her remaining engines sputtering. Where the nacelle had been ripped away, a jagged mess of exposed framework and charred, shattered Tritanium sparked in the void, flickering before fading into the darkness.

Two supporting destroyers erupted into fireballs.

"Sir!" The tactical officer said, blood trickling from a gash on his forehead. "Destroyer Intrepid reports missile lock! They're firing!"

On the screen, Alvarez saw a salvo of missiles streak from Intrepid toward the Hasha fleet. Alvarez leaned forward in his chair, following the missiles' trails across the viewscreen, allowing himself one moment to believe in miracles.

It was short-lived. The Hasha point defenses lit up, swatting the missiles from space with impossible ease. Their return fire was devastating. A blinding energy beam lanced out, and Intrepid vanished in a ball of fire, taking her sister ships with her.

"Weapons back online!" The XO shouted over the din of failing systems and wounded crew.

Alvarez clenched his fists. "Fire everything. Every damn missile we've got."

Trent shuddered as she unleashed her entire arsenal. Taipans and Scimitars streaked toward the Hasha ships, leaving fiery trails in the void.

On the bridge, even the alarms seemed to pause as the missiles streaked toward their targets.... only to detonate in brilliant flashes against glowing green shields, or disintegrate under relentless point defense fire. Not a single projectile reached its target.

More energy beams streaked from their capital ships, swift and merciless. Albion exploded outright, her death marked by a silent flash that lit up the bridge. Vanguard split in two, secondary explosions tearing through her broken hull.

Alvarez's world was coming apart. Literally. Trent shuddered and groaned around him, her hull breaching in a dozen places.

The bridge was a chaos of sparks, smoke, and the tinny blare of alarms that somehow cut through the ringing in his ears.

In that final instant, as the beam tore through Trent's hull, Captain Alvarez had a moment to whisper, "My God."

His world faded to black just as the first volley of shots rained down   on   the   planet   below.

Chapter 17

Forward Operating Base Charlie, Daalamas

Kliinat, Tau Ceti System

October 15, 2681

Carson stood in front of the briefing room, his shadow stretching across the flickering holographic map. The blue light bounced off the rough walls. He caught the sharp bite of tritium exhaust cutting through Kliinat's perpetual organic scent—a smell that still hit him like his first day. The chill crept through his collar despite the environmental controls, reminding him they were very far from home. Some Marines tapped their feet rapidly against the floor, others sat perfectly still with squared shoulders. He recognized the pre-mission tension he'd seen a hundred times before.

"Alright, eyes up," Carson said, quieting the room. "Tonight, we're going after the mobile Union base running their ground forces in this area. We've finally pinned it down. We need it in one piece, so we're going in subtle—no big bangs. We slip in quietly, close in without them noticing, and lock it down before they know what's happening. Let's run through the details one more time."

The map zoomed in on entry points, with lines and markers sketching their plan. "Echo Company's coming in from the northwest, Alpha from the east. The Griffins will drop us ten klicks out. We move in the dark. Non-lethal takedowns only, but don't take risks," he said, pointing out their exfil routes. "Keep your exit points in mind in case we need to bail. Galatea's running the show, and Dauntless fighters are circling outside Union sensors, ready to jump in if we need them. Once we've got the base, the Army Rapid Response teams will take over."

He scanned the room, noticing the newer Klii members sitting up straighter. "Combat is the anvil on which we forge our unity. Forward, the Light Brigade. Let's roll."

After the briefing, the Marines moved with purpose, their footsteps echoing through the ancient corridors. They exchanged tense glances under the soft, bluish lights that cast eerie shadows along the walls.

Carson led the way, accompanied by the distant hum of machinery and the sharp smell of ionized air. Gunny, walking beside him, tilted her head slightly. "I might have gone with something other than a reference to the light brigade, sir."

"What do you mean?" Carson asked.

"Last I checked, their gallant charge ended with them decorating Russian hillsides, sir."

"It's about the spirit, Gunny. About facing tough odds

together, as a unit," Carson said.

"Yes, sir."

As the armory doors hissed open, the room filled with the metallic clatter of Marines gearing up. Gunny was in her element, handing out M45 battle rifles, Mako grenades, flash bangs, and the specialized SHOCK Rifles designed for a softer touch.

"You keep babying that rifle, Gunny, and it'll start needing therapy," Carson said, watching her fuss over the weapon like a bear with her cub.

Rodriguez chuckled from his locker. "I think she likes it better than us."

"Only applies to you, Rodriguez." The corner of Gunny's mouth twitched upward as she kept her eyes fixed on the rifle's sights. Her comment sparked a wave of laughter among the Marines that mixed with the distant bustle of the base.

"Lock it up, boys," Williams said from the back. "Let's not broadcast our departure to those squids."

Gunny's smirk widened. "If they catch wind of us, it'll be the last sound they hear."

Maalek checked his SHOCK Rifle, eyeing Carson with a half-grin. "This would have made our early runs on Union bases much more interesting."

"Not a fan myself," Carson said. "One slip-up and you're the main attraction in your own personal lightning storm."

"How so?" Maalek asked.

"Synchronized High-Output Capacitive Knockout, Maalek.

Emphasis on knockout. If you get a jam and clear it wrong…50,000 volts zapping every hair on your body."

"It does indeed sound unpleasant," Maalek said.

Sousa, overhearing, chimed in. "Don't worry too much, Maalek. The amperage is low enough to keep it from doing any real damage. It's all about control, not barbecue." She said, then turned to the newest member of their team. "Speaking of control, you excited, Andaeer? The first op's always a memorable one."

Andaeer leaned forward slightly, his fingers drumming against his rifle's stock. "It is a pleasant change to have the advantage in numbers—and ammunition."

Carson watched his Marines gear up, ticking off each item in his head. SHOCK Rifles? Check. Comms? Check. Nerves? Triple check. With a nod, he signaled it was time to head out.

The Marines lined up, helmets secure, posture perfect. They moved with the fluid precision that only came from countless hours of drills. No wasted motion, no hesitation.

As they approached the hangar, the roar of engines grew louder. The Marines filed into their assigned shuttles. Carson took one last look at his team before boarding, catching glimpses of focused expressions, a finger tapping a rifle, a deep breath, a final equipment check. He boarded, hoping the mission wouldn't veer off course before it even began.

The journey to the drop zone, however, was anything but smooth. Turbulence shook the shuttles as they skimmed over the treetops, turning the dark forest below into a fleeting shadow on the monitors. Inside, Marines clutched their seats, the drone of the engines competing with Jones' choice of pre-mission music blaring through the speakers.

As "Fortunate Son" thumped through the cabin, Carson nodded along, the gritty lyrics painting a stark contrast to their situation—fighting for freedom in a place so alien, so far from anything resembling home.

"Brace yourselves," Jones' voice crackled over the intercom, dropping half an octave lower than her usual chatter. Carson had heard that tone before—it meant she was locked in but enjoying herself too much to admit it. "Keep a tight hold on your breakfast. We're about to dance with the turbulence."

"Stay sharp, everyone," Carson said through the static-filled comms. "We're almost at the LZ. Remember the plan and stick to your roles."

Gunny nodded. The dim lighting traced the recent dent in her helmet—a souvenir from their last drop that she'd refused to have repaired. Carson knew better than to mention it.. "You heard the captain. In and out. We make it quick and clean, and the Union's down one shiny base."

Jones's voice came through again, sharpening Carson's attention. "Drop zone in sight. Prep for deployment. Awaiting the green light."

Seconds later, the light flicked to green—a silent go-ahead that set everything into motion. The shuttles dipped closer to the treetops, their descent lost in the gust of wind through the woods. Ramps lowered with a quiet hiss, and the Marines stepped out into the night, their movements as soft as the shadows that cloaked them.

Maalek flowed through the shadows with the minimal movement that only came from years of combat—every movement measured, every step silent. "Stay close and keep it quiet," he told the team.

"Spread out," Carson said into the comms, his voice hushed. "Keep eyes on each other, but stay low."

As the team dispersed through the dense underbrush, their coordination was sharp and precise, honed from countless drills and live-fire exercises. Carson caught glimpses of his Marines through gaps in the foliage, blending with the dark, tangled vegetation. He nodded at Williams, who flashed a thumbs-up before slipping into the shadows toward her designated position.

The forest closed around them, its canopy a dark, shifting mass above. Carson's skin prickled beneath his armor. Every shadow demanded attention, every rustle needed classification. The weight of his rifle provided its familiar comfort. The faint earthy scent of the forest, mingled with the must of decay, filtered through his suit's environmental systems.

Maalek's fist shot up, signaling a halt. Carson eased in beside him, his movements calculated and silent. He opened a channel to Galatea. "Galatea, Echo Actual," he breathed into the comm.

The response was immediate. "Galatea here, send it, Echo Actual, over."

Carson glanced around, ensuring the shadowy woods would keep their presence concealed. "Galatea, Echo Actual. We're in position and awaiting further instructions. Over."

The static crackled in Carson's ear before the command came through. "Copy that, Echo Actual. Proceed with caution. Galatea out."

"Roger that," Carson said, his words lost in the soft rustle of leaves. He scanned his squad, their figures ghostlike in the dim forest light. "Stay sharp. We move on my mark."

With a nod, he signaled, and they moved as one—silent shadows melting into the dark woods.

Maalek took point again, weaving through the underbrush. Carson watched his team fan out, finding cover and sight lines. Williams settled in, SHOCK Rifle ready, while Andaeer matched Maalek's smooth movements.

As they pushed forward, the faint outlines of the Union base emerged from the darkness. The base's background hum carried through the ground into Carson's boots—generator cycles, life support systems, the subtle whine of sensor arrays. All standard frequencies, but something in their rhythm nagged at his combat instincts. Like hearing your own voice played back wrong.

"Echo One to Echo Two," Carson murmured into his comm. "We're set. Ready when you are."

"Copy, Echo One." Gunny's voice came through with the measured cadence that Carson had learned meant she was fully focused, already three steps ahead in her mind. "We're in position. Moving on my count. Three, two, one, go."

The Marines advanced, slipping through the underbrush. Sentries dropped to silent takedowns, their bodies swiftly hidden in the dark foliage.

Carson kept an eye on Andaeer as he approached a sentry. A quick move, a muffled zap, and the sentry crumpled into Andaeer's arms, lowered silently to the ground.

Nearing the base's center, Carson signaled a halt. Through his visor, he spotted two Marines by a tent, their laughter drifting on the night air. He nodded to Williams, who moved forward with predatory grace. A pulse from her SHOCK Rifle and one Marine slumped. As the other turned, confused, Sousa was on him, her rifle delivering a quick, quiet takedown. Carson watched Williams and Sousa work with the efficiency that came from too much practice—one fluid movement to catch the falling body, another to fade into shadow. The wet earth would hide their bootprints within minutes.

"Echo One to Echo Three," Carson said through his neural. "We're inside."

"Echo Three copies," Lieutenant Akitani said. She'd just transferred from Alpha Company, but she moved with their unit's rhythm now, anticipating orders before he gave them. The way she checked her corners, how she signaled—Carson could hardly remember when she'd been 'the new ell-tee' anymore.

Carson led them deeper, staying calm. They approached a clearing, and he signaled to hold. The base sprawled ahead, all mobile prefabs. Two soldiers came out of a command module, stretching, oblivious. Carson gave the signal; Maalek and Andaeer moved like ghosts, SHOCK batons ready. The soldiers' mouths formed silent 'O's as their bodies went rigid, then slack.

As Carson's team got into position, Alpha Company materialized from the darkness to the east, their shadows indistinguishable from the swaying vegetation. Carson caught fragments of hand signals through the foliage.

"Alpha Actual to Echo Actual, we're set to breach."

"Copy, Alpha Actual. Moving now," Carson said, low and steady.

But as they say, no plan survives contact. A shrill wail pierced Carson's audio dampeners. His gut clenched—someone had tripped an alarm. Rookie mistake or bad intel? No time to wonder. Sirens screamed, and harsh spotlights swept the area, throwing long shadows.

"Contact!" Williams called as armored figures appeared. Union soldiers burst from their prefabs, some still adjusting armor straps, others snapping fresh magazines in their rifles. Carson counted hostiles, muscle memory already categorizing threats and firing lanes. KODIAK mechs—smaller and quicker than YETIs—moved up, frames gleaming blue and white in the moonlight, red sensors pulsing.

The KODIAKs moved with that distinctive hydraulic grace that still set Carson's teeth on edge. Their chain guns tracked with cold precision, and the missile pods' red targeting lasers cutting through the mist like bloody threads. Each sweep of those beams made his skin crawl.

Gunny was a blur, her SHOCK Rifle up and firing. She emptied her mag into a KODIAK, the mech jerking as its systems fried. It staggered, sparking, before crashing down with a boom that shook the ground. But not all went down so easy; the other KODIAKs returned fire, their cannons thundering.

Carson ducked behind a thick tree, battle sounds ringing in his ears despite his helmet's dampeners. "Gunny, flank right. Williams, cover Maalek!" he shouted over comms. Williams nodded, laying down bursts of suppressing fire as Maalek maneuvered to a better spot.

Marines scrambled for cover, diving behind anything solid as bullets zipped by. Carson's comm buzzed with urgent calls, ammo requests, and pleas for fire support. The forest erupted; branches snapped, grenades boomed, and muzzle flashes lit up the dark.

The sharp chemical bite of weapons fire cut through his filters, mixing with the sweet-rot stench of burning vegetation. Carson's nose had learned to read battles through these smells—the acrid warning of overheated barrels, the metallic hint of spalled armor, the distinct tang of carbonite cartridges. Carson's visor lit up with data, enemy positions blinking, and his team's movements. The battlefield roared—rapid gunfire, thunderous explosions, and the eerie whine of ricocheting bullets.

Union Marines sprang into action, spreading out in the base. They crouched behind crates and buildings, eyes scanning. Officers shouted orders over the din. Snipers found high spots, rifles glinting as they picked off targets. Machine gunners unleashed hell, pinning Carson's Marines down.

"Echo Actual, Alpha Actual here. We're pinned down, taking heavy fire! Falling back to the perimeter," came the strained report.

"Copy that, Alpha Actual. Hold as best you can."

Crates exploded as Union Marines charged in on Puma vehicles, Stinger turrets blazing. Carson dove behind a downed KODIAK; Dirt geysered up in synchronized bursts, each impact marking a perfect firing pattern. The Union gunner was good— laying down suppressive fire exactly where Carson would have put it. Fighting against Marines who'd learned from the same manual always felt like playing chess against himself. Each impact against the KODIAK hull sent vibrations through his armor, a deadly drumbeat he felt in his teeth. The distinct ping-whine of 5 mm ricochets told him he should probably keep his head low.

"Suppressive fire!" Carson yelled over the roar. His team's responses crackled in his ear—frantic calls mixed with vicious return fire.

Gunny's voice cut through from across the field. "Hold the line, goddammit!"

Carson's jaw tightened until his back teeth ached, an old tell from his first combat drop that still surfaced when things went sideways. They needed more than just grit now; they needed air support, and they needed it yesterday. He activated his neural link. "Galatea, Echo Actual. Need immediate air support! Hostile vehicles approaching, multiple vectors!"

"Copy, Echo Actual. Mark your position," came Galatea's calm response.

Carson flicked on his IR beacon. "Galatea, Echo Actual. Position marked with IR."

"Roger that, Echo Actual. Air support inbound. ETA five mikes. Hold tight."

Carson switched channels. "Alpha Actual, mark your position. All units, prep for close air support!"

He slapped a new mag into his rifle with a click that felt too calm for the surrounding chaos. Sliding back into the fight, Carson rejoined his team, his rifle spitting fire as he moved.

∗∗∗

Jammer nudged the controls, the soft drone of the Dauntless fighter's engines as familiar as a worn-in leather jacket. Outside, the vast darkness of night stretched out in every direction, punctuated by the distant glimmer of stars. Ambient light bathed the cockpit, casting faint shadows across the sleek instrumentation panels. The holoscreen before him was alive with a ghostly blue dance of data—enemy locations, system check-ins, and mission parameters.

Each atmospheric pocket tried to knock Jammer's Dauntless off course, but his body had long ago learned to move with the turbulence instead of fighting it. The seat's familiar contours might as well have been molded to his spine—he'd spent more hours in this cockpit than in his own bunk lately. His suit recycled the same air he'd been breathing for hours—that distinct mix of ozone from the electronics, hot metal from the engines, and the ghost-scent of coffee that never quite left his flight suit. Some pilots complained about the staleness, but to Jammer it smelled like home. His gloved hands gripped the control sticks, each movement deliberate, each adjustment critical.

His comms pinged, and a call came through from Two Bit on the squadron channel.

"Jammer, did you ever think we'd be putting all that CAG training to real use? There's something about flying at night that just clicks for me."

Two Bit's voice hit him like unexpected turbulence, sending his carefully maintained professional distance into a momentary spin. He caught himself smiling at her familiar cadence before schooling his expression back to mission-ready neutral. Some dangers weren't listed in the flight manual. But damn if she wasn't the most wonderful, annoying, beautiful pain in the ass he'd ever flown with.

Then came Lunchbox's voice, jovial as always. "Anyone else got the munchies? How about we sweet-talk Gally into dropping us a midnight snack care package?"

Alphabet's chuckle filtered through. "Lunchbox, you're the only pilot I know who considers extra rations essential mission gear."

Jammer's voice cut in, steering them back on track. "Alright, let's run another systems check. I want to see all boards green."

"All systems green," Two Bit reported. "Weapons hot."

"Engines purring and ordnance primed," Lunchbox chimed in.

"Everything's looking five by five here," Alphabet said, sounding as steady as usual. "I hope Echo doesn't need us too soon. I'm enjoying the quiet." A beat, then with a note of disbelief, he said, "Oh hell, I just agreed with Two Bit."

Minutes dragged by as the squadron held their disciplined formations, skirting outside the Union's sensor range. Jammer's thoughts drifted to the mission ahead and the Marines on the ground, his mental preparation interrupted by Two Bit's familiar chatter crackling through the comms.

"Hey Jammer, remember that screw-up on Persephone? When Beaker fumbled with the live ammo and gave Packrat's Dauntless a new pinstripe?"

A chuckle escaped Jammer. "The Air Boss was so pissed I thought he was gonna smack Beaker with the broken stabilizer."

The familiar banter loosened the tension in Jammer's

shoulders, transformed the waiting from brittle to bearable. Even the turbulence felt more manageable with the squad's voices in his ears. Kliinat's air currents kept Jammer focused, his Dauntless shuddering now and then in the crosswinds. He made constant small adjustments—flying in atmosphere was tricky in its own way. No sharp turns up here unless you wanted to black out.

Glancing right, he saw Two Bit's fighter holding formation, her engine exhaust painting a brief, glowing trail in the cool air. Her Dauntless moved with an unexpected grace, a machine built for destruction showing an almost elegant poise. Jammer tracked Two Bit's Dauntless, her perfect formation flying both impressive and painful to watch. He knew every correction she'd make before she made it, could predict the exact way she'd adjust for the crosswinds. Regs about fraternization had never felt more like a wall than a rule, especially up here where they moved like extensions of each other's thoughts.

Shaking off the distraction, he refocused on the immediate. The comms snapped to life. "Saber Leader, this is Galatea. Echo Actual needs immediate air support. Hostile vehicles approaching. Position marked with IR."

"Saber Leader copies. En route to Echo Actual. ETA five mikes."

The casual chatter died instantly. Jammer's world narrowed to his instruments, his console, the visceral awareness of Two Bit's wing position. His breath slowed to the measured rhythm that always preceded combat, each inhale bringing sharper clarity. The squadron broke formation, diving toward the action, their engines thundering as they cleaved through Kliinat's thin atmosphere.

As they closed in, the familiar sounds of combat filled Jammer's comm—calls for backup, the crackle of gunfire, and the distant booms of explosions. Each transmission from the ground painted a clearer picture—Marines pinned down, needing air support five minutes ago. Jammer's mouth went dry as muscle memory took over, years of training narrowing his world to target acquisition and weapons release. They were the tip of the spear, and the Marines on the ground were counting on them.

"Galatea, Jammer. Visual on IR. Engaging hostiles now."

Jammer's cockpit was a kaleidoscope of lights. The holoscreen bathed him in a soft blue, outlining enemy placements, missile paths, and ally markers. His console flickered with orange and red, each light throwing eerie shadows over his visor. The seat vibrated beneath him, in tune with the thrum of the engines.

"Engage on my mark," Jammer said. Time seemed to stretch as his combat training took over. Every instrument reading burned clearer, every slight adjustment of his stick more precise. The background noise of his own breathing faded against the clarity of tactical awareness. "Let's give our people on the ground some breathing room."

The base erupted into view, alight with the flashes of combat. Jammer squeezed the trigger. The Vulcans' discharge rattled through Jammer's stick and up his arms, that familiar vibration that meant the rounds were feeding clean. His sister had called it 'the devil's purr'—a sensation that hadn't changed since atmospheric fighters first took to war. Explosions followed, deafening and destructive, marking their first strikes.

Jorge Sanchez

Suddenly, warning lights flooded his console in crimson waves—the color that bypassed thought and went straight to muscle memory. Jammer's hands were already moving through evasive patterns before his conscious mind registered the SAM alert tone, that high-pitched warble that featured in every pilot's nightmares—Mamba surface-to-air missiles.

"Saber Squadron, SAMs inbound! Break right, break right!" He shouted, his grip tightening on the controls. He yanked the stick back. The g-forces crushed Jammer back into his seat as he hauled the stick back, his vision narrowing as the Dauntless clawed for altitude. Blood pounded in his ears, fighting against the pressure. The ship groaned and shuddered, straining against the brutal forces. His cockpit erupted in a cacophony of alarms, bathing him in their urgent, pulsing glow.

Chapter 18

Mobile Union HQ, outside Daalamas

Kliinat, Tau Ceti System

October 15, 2681

The smoke stung Carson's eyes even through his helmet's filters, turning the battlefield into a blur of muzzle flashes and moving shadows. Their airstrikes turned the battlefield into a storm of fire, tossing debris and soldiers into the air. The ground bucked under his feet, and the wind carried a tang of burning fuel and charred tritanium as the strikes hammered enemy positions.

"That's one way to start a party," Carson said, feeling the heat even through his visor.

Union forces scattered, some making a break for it in their vehicles. A Dauntless caught one fleeing APC, turning it into a rolling fireball. Another swerved to avoid the metal rain, only to plow into a prefab building and go up in flames.

The night split with the high-pitched shriek of a SAM battery coming online, spitting missiles at the Dauntless fighters wheeling overhead. Smoke trails crisscrossed the sky as the fighters popped countermeasures, twisting and diving to shake off death.

"Rodriguez, that Mamba SAM battery needs to go down now," Carson said.

Rodriguez's shoulders settled into that familiar tension Carson recognized—the same coiled readiness he showed before every perfect shot. His fingers danced over the Ballista's controls. The targeting system activated, flickering as it struggled to lock onto the SAM through the smoke and debris. "On it," he said, adjusting his stance.

"Anytime now, Rodriguez," Carson pressed, impatient.

"Almost there, Captain," Rodriguez said. A brief pause, then, "Getting a lock."

The SAM battery launched another missile, tracing a fiery arc against the night sky. Carson's jaw clenched as he watched the missile's trajectory.

"Seconds stretched, until the launcher emitted a steady beep. Rodriguez's grin spread. 'Locked on!'"

The rocket shot from its launcher, tracing a fiery arc into the night sky before diving toward the SAM battery. It unleashed a firestorm on impact, igniting the battery and setting off a series of explosions. Carson and his Marines braced themselves, leaning into the shockwave as it rolled over them.

"Nice work, Rodriguez!"

"This is Echo Two, Dragonfly machine gun's got us pinned," Gunny said through the comm.

Carson tapped Maalek's shoulder, pointing to a prefab on their right. Bright tracers streaked from the rooftop, zeroing in on Gunny. "Maalek, take your squad and take out that machine gun nest."

Maalek and his team darted between cover, bullets snapping around them. The machine gun pivoted, unleashing hell and pinning them down.

"Maalek, we need that gun down now," Carson said with a hefty dose of urgency.

"Roger that, Skip. On it," Maalek said.

Using every dip and bump in the terrain, Maalek's squad snaked around to flank the prefab. A few quick hand signals, and they lobbed a salvo of grenades. The nest went up in a chain of explosions, silencing its deadly chatter.

"Machine gun neutralized, Captain," Maalek said. His voice carried that particular flatness that Carson had learned meant everything had gone exactly according to plan—probably better.

"Good work, Maalek," Carson acknowledged.

Threats cleared, Carson waved his troops forward. "Move up. Alpha's hitting them from the east. Let's shut the box."

The Marines surged ahead, boots churning dirt, rifles primed. Gunny took left, Williams right, Carson leading center, eyes peeled for hostiles.

"Echo Actual to Alpha Actual, we're moving in. What's your status?"

"Alpha Actual here. We're slugging it out on the eastern edge. They're dug in, but we're gaining ground."

Carson's rifle cracked as he dropped a soldier attempting to break cover. "Keep pushing. We've got them cornered."

Gunny scored two quick shots with her M45, taking down another Marine, then turned to Carson with a raised eyebrow. "Captain, a little heads-up about the fireworks would've been nice."

Carson flashed a brief grin. "Where's the fun in that, Gunny?"

Echo took the prefabs in sequence. Room clear. Corner check. Door breach. Alpha's gunfire echoed from the east wing, keeping pace Carson and Gunny led their teams, navigating the labyrinth of equipment and buildings to secure critical areas like the communications center and vehicle maintenance.

"Echo Two to Echo Actual, we've secured the comm center. Downloading intel now," Gunny said over the comm.

"Top-notch," Carson said. "Akitani, what's your status?"

"Akitani here. Eastern section's locked down. Minimal resistance encountered."

"Roger that. Stay sharp," Carson said. As soon as the call ended, his comm crackled to life again.

"That you down there, Skip?" Jammer said.

"Jammer, thanks for the assist. You guys still airborne?" Carson asked.

"All SAMs neutralized or evaded. Skies are ours. Looks like I pulled your chestnuts out of the fire again."

A grin broke across Carson's face. "Next drink's on me. Heard the chief brewed a new batch of moonshine."

Jammer laughed. "Trying to poison me as thanks, wow. We're RTB, Hammer squadron's coming to relieve us. Over and out."

***

Carson led Echo Company as they busted into the old command hub, a dim warren of scattered gear and slapped-together walls.

"Williams, you're up," Carson said.

Williams' rifle muzzle tracked her eye line—door frame, corner shadow, ceiling vent. At each corner, she coiled—ready to spring—then whipped around. Every move was razor-sharp, no wasted energy. The squad moved as one behind her, each Marine a mirror of Williams' deadly precision.

"Clear on the left," Williams said, peering through a doorway.

Carson joined her before signaling the squad to continue. They swept the building end to end, disarming the holdouts.

As they cleared the command post, a hail of bullets from a nearby storage building sent them diving for cover. Rounds pinged off plasteel and kicked up dirt geysers around them.

"Union Marines regrouping!" Williams yelled. "They've dug in at that storage building."

"Williams, Maalek, take the left flank. I'm going straight in," Carson said.

Echo Company lit up the building, pinning the Union troops while Williams and Maalek slipped left, using every scrap of cover. Carson led his squad in a push timed to the steady beat of suppressing fire.

"Breach and clear!" he barked, kicking in the door. They poured in, rifles up, driving deep into enemy territory.

Union soldiers fired back from behind crates and jerry-rigged barriers, but buckled under Echo's coordinated assault. Carson's team swept through, leaving no corner unchecked.

"Area clear," Carson said after a final sweep.

They gave the building a once-over for surprises or stragglers. Carson caught his breath, his pulse still hammering from the fight's rush.

Just as they were about to push on, Carson's comm crackled. "Echo Actual, we've got movement up north. Looks like Union's gearing up for a counter."

"Copy that, Echo Two. Dig in and hold tight. Cavalry's coming," Carson replied.

He turned to his team. "Rodriguez, Maalek, with me. Union's trying to regroup. We can't let them get set."

"On it, Skip," Rodriguez nodded.

The Union Marines had holed up in a big prefab bristling with antennas. Dragonfly machine guns on the roof spat lead, keeping Gunny and her team pinned down.

Carson led his squad behind burnt-out Puma IFVs, setting up a nasty crossfire. He raised a fist, then dropped it.

"Light 'em up!" His command sparked a firestorm aimed at crushing the Union's last stand.

Rifles cracked as rounds tore through the air. Echo

Company's first volley shattered windows. The second caught three gunners mid-stride. Maalek's grenade took the radar array, showering the roof with white-hot fragments and screaming electronics. The The Union's resistance collapsed in stages—first the irregular pause between return shots, then the telltale scramble of boots on metal as positions were abandoned, finally the distinct sound of weapons hitting the ground that every combat veteran knew meant surrender was imminent.

"They're falling back inside!" Gunny's voice cut through the gunfire.

"They're falling back inside!" Gunny's voice cut through the gunfire.

"Don't let up," Carson barked into the comms.

Echo pushed forward, bullets whizzing by as they used every dip and bump for cover.

Movement left. A Union Marine rounded the corner, rifle half-raised. Carson's trigger broke twice. The Marine's chest armor caught the first round. His throat didn't stop the second.

Gunny dropped two more trying to dash for cover, her M45 bucking in her arms. Williams laid down a stream of covering fire, giving Maalek's squad the chance to flank and break the enemy line.

"All units, push in," Carson ordered.

"Echo Actual, Alpha's rolling in from the east—we've got 'em boxed," Gunny reported.

"Copy that. Wrap it up," Carson replied.

Echo and Alpha tightened the noose. They swept the

building, mopping up the last pockets of resistance. The remaining Union troops dropped their weapons in surrender.

"Echo One to Echo Actual, all buildings secure. No hostiles remaining," Williams radioed in. Her words came clipped, measured—the way Williams always spoke after prolonged firefights, when the adrenaline was bleeding out but the trigger finger wasn't quite ready to relax.

"Alright, Echo Company," Carson said. "We've got plenty ahead. Let's get moving."

***

As the dust of battle settled and the last Union soldier lay disarmed, Carson directed his Marines to tighten the perimeter. They flowed into defensive positions with practiced motions. No voices now, just the click of safeties and the rustle of boots on the ground. The base settled into that particular kind of quiet Carson had learned to hate—the hollow aftermath of combat where every groan of wounded meant someone he'd failed to protect. His armor's filters couldn't quite mask the copper-sweet smell of blood mixing with burnt electronics.

Griffin shuttles thundered down, kicking up whirlwinds of dust and ash with their powerful engines.

"Set up triage here," Carson said, pointing toward a section near the base's central structure. "Treat everyone—Colonial, Union, whoever. No exceptions."

Gunny took charge of the medics, barking orders and manhandling stragglers into position. "Walking wounded, my left. Critical, center. Get those ReGen Shots moving." Medics who'd been hesitating found themselves obeying before they realized she wasn't medical staff. Carson had seen that same tone stop a platoon in their tracks during a hot firefight. Stretchers rolled out, and the parade of the injured began—a mix of Colonial grays and Union blues blurred by blood and grime.

Carson moved through the triage area like it was another tactical environment—because it was. His boots found the clean paths between blood pools automatically, body turning sideways to slip past rushing medics without breaking their stride. The battlefield just shifted forms here; instead of tracking muzzle flashes, he tracked facial expressions, cataloging which wounds needed attention first. He paused beside a Colonial Marine, her arm wrapped more in hope than skill. "You'll live, right?" He quipped, one eyebrow arching. "We're short on hands, even the slightly leaky ones."

The Marine's attempt at a smile turned into a grimace halfway through, but her eyes held that stubborn spark Carson knew too well—the one that kept soldiers fighting long past when their bodies begged to quit. "Only if you promise no push-ups, sir."

"Deal." He gave her shoulder a reassuring pat before moving on through the sea of makeshift beds.

He paused next to a young Union private, just a kid swimming in a uniform a couple sizes too big. Carson dropped to one knee to meet his eyes. "Name's Carson. What's yours?"

"Jamie, sir." The private's words came out steady enough, but Carson caught the slight tremor in his hands, the way his eyes darted between Carson's face and the chaos of the triage area. Probably his first real firefight. Carson's gaze landed on the burn marks scarring the right side of the boy's face and the singed hair above his ear. "That sting?" he nodded toward the wound.

"Yes, but I think the medics are really busy, so..."

Carson pulled out a DermaGel patch from his kit. He leaned in, lowering his voice. "You got family, Jamie?" He began applying the soothing gel, careful not to press too hard on the burned skin.

The kid flinched, balling a fist as Carson smoothed the DermaGel into place. "Yeah, sir. My ma and two sisters back in Eridani."

"You're gonna see them again sooner than you think, alright?" Carson said, trying to reassure him. "Okay, how's that feel?"

"Better, sir. Thank you."

Carson gave him a firm pat on the shoulder as he stood, sweeping his eyes across the triage area.

The field hospital pulsed with its own combat rhythm—the snap of med kits opening, the zip of DermaGel patches, the low hiss of ReGen Shots being administered. Carson's nose had long ago learned to catalog the scents: the sharp bite of antiseptic trying to mask the metallic tang of blood, the acrid smell of burnt armor plates, the distinct odor of fear-soaked uniforms. Portable lights cast a sickly glow over everything—blood-stained bandages, scorched gear, and wounded Marines. The med teams moved with that particular exhausted precision Carson had seen before—hands steady even while their legs wavered, eyes sharp even as dark circles deepened beneath them. Combat medicine was its own kind of warfare, fought with bandages instead of bullets.

The fragile quiet shattered as a Colonial Marine started seizing. "Medic! We need help here, now!" Rodriguez's urgent shout rose above the hum of activity, grappling to steady his thrashing squad mate.

A Union medic, her arm bound in a makeshift sling, barreled through the crowd to their side. "He's seizing! He needs diazepam, now!" Her eyes darted around, landing on the open kit at Rodriguez's feet. She snatched an injector and administered the drug. The convulsions soon subsided.

She finished tending the bullet wound that Rodriguez had been working on. "Make sure you stabilize that arm, use that sling in the kit," she told him. Rodriguez nodded.

"Thanks, Lieutenant...," Carson said, eyeing the insignia on her uniform.

"Cho," she said, her name delivered with the clipped efficiency of someone who'd learned to save her breath for what mattered, her good arm already reaching for her next patient as she spoke.

Carson watched the medics work, a whirlwind of activity. The air reeked of blood and burnt metal, telling the story of the day's fight better than words ever could. As they started moving out the worst cases, a Union Major walked up, hand out.

"Thanks for looking after our wounded, Captain."

Carson shook it. "You'd have done the same."

"I'd like to think so," the Major said.

Not everyone agreed. A scoff from a group of Union POWs nearby caught Carson's ear. He glanced over, taking in their stiff backs and faces smeared with dirt and defiance.

One prisoner, towering over the rest, fixed Carson with a hard stare. His face carried the kind of hardened lines Carson recognized from too many mirror checks after battle—the sort of anger that came from watching too many friends get shipped home in boxes. The man held himself with that rigid posture that screamed career Marine, even in defeat. "What're you playing at? Think you're heroes, saving the guys you just shot?" His voice was gravel and grit, each word laced with resentment.

"I'm not playing at anything," Carson said. He let the words settle between them, giving them the weight of combat-earned truth rather than rushing to fill the silence. Around them, the organized chaos of triage continued, but his focus narrowed to this moment—one veteran recognizing another across enemy lines. "Right now, it's about keeping people alive—that's everybody."

The man glared for a long moment before giving a grudging nod. "Don't make us pals," he grumbled, looking away toward the medical tents.

"No, it doesn't," Carson said, watching him turn. "And that's okay." He swept his gaze over the camp as night crept in.

He wandered over to Gunny, who was managing the supply distribution. "How's everyone holding up? Is Maalek okay?"

"Stoic as ever, but this isn't easy for any of them," Gunny said, nodding toward Maalek, who helped a young Klii soldier bandage a Union Marine. "But if showing some mercy plants a better seed, it's worth the effort."

"Let's hope," Carson said, sweeping his gaze over the field hospital.

As the shuttles made their final preparations and medics

packed up their kits, a Marine watching the east entrance raised his voice, and his rifle. "Something's stirring in those woods there." Moments later, a disheveled and frantic figure burst from the tree line.

"Wait! Don't shoot! I've got something you need to hear!"

Carson's shoulders carried the familiar weight of too many hours in combat armor, and his trigger finger still twitched at unexpected movements—the body's way of saying it wasn't done fighting yet, even if the mind knew better. He waved his men to lower their weapons. "And you are...?"

Weber. Dr—" The man's chest heaved between words. His lab coat was torn, hands shaking as they gripped a datapad. "Engineering section. There's—" He sucked in another breath. "Intel. Critical intel." His eyes kept darting to the tree line he'd emerged from.

"Intel that warrants getting shot?" Carson asked.

Weber, panting, stumbled over his own words. "They— they've got spies in Arcturus, scheming against the emperor! And—just as crucial—someone needs to feed my cat. He's very particular about his schedule."

Carson sighed. "Alright, Weber. Let's get you inside and sort this out."

And   now   he   had   this   to   deal   with.

Chapter 19

Forward Operating Base Charlie, Daalamas

Kliinat, Tau Ceti System

October 16, 2681

The mess hall was alive with morning chatter. The smell of synthetic bacon and eggs mixed with the fresh breeze coming through the open windows. Trays clattered, and laughter punctuated the air, lightening the mood despite the faded unit insignias on the walls that hinted at harder times.

Maalek's hand hesitated over each serving spoon, his muscles still tense from last night's firefight. The familiar Earth dishes triggered memories of shared meals after other battles, other losses. His fork found the synthetic eggs on muscle memory alone. Earth food still felt like borrowed comfort—a taste of someone else's home that had somehow become his own after too many post-training breakfasts. He headed over to Gunny's table, where his squad had gathered.

As he got close, he caught Gunny mid-story, waving her fork like a prop. "There we were, engine on fire, dropping like a rock!" Her hands traced the ship's descent, the fork playing the part of their doomed vessel. Maalek slipped into an empty chair, finding himself drawn into the tale.

The door swung open, and Carson walked in, wearing a look of fatigue but still sharp-eyed. A few heads turned, conversations dipped, then picked back up. He loaded a plate and made his way through the tables.

"Morning," Carson said, pulling up a seat next to Gunny and Maalek. "What'd I miss? This the one about that moon... what was its name again?"

Gunny scrunched up her face, thinking. "2MASSJ11... something."

"Yeah, that's it," Carson nodded, digging into his eggs. "Man, Jones pulled off one hell of a save that day. Pretty sure my armor still has the burn marks to prove it."

Conversation died in stages—first the war stories, then the jokes, finally even the routine grumbling about synthetic eggs. Only the soft clink of metal spoons against trays remained. Maalek sensed the exhaustion from last night's battle settling over the group. Even the usually animated Williams sat quietly, hands wrapped around her mug.

Gunny broke the silence with a bit of good news. "Corporal Sousa's going to be okay. Her visor saved her—it's just a scratch. Doc says she'll be back on duty next week."

Across the table, Andaeer's shoulders dropped a fraction, his breath escaping in a slow exhale that carried the weight of waiting for news about a squad mate. "That is good news. She is a stout and resilient warrior."

The familiar buzz of the mess hall slowly crept back in, punctuated by occasional bursts of laughter from nearby tables.

Carson's shoulders squared at the neural chime, his coffee cup freezing halfway to his mouth. Maalek recognized that instant shift from mess hall casual to combat ready.

"Major Lewis," he said, pushing his chair back with a sigh. "Seems Weber's decided he'll only talk to me. Maalek, want to tag along? Could use an extra set of ears." He snagged a piece of toast, washing it down with the last of his coffee.

Intrigued, Maalek nodded and finished his breakfast quickly. The synthetic eggs left a peculiar aftertaste as he stood to follow Carson out of the mess hall.

They made their way through the base, the weak morning sun casting long shadows. Rows of armored transports lined the yard while maintenance drones buzzed overhead. The sharp scent of Tritium fuel mixed with the constant hum of machinery. Every so often, the crisp sound of a patrol changing shifts cut through the morning air.

"How are you holding up, Maalek?" Carson asked, his voice mingling with the crunch of gravel under their boots.

"War is not unfamiliar to me, Skip. Loss is an old companion, yet we must continue for those who cannot," Maalek said. A squad of Marines rounded the corner at double-time, their formation still sloppy at the edges. Their boot strikes didn't quite sync up—the kind of small detail that marked them as green recruits. Three months in combat would fix that, if they lasted

"Can't argue with that. It never gets easier, does it? We just keep going," Carson said, glancing at Maalek. "After all these years in the thick of it, what's the one thing that's stuck with you?"

Maalek pondered this as they neared the briefing building. "Resilience," he said after a thoughtful pause. "Not just to keep fighting, but to rebuild. To forgive."

Carson's lips curved into a small smile. "They always said it's the little things that count. Took me years to really understand that. That's what I've learned."

Their conversation died down as they reached the entrance. The guards snapped to attention, rifles ready. Carson gave a brief nod. "Morning, Sergeant."

"Morning, Captain. Lieutenant," the guard said, maintaining his formal posture.

They stepped up to the checkpoint, leaving the open air and morning sounds behind. Carson breezed through the familiar routine, Maalek following his lead.

The scanner's field crawled across Maalek's skin like static electricity, triggering old muscle memory from Union checkpoints. His fingers still wanted to reach for weapons that weren't there.

"Stay close," Carson warned as the door slid open. "This place is a labyrinth. I ended up in a supply closet my first time through."

The briefing building swallowed them in layers—first the outside air died, replaced by recycled chill, then the morning birds faded under the hum of security systems. Even their footsteps changed tone, from gravel crunch to the particular hollow echo of concrete flooring.

The interior screamed military efficiency. Harsh lights carved sharp shadows on bare walls, tightening Maalek's chest. The air tasted sterile, buzzing with hidden tech and muffled voices behind closed doors. Every office looked like its own fortress in a maze of brass and bureaucracy.

At another checkpoint, Carson flashed his ID with a casual flick. Maalek fumbled with his, like he was holding some ancient relic.

They headed down an endless corridor, their footsteps muted by thick tiles. Screens plastered the walls, spitting out data and battle plans. Up above, stern-faced military legends glared down from their frames, like they were watching all the comings and goings.

The air carried that distinct mix of military efficiency—three-day-old coffee from endless briefings, industrial cleaner that never quite masked the electronics' ozone bite, and the faint anxious sweat of junior officers waiting outside command offices. Carson and Maalek pulled up at "Briefing Room C." Major Lewis stood by the door with parade-ground posture, the kind of officer whose collar brass caught every available light. Even his frown lines seemed regulation-issue. His uniform was so crisp it looked like it might crack if he moved too fast.

"Captain, Lieutenant," Lewis nodded, all business. "Weber's inside. He's on edge. Got left behind when the Union pulled out. Keeps going on about missing scientists and strange goings-on."

Carson's eyebrow shot up. "He asked for me specifically?"

"Wouldn't talk to anyone else. Said something about last night?"

Carson frowned. "Drawing a blank, but let's see what he's got."

Maalek's ears perked up at the mystery.

The door whooshed open, hitting them with a blast of cold air. The interior looked like a mini command center: walls of consoles, a massive holoscreen, and a table littered with cups.

Weber's boots traced the same six-step pattern across the floor tiles, each turn precisely matched to the last. His lab coat showed three days of wrinkles and what looked like scorch marks along one sleeve. A fluffy gray cat was perched by the console, giving them a look that said it owned the place.

Maalek couldn't help but stare at the cat. "Such a small creature, yet it seems to command the room," he murmured.

"Lieutenant Maalek," Carson introduced. Weber stopped his pacing, looking both relieved and terrified.

"Captain, Lieutenant, thanks for coming," Weber's words came out clipped, controlled—the voice of someone who'd rehearsed this conversation a hundred times in his head. His fingers kept finding the scorched edge of his lab coat, tracing the burn pattern like a worry stone. "That's Mr. Whiskers. He's stuck with me through this whole mess."

Carson pointed to a chair. "Lewis says you wanted to talk."

Weber sat, his hands trembling. "There are rumors— scientists and officers disappearing. It's happening more and more in the frontier systems, at the edge of Union space. I needed a backup plan, you know?"

Carson and Maalek traded glances. "Let's hear it," Carson said, leaning in.

Weber hunched forward, his voice dropping to a whisper. "I hacked into a console. Found something big. In return, I want safe passage to the colonies—not some POW camp—and Mr. Whiskers comes along for the ride."

Mr. Whiskers' tail cut through the air as if in agreement, each twitch marking a different console like a furry targeting system. The cat's eyes tracked movement with the same intensity Maalek had seen in sniper teams.

Lewis's face soured. "We need to verify this intel first."

Weber's boot heel clicked against the floor tiles—tap-tap-tap-pause, tap-tap-tap-pause—with the precise rhythm of someone trying very hard to appear calmer than they felt. "The Union's working with an Arcturian faction. They're plotting to topple their emperor."

Carson's hand froze halfway to his coffee. Lewis's datapad clattered against the table. In his years of combat, Maalek had seen that particular stillness only twice—both times right before everything went sideways. "Damn," Carson breathed. "You weren't kidding about this being big, Doc."

Weber spilled rapid-fire details: "I've got names, Arcturian contacts, everything. It's a small group, but they've wormed their way into everything—military, government, even day-to-day operations. With the Union backing them... who knows what's coming next."

Lewis's brow furrowed deeper with every word. "Alright, Dr.

Weber, you've got yourself a deal. Show us what you've dug up."

Weber brought the holoscreen to life, data cascading across it in a dazzling light show. Carson and Maalek leaned in, their faces growing grim as they waded through the sea of information.

"Give us a minute, Dr. Weber," Lewis said, nodding towards the door. Once outside, he turned to Carson. "I'm calling this into General Intelligence. You need to loop Antonov and Mori in. The fleet's got to go on condition one—we've got Arcturian officers in the mix now."

Carson gave a quick nod. "I'm on it, Major." He waved Maalek over and found a quiet corner.

Tapping his ear, Carson fired up his comm. "Galatea, priority one secure line."

Maalek listened in as the call connected. "This is Lieutenant Daniels on Galatea. Secure channel open, Captain. Authentication, please."

"Carson, Echo Company, 2nd Battalion, 5th Marines. Delta-Charlie-Niner-Two," Carson rattled off without missing a beat. "Need an immediate secure line to Admiral Antonov and Captain Mori on a priority one channel. Urgent operational intelligence."

"Verified, Captain. Stand by," Daniels said.

Carson's chin dipped a fraction of an inch—the same minimal movement he used to signal 'ready' before a breach. Combat habits died hard, even in conference rooms.

"Maalek, I'm patching you in," Carson said. "Fill any gaps I miss."

"Got it, Skip."

Maalek's neural buzzed, connecting him to the call.

Antonov's voice carried that particular edge admirals developed after too many interrupted meetings. "This better be important. I just left a call with the Secretary of the Navy."

"Admiral, we've got solid intel on a Union-Arcturus faction plot to overthrow the Emperor," Carson said, cutting to the point.

"Mori here. Go ahead, Captain."

Carson shifted towards Maalek. "Maalek is with me; he was present at the briefing. I patched him in."

"Admiral Antonov, Captain Mori, I can confirm that the intelligence we have received from Dr. Weber is substantial and alarming," Maalek said.

Carson took the lead, outlining Dr. Weber's defection and the rather unusual stipulations involving his cat. Maalek paid close attention to the unfolding dynamics, noting how the urgency of the intelligence seamlessly united everyone across the command chain.

"Prepare Dr. Weber for transport to Galatea for a comprehensive debrief," Antonov said.

"Affirmative, Admiral. We'll ensure Dr. Weber and… Mr. Whiskers are ready for immediate extraction," Carson said with a slight pause at the mention of the cat.

"Keep this channel open," Mori said.

"Understood, Captain. Carson out."

The line clicked off, and Carson turned to Maalek. "Let's

move. We've got a scientist and a cat to wrangle, but first, let's grab   some   real   coffee."

Chapter 20

Briefing Room, CCV Galatea

Kliinat, Tau Ceti System

October 17, 2681

Mori strode down Galatea's narrow corridor, mind racing. Arcturians teaming up with the Union to overthrow their Emperor was almost too wild to believe.

She exchanged salutes with her crew as she passed. These days, even the most loyal salute could be hiding something sinister. She pushed aside that nagging thought. This was no time for paranoia.

Grant, the XO, the chief engineer, the CAG, and the Master Chief Petty Officer were already in the briefing room when she walked in.

"At ease," she said, taking her place at the table. "Here's the situation: An Arcturian faction is working with the Union, trying to overthrow the Emperor. The Imperial Nightguard's already rounding up suspects, and we're at Threat Level Critical. Eddie has sent you all a detailed report. Master Chief, I want a full sweep—checkpoints at every critical system. We're also changing all encryption codes."

Chairs creaked. Datapads clicked. Then the strategies began, each officer leaning slightly forward in their seat.

"Are we talking about a full system reboot?" The MCPO asked, already tapping away at his datapad.

"Not yet," Mori said, letting the possibility hang in the air for a moment. "For now, restrict critical system access to senior staff."

"Yes, ma'am," he nodded, jotting down orders.

The engineering officer fidgeted in his seat. "With all these security tweaks, we should expect some hiccups," he said.

"Yes," Mori said. "Keep an eye out and jump on any issues fast. And until we sort out this mess, all Arcturian officers are off-duty fleet-wide."

The XO's eyebrow shot up. "That's a bit extreme," he said.

Mori's jaw clenched, her eyes scanning the faces around her. She leaned forward. "But necessary." She said, letting the word hang in the air. "It's temporary. We're not taking chances until we get a handle on this." She turned to the Chief. "I want an extra squadron of fighters ready to scramble at a moment's notice."

"Roger that. We'll have our birds primed and ready," the MCPO confirmed, with a nod from the CAG, who started tweaking the flight roster.

Then came the tricky part. "And Talyn," she said, "will be confined to quarters."

Grant's shoulders stiffened, his fingers drumming a quick pattern on the table. The other officers shared uneasy glances.

"XO, review everything Talyn's touched," she said. "We've got our work cut out for us. Dismissed."

Grant was pacing outside the briefing room, chewing his lip. He stopped short when he spotted Mori.

"Skipper, do you have a minute?" he asked.

"Walk and talk, Mr. Grant," she said, nodding down the corridor. "I'm fashionably late for a call with the High Daimar."

Grant fell in step, his eyes darting around the hallway. "Permission to speak freely, Skipper."

"Floor's yours, Mr. Grant."

"Is locking up Talyn really necessary? He's been solid gold as an officer."

"I know, Mr. Grant," Mori said, returning a salute from a passing junior officer. "But we can't take chances on this one. Keeping the ship and crew safe is job one. It's a precaution, not a punishment."

Grant nodded, his fingers tapping out a nervous beat on his leg. "Yes, Captain. But the crew... he's become part of the woodwork here. This could stir up some... let's call them ripples."

"It's gonna be a fun few days," Mori said with a wry smile. "And congrats, you're now our Morale Officer. No pay bump, but fame and glory await. Keep those ripples from turning into waves."

Grant's face brightened a bit. "I'll give it my all. And as my first official act, I'm bringing back intramural Breakball."

"Just make sure MedBay's prepped for that," Mori quipped, her smile lingering as they walked. She paused as her datapad pinged with a message from comms.

"Captain, High Daimar Aldwynn's waiting on vidcall in your office," the message read.

"Go stretch those morale officer muscles, Mr. Grant. I've got a call to make," Mori waved him off. "We'll chat later, perhaps over coffee—if the MedBay isn't packed by then."

Grant saluted. "Understood, Captain. Good morning."

Mori slid into her seat just as Antonov settled in across the table. The screen flickered to life and snapped High Daimar Aldwynn into focus, his stern face filling the frame. Even through a screen, his presence was commanding. He was Arcturian military prestige personified in his black uniform, the Imperial Nightguard's silver pin—a shield crossed by sword and spear—glinting on his lapel. His crest was decked with gem-studded chains and ancient coins, symbolizing his lofty status.

"Captain Mori, Admiral Antonov," he said with a curt nod. "The emperor is most grateful for your uncovering of this treacherous scheme." His voice was as heavy as the medals pinned on his uniform. "And I thank you for your alacrity in taking this call."

"We serve at the pleasure of the High Daimar," Antonov said. He inclined his head slightly.

"Gratitude. I shall be brief, for time presses. The primary conspirators are in chains, but shadows are long and deceitful. They've laid false trails and marked loyal Arcturians as traitors. Our vigilance must be unrelenting."

Mori nodded, her face set. "We are securing critical areas and conducting thorough systems reviews."

Aldwynn hit a button, and the room went dark, replaced by the eerie light of a holographic display. It showcased the Imperial Nightguard in action—raids on warship strongholds and Arcturian colonies. The images were stark— elite units moving with a precision that was both impressive and chilling.

Mori's hands remained folded on the table, her nails pressing crescents into her palms as the Nightguard's footage played. One scene showed them storming a small outpost; doors blew open, and dark-armored soldiers poured through like a flood. They took down the suspects with extreme prejudice.

The scene shifted to an officer being dragged from his quarters, his protests cut short by the butt of a rifle.

But it was the next scene that really got to Mori. The calm facade shattered on a battleship's bridge as doors blew open, revealing a squad of Arcturian Marines. Dressed in Navy black and red, they rushed in like a tidal wave.

The XO spun around just in time to catch a baton to the stomach. He doubled over, gasping, before being shoved to the deck, cheek pressed against cold metal.

An ensign made a desperate grab for his sidearm but was too

slow. A stun baton came down hard, hitting his arm with a sickening crack. His scream was cut short as his head slammed on the deck, pinned down by an imposing Marine with a face chiseled from stone.

At a curt nod from the Captain, the Marines yanked the men to their feet. The ensign swayed, but managed to keep his feet. The XO glared at the Captain, a trickle of blood running from his split lip that he didn't bother to wipe away.

With a snarl, the Captain lashed out. The back of his hand cracked across the XO's face, snapping the man's head to the side. He then turned to a nearby Marine and snatched the stun baton from the soldier's grip. In one fluid motion, he swung the baton into the ensign's abdomen. The young officer crumpled, held up only by the iron grips of the Marines flanking him.

The High Daimar's stern voice snapped Mori back to reality. "As you see," he said, "the Imperial Nightguard is committed to eradicating this threat. Rest shall not find us until every conspirator lies in chains."

Mori nodded, her face tight. "Understood, High Daimar. We appreciate your efforts."

The High Daimar's gaze sharpened, as if trying to reach them through the screen. "Captain Mori, be clear: the conspirators are cunning, deep in resources. Deception, cloaked as friends or allies, is their tool. Ruthlessness, in unearthing serpents from their dens, is ours."

"We will remain on high alert, High Daimar. The safety and security of the fleet are our top priorities," Mori said. "Any serpents will be swiftly eradicated."

The High Daimar's stone-faced expression cracked for a

moment, approval flickering in his eyes. "Would that you had been born an Arcturian, standing with us as kin, shoulder to shoulder."

His tone hardened again as he continued, "Raids persist, and traitors are exposed daily. Those apprehended may consider themselves fortunate if merely stripped of their adornments. The shame may compel some to choose an end by their own hand." He shrugged as if he was discussing the weather forecast. "This, however, is of no consequence to us. I shall update you on any developments." The screen went black, leaving the room in a heavy silence.

Antonov turned to Mori. "Make sure all security protocols are updated. We can't afford to let our guard down for even a moment."

Mori gave a sharp nod, her jaw set. "It's already in progress, Admiral," she said.

A ghost of a smile touched Antonov's lips. "Of course it is. I have to update the chancellor and president of the Senate. Join me in my cabin later to discuss this in more detail."

Mori cut the call with High Daimar Aldwynn and took a steadying breath before leaving her office. She straightened her uniform—a little ritual to get her head on straight—and stepped into the corridor. The usual buzz carried a sharp, nervous edge. Fragments of conversation quieted as she rounded corners, but not quite soon enough:

"They should just ship the whole bunch back to Arcturus."

"Did you hear about Talyn? What, are we on some kind of

witch hunt now?"

"I heard they're rounding up all the Arcturian officers. Next stop, POW camps."

The usual easy chatter of the corridors had given way to clipped responses and half-finished conversations. Even the regular card game in the mess had disbanded early.

As she neared the bridge, two Marines snapped to attention. Mori gave the slightest of nods, all business. "With me," she said, and they fell in line as she entered the ship's nerve center.

Talyn was at his post, his usual Arcturian black and red swapped out for Colonial Navy grays. The bridge crew's movements had changed—subtle course corrections around his station, careful distances maintained.

The bridge fell silent as Mori approached. "Sentar Talyn, you're to come with us to your quarters," she said. She adjusted her collar, an unnecessary gesture that took longer than it should have.

Talyn met her gaze, his face a mask, emotions locked down tight. He gave a sharp nod, stepping away from his console. "Of course, Captain. I'll comply without delay."

The Marines, respectful but alert, escorted Talyn through the ship. Sailors froze mid-task, eyes following the group, whispers trailing in their wake. The hiss of doors and the steady clack of boots on metal ratcheted up the tension. In the elevator, a junior officer, nose buried in his datapad, bumped into the group. He took half a step back, datapad clutched tight. "I'll, uh... catch the next one," he stammered, backing away.

The elevator hummed. No one spoke. No one moved. Soft

lights traced their wordless journey into the ship's heart. When the doors opened, the bright corridor stretched out before them, shadows dancing slightly.

Mori's thoughts churned as they neared Talyn's quarters. The corridor's silence felt heavy as she motioned the Marines into position. The soft click of the door sounded like a judge's gavel as she waved Talyn inside.

"May I come in, Talyn?" Mori broke the tense quiet.

"Certainly, Captain. Please enter," Talyn said, stepping aside.

His quarters were a small museum of Arcturian culture—coins, a dagger on the wall, a traditional rug on the floor. A holo-frame flicked through pics of Arcturus, a younger Talyn in armor, and a group shot with his fellow officers from Galatea.

Talyn gestured to a chair, but Mori stayed standing. "Thanks, Talyn. This won't take long. I'm sure you've heard the rumors— a faction back home plotting with the Union to overthrow the Emperor."

Talyn's stance was rigid, his face giving nothing away. He gave a slight nod.

"For now, you're confined here. A Marine guard will remain at your door. Is that understood?" Mori knew she had to set the boundaries and personal feelings aside. This was about protocol, not friendship.

"Your orders are clear, Captain," Talyn said, his voice as neutral as his face.

"We'll make sure you're taken care of—exercise time and all. The guards will have your schedule," she said in a softer tone.

"Thank you, Captain," Talyn said as Mori turned to leave.

The door shut with a solid thud, closing off the room—and their conversation—behind her.

***

The daily reports blurred together on her screen. She'd read the same maintenance log three times before the comm's ping cut through.

"Captain Mori, Lieutenant Daniels here. We've got a situation on the bridge. It's about our comm sweeps."

"What's the problem?" Mori asked, already heading for the door.

"It's... something you need to see for yourself, Captain. It's not good."

"Understood. I'm on my way."

Mori hit the bridge elevator, her mind racing as it climbed. She checked her watch. Not even midshift, and the day was already writing itself into the logs.

As soon as Mori stepped onto the bridge, Daniels approached.

"What've you got, Lieutenant?" Mori asked, leaning in, eyes locked on the comms officer.

"Captain, I stumbled on something odd—an unauthorized data packet beamed out via the quantum entanglement transmitter," Daniels said. She paused, her eyes flicking to her notes. She pursed her lips and let out a small sigh before continuing. "It happened during Talyn's shift, but there's a catch," Daniels said, hesitating.

Mori drummed her fingers on her thigh. Her gaze swept

from Daniels to the console and back. "Lieutenant, the details, please."

"The timestamps don't line up. The transmission time and the transceiver's hard-coded time are off. The odd thing is Talyn was running a meditation group in the rec room when it happened. He wasn't even at the controls," Daniels said, looking as confused as Mori felt.

Mori studied the timestamp data again. Each number raised new questions, and somewhere in those questions lurked her answer.

"Any chance we can see what was in that packet?" Mori asked, her gaze sharp.

Daniels shook her head. "No luck, Captain. The logs are scrubbed, buffers too."

Mori tapped her comm. "XO, get the senior officers to the briefing room. Now." She turned back to Daniels. "You're with me, Lieutenant. We need to sort this out."

Galatea's corridors closed in on her when Mori marched out of the bridge, each intersection another decision point with too many possibilities.

Her officers spaced themselves around the table, datapads aligned with military precision. Mori tried to crack the tension with a bit of humor. "So, who had 'two crisis meetings in one day' on their bingo card?" she quipped, then got straight down to business. "Thank you for dropping everything to get here. We've got a serious problem on our hands. Someone sent an unauthorized data packet from our QE transmitter during Talyn's shift. But here's the twist—the timestamps don't match his duty log, and he was somewhere else at the time. Looks like we've got an uninvited guest playing with our comms."

Daniels jumped in with the technical details. "The transmission time and the transceiver's hard-coded timestamp are out of sync. This wasn't an accident—someone manipulated the logs."

The XO, sharp as ever, suggested, "We should cross-check all on-duty personnel and their access levels during the incident."

"Yes," Mori nodded. "I want a full security audit. Check against all alibis during the transmission time and review all related security footage."

Commander Liu, head of IT, chimed in with a proactive step, "I'll have my team run a diagnostic on the entry logs to the transmitter room. We might catch an inconsistency in the access records."

"Good," Mori said. "I expect updates every two hours. This is our top priority— turn this ship inside out if you have to. Dismissed."

With the room clearing out, Mori needed a breather. She headed for the observation deck. Through the viewport, space stayed constant. Unchanging. No conspiracies among the stars.

The usual between-shift bustle had taken on a mechanical quality. Crew members moved with purpose but kept their eyes forward, their conversations low. Gone were the easy smiles and relaxed postures of last week. Instead, Mori caught sight of tightened jaws and furrowed brows, eyes that flicked away a bit too fast. The ship's hum felt distant, hollow.

Mori returned each salute, keeping her expression neutral, but inside, her mind was racing. This was suspicion doing its dirty work. The whole mole situation had everyone on edge, creating an undercurrent of tension throughout the ship. She could almost hear the unspoken questions hanging in the air: A traitor? Here? On Galatea?

It hit her then, a sobering realization. This unease, this shift in atmosphere—it was eating away at her ship's spirit. Mori set her jaw. They were still a team, still united in purpose. Her job now wasn't just to find the mole. She had to keep her crew's trust intact, be the steady hand that would guide them through this storm.

Mori stepped into the elevator, her finger hovering over the control panel for a moment before selecting the deck. In the empty elevator, her shoulders dropped a fraction. Three decks to go. Time enough to exhale.

The observation deck's viewport showed streaking stars and nothing else. She checked the duty roster, closed it, checked it again. Each name carried new weight. It was like a jigsaw puzzle from hell; none of the pieces fit, and she hated sloppy work.

The comm chime in her head interrupted her thoughts. Talyn, requesting a meeting. Mori sighed, and for a moment she toyed with the idea of delaying. She checked the time. Three urgent reports waited on her desk, and the mole's transmission data still needed review. But Talyn wouldn't reach out without good reason.

Mori sent an affirmative, then turned from the viewport. Had Talyn discovered something about the Arcturian plot? Or was this a personal plea against the confinement? Either way, it meant more complications in an already tangled web. Never a dull moment on Galatea these days, that was for sure. And somehow, she had a feeling things were about to get even more interesting.

With reluctance, Mori left the observation deck and made her way back to the elevator. Somehow, the walk seemed longer than usual.

She took a deep breath outside Talyn's door, steeling herself for whatever was coming. She hit the chime, and the door slid open with a soft hiss.

In his cabin, the usual vibrancy had given way to a somber atmosphere. Talyn seemed transformed—not by his environment, but by circumstance. Talyn stood at parade rest, his uniform collar stark against bare crests where ceremonial chains should have hung. The room's collection of Arcturian artifacts cast shadows behind him. He handed a polished wooden box to Mori, his voice carrying that formal Arcturian tone.

"Captain," he began, "these badges stand testament to honor—relics I find unworthy to bear. Disgrace fallen upon Arcturus, and by extension my person, weighs heavy. I am prepared to take leave of Galatea should you deem it so, but I would beg favor to remain. A spy lurks among us, and rest shall not find me until this shadow is brought to light, that honor may once more grace my people."

Mori eyed the box, then locked eyes with Talyn, looking for any hint of deceit but coming up empty. She weighed the box in her hands. Years of earned honors, against days of suspicion. Her fingers closed around the lid. "I'll hang onto these for now," she said. "Not because I think you're guilty. We clear this mess; you get these back."

Talyn lowered his head and shoulders in a deep, formal bow. As he straightened, his voice carried a solemn tone. "Gratitude, Captain. I will not fail you. Know that my loyalty remains with Galatea, regardless of the outcome."

Her reply was short and sweet, hiding the storm brewing inside. "Alright, Talyn, you're in, but you'll be under Lieutenant Grant's watchful eyes," she said. "And when you take these back, it'll be because we'll have done our job."

As Mori walked out of Talyn's quarters, the box felt heavy in her hands, but there was a flicker of hope, too. Trusting Talyn was a gamble, no doubt. She traced the Imperial seal on the box with her thumb before tucking it away. If they were gonna catch this mole, they'd need every trick in the book—and then some.

Chapter 21

Deck Six, CCV Galatea

Kliinat, Tau Ceti System

October 21, 2681

Carson keyed his neural, checking the time before his meeting with Mori. Five minutes early was regulation-perfect, though he'd probably spend those five minutes second-guessing why he was counting minutes at all. A mixture of ozone, cleaning chemicals, and machine oil enveloped him like an old, annoying friend.

His last awkward conversation with Mori still played in his head. That moment would haunt him, like when a server brought his food and said, "Enjoy your meal," and Carson answered, "Thanks, you too." That little gem made an appearance every few months.

Jorge Sanchez

Deck Six buzzed with activity. Carson had cranked the temperature down to a brisk 18 degrees. He caught Akitani hiding a shiver during Second Platoon's hand-to-hand drills — good. Nothing sharpened focus like remembering those frost-bitten mornings at Thebes. The rhythmic crack of M45s from the range meant First Platoon was running their qualifications right on schedule.

Third Platoon gathered around Gunny in a quieter corner, soaking up tactical knowledge like sponges—heavily armed sponges. Nearby, the 2nd Battalion's other companies undertook physical training or navigated the obstacle course. Echo Company had some wrinkles to iron out, and what better place to do it than Galatea?

He looked back at the procession of Union prisoners in their distinct orange jumpsuits, marching under the strict gaze of the Military Police. Given the lack of resources in Kliinat, they had been brought to Galatea for medical care.

Carson's gaze drifted to a nearby training area, where Talyn was working out alone. The blue-skinned officer was hard to miss—a 6'3" mountain of muscle moving like liquid lightning as he unleashed a series of strikes on a training dummy. Two Marines stood nearby, on "guard duty". But their slack-jawed expressions suggested they were more captivated by the impromptu martial arts display than focused on their actual job.

Carson mused that if Talyn was a spy, he was either the world's worst at staying inconspicuous or the best at hiding in plain sight. Watching his fluid movements, Carson couldn't help but think that keeping skills like that cooped up was a waste of good talent. His attention shifted as someone called his name.

"Lieutenant, I have some good news. Your shipment arrived," said the supply officer, a Klii butterbar whose enthusiasm seemed almost illegal in the dull military environment. She handed Carson a datapad, her smile as bright as the screen she presented.

He received approval for his new "toys"—that batch of thermal knives adapted from the Klii Scouts, which would soon become bayonets for his troops' M45s. Considering how impressive those knives had been in the field, Carson had been really looking forward to them. His fingers itched as he signed the screen. Those knives would give his Marines an edge— assuming they didn't slice their own fingers off first. He could already hear Gunny's creative cursing during training.

He held on to the datapad as the Lieutenant tried to take it. "Thanks, Lieutenant. You'll let me know as soon as they get here, right?"

"No, I'll keep them and sell them to Charlie Company unless you give back my datapad, sir," she retorted with a grin that suggested she might not be entirely joking. Carson was impressed; her English was impeccable, and her sense of humor was sharp. She snatched the datapad from his grasp, flashed him a smile, and saluted. As she turned to leave, she snapped another salute at Maalek, who was approaching.

Carson waved Maalek over, then turned back to the mats where Sousa and Andaeer were sparring. Sousa gave the Klii a demonstration of hand-to-hand combat that looked more like a demolition derby. Andaeer became intimately acquainted with the mat.

Rodriguez and Muller, one sporting a swollen eye and the other a sling, urged him on with a bit too much enthusiasm. Carson noted their injuries with a wary eye, wondering if they were a preview of what awaited anyone brave or foolish enough to spar with Sousa.

Andaeer kept going, even despite the mismatch. Each time he hit the ground, he popped back up like one of those inflatable clown punching bags, ready for more. With her deceptive speed and sharp moves, Sousa always had another trick up her sleeve, keeping Andaeer on his toes—and frequently off his feet.

Sousa's vicious shoulder throw sent Andaeer crashing onto the mat with a thud that made Carson wince. Shaking it off, Andaeer was up again in a heartbeat, determined to get in at least one good hit before the bell.

"Maal, I hope you're right about this healing ability of the Klii. Andaeer's gonna be sporting shades of green and purple after today. Ouch, there he goes again. Maybe the next guy to spar with Corporal Sousa should get armor. And a helmet."

Maalek nodded, his eyes tracking Andaeer's enthusiastic attempts to turn his bruises into badges of honor. "Ah, yes. Andaeer will heal after a few hours. His pride, well, that might take longer. He does seem to be enjoying the fight a great deal. Oh, he landed on his head there. Maybe we should provide head protection," Maalek said.

Carson chuckled, impressed by Maalek's grasp of the situation—and of English. "You know, Maal, your English has gotten pretty darn good. All the Scouts have improved. And here I am, struggling to string two words together in Daal. The last time I tried to order a beer, they handed me a bowl of soup instead. I was too embarrassed to correct them, so I ate it."

Maalek inclined his head. "Thanks, Skip. We study hard and are eager to learn. Though Daal is challenging, you will master it soon. Beer and soup do sound similar; do not be discouraged."

Carson paused, a slight tilt to his head. "Do they really?"

"No, not at all. I just wanted to be supportive."

Carson laughed. "You really are the worst. Anyway, it's impressive how far you've come along in so little time."

"I've read some books you recommended, and I try to catch the Colonial radio broadcasts when I can. It helps. I particularly enjoyed The Charge of the Light Brigade. Fascinating story. Did that really happen?"

"Yeah, it did. It was a classic Charlie Foxtrot—cavalry charging straight into artillery. Total mess, but those guys didn't flinch. Rode right into a hail of cannon fire. Balls of steel, that."

"What gallantry," Maalek said.

The word 'gallantry' hit too close to home. Carson's father had shown the same kind of gallantry in his final charge on Platea. His voice caught for just a moment, and he cleared his throat, focusing on a point somewhere past Maalek's shoulder. "If we ever have to make a suicidal charge, I want a poem written about it. Or a song; no, both—a poem and a song. And a film..." He forced a grin, but his fingers drummed a restless pattern against his thigh. "Speaking of which, I've got more books for you if you're interested."

Maalek's eyes lit up. "Yes, thank you. I am very interested. I have also joined a small discussion group with Marines from Bravo Company. My pronunciation needs work, but I am optimistic that it will become passable with more practice," Maalek said.

Carson gave Maalek a playful shove. "You're kidding, right? At this rate, you'll be speaking English next week. Wait, I mean, you'll speak better English than I—no, me." Ah, damn it.

They stood in companionable silence, taking in the scene of intense training exercises. Despite his anxiety, Carson found comfort in Galatea's rhythm—the soft buzz of inertial dampeners, soothing blue lights, and the gentle hum of air scrubbers. Turning to Maalek, he said, "So, I heard you got a little lost earlier?"

Maalek shifted his weight, tugging at his collar. "I see scuttlebutt travels as fast aboard ship as it does back home. I am not yet accustomed to the neural interface. Ended up in the hangar, somehow. The air boss did not seem pleased to see me there," he said.

Carson placed a reassuring hand on Maalek's shoulder. "Don't take it to heart. He's never happy to see anyone."

"He was kind enough to reset my neural, at least."

"After dinner, I'll go over the menus with you. Don't worry. You'll wonder how you ever lived without it in a few days. Whoa, watch out!" He yanked Maalek to the side as a platoon of Marines charged past them, their boots thumping in unison on the rubberized deck. The shortest was a woman towering over six feet, who looked like she could wrestle a tank and win.

Maalek's eyes followed them. "Is that a new company? I haven't seen them before. They look formidable."

"They're Hell Divers," Carson said, watching the Platoon disappear around a corner. "They arrived yesterday."

"Hell Divers? What in the Goddess is a Hell Diver?" Maalek asked.

"Remember when we secured that shuttle crash site? A squad of Hell Divers was aboard on their way to Naadan. They're orbital drop troops," Carson said.

Maalek's brows furrowed. "They are what?" he asked.

"Hmm," Carson hummed quietly, taking a moment to think. "Okay, you remember the Archangels, right?"

Maalek's expression shifted, and a flicker of dread crossed his face. "How could I forget them? They arrived during the first wave of the invasion, iron that rained from the sky. And that sound... I never wish to hear it again."

Carson raised his hand, mimicking a dive. "Yeah, their suits make high-pitched whines when they dive. It's designed to intimidate their enemies, and I'll be dammed if it doesn't give me the willies. Archangels and Hell Divers are shock troops that jump from ships in orbit, which is already bananas." Carson lowered his voice. "Union Archangels are the best soldiers to have ever taken the field of battle." The admission came easier than it should have. "If you ever tell anyone I said that, I'll deny it and bust you down to private." Some things were true whether you wanted them to be or not.

He paused for effect. "But Hell Divers are right there with them. Only one percent of recruits make it through their selection process. They excel at taking out high-profile targets and generally blowing shit up. On paper, they're the Naval Special Warfare Group, but in the field, they answer to Keres,

Jorge Sanchez

Iron Demons, or—most commonly—Hell Divers. Athens sends them in when someone needs a swift boot up the ass."

Maalek's eyes widened. "I must admit, jumping from orbit sounds quite exhilarating."

Carson couldn't help but laugh a little. "Or quite suicidal. Divers from Cassiopeia stormed that Union garrison on Egeeo." He snapped his fingers to emphasize, "Just like that, three thousand troops surrendered. Everyone knows they're augmented with cybernetics, but it's all hush-hush. Look at them; they just ran a four-minute mile and are not even panting."

"I recall that mission, but the city is called Aageo, and I would caution you, as a friend, not to mix those up around a Klii woman unless you enjoy being stabbed."

Carson grinned. "Thanks for the tip. I'll do my best not to get murdered by the next Klii lady I talk to. Anyway, I need to go see the Captain. I don't wanna let the cat out of the bag yet, but I have something fun in mind to celebrate the activation of Echo. It's long overdue, but I need the green light to make it official."

"Are you sure you should keep this cat trapped? Are there no regulations against it? Please don't do it on my account," Maalek said, his brow furrowing.

Carson laughed. "Don't ever change, Maalek. See you at chow. Save me a seat?"

"As always."

The prisoners' whispers faded under the sound of Carson's boots on metal. The familiar mix of disinfectant and sweat hung in the air, but it felt different here, heavier. Overhead lights flickered across faces wearing his enemies' uniforms—or maybe just the other side's uniforms, when he really thought about it.

"Jamie, right?" Carson approached a familiar face in the crowd. The MP stepped aside with a nod.

The private had filled out since Carson had last seen him, and though the burn mark had faded, the DermaGel patch was a reminder of how things could have gone differently. For either of them.

"Captain Carson." Jamie's salute was crisp despite the awkward looks from the other prisoners.

"You seem to be doing much better."

Jamie smiled. "Yes, sir. It doesn't hurt much anymore. Might leave a little scar, but that's okay."

"Think of the scars as giving you an air of mystery." Carson glanced at the medical bay down the corridor. "How are they treating you here?"

"Real well, sir. Better care than I would've gotten..." Jamie trailed off, then straightened. "Your docs are top notch."

"Getting along okay with the others?"

Jamie's eyes flickered to his fellow prisoners before returning to Carson. "Yes sir. We look out for each other, you know how it is."

Carson nodded. He did know—it was the same way his Marines stuck together, the same bonds that kept units whole under fire. "Your family know you're okay?"

"Yes sir. They let us send messages home last week." Jamie's voice softened. "My mom was pretty worried."

"Moms tend to be that way." Carson checked his neural reluctantly. "Listen, I gotta run, but I'll check in again. Keep your head up, Jamie."

"You too, Captain." Jamie snapped another salute, this one less stiff than the first.

Carson stopped short of the elevator, thinking about the prisoners and how it could just as easily be him in their place. Pushing these thoughts aside, he pressed the elevator call button, and the familiar sound brought him back to the moment. He stepped in but heard a familiar voice as the doors closed.

"Skip, hold the door!"

"Jammer, I thought you were already on Corinth." Carson held the door to keep it open.

Jammer hustled into the elevator with Two Bit, clad in running shorts and sweat-soaked t-shirts, looking like they'd been running laps along the entire length of Galatea. As they caught their breath, Jammer brushed some stray hair from Two Bit's forehead. Carson noticed the gentle gesture as he turned away, raising an eyebrow. "We got held up. Our birds got firmware updates, but the simulators aren't ready. We're riding shotgun on Atalanta. Scuttlebutt says you're coming along for a 96er."

"That's the plan. I haven't had that long of shore leave in a while," Carson said, releasing the door. "Still need the final nod from the Skipper."

Jammer clapped Carson on the shoulder. "Hey, congrats on the promotion. Well-earned. Oh—this is Two Bit, by the way. Two Bit, meet Matt Carson. We wrecked the Breakball fields at the Academy together."

"Oh, I remember you; I lost three hundred creds on that Diamond Bowl when your last try covered the spread." Two Bit extended a sweaty hand, which Carson shook with a chuckle.

"Sorry about that."

"Don't be. Sure, I lost some coin, but we beat those snobs from Thebes Polytechnic."

The elevator chimed Carson's floor, and the doors whooshed open. "Catch you guys in Corinth then," he said, bumping fists with Jammer. "Rock Bottom, first round's on me."

You're on," Jammer said with a grin. As the elevator doors closed, Carson caught the casual drift of Jammer's hand to Two Bit's back. He filed that detail away without comment—some things weren't meant for official notice. He brushed the thought aside and stepped out of the elevator.

"It was nice meeting you, Two-Bit. Sorry you're stuck with this nugget, but someone's gotta show him where to point the business end of a Dauntless, right?" He said.

Jammer flipped Skip off as the doors slid closed.

He stepped out, checked in with the Marine guard, paused outside the Captain's quarters, and pressed the chime. He straightened to full attention as he waited for the go-ahead.

"The captain is ready for you, Captain," Eddie buzzed in his ear.

"Thanks, Eddie," Carson said, pushing through the door to

find Mori multitasking. She sat at a small table with a coffee and a bowl of fresh fruit, scrolling through her datapad.

She glanced up, inviting him in with a wave. "At ease, Skip. Come, take a seat. Sorry, I'm covering a watch soon and trying to catch up on the news from home. Mind if I eat while we talk?"

Carson settled into the chair opposite Mori, shifting to a comfortable position as he sank into the plush cushion. "Not at all, ma'am."

Mori gestured at her screen. "The Badgers might pull off their first three-peat in twenty years."

"Ugh, I hope not," Carson said with a grimace. "I can't stand them. Always been a Ramjets fan. It's not even the team; it's those insufferable Badger fans from Gaia."

Carson's gaze shifted around the Captain's office, catching sight of a picture hanging on the bulkhead. It depicted a younger Mori with her parents on a ski trip in Kedros, a famous mountain resort on Gaia. Next to the picture hung a framed blue-and-white striped flag emblazoned with Gaia's crest. His eyes landed on the brass pin on her lapel, an award given to top graduates from the prestigious military prep school in Thessaloniki, Gaia. Mori cocked her head, eyebrow raised.

A memory dawned on Carson. "Aaaand I forgot you're from Gaia. Beautiful place, isn't it? I've always said it's the best Colony. Really great, excellent food, terrific people. Everybody agrees, believe me. Uh, did I say insufferable? I meant those Badger fans are incredible."

Mori's eyes narrowed with a glint of amusement, and she smiled. "As soon as the meeting ends, please report to the

Master-at-Arms for a keel hauling. I agree, though. I've always preferred the Spartans. Same planet, less glitzy, better fans. So, what brings you to my neck of the woods? Is this about the request from last week?"

Carson exhaled, his tension dissolving. He survived another classic foot-in-the-mouth moment. This one would make him cringe years down the line—add it to the list.

"Yes, ma'am. I wanted to do something for the company so they have something to look forward to."

Mori tapped on her datapad. "Have you worked out the logistics of the trip?"

"Yes, ma'am. I have a draft ready. I can have it in your inbox this afternoon for your review," Carson said.

"No need. Request approved. Let Eddie know if there are any forms I need to sign. Anything else?" Mori asked.

Carson blinked, caught off guard by her brisk approval. "Uh... no, ma'am. Thank you."

"You seem surprised," Mori said.

"I was prepared to argue my case. Sorry, Captain, you just threw me off for a moment."

"Your request is straightforward; I don't need to overthink it. I've got a few minutes left to kill, care to join me for a cup?"

Coffee. With the Captain. Carson's brain stuttered over those four words. He managed to say 'yes' before his overthinking could catch up.

He managed a nod. "Yes, thank you, ma'am. Coffee sounds great."

Jorge Sanchez

The conversation shifted from Breakball to personal stories as she poured him a cup. The familiar scent of coffee grounded him, made this feel less surreal. 'So, how'd you become a Ramjet fan?' she asked.

Carson wrapped his hands around the warm mug, grateful for something to do with them. "My dad was a big fan. We watched every game together."

"Your dad was a Marine, right?"

Carson blinked, surprised she knew. "Yes, ma'am. He died defending Thebes in the Second War," he said.

"The tide turned after Thebes. You must be proud."

"Proud and grateful," Carson said, the memories bittersweet. Mori's hand brushed his—a gesture so unexpected that Carson's next breath caught in his throat. She withdrew, and suddenly the coffee cup seemed like the most interesting thing in the room. "I'm sorry, ma'am, I don't mean to walk down sad memory lane. What about you? Have you always liked Breakball?"

"I wasn't a Breakball fan until you helped us beat Army in the Winter Classic. Now I can't get enough," Mori shared.

Their conversation flowed from there, easy and comfortable, as they talked about the Academy, their favorite vacation spots, and the shared sacrifices of life aboard a carrier. Carson knew he'd dissect every moment of this conversation later, adding it to his mental archive of overthought interactions.

Chapter 22

Observation Deck, CCE Atalanta

Athenian Space

October 28, 2681

Maalek, Andaeer, and Sousa wedged themselves around a prized viewport on the cruiser Atalanta. The observation deck buzzed with scrappy energy as Marines crammed together, vying for a glimpse of the approaching space station. Maalek, with a sharp glance, noted the way Sousa and Andaeer stood a little too close, their fingers brushing as they pointed out details to each other. He arched an eyebrow, wondering if more than a martial arts partnership was brewing. Along with Williams and Rodriguez, they were the company's top guns—a fact they never let anyone forget, whether they wanted to hear it or not.

As the looming shape of Corinth Station drew nearer, the human Marines offered an enthusiastic play-by-play to their

Klii comrades. Atalanta had made her grand entrance into Athenian space at a designated jump point, cruising past the system's vigilant defenses and the watchful destroyers of the Home Fleet. They'd glided at sub-light speeds for six hours, during which Maalek read about their destination. When the station came into view, a buzz of anticipation swept through Echo Company.

As the massive silhouette of the juggernaut CCV Callisto came into view, Maalek's grin spread ear to ear. "Andaeer, look there. She looks like Galatea."

Andaeer, without shifting his gaze from the ship, nodded. "She is beautiful. And those rail gun batteries—are they not a sight? Each one has its own reactor, sucking power like a Taepyr pup in spring. They are rarely deployed, except for show... or a showdown."

Carson strolled up, his gaze fixed on the metal colossus before them. "Impressive, isn't she?"

Maalek shuffled, awestruck, "It is incredible. Words cannot do it justice."

Carson clapped him on the shoulder. "You think this is something? Wait until we're inside the station—over two hundred levels of Athenian might and marvel. We're dining at the officer's club tomorrow—best view in the galaxy."

Carson turned to address the gathered Marines.

"All right, everyone, listen up. Listen up, I said. We're docking in about ten minutes. Once we receive clearance from the station and the captain, we'll line up by squad and platoon at the passageway. Follow your squad leaders and lieutenants." He raised his datapad above his head.

"Make sure you have your orders pulled up on your datapads to speed things up at border control. My Klii Marines, stick with your human squad mates until you get your bearings. Everyone, check your itineraries and room assignments on your datapads, and be sure you're at the commissioning ceremony an hour before the start time. All right, have fun, enjoy the sights, and see you here in two days at 0800. If you're confused, ask the guy next to you."

An excited murmur spread while Marines headed to the lower deck.

"Maal, you're with me, Gunny, and Lieutenant Akitani unless you wanna hang out with the rank and file."

"Actually, Skip, could you help me with something more personal? I would like to purchase a gift."

"Let me guess—something for a particular lady?" Carson said, leaning in with a grin. "I'm betting ten creds I can guess her name."

Maalek answered his question with a dignified lift of his chin. "It is for someone close, yes. And she is indeed a woman."

"Well, she sounds very special, this mysterious woman," Carson said.

"Oh, this is one of your human customs. What do you call it? Busting chops? It is quite amusing."

Carson chuckled. "Come on, I have another surprise for you. And yes, I will help you pick out a gift for Adaara. I know the perfect place. She's going to love it. Now, follow me."

Navigating through a sea of Marines with the practiced ease of seasoned soldiers, Maalek and Carson descended a couple of flights of stairs to the command deck. They approached the bridge, where the sentries snapped to attention. Carson returned the salute. "Carson, Echo Company. I need a word with Captain Anderson," he said.

"Hold one, sir," one of the Marines said as he activated his neural implant with a touch to his ear. After a quick, whispered exchange, the bridge doors swung open. "You're clear to enter, sir."

"Thank you. Come on, Maal."

Captain Kenny "Gumball" Anderson greeted Carson with a half-hug and a playful jab. Maalek hung back a little, his eyes darting across the intricate dance of holoscreens, control stations, and flickering lights.

"Hey, Skip. What's up? Did you get lost again? We're trying to dock the old girl. Ensign Robertson here hasn't quite mastered the art without decorating her with scrapes, so we're all telling him how to do it," Anderson joked, drawing a reluctant grin from the young officer. "Sure beats peeling potatoes in the galley, though, right Robertson?"

"Yes, sir, and it's certainly better than chopping ghost reaper habaneros," Robertson said with a wry smile.

"That's why we're here, Kenny," Carson said. "Mind if we shadow the bridge for the docking? This is Maalek; it's his first time in Corinth—first time in space, actually."

"No kidding?" Anderson extended a hearty hand to Maalek. "Pleasure to meet you. Sure, park it by the navigator. Best view in the bridge. Goldstein, make some space, will ya? And Skip," he said with a pointed finger, "try not to break anything."

Maalek settled into his designated spot, awestruck by the metal titan displayed before him. He couldn't believe he'd been scavenging in war-torn ruins for ammo and rations just months ago. Now, he was cruising to a space station in the heart of a galaxy-spanning civilization. Carson leaned over, nodding toward the screen that provided a panoramic view from the cruiser's front cameras. "It's almost like looking out an actual window, right? It can even give you vertigo if you stare at it too long."

The station grew closer, revealing itself as a hive of activity. Ships docked and departed, elevators shuttled between levels, and tiny figures hinted at the bustling life aboard. Maalek's hand drifted to the pendant beneath his uniform—Sanya would have loved this view, this moment of pure wonder.

Leaning closer to Carson, he said, "Skip, this is incredible... thank you."

Carson's smile was genuine. "My pleasure, Maal."

Maalek sat in awe as Atalanta drew closer to Corinth. Anderson approached them to attend to a matter at their station before returning to his chair, giving Carson a friendly pat on the shoulder. Maalek leaned in to speak to Carson again. "You seem to have a close bond with Captain Anderson," he said.

"Kenny and I were roommates at the Academy during our second and third years," Carson said.

"Forgive me for prying, but I thought only Navy officers went to the academy."

"Well, mostly. I wanted to be in the Navy and command a ship, but I didn't have the head for it like Kenny or Captain

Mori. The best I could hope for was a position as a deck officer on a frigate or destroyer. I could have worked my way up the chain, but when the war started, they needed more Marine officers than tugboat drivers, so I went for a commission in the Marine Corps during my junior year. I don't regret it."

"For what it is worth, I am glad of it. You are a fine officer and an even better friend."

"Thanks, Maal. That means a lot."

The ship twitched, interrupting their conversation and causing Maalek to tighten his grip on the armrests. "It's the station's tractor beam," Carson said, noticing his discomfort. "They're pulling us in for docking. It'll smooth out in a second."

As Maalek relaxed, he returned to the holoscreens, which now detailed their approach. The ship nestled into its berth, docking clamps latching on as a jetway reached the airlock. Anderson stood, announcing, "Nicely done, everyone. XO, you have the deck. I'm off to deal with the paperwork."

Carson and Maalek left their seats and joined Anderson on their way out.

"Thank you, Captain," Maalek said, shaking Anderson's hand, "I am in your debt."

"Anytime, Maalek. You boys riding back with us, right?" Anderson asked them,

"Yeah, as far as Alexandria, then we're catching Ajax. Yuri has her," Carson said.

"Are you telling me the Navy was desperate enough to give Crazy Ivan a ship? And a heavy cruiser, no less."

"You got any plans after dinner tonight? I'm taking Maalek

and the guys to Rock Bottom," Carson said.

"If you're buying, I'm there. Call it 2200?"

"Cool, see you there."

As Maalek and Carson reclaimed their seabags and exited their berths, the bustling energy of Echo Company surrounded them. The passageway buzzed with the hum of anticipation as the airlock swung open, and the station's security—C-Sec—waved them through. They cleared border control, their datapads and IDs scanned by omnipresent security, and entered Corinth Station's expansive arrival hall.

Electronic figures materialized from thin air, offering salutes that Maalek nearly returned before realizing they weren't real soldiers. The walls themselves seemed alive with moving images - weapons that would have changed the course of their rebellion, places he'd never imagined existed, foods he couldn't begin to name. As some Klii Marines snapped pictures, capturing their first moments on this monumental structure, Maalek absorbed the vibrant scene with a sense of wonder.

Carson leaned in and said, "This is one of the military arrival gates, pretty ordinary, but if you need any last-minute shopping, Red Rocket has a bit of everything. Come on, we'll take the elevators to Tier Two."

Ordinary? Maalek blinked at Carson's casual assessment. He'd seen wonders today that would fill the great halls of Daalamas with gasps and whispers, and here was his friend calling it 'ordinary.' Sometimes the gap between their worlds felt both vast and insignificant at once. They merged with a group of Marines and queued for the elevators. Inside, Maalek gripped the handrail as they surged upwards. Moments later, the doors slid open and they walked into a massive open space, a marketplace that stretched as far as he could see. Above, a tram glided along its suspended track. A lush green belt adorned with flowers and benches divided the walkway, creating an inner and outer ring.

The air, fresh with a floral hint, appeared designed to soothe and invigorate. Around them, people moved with the easy confidence of those who'd never known occupation, lounging in cafés, browsing shops, treating wonders as commonplace. Through the enormous windows, ships drifted past like sea creatures in an ocean of stars. Maalek watched a child point excitedly at a passing freighter, her mother barely glancing up from her datapad—such different worlds they'd grown up in.. Animated holograms and eager salespeople promoted everything from high fashion to rare galactic delicacies.

Station residents approached with genuine smiles and enthusiastic greetings, many asking to take pictures with their new allies. Maalek tensed at each request—not from the attention itself, but from how swiftly and completely his world had changed. Just months ago, he'd been fighting in the ruins of his city. Now strangers wanted to shake his hand and welcome him to their home among the stars. Carson clapped him on the shoulder, grinning at his obvious discomfort with all the attention.

He paused often, drawn to the colorful displays and the sheer variety of goods. Each stall and storefront brought a fresh wave of sights and sounds, each more intriguing than the last. Carson was more than happy to point out this and that. Despite the floating advertisements and artificial sky, the heartbeat of the market felt as familiar as Daalamas' evening bazaar. Voices haggling over prices, the dance of buyers and sellers, even the way people clustered around popular stalls—some rhythms of life remained constant, whether under open sky or station lights. Here, in the heart of Corinth station, Maalek found himself relaxing. This was a slice of home, light-years from Kliinat.

Carson paused and swept the hall with his hand. "We call this the promenade. Every level on Tier Two has one just like it or close enough to make no difference. There's one on Tier One that's just a park. That's my favorite. You can picnic, walk, jog, play with your dog."

"What's a dog?" Maalek asked.

"Oh, boy, you'll see. First, I have another surprise for you. We're going to meet Gunny and Akitani at the best ice cream parlor in Athens, and then we'll go find that gift," Carson said, leading the way through the promenade.

Maalek followed Carson through the bustling corridors of Corinth to Gaewynn's Creamery and Confections, a favorite among the Colonial forces. Exotic fruits and warm pastries filled the parlor with their rich aroma. Inside, the decor was colorful but not flashy, with furniture mimicking moons, planets, and stars. Soft ambient lighting created a welcoming atmosphere.

"You have to get the Gooseberry Sundae, Maalek. It's a tradition here when we dock at Corinth," Carson said as they sat next to Gunny and Akitani at a table shaped like a small moon.

Gunny nudged a paper cup filled to the brim with ice cream

toward Maalek. "Try this in the meantime, Lieutenant. It's Starlight Strawberry—topped with chocolate and caramel," she said. The caramel was rich, its sweetness enhanced by a hint of buttery smoothness, balancing the tangy strawberry in a perfect blend of flavors.

Gaewynn approached with a warm smile, her teal skin and lilac eyes unlike any being Maalek had encountered. But her merchant's welcome was familiar enough—the same careful attention he'd seen from spice traders and cloth merchants in Daalamas' markets. Her head crests, woven with metallic threads that caught the light, marked her as someone who took pride in her work, just as the market women back home wore their finest scarves while tending their stalls. She handed Akitani a towering bowl of neon green and bright blue ice cream. "Here's your Atomic Nebula, Lieutenant."

"And what can I get for you, Skip?" Gaewynn asked with a knowing smile.

"C'mon, you have to ask?" Gunny said, pushing an empty dish aside.

"You're in luck, Skip, I got a fresh delivery of gooseberries," Gaewynn said, turning to Carson.

"Thanks, Gaewynn. This is Maalek, by the way. Maalek, meet Gaewynn."

"It's a pleasure, Maalek. Welcome to my little slice of the galaxy," she said, her smile broadening as she shook his hand, clearly proud of her cozy establishment.

Maalek's eyes swept over the walls, which were adorned with glowing Arcturian glyphs and colorful depictions of fruit. "This place is incredible... I feel like I am stepping into a story," he said, lost in the ambiance.

"The universe is full of stories, Maalek. We aim to make each scoop here a memorable tale," Gaewynn said. "That way, you'll come back for more." Her laughter blended with the parlor's background music.

A Colonial Army Praetorian entered as they chatted, wearing a scowl that cooled the warm atmosphere. "Make sure it's all there this time, Gaewynn. No mistakes," he said, skipping over pleasantries.

Gaewynn's smile stayed fixed in place—the same one she'd probably given thousands of difficult customers before him. "Of course, Sergeant. One moment." She collected empty cups from their table, each movement practiced and professional.She met him at the counter, where a vibrant display of ice creams and toppings sparkled under the soft lighting.

After the Praetorian left, the relaxed ambiance returned. "Praetorians," Carson said with a roll of his eyes.

Scraping the last bits of her ice cream, Gunny gave a theatrical sigh. "Back in your Navy days, you used to spout poetry, Gaewynn. 'You ply ear with honeyed tongue,'" Gunny teased, mimicking Gaewynn. "Now it's all 'super great this' and 'awesome that.' What happened to our mystical ice cream priestess?"

"The heart swells at such gilded words, Gunny. But what can I say? Commanding a ship is a bit different from commanding a scoop. And even a starlight merchant has to adapt to her customers. But don't worry, the magic's still in the mix." She turned to Maalek. "Since it's your first visit, I'd like you to try a new flavor I've been perfecting. It's made with Butter Fruit from Kliinat and spices from Arcturus."

Maalek's eyebrows rose at the mention of Butter Fruit. "I am honored," he said, genuinely curious about how this familiar taste from home would blend with something so exotic.

"Don't forget, we have lunch reservations in an hour," Akitani said, muffled by another spoonful of ice cream.

"We'll meet you there," Carson said, checking his datapad. "Maal and I have a few errands to run first. And tonight, we're all heading to Rock Bottom. Don't make any plans, alright?"

Chapter 23

Tier Two Promenade, Corinth Station

Athenian Space

October 28, 2681

The rich cocoa aroma enveloped Maalek and Carson as they entered a quaint confectionery. The storefront featured a brown façade with vibrant orange trimmings, a large display window showcasing delicate chocolates in colorful foils arranged into pyramids, and baskets brimming with dried fruits and sweets. The small awning above the entrance displayed the name "Leander's" in a flourish of attractive cursive.

A young girl with platinum shoulder-length hair and a small gold ink tattoo of a dove on her cheek approached them. Surprise flashed across her face, quickly replaced by a warm smile. "Welcome to Leander's. Would you like to sample our new truffles? They're handmade in Athens, with a fresh strawberry jam center," she said, offering a silver tray piled with dark chocolates.

Maalek's eyes lit up as he popped one into his mouth. "By Grabthar's Hammer, I cannot quite describe it in your language without doing it a disservice," Maalek said with delight.

"Not bad, right, Maal?" Carson said.

The girl thanked them with a graceful curtsy. "Thank you, sir. My grandfather crafts all our chocolates in our family workshop. He will be thrilled to learn that his creations have impressed such a distinguished guest.

Carson stepped forward and shook her hand. "I'm Skip, and this is Maal. He's looking for a gift, and I figured your chocolate-covered beans and peppers would hit the mark."

Her eyes lit up. "A pleasure to meet you both. My name is Amelia. Give me one moment, and I'll bring out some samples," she said with a broad smile.

"Thank you. We need the best, Amelia. She's a special friend," Carson said, winking.

Maalek wandered the store, marveling at the variety of confections while sipping a small espresso that another attendant offered him. The smooth texture and rich, bittersweet flavor—tinged with caramel—was a revelation compared to the coffee aboard Galatea. "Skip, all these wonders, it is overwhelming," he confessed.

"If you think that's good, wait until I treat you to a Mochaccino after we're done here," Carson said.

"It is funny how we once thought our small planet was the

center of the universe. It is humbling to realize we are just another grain of sand in a vast sea."

"We all have small universes of our own, don't we? Growing up in Alexandria, I didn't grasp how big the galaxy was or how many new friends I'd make," Carson said.

"Irony that we have the Union to thank for that," Maalek said.

"In a way. They broke one tenet of human exploration, though. We're not supposed to contact species or civilizations that have not achieved FTL travel. And there are a couple that we're keeping an eye on. One is still in its Bronze Age, but the other launched its first satellite a few years ago."

"I have heard of this rule. It is self-imposed, is it not?"

"It is, but it had never been broken until the Union invaded Kliinat."

"What about the Arcturians?" Maalek asked.

"That's some story. The Arcturians reverse-engineered the FTL drive from a ship that crashed in their system. Things didn't go well when we made first contact, which became the First Contact War. After the truce, they let us poke around the wreckage. We got some interesting upgrades based on tech we found on it."

"Fascinating," Maalek said. "A century ago, we Klii were mastering powered flight, and you humans were already pushing the frontiers of space."

Amelia returned, bearing a tray of chocolate-covered coffee beans and fiery peppers. "This mix would make a splendid gift box. Please, try as many as you like," she encouraged.

Maalek tried one of the recommended beans—a swirl of white and dark chocolate over an arabica bean sprinkled with cayenne pepper flakes—and was delighted by the intense burst of flavors. "By the Goddess. Simply perfect. I'll take a box."

Carson picked a second bean from the bowl. "One for me, too, please."

"Oh, is it for a particular friend? I bet ten creds I know who she is," Maalek said.

"You're hilarious, Maalek."

Carson and Maalek walked out of Leander's with two boxes of chocolates each.

Chapter 24

Captain's Quarters, CCV Galatea

Kliinat, Tau Ceti System

October 28, 2681

Captain Mori savored the crisp air of her quarters. The climate control was doing its job, keeping the room invigoratingly cool. She'd just finished her workout, sweat still beading on her temple as she sat down for breakfast.

Her table looked even more appetizing after the burn of her workout: fresh fruit glistening with juice, whole grain toast perfectly crisp, fluffy pancakes soaking up syrup, and vat-grown sausages sizzling in their own juices. The rich aroma of strong coffee completed the scene. Mori poured herself a cup and savored that all-important first sip.

As she ate, her mind ticked through her mental checklist. The unauthorized transmission topped the list, a persistent itch she couldn't scratch. Every lead so far had fizzled out. She'd have to nudge the investigation in a new direction soon.

A soft chime interrupted her mental checklist. "Come in," she said, setting down her cup with a clink.

The XO strode in, his brow furrowed. "Captain, Grant and Talyn think they've got something on the transmission."

Mori's fork paused halfway to her mouth. So much for a quiet breakfast. "I'll have Eddie set up a meeting—"

"They're actually right outside, Captain."

Of course they were. Mori nodded toward the empty chairs, shifting mental gears. "Bring them in."

Grant and Talyn entered, their eyes darting between Mori and her half-eaten meal. Mori waved away their hesitation. "What have you got?"

Talyn leaned forward, meeting Mori's intense gaze. "Fragments of the data packet or access code are recoverable by analyzing the system's memory buffers."

The XO's eyes narrowed. "Daniels said those buffers were flushed, Talyn."

"The transmission buffers, yes," Talyn countered. "But the transceiver buffers stand overlooked."

"We've sent and received petabytes since that leak," the XO argued.

A flicker of hope crossed Talyn's face. "In studying the transceiver's documentation, we learned that the recent firmware update expanded the buffer capacity. Echoes of the transmission may yet remain."

Mori considered this, weighing the possibilities. It was a long shot, but long shots were all they had right now. "Alright," she said, decision made. "Grant, set it up. Work with Commander Liu. If there's a thread to pull here, I want you tugging until the whole thing unravels."

Grant shot to his feet. "On it, Captain. We'll need full access to the comm suite."

"You've got it," Mori assured him. She fixed them both with a stern look. "I want updates the moment you have them. Clear?"

"Yes, Captain," they chorused.

As the door closed behind them, Mori returned to her breakfast, eyeing the now-cold pancakes with a rueful smile. She pulled up the day's schedule, then closed it without reading, her fingers already reaching for her comm. If Grant and Talyn were right, this could crack the case wide open. If not... well, they'd make that FTL jump when they came to it.

One thing was certain: it was shaping to be a long day. Mori drained her coffee and stood, rolling her shoulders. Time to get to work.

✶✶✶

Captain Mori stared at the logistics report on her screen, the numbers blurring together. She'd been at it for hours, but her mind drifted back to the morning's discussion about the rogue transmission. With a frustrated sigh, she pushed away from her desk and stood, stretching muscles stiff from too much sitting.

She was halfway through brewing a fresh cup of coffee when her comm unit chirped. Grant's voice crackled through, words tumbling faster than usual despite the late hour.

"Captain, we've hit on something. We've found fragments of the data packet in the buffer. It's patchy, but it's a start."

Mori paused, absorbing the news. "Good work, Mr. Grant. Keep at it. Any crumb could lead us to the bakery."

"Roger that, Captain. We'll keep chiseling away and update you on the chips we uncover," Grant said.

After ending the call, Mori tried to refocus on her reports but found her attention waning. She closed the logistics report and grabbed her coffee. The IT hub would have better answers than her paperwork.

The corridors of Galatea hummed with the ship's usual activity, but Mori noticed the undercurrent of tension. News of the investigation had spread despite her efforts to keep it under wraps. Her steps matched the rhythm of Galatea's heartbeat and the murmurs of her crew.

Arriving at the IT hub, she found Talyn, Grant, and Commander Liu awash in a sea of glowing screens. The IT hub smelled like overworked processors and hours-old coffee. Her team had claimed their territories among the scattered datapads and spare consoles, their faces lit by scrolling code. The room snapped to attention at her arrival, but she eased the formality. "As you were."

Liu greeted her with a nod. "Captain, following Talyn's lead, we've managed to extract data from the buffers."

Mori leaned closer to the monitors, her coffee forgotten. "What have we got?"

"We've isolated segments of an access code," Liu said,

pointing at the display. "They're encrypted fragments, but should be enough to tighten our net. We'll compare them with personnel logs and biometric entries."

Hours slipped by as the team dove into their work. The scent of pizza softened the sharp edge of their mission. Chairs scraped closer together as boxes were passed around.

Talyn picked up a slice of pizza with a mixture of curiosity and caution. "Is this typical sustenance during extended operations?" He asked, attempting to fold his slice as he'd seen Grant do.

"It's the staple of midnight breakthroughs," Grant said, watching Talyn navigate his first bite.

Talyn took another measured bite, then reached for a second slice. "Surprisingly adequate," he said, earning a laugh from Grant.

"The late shift does have its perks," Mori said with a smile, taking a seat and grabbing a slice for herself.

Liu joined in the conversation. "It's not Filippi's Pizza, but it'll do for now. We should grab a pie from Corinth next time we're docked."

"Agreed," Mori said, turning to Talyn with a smile. "You'll have to join us, Talyn. It's an experience not to be missed."

Talyn, hesitating before another bite of his pizza, nodded. "This differs greatly from Arcturian rations. I begin to grasp the appeal."

Grant laughed, "Wait till you try it with extra cheese. It's a game-changer," he said.

With a round of light-hearted comments winding down,

Mori steered the conversation back to their task. "Let's keep the coffee coming and order more of these... adequate pizzas."

As the afternoon unfolded, the focused hum of activity was punctuated by the rhythmic tapping of keyboards and the occasional rustle of pizza boxes. But despite their efforts, they kept hitting dead ends.

Liu pushed her glasses up for the dozenth time that hour. "Another dead end." She reached for her coffee, found the cup empty. Again. "Every time we think we're close to cracking this encryption, it morphs on us."

Grant leaned back in his chair, stretching. "And the signal trace keeps bouncing us around the ship's systems. It's like trying to catch smoke."

Mori frowned, her mind racing. "What about bypassing the bridge systems altogether? We can write a program to trace the signal back to the source, assuming the fragment has part of the transmitter ID."

The room fell silent for a moment before Liu let out a groan. "Of course! We've been so focused on decryption that we didn't even think... if it's brute force, we'll need Eddie's help. There are some security locks in place, but with your authorization, Captain..."

"You've got it." Mori's fingers tapped a quick rhythm on her armrest as she nodded to Liu. "Whatever permissions you need, they're yours."

With renewed energy, they set to work. Hours slipped by as the team grew tense and frustrated with each passing minute. Just as Mori considered calling it a night, Liu straightened in her chair, her fingers flying across the keyboard with renewed speed.

"We got it! The trace was successful—the rogue signal originated from life support."

Mori leaned forward, heart pounding with anticipation. "Life support? That's a restricted area."

"Precisely," Liu said, pushing her glasses up her nose again. "I'll pull up the details on who's had access in the past week. With any luck, we'll narrow down our list of suspects."

Mori nodded. "Cross-reference that list against crew transfers in the last six months."

"Yes, Captain."

"Great work, everyone," Mori said. She measured each word carefully, her hand flat against the console. "Let's pause here, gather some rest, and reconvene with fresh eyes."

As the team filed out, Mori lingered, staring at the screens filled with data. The evidence lined up too neatly. In Mori's experience, conspiracy was messier than this. She pulled up the duty logs again.

With a shake of her head, she left the IT hub. Tomorrow, she vowed. Tomorrow, they'd crack this wide open.

✶✶✶

Captain Mori rubbed her temples, washed in her console's soft blue glow. "Eddie, ask Lieutenant Grant and Specialist Talyn to come to my office."

She leaned back in her chair, eyes fixed on the dossier before Her. Specialist Harper's face stared back, clipped in the top right corner of his impeccable service record. The circumstantial evidence linking him to the rogue transmission was troubling but inconclusive.

The door chimed, interrupting her thoughts. "Enter," she said.

The two officers walked in. Grant's fingers drummed against his thigh, his weight shifting from foot to foot. Beside him, Talyn maintained parade rest.

"At ease," Mori said, gesturing to the chairs across her desk. "Let's talk about Harper."

Grant leaned forward. "Captain, I know it looks thin, but—"

Mori held up a hand. "I've read your report, Lieutenant. What I don't need are your gut feelings. This isn't just about evidence; it's about the implications."

Talyn's crests rippled. "I understand. The consequences loom severe should error in judgment be made. Not for us alone, but for relations between humans and Arcturians."

Mori nodded. "Exactly. We're not just accusing a crewman of espionage. We're potentially upending the lives of everyone on this ship." She stood, pacing behind her desk. "If Harper is innocent, we're looking at JAG involvement, possible civil suits, and the crew's loss of trust."

"But if he is guilty," Grant interjected, "and we do nothing..."

"I know, Lieutenant," Mori said, her voice tight. "That's why we need to tread carefully here." She turned to Talyn. "You mentioned a possible strategy in your report. A sting operation?"

Talyn nodded. "When a man is pressed, lies flow with greater ease. I have formed a strategy—to approach Harper under guise of complicity. It may provoke confession, or at minimum, provide more concrete evidence."

Mori considered this, drumming her fingers on the desk. "It's risky, Talyn. You'd be putting yourself in a difficult position."

"Duty to ship and mission compels action, regardless of risk," Talyn said.

Mori nodded slowly. "Alright. But we're not moving on this without proper authorization. Eddie, get me a secure line to Major Lewis from Naval Intelligence and loop in Admiral Antonov. We need their sign-off on this operation."

Thirty minutes later, Mori faced the stern visages of Admiral Antonov and Major Lewis on her viewscreen. Antonov's jaw tightened with each detail of the plan.

"It's a delicate situation, Captain," Antonov said, his voice gruff. "If Harper is innocent, we could be looking at a public relations nightmare."

Major Lewis's mouth tightened into a thin line. "Not to mention the potential damage to our own investigations."

"I've considered the risks," Mori said. "But if Harper is our mole, we need to act before he can do more damage."

Antonov and Lewis exchanged a look. "Very well, Captain," Antonov said. "You have authorization to proceed. But I want real-time updates on this operation. If anything looks off, pull the plug immediately."

"Understood, Admiral. Thank you both," Mori said, ending the transmission.

She called Grant and Talyn back into her office. "We're a go. But we do this by the book. Grant, coordinate with the Master-at-Arms. I want every precaution in place."

As Grant disappeared to pull strings, Mori traced the same path across her cabin floor—from viewport to desk and back again, checking her comm with each pass. One wrong move would compromise the entire operation. Talyn's plan was a gamble, but it was their best shot.

Later that afternoon, Mori headed to the security room, quickening her pace. She checked her comm one last time before walking through the door. All pieces were in place.

She stepped into the security room, lit only by the glow of monitors. Grant and the Master-at-Arms were poised over screens, waiting. The air was cool and dry, tinged with the faint metallic scent of recycled oxygen. The security room's recycled air felt thick in her lungs. No one spoke above a whisper.

"Initiating operation," Mori said quietly into her comm. "Talyn, you're clear to proceed."

On the main screen, they watched as Talyn entered the life support bay. The cavernous room hummed with the steady thrum of electronics—great cylindrical tanks and a maze of pipes stretched from floor to ceiling. Harper stood at a control panel, his back to the door.

Talyn's approach was casual, almost nonchalant. "Specialist Harper," he said, his voice carrying easily in the ample space. "A moment of your time."

Harper's shoulders stiffened, his hand pausing over the control panel."Sentar Talyn? What can I do for you?"

Talyn moved closer, his voice dropping. "Your machinations,

stripping honor from my name, stand remembered. Yet let past grievances fall to shadow. The packet has been well received, yet HUMMINGBIRD is not satisfied."

In the observation room, Mori leaned forward, her eyes fixed on Harper's face. Harper's hand twitched toward his pocket. His eyes darted to the exit, then back to Talyn.

"What is this, a joke?" Harper stammered, taking a step back. "Who the—"

Talyn closed the distance between them, his face inches from Harper's. His crests flared and stiffened, sharp edges catching the light. "Bite down tongue and open ears."

Harper nodded, swallowing hard. His eyes darted around the room, looking for an escape that wasn't there.

Talyn's voice dropped to a threatening whisper. "The information stands incomplete. HUMMINGBIRD wants the schematics. Deliver them, lest the endless voids of this ship become your eternal rest." As he spoke, his fingers drifted to the hilt of his dagger, tracing its outline in a pointed gesture.

Harper's face drained of color. He licked his lips, a bead of sweat forming on his brow. "Look, I don't have direct access to what you need, but... I can figure something out. It'll cost you, though," he said, his voice quavering. "A lot more."

"Wisdom guides your tongue, Harper. Provide us details with haste."

Mori leaned closer to the monitor, her fingers pressing into the edge of the console. She nodded to the Master-at-Arms. "Move in. Now."

Marines flooded the life support bay, their boots echoing on the metal floor. Harper's hand twitched toward a concealed weapon, but Talyn was faster. With fluid grace, he disarmed Harper and pinned him to the deck.

Mori exhaled slowly, watching the Marines secure Harper. But she knew this was just the beginning. Harper's confession had hinted at a larger conspiracy, a tangled web they'd need to unravel piece by piece.

"Excellent work, Talyn," she said into the comm. "Bring him in. We've got a long night ahead of us."

Later, after hours of debriefings and reports, Mori found herself back in her quarters. She traced Harper's interrogation transcript with her finger, each line raising new questions. Harper's confession had started with Union contacts and ended with Arcturian collaborators. She'd need more coffee before tackling that mess.

Her thoughts were interrupted by a knock. The door hissed open, revealing the XO, his expression more unreadable than usual. He stood at attention, chin lifted slightly. "Permission to enter, Captain."

Mori turned from the viewport, eyebrow raised at this late-hour appearance. "Granted," she said. The XO's late-night visits usually meant crisis, not conversation.

The XO walked in, his usual stoic expression softened slightly. "Hell of a day, Captain," he said, forgoing the usual formalities.

"That's one way to put it. What's on your mind, XO?"

He closed the door with a soft click. For a moment, he stood there, as if weighing his words. "I think you made the right call with Talyn," he said. His usual rigid posture had softened a fraction. "It's going to change some minds around here."

Mori raised an eyebrow. "High praise, coming from you. Think the crew will fall in line?"

"They'll have to," he said. His words carried the same steady rhythm as a warning shot. "Or they'll answer to me."

"Thanks, XO," she said.

He nodded, the smirk blossoming into a genuine grin. "We gave the Union a good wallop today. They'll be back, but we've got the edge for now. And we'll be ready when they try again."

As the XO left, Mori pulled up Harper's preliminary interrogation report. The Union connection was solid, but fragments of his confession hinted at a larger network. She marked several names for Naval Intelligence to investigate, then checked the time. Four hours until her next shift.

She stretched, feeling the day's tension in her neck. Time enough for sleep, if she could manage it. But first, she needed to update Talyn's security clearance. After today, he'd earned it back.

Chapter 25

Tier Six, Corinth Station

Athenian Space

October 28, 2681

Carson pushed through the doors into Rock Bottom, the station's famed bar on the lowest level, where good vibes outweighed the weak gravity. The air buzzed as a motley crew of spacers, station workers, and military personnel gathered to unwind before a breathtaking space view... if you weren't already breathless from the booze.

Despite its compact size, Rock Bottom could pack in two hundred souls eager for some revelry. To the right, booths with well-worn cushions hugged the walls. Opposite them was the main attraction: a horseshoe-shaped bar that served as the pulsating heart. Its polished surface reflected a rainbow of liquor bottles under warm lights, each lined up like a soldier at the ready. Scents of oak, spiced rum, and a note of smokiness wove through the air.

Carson's path to the back turned into a tour of open tabs and waiting shots. The Mezcal with the Alexandria crew was just good manners. He had a beer with Jammer and a few of the pilots from Galatea and Callisto. By the time he reached his table, he saw signs of a party already in full swing—two empty tequila bottles and a large bowl half-filled with spent limes. Anderson was already deep in storytelling, captivating the audience around him.

"We had finished morning inspection," Anderson said, raising his voice to be heard over the crowd, "and it was Carson's turn to fetch breakfast for the squad. But on that particular morning, dear listeners, our hero was preoccupied with a plan he'd been hatching all week—even though his pal Kenny had tried to talk some sense into him."

Anderson leaned forward, lime wedge poised between his fingers like a conductor's baton.. "He'd been practicing all week, planning the perfect moment to ask Mori out. Going over his lines in front of mirrors, mumbling to himself during drills— completely smitten and utterly distracted. Now, we're talking about a second-year going up to a firstie, and not just any firstie, but the gorram Brigade Commander. So there he was, tray in hand, his mind buzzing with lines like, 'Would you honor me with your company at dinner?' In a world of his own, oblivious to everything else."

Akitani shook her head, suppressing a laugh. "Oh, please tell me he didn't actually say that."

"He almost did, and believe me, that wasn't even the worst

one," Anderson said, laughing. He downed his shot and signaled for another. "Caught up looking at Mori, who'd just stepped up behind him, he missed Yuri—Captain Dasayev—walking right into his path."

Anderson clapped his hands. "And boom!" he said, acting out the collision. "Breakfast-ocalyspe. Carson collides with Yuri, and the tray goes flying—applesauce, coffee, eggs—like a buffet missile."

Gunny, handing a lime wedge to Akitani, grinned. "Oh, it gets even better."

Anderson leaned in, lowering his voice. "And who gets caught in the splash zone? Carson, Mori, poor Yuri, and—wait for it—Commandant Burke himself. Covered in breakfast, the commandant's face turned a shade of pure fury."

Gunny chuckled, then coughed as the tequila caught in her throat. "I'll never get tired of this!"

Akitani covered her face with both hands, peeking through her fingers. "Oh gawd, I'm feeling secondhand cringe."

"The aftermath was legendary," Anderson said, his smile wide. "We all ended up on mess hall cleanup duty. We made Carson do an extra week of chores in the dorm as a souvenir. And did he ever ask Mori out?" Anderson looked around before delivering the punchline. "Not a chance. He spent the whole day too embarrassed to even look her way." He downed another shot and added with a twinkle in his eye, "That incident buzzed through the Academy for years. Mori gave her presentation on asymmetrical warfare that day, still splattered with breakfast. Didn't miss a beat. Legend has it, the next day, she received a massive bouquet with a simple card reading 'sorry.'"

Carson, sliding into the seat next to Anderson with a smirk, chimed in. "I can't believe you guys are eating this up. That's not how it went down—at all."

Anderson slid the tequila bottle closer to Carson. "Go on then."

"Well, maybe you got a few minor details right." Carson grabbed the shot glass from Gunny and bit into a lime, his face scrunching up. "I thought I was done for after that debacle. To this day, I can't look at applesauce without breaking into a cold sweat."

The night deepened, and Rock Bottom swelled with the usual crowd, ready to drink beneath the stars. As a prime window table freed up, Carson and his crew snagged it just ahead of a squad of Colonial Army Praetorians.

The Praetorians' table went quiet. A few meaningful glances passed between both groups, measuring the old rivalry—sometimes friendly, sometimes not, centered on budgets, recruits, and bragging rights. Soon, more of Second Platoon filtered in—Williams, Sousa, Rodriguez, Muller, and others. They pulled together a few tables under the watchful glare of the Praetorians. Carson counted three failed attempts to flag down a server and took matters into his own hands. He returned from the bar victorious, brandishing two bottles of Alexandrian Rye Whiskey.

The victory lap back to his table lasted exactly three steps, however, as he bumped into a towering Praetorian on his way back. "Sorry, my man," he said, reaching for the friendly tone he usually saved for customs officials.

The Praetorian whirled around, his height casting a shadow

over Carson. "Watch where you're going, Marine."

Carson, ever the diplomat, took a step back. "Yep, totally my fault. Let me make it up to you—next round's on me."

"Nah, keep your creds." He then gave Carson a firm shove, sending him stumbling into another patron and causing a cascade of spilled drinks. Conversations died mid-sentence. Chairs scraped back from tables. The bartender reached under the counter.

Carson straightened his jacket with the careful precision of a man counting to ten in his head. Marine captains weren't about starting brawls with elite Army units but about setting the standard.

"Enjoy your evening," he said. His smile had all the warmth of a captain filing paperwork.

Carson wiped his jacket with a napkin. The Praetorians' voices carried just loud enough to hear "alien zookeepers." Carson took another sip of his drink.

Typical Praetorians, always jerks, he thought.

Rodriguez's hand tightened around his glass."Everything okay, Skip?" he asked, glancing between Carson's soaked jacket and the Praetorians' table.

"Yeah, just a misunderstanding," Carson said with a smile that didn't quite reach his eyes. He attempted to dry off his jacket, turning in time to catch a burst of laughter and a chorus of animal sounds coming from the Praetorians' table. Rodriguez pushed back his chair, already rising, but Carson tugged him back down.

"Easy, Rodriguez. Let me smooth this over," he said, slipping into his metaphorical diplomatic boots. With a dose of his trademark charm, Carson approached the Praetorians' table again, plastering on his best recruitment poster smile. "Look, guys, we're all on the same team here. How about a peace offering? First round of Athenian Gin on me."

The Praetorian made a sound somewhere between a laugh and a threat. "What was that, mate?" one Praetorian sneered. Before Carson could reply, another firm shove from the side sent him tumbling back into a table. He found himself studying the ceiling, then remembering why standing up seemed like a good idea.

That was the spark in the powder keg. Rodriguez, Andaeer, and Maalek didn't need further invitation, springing into action with the brute force of brawlers rather than the finesse of warriors. A chair splintered against the wall. Glass crunched underfoot. Someone laughed—until a fist found their jaw. The cramped space of the bar left no room for maneuver, pulling everyone tighter into the fray. Andaeer snatched a Praetorian by the throat, lifted him like a trophy, then introduced him to the nearest table. The table lost.

It was mayhem. Patrons hurled glasses and bottles like missiles. Seeing a spacer aim a kick at Carson, Gunny cleared three tables in two strides, leaving overturned chairs in her wake. She tackled the spacer and delivered an elbow strike that surely reset the poor guy's sense of direction.

Carson, back on his feet but staggering, ducked, dodged, and dealt blows. The clatter of breaking glass and furniture enveloped the bar. "So much for a quiet drink," he said to himself. Rodriguez's shout mixed with the whistle of incoming furniture. Carson's dive for cover was pure reflex. "Thanks,

Frankie!"

His thanks were cut short by another punch, landing on his cheek like a railgun slug and lighting up his vision with a burst of stars. He crawled to the sanctuary of an overturned table, wiping at the blood trickling from his nose. This was *not* the kind of mixer he had planned.

As the brawl escalated, a station worker sneaked up to attack Rodríguez with a bottle. Jammer's haymaker spun the guy around. Two Bit stepped in—crack!—and suddenly the station worker had urgent business with the floor.

Anderson found himself tangled in a scuffle with a spacer. Both sported matching bloody noses when Gunny wrapped her arms around the spacer's waist, lifted him like a practice dummy, and introduced him to gravity with a thud that resonated all the way down to Athens. The bar was a whirlwind of fists, shouts, and the sharp tang of spilled drinks.

Battered but resilient, Carson plunged back into the mix, only to be blindsided by two Praetorians who grabbed him by the jacket and flung him across the bar. He hit the wall hard enough to rearrange the bar's artwork. The resulting crash got lost in the symphony of breaking furniture. A jolt of pain surged from his neck straight to his spine. Carson against the wall, testing his shoulder. Left, right, up—nope. Definitely not up. Assessing his battle scars—swollen eye, bloody nose, and a tooth that wobbled in a way that promised trouble—he realized this night would leave more than just memories.

As Gunny approached, Carson pushed himself upright, trying to look more captain than casualty. The doors slammed open. C-Sec poured in, stun batons crackling, looking eager to add to the evening's collection of bruises. Carson, squinting through his good eye, managed a wry grin at Gunny. "Is it your turn to talk to them or mine?"

Gunny bent down, rescued an unbroken bottle of rum from the wreckage. The cork came out with her teeth—she took a long swig before answering. "Yours, I think," she said, wiping her mouth with the back of her hand. "I had the pleasure last time."

Chapter 26

Tier Six Holding Cells, Corinth Station

Athenian Space

October 29, 2681

Carson shifted on the plasteel bench that pretended to be a bed. He sprawled out, hands behind his head, sniffing the lingering aroma of stale beer and whiskey on his shirt. He rolled onto his side, gazing out through the bars, giving up on the notion of sleep. The cell buzzed with Echo Company's greatest hits, each story getting louder and more impressive with every retelling.

In her usual style, Gunny was already at the bars, giving the guards a piece of her mind. "This is some bullshit. Why don't you have those army plonkers in here, too?"

"Because a dozen witnesses say you guys started the fight.

Lucky there are no charges, or you'd be planet-side already," a guard said.

"C'mon, that's a load of crap, and you know it, Billy. That plug-ugly asshole started the whole thing. Did you even look at the videos from the security cameras? It's clear-cut self-defense, as open-and-shut a case as they come."

Billy sauntered over, coffee in hand, his uniform sagging in a way that did him no favors. "Gunny, gimme a break, will ya? I don't make the rules. As soon as the commander arrives, we'll figure out what to do with you. You'll likely spend a few days in the slammer and pay a fine, and then you can go to some other station and ruin some other guy's day."

"Is this because I wouldn't go out on a date with you? It's been ten years, Billy. I know it's hard, but you need to get over me."

Billy's coffee mug couldn't hide his eye roll as he retreated to his desk.

Carson listened to the exchange with a smile, turning to Maalek, who slid beside him on the bench. "Skip, I'm not sure what comes next, but I am glad to face it with my brothers and sisters here."

Carson nodded. He was no stranger to the insides of a holding cell, but the timing couldn't be worse. He thought of Anderson, who'd somehow slipped away—a talent he'd honed since their academy days.

"I'm sorry things got this crazy. Not exactly the shore leave I'd pictured," Carson said.

Maalek's wry smile returned. "Nor I, but I must admit, it has been some time since I had such a spirited fight. I can already envision Andaeer retelling his part, with advantages, to our friends in Daalamas."

"Maalek's right; we sure gave those grunts what for, didn't we, Captain?" Muller said.

"We?" Gunny released the bars and approached. "Oh yeah, you really took it to them, Muller."

"What do you mean? I was right in the mess of it. Look at this cut on my forehead."

Williams gave Muller a dismissive shove. "Shut up, Muller. We all saw you ducking behind the jukebox."

The cell door swung open with a clang that silenced the room. Anderson stood at the door with a slight grin as if he'd walked into a surprise party instead of a cell. "Party's over, folks. Let's go before they change their minds."

As the Marines shuffled out, Anderson motioned for Carson to hang back. Once the crowd noise had faded, he leaned in. "Okay, the C-Sec commander was none too happy and insisted that you guys spend at least a week in the joint. He left me no choice but to call in the big guns. Captain Mori threatened to jump her entire carrier group here and talk to him in person."

Carson rubbed the bridge of his nose and shook his head. "Oh, God, Kenny, why? I wonder the record for making Captain and being busted back to Lieutenant."

Anderson suddenly found his boots fascinating. "About that... I might have left something out. Just a teeny bitty, nothing little detail."

"And what's that?" Carson's stomach churned, unsure if it

was from nerves or the night's drinking—or both.

"Captain Mori called the Old Man."

"The Admiral got involved over some bar fight? Kenny, are you trying to get me kicked out of the Navy?" Yes, anxiety was taking the lead now.

"It was her idea. She wasn't sure if she'd have enough juice, which she did. Antonov is, um, going to talk to you tomorrow. But don't worry, maybe it won't be so bad."

"I'm not sure that makes me feel any better. I bet that's what the Arcturians thought before Antonov took their entire Navy to the woodshed."

"Oh, one thing Captain Mori insisted on is that you guys pay for damages. Well, we guys."

Carson nodded, then sighed. "I'll talk to C-Sec tomorrow and get that taken care of. This one's on me."

Carson signed back into the barracks after Anderson departed for his ship. Learning of the scuffle with the Praetorians, the Marine officer handed him vouchers for a complimentary breakfast at Café Lupin, a high-end French restaurant on Tier Two.

Back in his room, Carson tossed his booze-drenched uniform into the auto cleaner and jumped into the shower. The stream flushed away the night's debris, stinging his cuts but clearing the grime. Once dry, he dressed in a clean T-shirt and briefs, applied DermaGel to his bruised eye, swallowed some painkillers, and collapsed onto his bunk.

***

Carson rose early, aware of Antonov's habit of greeting dawn galaxy-wide. There was even a chance Antonov hadn't slept, given he'd just arrived in Athens. Carson moved his head from side to side in front of his vanity mirror, assessing the damage from the previous night's brawl. The mirror showed progress—his eye had faded from purple to a sickly green, courtesy of DermaGel. His shoulder ached, and his crooked nose required a quick adjustment, which he performed with a practiced hand. He swallowed another pair of painkillers, hoping to dull the persistent throb in his head. He dry-swallowed another antacid. The morning's third.

Carson sat outside Antonov's office, fingers drumming against his thigh until he forced them still. After a nerve-wracking hour, an assistant emerged and ushered him in. She closed the door behind him, leaving him face-to-face with Antonov, who was engrossed in his datapad but gestured for Carson to sit.

"Good morning, Captain. Please sit down," Antonov said without looking up.

"Thank you, sir." Carson settled into the chair. He counted the tiles on the floor, a habit from Academy days. Beneath him, he heard a rhythmic tapping—it was his foot. Antonov appeared not to have noticed.

"I would ask for your version of events, but I've already read the C-Sec reports, so let's skip that," Antonov said.

Carson blinked. His mouth felt like he'd swallowed half of Alexandria's desert. "I'm prepared to accept any punishment you deem necessary, sir."

"Are you, now? Do you understand the position this puts me

in? I have to explain to Prime Adaara and her Council why Echo Company, Marines I personally vouched for, spent the night in a C-Sec holding cell. And then I get to brief the Chancellor on why this elite unit is redecorating station bars."

"Sir, I—"

Antonov interrupted with a raised hand. "It's best if you let me finish."

"Yes, sir." Carson wiped sweaty palms on his legs. Forget getting knocked back to Lieutenant. With any luck, he might only be knocked back to private. Antonov stared at him, silent, for an eternity.

"You're fortunate we have the entire interaction on record, or this conversation could be taking a very different tone," Antonov said, picking up his datapad and handing it to Carson. "A reprimand from a flag officer will be added to your personnel jacket. Sign here."

Carson took the datapad. He scrolled to the bottom of the form and signed his name with his finger. His signature came out steadier than expected. He handed the datapad back to the Admiral, who also signed his name and then put the datapad on his desk.

"Alright, that's the official part done. Now, here's some advice: Things are not like they used to, son. You need to use better judgment. Being a victim of circumstance is not a good enough excuse anymore."

"Yes, sir." Carson kept his face neutral. The Admiral wasn't done yet.

"You might want to remember that sometimes, the best

action is inaction. It would have served you well last night. Understand?"

"Yes, sir, I think I do."

"Good. Did you at least win?"

Carson touched his mostly-healed black eye. "It wasn't even close."

Antonov's expression softened. "Your dad and I found ourselves in a few scraps back in the day. I'm glad to see the Marine spirit is still alive. Alright, dismissed."

Carson shot to his feet, saluted, and walked out. Three corridors away, Carson found a wall to prop up while his legs remembered how to work.

***

The commissioning ceremony and company dinner went without a hitch. Still, Carson had his fill of Corinth Station and looked forward to boarding Atalanta for the trip home. Maalek met him at the elevator the following morning, and they walked to the ship together.

Maalek headed to his berth, but Carson detoured to the bridge to talk to Anderson. His men needed more training in zero-g conditions, and he hoped they could use a full deck. They had trained on their way to Corinth, but it had turned into an unmitigated disaster, and he wanted the Klii to log a few more hours. Maybe this time, their stomachs wouldn't turn themselves inside out. He found Anderson on the bridge, going over pre-departure checks. The Marine sentries waved him in, and one even gave him a fist bump.

If we could harness the power of scuttlebutt, we wouldn't

need FTL drives, he thought.

"Missed you at dinner last night, Kenny," Carson said.

Anderson's grin surfaced from behind his console. "Yeah, sorry, I'd already made plans. How was it?"

"Great, actually. I'm happy my guys saw Callisto push off. Where did you run off to?"

"I ended up hanging out with the bridge crew from Ulysses. They always put on a good poker game. You're looking at a man who won a three-hundred cred hand with a royal flush," Anderson said.

"You must be getting better. I still remember how we cleaned you out playing Go Fish."

"Well, you're also looking at a man who lost a four hundred cred hand to a pair of jacks."

Carson shook his head. He had a lot of fond memories of Anderson and their Naval Academy days. It was good to see that his friend hadn't changed much. "You've never been good at reading a bluff."

"How did it go with Antonov? You're here bugging me on my bridge instead of riding a military transport back to Athens, so I'm guessing it's not all bad?"

Carson leaned against Anderson's console. He straightened his collar, the ghost of Antonov's reprimand still hanging in the air. "He wasn't thrilled, but it could've been worse. Everything's good."

"I told you. You need to listen to your pal Kenny more often."

Carson punched Kenny on the shoulder. "You're the one who

created the whole mess to begin with, but never mind that. Did you look over my training request?"

"Yeah, shouldn't be a problem, you ingrate. I can only give you a portion of the deck, and we can turn off the grav generators in the common room again. That seems to have worked last time? But... detail a cleaning crew once you're done. The Chief Steward wasn't too happy, and I don't want to piss off the man who cooks my food."

Carson tapped the edge of Anderson's console, weighing the options. Using the entire deck, they could practice multiple scenarios at once. However, the constraints of a single room meant they could focus on specific exercises. "Yeah, yeah, I can make that work. I bet Gunny can adjust her close-quarters zero-g scenarios to make it newbie-friendly."

"Okay, the room's all yours, but after we jump. I like keeping the ship at condition one while we're in Athenian space."

"Sounds good, thank you. It'll give us time to prep, too. Speaking of, how's the itinerary looking?"

"Right on schedule. Should be in Alexandria in two days to drop you off. Why, do you have plans?"

"I hoped to go planet-side, so if we're running on time, it sounds like I'll have at least a few hours to spare." Carson had been looking forward to spending quality time with his family. It would help to recharge the old batteries, too. His mom's breakfast spread and Gianna's morning chatter were only two days away

"Oh, you're going to see Gianna? If you do, tell her I said hello and that I'm still waiting for her to make an honest man out of me. Also, mention to her I'm the dashing Captain of a warship and that I just saved you from being drummed out of the Navy like a common scoundrel."

"She's married, you dolt. Anyway, where are you headed after this?"

"We're going to Antares to give Battle Group Delta some teeth. Intel says we'll see heavy action."

"That's the Imperial Arcturian Fleet auxiliary, right?"

"Yeah, they're guarding the mining systems to free up Fifth Fleet for offensive operations. Union wolf packs have been hitting the freighters and mining vessels hard, so we'll run interference."

Carson adjusted his stance. The warlike Arcturians shot first, asked questions later, and then shot again—not exactly reassuring. They looked forward to a glorious death in battle, which put the Colonial Navy in very dicey situations. "Be careful, will ya? If you wanna lose more creds later, I'm teaching Maalek and Andaeer Texas Hold 'Em after dinner. You and your creds are welcome to join."

"I'll be there, and Skip, thanks for one hell of a fun night." Anderson pointed to the slight cut on his right eyebrow with a smile.

"Any   time,"   Carson   said.

Chapter 27

Admiral's Quarters, UNS Repulse

In Transit, Betelgeuse System

October 31, 2681

Admiral Stevens paced his cabin, bourbon in one hand. The old wood paneling around him felt like it was closing in, but the caramel-oak flavor of his drink kept the walls at bay—for now.

Images of the recent battle haunted him, each scene hammering home the same ugly truth: they were just buying time. If they could somehow secure an alliance with Athens, there might still be a chance to halt the Hasha's advance and recover lost ground—hell, at this point, he'd take just fighting them to a draw. His eyes landed on the framed schematic of Repulse, the crown jewel of the Union Navy. Her massive silhouette dwarfed the other ships in the fleet diagram, a symbol of Union engineering prowess and firepower. Stevens caught his reflection in the glass—god, when did he get so old? The man staring back at him was far from the idealist cadet who'd joined the navy so long ago.

If only he had a hundred more dreadnoughts like her. Maybe then they'd stand a chance.

He slumped into his chair and pulled up the footage from the Eris system jump point. The holoscreen cast a pale orange glow, looping the nightmare over and over. He'd seen it a thousand times, but it never got easier. The fleet charged, and then... the Hasha unleashed their EMP weapon.

Lights flickered and died, engines sputtered into silence, and life support systems failed. Artificial gravity cut out, plunging crews into a terrifying weightlessness. The once-formidable warships became lifeless husks, their defenses shattered, their communications reduced to static.

A barrage of missiles and energy beams tore into the defenseless fleet. Crews slammed into bulkheads or tumbled through corridors that no longer had an up or down. As hulls breached, the vacuum of space silenced screams and snuffed out lives. The final salvo of missiles reduced the proud Third Fleet to drifting wreckage, a graveyard of twisted metal and scattered debris.

Civilian evacuation ships met the same brutal end. Over twenty thousand lives were lost in minutes—a merciful fate compared to the colonists who were slaughtered by orbital strikes or suffocated by terraformers that choked their world with sulfur dioxide.

Every replay carved the disaster deeper into his mind. Right as he reached to play the footage again, his door chimed. He downed the last of his bourbon, grateful for the interruption and the numbing warmth that followed.

"Yes?" He cleared his throat, pausing to steady himself after what he'd just seen.

"It's Lieutenant Koothrapali, sir."

"Enter."

The door opened to reveal Lieutenant Koothrapali, who had become his aide on Repulse despite her lower rank in engineering. Something about her reminded Stevens of his estranged daughter—filling a gap he hadn't realized was there. And she had an uncanny knack for showing up right when he needed her.

They had more in common than most knew. Both had clawed their way up from the bottom—her from the Martian slums, him from Earth's undercities. She'd traded gang life for a Navy uniform, making the tough calls Stevens knew all too well. He respected that.

Koothrapali paused just inside, giving the cabin a quick once-over. A thin scar near her temple caught the light—a reminder of her past or maybe a badge of determination.

"Yes, Lieutenant?"

She held out a datapad. "The latest casualty reports and colonial FTL analysis, sir."

"Thank you. You can set them on my desk," he said, each report adding to the weight he already carried.

As she did so, Stevens noticed a slight change in her expression—a momentary clench of her jaw. "Anything else?" he asked, seeing past her usual stoic professionalism.

She hesitated. "Sir, you've skipped meals. Shall I get you something from the mess? Something light?"

The disturbing images from the video had killed his appetite, but perhaps he could stomach a strong coffee. "No, thank you, but if you can scare up a cup of black coffee, I'll be in your debt."

She gave a small smile and saluted. "Right away, sir."

Alone again, Stevens found himself thinking about Koothrapali. Her warmth and grit were rare commodities these days. Sweet kid, he mused, feeling some of that warmth seep into the chill of his cabin.

But duty called. Stevens pulled up a top-secret file on his holoscreen, punching in his access codes with steady hands that belied the knots in his stomach. The screen lit up with Operation TORCH—their Hail Mary at stealing Colonial FTL tech.

Sure, it was a desperate move, but what choice did they have? The Arcturian purge had killed any hope of inside help or sneaking data on those FTL drives. With the hardliners in charge, there'd be no splitting their ranks now. And the Colonial Navy had dismantled their carefully cultivated spy network, leaving them blind. Now, they were banking on pure brass to turn this conflict around.

It wasn't the most honorable path, but wars weren't won on honor alone. Stevens signed off on the order, praying this wouldn't be their last play.

After sending the orders to headquarters, he leaned back, staring at nothing. Maybe the inevitable wasn't so inevitable after all. They still had moves to make, and he'd be damned if

Jorge Sanchez

he didn't play every last card they had against the Hasha. Right
down   to   the   bitter   end.

Chapter 28

Deck Six, CCE Atalanta

Fenris System

November 3, 2681

Maalek skimmed the datapad, accompanied by the comforting rhythm of Atalanta's systems. Yesterday's zero-g training had gone well enough, but the thought of his arms and legs flailing about still made his stomach flip. He planned to get more practice on Galatea's deck—maybe on an empty stomach next time.

Echo Company Marines and off-duty sailors packed the rec room, shuffling cards and swapping stories. The warmth of the room, mixed with the smell of fresh coffee and replicated food, was a nice contrast from the cold emptiness outside. Laughter punctuated the air, rising above the general chatter and the clinking of chips.

With Atalanta gearing up to jump from Vigo to Fenris, Maalek settled into his chair, which creaked under his weight. He turned on his personal datapad to draft a message to Adaara. Their last jump had been cut short by a distress call—a freighter in the Antares system with reactor trouble. This meant postponing their dinner plans on Kliinat again, and it was anyone's guess when they'd next find the time.

Maalek found himself spinning tales of his adventures among the stars as he typed, but a twinge of guilt over moving on from Sanya nagged at him. Deep down, he knew Sanya wouldn't have wanted him to put his life on hold.

The announcement of the upcoming FTL jump sent Maalek's heart racing. No matter how many times he'd done this, he still couldn't shake the jitters. Somehow, it was even worse than the disorientation of zero-g. As the ship made the jump, a slight vibration ran through the deck. Funny how something that used to be such a wonder became so routine

Maalek stood up, thinking a drink might calm his nerves. But before he could take a step, the ship shuddered. He froze, looking around. The human Marines didn't seem bothered—a good sign. Then, another jolt threw him off balance.

Everything else faded into the background as Maalek's senses went on high alert. He strained to pick up any hint of trouble. The lights started flickering, screens blinked on and off, and weird shadows danced along the walls as the ship groaned. Then a shockwave hit, and everything that wasn't bolted down started rattling like it was trying to shake itself apart.

Then came the blare of the general quarters alarm, breaking through the commotion. At the same time, the Captain's voice blasted from every speaker.

"General quarters, general quarters. All hands to battle stations. The ship is under attack. This is not a drill."

What in the Goddess?

Maalek's heartbeat thundered as his mind raced through a million scenarios. Combat was always the same whether on the ground or in space: stay alive, protect your comrades, and make the enemy regret waking up.

The lights shifted to red, and the ship shook again. Sailors bolted from the rec room while some Marines stared in shock. The GQ announcement repeated, and then a massive explosion rocked the deck plates, followed by another jolt. Overhead, lights started sparking and flames shot out of a vent. The fire suppression kicked in, dousing everyone in sticky fire retardant.

Maalek grabbed a passing chief petty officer, clutching the fabric of his uniform.

"What is happening, Chief?" he asked.

The chief snapped. "No idea, sir, but I need to get to my post."

The ship lurched, then just... stopped. Maalek went flying, face-planting on the deck. People were screaming as they bounced off walls in the tight corridors. He struggled to his feet, using the bulkhead for support. His head was spinning, and when he touched his forehead, his hand came away bloody.

Just as he regained his balance, a message from Carson pinged in his neural. "Echo Company, this is Carson. Atalanta is under attack. Engines and critical systems are offline. Dart shuttles with boarding teams are en route. Report to Deck Three immediately. A Colonial Navy warship is not going to be boarded on our watch. Things will get frisky, so I want everyone to load up with armor-piercing slugs. Gunny will get you sorted as soon as you arrive at the armory. Oorah."

Maalek pushed through the tide of sailors rushing past, shouldering his way to the armory. He arrived to find Gunny orchestrating the distribution of weapons and armor. She had Marines lined up in neat rows, filling the passageway. Maalek squeezed his way to the front.

"Corporals, sergeants, lieutenants, front and center!" Gunny said, quieting the chatter. "Everyone else, find your squad and line up. I said line up! Muller, get your ass to your gorram squad, or I swear I'll space you myself. Lieutenant Akitani, get that platoon in order... ma'am." She was everywhere at once, checking gear and readiness.

Maalek knew she didn't have the horsepower to order an officer to do much of anything. Still, he figured no one was dumb enough to argue. After gearing up, he joined her as she inspected the Marines.

"Gunny, this voyage continues to exceed my wildest expectations. I can now check 'space-borne combat' off my bucket list," he said.

"Join the Navy and see the Universe, Maalek. They just forget to mention the shooting part." She lowered her voice. "Stay sharp, okay? In these enclosed spaces, all it takes is one hole or a bad ricochet for things to go tits up. I hate fighting in these friggin' tin cans. It's goddamn unnatural."

Carson arrived, armored and armed. "Gunny, sitrep."

Gunny snapped to attention. "Almost set, sir. Squad leaders are kitting everyone up." She glanced back. "Where do you figure they'll hit? Engineering, bridge, life support, ops?"

"On a Hera-class cruiser, ops and life support are also in engineering. But yeah, that's what I'm thinking."

"Keg of beer says these are S3 commandos. I haven't tangled with them since Teegarden," Gunny said.

"S3 commandos? I'm not familiar with that designation," Maalek said.

Gunny turned to face him, her expression stern. "Special Space Services. Tough SOBs."

"But not tougher than depleted uranium rounds," Carson said. "They're in for one nasty surprise if they think they will take Atalanta with us on board. Let's do one last check."

They stopped at Muller, who was fumbling with his chest rig. "Gunny, this thing's busted. It's all loose. This ship gear is FUBAR. Can I fix it or chuck it? I don't need armor to waste some Union squids."

Williams, struggling with her rig, pulled and tugged at the straps. "And mine's too tight around the shoulders. Is there a trick to these things? How am I supposed to move in this?"

Gunny, frowning, scanned their rigs for a moment before replying. "Did either of you geniuses check the back straps?"

They both paused, examining their equipment. Muller found the adjustment tab and pulled it. "Got it," he muttered, glancing away.

Williams adjusted hers, too. "Oh, that's better. Thanks, Gunny."

Gunny smirked. "Next time, try not to let the gear outsmart you before you spill stupid all over the deck."

Carson huddled with his lieutenants. "Just got word from Kenny—Captain Anderson. All the Darts are latched. One breaching team is already above engineering on Deck Four, another is amidships on Deck Eight, and the last is on its way to the bridge. Maalek, take First Platoon to engineering. Gunny, take Third Platoon to Deck Eight and head off the breaching team there. Akitani, you and Second Platoon are with me. We can't let them get a beachhead."

Maalek joined his platoon. The air filled with the sounds of armor straps zipping, air seals locking, and magazines clicking into place. Every face was stone-cold focused. They turned to Carson, who raised his fist.

"Two-five, retreat?" Carson said.

"Hell!" came the immediate reply.

"Retreat?"

"Hell!"

"Good   hunting,   Marines.   Oorah."

Chapter 29

Deck Four, Engineering, CCE Atalanta

Fenris System

November 3, 2681

Maalek, at the rear, let his seasoned Marines take the lead. They maintained radio silence, though Carson updated him through the neural link as long as possible. Once the Union Marines boarded, they jammed ShipNet, leaving Maalek and Echo Company blind.

The signal to halt arrived without warning. Maalek tapped the Marine in front of him and moved forward. She nodded, turned, and aimed her rifle down the corridor.

"What is the issue?" he asked, reaching the lead Marine.

The corporal turned, displaying his tablet. "This route leads to engineering, but there's a four-way junction ahead. We can place mines here and here to limit their cover options. Once we fortify engineering, we can funnel them to the center."

"Agreed. Detail a team. I will take the rest of the platoon and prepare defenses."

"Yes, sir."

The engineering room was locked down with all hatches sealed. Maalek knocked and addressed the camera. Moments later, a Sailor in combat armor swung the door open.

"Thank God. Come in, sir."

The Sailor gripped his rifle with white knuckles, finger on the trigger, the barrel aimed straight at Maalek.

"We got it from here, specialist," he said, gently moving the barrel away with two fingers.

"Yes, sir, thank you."

Inside, red emergency lights revealed the engineering room's vast area. Holoscreens, flickering with error codes, lined the walls. Six rows of workstations stretched across the width—potential defensive sites but vulnerable to crossfire from two side doors.

A large hatch opened to the reactor room—shielded and spacious—making it an ideal triage station. Above, thick cables and hoses crisscrossed the ten-meter-high ceiling. The catwalks that spanned the room's length offered access to the wires and would serve as excellent sniping positions. The front row of consoles would provide good cover, more so if he deployed portable shield generators. After ten tense minutes of preparation, Maalek's neural link crackled to life.

"They're here, sir. We're pulling back to engineering," came the report.

"Roger that," he said.

His Marines, who had just laid mines in the passageway, had made contact with the boarding party. Maalek strode to the front hatch and turned to face his platoon. Adrenaline sharpened his focus; the fate of Atalanta might hinge on their ability to hold engineering. His Marines exchanged nervous glances—some were green, untested in combat. But he knew they would hold.

"First Platoon, we hold this line to the last," he said, his finger jabbing toward the deck. "This is our ground. We are the wall the Union will crash against. If we fall, Atalanta falls—and we will not fall. Oorah!"

"Oorah!" they thundered in response.

As the team dashed through the hatch, Maalek covered their retreat with his M45 as bullets sliced past him. His covering fire bought his Marines precious seconds. He slammed and secured the hatch as the last Marine stumbled through.

Breathless, the corporal said, "Counted twenty-two, sir—S3 commandos with mechs, breaching guns, and plasma torches. A grenade exploded at the junction—blast missed me by inches."

Maalek surveyed the room, eyeing the plasteel bulkheads with a critical gaze. They weren't thin, per se, but against explosive rounds, he had his doubts. "Will these bulkheads hold?"

"Maybe a few minutes. Breaching ships is what they do, sir."

Of course.

"Take position on the right, cover the primary hatch. Be careful of crossfire from those side doors," Maalek said.

The corporal looked around the room. "Yes, sir. We'll hold them as long as we can. Not much cover, but the shields should—"

The hatch exploded inward, hurling shrapnel across engineering. A sharp piece caught the corporal in the chest, dropping him to the deck. Union troops poured in, unleashing a hail of high-velocity depleted uranium rounds. More explosions rocked the room, tearing new breaches in the bulkhead.

Maalek lunged, grabbing the wounded Marine and dragging him to safety. That's when he spotted two plasma grenades skittering across the floor. Without hesitation, he threw himself over the Marine and shouted:

"Plasma grenades! Take cover!"

His warning echoed as Marines scrambled for what little protection they could find. The grenades detonated, filling the room with lethal fire. Maalek rose, shaking off the impact. His ears rang, muffling the battle's clamor, and his visor's displays flickered and jumped, overlays misaligned and threat indicators skittering across his field of view. The corporal stirred beneath him, gasping but alive, his armor having absorbed the worst of the blast.

First Platoon, undeterred, unleashed a barrage of return fire as the injured were moved to safety. Despite his impaired vision, Maalek rejoined the fight.

He crouched behind an engineering station with Muller, finding it a decent vantage point. Another explosion shook the bulkheads, and Maalek instinctively ducked. A fresh breach opened ahead, revealing a heavy machine gun that sent the Colonial Marines scrambling for cover.

His back was against the workstation as he turned to Muller.

"They really mean to take this room, don't they?" he said, using the contractions he'd picked up from the Marines.

"But we're not gonna let them, right, sir?"

"Absolutely not."

Muller grimaced. "They've got a couple of Dragonfly heavy guns set up, and two of those light FENIX mechs are blocking our way. Getting through that debris and into their crosshairs doesn't look too appealing."

Maalek popped up, fired his M45, and then grabbed a frag grenade from his belt. He tossed it over the portable shields, watching it sail through a breach before detonating on the other side. A bullet zipped past his shoulder armor, sending him ducking back into cover. He then caught sight of a massive mech as it lumbered through the primary hatch, spitting supersonic rounds with its rail gun.

"We need to hold this position," Maalek said, his mind racing. "I'm going to flank that mech on the right. I've dealt with Union mechs before. Keep the pressure on here."

Muller slammed in a fresh mag and let loose a burst from his M45. "Hold the line. Got it, sir."

***

For fifteen minutes, Maalek and his platoon held off two

fierce assaults. The enemy mechs were scrap now; by his count, the S3 commandos had lost at least a dozen of their own. His snipers, perched on the catwalks, had taken out three attack drones the commandos sent through the breach. Maalek could feel it—one more push, and they could end this fight.

The emergency lights cast a feeble glow, struggling to cut through the gloom of engineering. Still, Maalek could make out his Marines and Atalanta's crew trading fire with the persistent attackers. Overhead, conduits crackled and snapped, showering sparks and filling the air with acrid smoke and toxic fumes. Thank the Goddess for helmet filters. They'd kept the Union forces from overrunning engineering but at a cost. Six Marines from Two-Five and two techs were dead, with four more Marines fighting for their lives in the reactor room as medics worked to stabilize them.

Maalek let out a breath, catching Muller's eye.

The young Marine flashed a confident smile and made a "V" with his fingers, pointing at the nearest breach. "We call it the Odessa Two Step back home," Muller said. "My old man called it the double whammy. Never really got what he meant by that."

Maalek grinned back. "Andaeer and I had something similar," he said. "He called it the Qaar, after a mythical two-headed sea monster from the Sea of Tranquility."

"On your count, then," Muller said, snapping in a fresh magazine.

Maalek counted down from three on his fingers. He and Muller popped up together on zero, laying down controlled bursts in all directions. The portable shields had failed five minutes ago, and the Union Marines were pressing their advantage. Maalek heard a grunt to his right. He dove for cover, but Muller wasn't so lucky. The Marine collapsed, clutching his throat as blood seeped through his fingers. Maalek dropped his rifle, pressing his hand over Muller's in a desperate bid to stop the bleeding.

Maalek opened a channel through his neural implant. "Medic! Marine down!" One hand still on Muller's wound, he fumbled through his kit with the other, searching for a ReGen Shot. Finding one, he yanked the cap off with his teeth and jammed it into Muller's neck. The shot hissed, pumping its cocktail of meds, painkillers, and stims. Muller tried to speak, but all that came out was a wet, choking sound, blood bubbling from his mouth.

A Navy corpsman came sliding in, ducking as 5 mm rounds from Union rifles pinged the air around them. "I got him, Lieutenant. Keep your hand there." He pulled out another ReGen Shot, but as he prepped to inject Muller, the young Marine's face went slack. The corpsman grabbed a scanner from his belt, held it to Muller's ear, and sighed. "He's gone, sir. Neural readings confirm KIA. Nothing more I can do." His comm chirped, and he answered, "On my way." With that, he was off, sprinting toward the starboard side of the room.

Maalek placed his hand on Muller's chest and closed his eyes. "Ancestors, welcome this brave warrior. He crosses the Great Sea with steed and blade to join your grand banquet. Hold my place by the fire, for I, too, shall join in time."

The enemy gunfire was tapering off. Maalek realized the Union forces were probably regrouping. This is it, he thought.

He grabbed his last grenade and hurled it over the barricade.

Opening the platoon channel, he shouted, "Two-five, retreat?"

"Hell!" the platoon answered.

"First Platoon, push forward!" Maalek slammed a fresh mag into his M45 and vaulted over a crate just as his grenade went off. He fired through the smoke, unflinching when a 5 mm round pinged off the deck and cracked his visor. His Marines advanced, step by step; two went down, but the rest kept coming. Maalek pressed himself against the bulkhead, firing through the hatch. As he moved up, he let loose a barrage, dropping a retreating commando with a clean shot through the helmet visor and catching another in the leg.

Another squad burst through a breached section, their M45s hammering away as they laid down suppressing fire. Three more commandos fell.

A helmet on the end of a barrel waved from behind a column—Maalek had to yell "Cease fire!" three times before his Marines eased off the trigger. From the smoke, a tired voice called out.

"We surrender!"

***

Two Navy corpsmen worked on the six wounded Union soldiers while a pair of Marines kept watch over the three prisoners. A line of twenty-three body bags stretched along the passageway, Union and Colonial alike. Maalek walked the somber line, his heart heavy. He knelt at each bag, placing his hand on it to offer a blessing.

As the adrenaline ebbed, Maalek tasted the bitter tang of propellant in his mouth. His pulse, rock-steady during the fight, now skipped and jumped as his body tried to remember what "normal" felt like.

Carson's voice cut through his thoughts on the neural link. "Echo two-one, Echo actual. Sitrep."

Maalek took a breath, trying to clear the taste from his mouth. "Echo actual, echo two-one. Engineering is secure, sir."

"Oorah, Maal. Well done."

"Thank you, Skip. We have a significant number of casualties. Requesting backup to transport our wounded to MedBay and to secure the prisoners."

"I'm sending two squads your way. The other boarding team surrendered, but stay sharp."

"Understood."

"Also, Andaeer is wounded; he's in MedBay now. I thought you should know."

A chill ran through Maalek at the news, old fears bubbling up. He pushed them down, forcing confidence into his voice. "Thank you, Skip. Andaeer is a rugged warrior, but I will pray for his swift recovery."

"Okay, Maal, Echo actual out," Carson said, cutting the connection.

Maalek pulled off his helmet, rubbing his scalp as he leaned against the bulkhead with a relieved sigh. Another battle survived. He wondered about the unseen forces that kept sparing him, but couldn't help but be grateful. Tonight, he'd pray not just for his fallen comrades, but for all the lives lost, friend and foe alike.

Chapter 30

Deck Six, CCE Atalanta

Fenris System

November 3, 2681

Carson picked his way across the scorched deck toward the bridge. His right knee had locked up again, but he'd only just noticed. A few minutes of walking would sort it out. He slung his M45 over his shoulder before rounding the corner. The adrenaline crash was setting in, leaving his hands with a slight shake.

He popped his helmet off, welcoming the hiss of the breaking seal. The ship's stale, recycled air wasn't a fresh mountain breeze, but it beat his armor's supply. His fingers found a new dent above his right ear—a little memento from that firefight near the ship's library. When did that happen? Probably during that hail of bullets before Andaeer took out the gunner.

He set his helmet down and checked his pocket for a protein pack. No luck. Chow would have to wait. Atalanta's Marine Detachment marched by with prisoners headed for the brig. A corpsman hurried past, trailing the sharp smell of antiseptic and blood as he tended to the wounded. Two Sailors hustled by carrying the fallen, burdened but moving with purpose.

Carson shook his numb right hand, trying to regain some feeling, and pressed toward the bridge. He picked his way through the battle's leftovers—abandoned gun nests, busted shields, and scattered junk. Each step on the charred deck was a reminder of the day's fight. The air scrubbers hummed, battling the mix of ozone, propellant, and that unmistakable coppery scent of blood.

The Marines guarding the bridge snapped to attention, throwing sharp salutes. A lieutenant with a tired smile and battle-scarred armor nodded at Carson.

"Thanks for the assist, Captain. The Union didn't see you coming; your Klii fighters are very impressive. Beers on us next shore leave."

Carson nodded back. "Your Marines did the heavy lifting. And don't think I won't take you up on that beer. Captain Anderson free?"

"Pretty sure he's expecting you, sir. Head on in."

Carson stepped onto the bridge to find Anderson pacing, sporting a nasty lump on his forehead. Back at the Academy, Anderson had been known for his laid-back style, but he'd slipped into command like it was a second skin. Carson couldn't help but admire how his old friend handled the pressure, every inch the seasoned captain.

"Keep the Gorgon turrets on that cruiser. Don't let up until I say so," Anderson was saying. "And someone tell me we've got engines back. What's the word on the Nyx batteries?"

"Locked and loaded, sir," a bridge officer said.

"Arm tubes one through six. Fire when ready."

"Arming now, aye."

The helmsman chimed in, "Skipper, starboard engine's back up. Engineering says port needs another five to reboot."

"Good. Astrogator, plot an FTL jump to Athens."

The Astrogator looked up, worry etched on her face. "We lost a tritium tank, sir. I'm down to manual calculations. Might not have juice for three jumps."

"I need options, now."

"Got a couple." She tapped her temple with a grease pencil. "One jump to Alexandria, but they can't handle a ship our size. We could refuel, drop off wounded, then push to Athens. Seventy-two hours transit. Or two jumps, forty-eight hours to Kliinat."

"Kliinat it is. Hull breaches sealed yet?"

"Working on it, sir. Twenty minutes, tops," an engineering officer said.

"Tell them to step on it unless they want to make an FTL jump in EVA suits." Anderson spotted Carson and waved him over. "Hey, Skip. C'mere, you beautiful bastard." He pulled Carson into a bear hug, messing up his hair. "You saved my ship. I owe you one."

"I wasn't looking forward to ending up on a Union prison

barge, and your MarDets kept the S3 commandos on their heels. Team effort all the way. We're all on the same boat, after all," Carson said.

"Literally. Well, we're almost clear of them. That cruiser can't keep up with us in a fair fight. It's basically a destroyer that's wearing daddy's suit, and they're taking a licking. Engineering, where's my port engine?"

"Back online, sir."

"All head flank. Let's get the hell out of here," Anderson said.

"Kenny, looks like you've got this under control. I'm heading to MedBay to check on my Marines."

"I'll tag along. XO, you have the deck."

"I have the deck. Good evening, sir," the XO said.

Carson trailed Anderson through the narrow passageway, pausing as the Captain checked on his crew and Marines. The bulkheads told the story of the battle—laser burns, bullet dents, and dark stains where medics had patched up the wounded. Where Gunny had faced off against the S3 commandos, twisted metal and shattered conduits created an eerie obstacle course. Anderson ran his fingers over a deep gouge and let out a long sigh.

"It could've been worse," Carson said. "Atalanta's banged up, but she's steaming under her own power," Carson said.

"It's just that she's my first command, Skip. You know what they say about firsts."

"I don't, actually, and frankly, hearing you right now, I'm not sure I want to."

Jorge Sanchez

They stepped into a MedBay that was a buzz of activity. Techs and corpsmen rushed about, tending to wounded that spilled out into the passageway. Injuries ran the gamut from burns and shrapnel to concussions and broken bones—courtesy of the ship's sudden stop.

The worst cases were tucked into AutoDocs, sedated into medically-induced comas. The rest, mostly Echo Company Marines, were under the watchful eye of the ship's medical staff.

At least the ship has plenty of ReGen Shots, Carson mused.

Carson's eyes fell on a row of gurneys holding the shrouded forms of fallen Echo Company Marines. He snapped to attention, saluting. "Fair winds and following seas."

Anderson joined him, throwing an arm over his shoulders. "Hell of a butcher's bill. Lost five at Alpha Centauri, scrapping with the Union Combined Fleet. That felt like a punch to the gut. This is something else."

"Don't think I'll ever get used to it," Carson said. "Why'd they even try to board us?"

"They did it during the First War of Independence for who knows what reason. My great-uncle spent two years as a POW until the armistice. He's a legend in the family. That man never broke and hated the Union until the day he died. Bitter to the very end. I want to be just like him."

Carson touched the ID tag on the nearest body bag—Muller, Frederik, Pfc. He closed his eyes, rubbing his forehead.

"War's a bitch, isn't it?"

"Yeah," Anderson said, "but I still want to jump to Sol and shove a couple of missiles right up their ass."

Carson wove deeper into MedBay, navigating the gurney maze with nods and shoulder squeezes. The antiseptic sting clung to every breath, mixing with the white noise of beeping monitors. He pushed past the sterile sharpness, focusing on his wounded Marines under the harsh lights. As he made his rounds, the backdrop of beeps and hushed conversations underscored his words of encouragement.

"How're you holding up?" Carson asked, reaching Andaeer's gurney.

Andaeer managed a small smile. "I have stopped bleeding, and the wound is closing. It still hurts, but it could have been worse." He lifted his shirt, revealing a tender spot below the bandage. "Right here is our Midean Sack, like your human liver. The bullet missed it by a Kaava's tooth. A hit there, and no Klii comes back."

"Sometimes it's better to be lucky than good," Carson said.

"We have a saying, too: Fortune visits a fool but does not stay for dinner," Andaeer said, shifting in his bed. "Remember when you found us in Daalamas?"

Carson nodded. "One of our team, a young girl named Tyreen, was shot right there; she died in seconds. She would have made a fine Marine."

"No doubt about that. Doesn't your armor cover that spot? Thought we'd sorted that out."

"My personal armor does, but the armor on the ship does not."

"I'll make a note. We need to fix that."

"Thank you, Captain." Andaeer lowered his voice. "If I may

be honest, I am unsure why I am still here. The doctors do not know what to do except look at the wound and take pictures. This bed will be more useful for the seriously wounded."

"I'll see if I can do anything, but I won't let doctors tell me about soldiering, so I won't tell them about doctoring. Oh, looks like you've got more company."

Carson stood as Sousa and Maalek approached.

"Don't baby him too much, Maal. He's already milking it," Carson joked. "Made me fluff his pillow and everything." He gave Andaeer a pat on the shoulder before moving on.

Anderson was making his rounds, too, bringing a much-needed light touch to the somber MedBay. As the Skipper approached, the crew's mood lightened, with more than a few smiles breaking through the fatigue.

Carson found Akitani perched on a gurney, left arm in a sling, trying to flag down a passing medic. He settled in beside her, draping an arm across the back of the gurney.

"How're you holding up, Lieutenant?" he asked, his expression softening.

Akitani's eyes narrowed, her good hand gripping the rail. "I'm fine, Skip, but these quacks are keeping me here over a stupid broken scapula!" She leaned forward, raising her voice. "I've got a spare, don't I? What the hell do I need two for?"

A nurse passing by gave a questioning look but kept walking, shaking her head slightly.

Akitani's gaze darted to the Marines that leaned against the wall or lay on the floor, waiting their turn. Her jaw clenched and she turned back to Carson. "I want out. My Marines need this bed more than I do. Tell 'em I'm five by five, Skip."

As another medic hurried past without acknowledging her, Akitani's frustration peaked. She sat up straight, her face flushing. "Hey! You with the datapad!" The medic froze mid-step, along with several others nearby. "Yeah, you! I'm not some invalid. I've got one good arm and two good legs, so if—"

"Lieutenant." Carson placed a hand on her good shoulder, applying gentle pressure. His eyes met hers, one eyebrow slightly raised.

Akitani's tirade halted mid-sentence. She closed her eyes and took a deep breath. "It's just so…" Her jaw worked silently, teeth clenched for a moment before she spoke. "Ugh, so damn frustrating."

Carson's hand remained on her shoulder as he smiled. "Need a scapula donor? I'll grab Gunny. She's about your size. Bet she's got extras. That woman ain't natural—told me once she feeds off fear from new recruits. I believed her till I caught her demolishing a bag of cheese crisps."

That made Akitani grin. "I can take a ReGen Shot and rest in my bunk."

Carson sighed, running a hand through his hair. "I just had this conversation with Andaeer. I know you think you're fine, but we'll let the doctors make that call."

"Bollocks. 'Tis but a scratch."

"You're not seriously asking me to pull rank, are you?" Carson said, fighting a grin.

"I'm *fine*, Skip."

Carson leaned in. "Lieutenant Elizabeth Akitani, you will stay here and follow the medics' orders to the letter. Copy?"

She nodded, tight-lipped, settling back. After a moment of silence, she leaned forward. "How bad was it?"

"Ten, so far. Muller, Kent, Ortega, Aaria, Bertolucci, Drystaan, Adebayo... and a couple of guys from First Platoon are in the AutoDoc. They hit us hard in Engineering. Could have been worse, all things considered."

Akitani gave a slight nod. "Gunny told me those squids ran into a buzz saw when they met Maalek and his guys."

"Yeah, for once, I'm actually looking forward to the after-action report."

Her gaze drifted to where orderlies were moving the body bags. She bit her lip. "Can we wait till we're back at base for the memorial...?"

Carson got the unspoken question. "Gotta check with Anderson, but a ship this size has a decent morgue. We'll do it proper in Persephone or on Galatea. If not, they'll join their brothers and sisters among the stars."

She squeezed his hand, her gaze dropping to the floor. "Skip... when it's my time, I want to go the same way. Out there, with my family." A tear escaped, and she wiped it away. "You'll make sure, right?"

"Okay, first off, you're mental," Carson said, squeezing back. "But yeah, I'll make sure. Now, let's save that talk for a few decades, alright?"

Her smile was weak but genuine. "Copy that."

Anderson strode up, cutting into their chat. "Lieutenant Akitani, is this ruffian bothering you?" he said, mock-serious.

"Yes, he is most insufferable," she said with a playful grimace.

Anderson grinned. "Don't I know it. Hold on, I'm getting pinged from the bridge." He stood silent for a couple of heartbeats. "Thank you, XO. I'll take the call in my quarters, Anderson out. Skip, Antonov wants a recap. Why don't you join me?"

"Sounds good. But first, let me grab ice for that thing that keeps growing on your forehead," Carson said.

"You're a forehead. See you later, ell-tee," Anderson shot back to Akitani.

As they left, Carson spotted a nurse handing Akitani a clean jumpsuit and shooing her off the bed. She looked thrilled.

Carson flopped onto the couch in Anderson's cabin, sinking into the cushions as if he belonged there. The cold whiskey glass felt good in his hand. They clinked glasses and knocked back their drinks in sync.

"Damn, this is good," Carson said, squinting at Anderson. "When did you develop taste? Back at the Academy, you drank nothing but that shitty light beer... what was it called? Hop-Lite?"

Anderson chuckled. "That's the one. And also, how dare you? I'm a connoisseur. I enjoy fine libations, like any red-blooded Navy Captain."

"Well, my glass is empty. Pour me some more libation."

Anderson obliged, uncorking the whiskey with a flourish. He filled Carson's glass and set the bottle down. "Alright, Skip, let's do this."

Carson nodded, and Anderson tapped his comms. "Get the Admiral on the line."

After a brief pause, an operator's voice came through. "Admiral coming online, Captain Anderson."

Admiral Antonov's stern face popped up on the holoscreen. "Captain, I trust everything is well? I received a preliminary report from your XO. I'm pleased to learn you repelled the boarding attempt."

"Thank you, sir. And sorry for making you wait; Skip and I just came from MedBay. He's here with me. I figured he could add color to the details," Anderson said.

"Well done, Captain Carson. Give my regards to your team."

"Will do, Admiral, thank you," Carson said.

Anderson cleared his throat and dove in. "As you know, we answered a false distress call. A Union cruiser was waiting, one of those Asunción-class boats modified to carry Dart shuttles. They hit us with an arresting field and disabled the engines. Three S3 commando teams boarded us, but we retained control of the ship. We have fifty and counting casualties, including sixteen KIA. We also have twenty-two prisoners."

"You're on your way to Kliinat, is that right?" Antonov asked.

"That's right, sir. Lost a fuel tank in the scrap. We need better facilities to handle our wounded."

"Understood. Titan dock is prepped for your arrival. We'll have medical and repair teams ready. Navy Intelligence will handle the prisoners. Make best speed to Kliinat, and stay alert. We've had more boarding attempts between yesterday and today. I expect a full report by EOD. Carry on, Captain."

Antonov signed off.

Anderson turned to Carson with a grin as the Admiral's image faded. "Feel like helping with this report? Just like old times."

"Sure, but you'd better feed me. I'm starving."

Chapter 31

Captains Quarters, CCV Galatea

Kliinat, Tau Ceti System

November 4, 2681

Mori eased out of her yoga poses, muscles humming from the stretch. She flowed from the pretzel-like yoganidrasana into a high plank, twisted into astavakrasana, and finished with bhujangasana. Her arms shook—today's workout had run twenty minutes over. "Not too shabby," she murmured, grinning.

She wiped the sweat off her brow, snagged her towel, and padded into the sitting room. The scent of Athenian coffee reached her—comfort in a cup. Breakfast waited on the tray: oatmeal, fruit, and eggs that were too good to be plant-based. After a big gulp of water and tossing her towel in the hamper, she settled at her desk to scan the morning updates.

A new message from Clara caught her eye, a digital postcard from her friend's cushier life on a cruiser. Clara's stories about ship life and Academy memories made Mori smile. She clicked through the attached photos—her and Clara laughing on their first day at the Academy, and a younger Mori hugging Captain Biyombo, his face beaming with fatherly pride.

The photos stirred up memories. After her rescue, Mori had spent days at Corinth Station, getting grilled by Naval Intelligence and Internal Security. When they learned she'd been on the bridge during the Valorous Hope attack, the questions got sharper. Even the General Intelligence Directorate spooks had shown up. But after each session, there was Lieutenant Biyombo, like clockwork, always with something sweet or a warm cup of tea.

Mori brushed away a tear, chuckling at life's knack for mixing bitter and sweet. Her past was full of these moments—underscoring the grit and friendship that had always pulled her through.

Mori's quiet moment with her coffee and memories shattered as her datapad lit up with an urgent orange alert—the kind that screamed 'trouble' in big, flashing letters. A fleet-wide message from the Admiralty pinged her neural, words blazing across her vision.

Just like that, Captain Mori was back, adrenaline surging. Her ship might turn into a war zone while she was still in her yoga pants. If the Union thought they could make a move on Kliinat, they'd be getting a face full of Galatea's teeth.

She pulled up the priority message. The screen was a nightmare of reports—boarding attempts and lost ships all over colonial space. A cruiser gone, vanished with all hands, and a destroyer MIA. What in the hell?

The general quarters alarm wailed through her cabin, the XO's voice booming over the 1MC, calling all hands to battle stations. Mori was already moving, muscle memory kicking in. She bolted for her bedroom, yanking tactical pants over her leggings, fumbling with fasteners while hopping towards her gear.

She laced her boots in record time, snagged her jacket off the hanger, and shrugged into it while sprinting for the door. She opened a comm channel to the XO. "Captain here. On my way," she said, entering the elevator and hitting the button for the bridge. "Come on, you piece of junk, move it."

Those thirty seconds crawled by, each one stretching longer than the last. The doors swooshed open, and she burst onto a bridge humming with frantic activity. The Marine sentry snapped a crisp salute.

"Captain on deck," he said, standing at attention.

Mori returned the salute with a quick "At ease." She scanned the bridge, taking in her crew's razor-sharp focus. Sliding into her chair, she flicked on the holoscreen.

The XO approached with updates. "Missile batteries are hot, alert fighters are scrambling, and engines are spooling up."

"Good. CAG, keep a wing of interceptors on standby," Mori said, eyes glued to the screen.

"Aye, Captain."

"Did you catch the report?" the XO asked, tacking on a hasty "Captain" after Mori's sharp glance.

"Read it twice now."

Carrigan paused, his face hardening. "Union's lost their damn minds if they think they can board a Strike Carrier with Fourth Fleet keeping watch."

"Desperate times, desperate measures," Mori said, eyes narrowing at her screens. "They might send one ship or the whole damn Expeditionary Fleet. Let's not get cocky."

"Yes, Ma'am," Carrigan nodded, turning to relay orders.

"Talyn, all guns locked and loaded. Safeties off," Mori said.

"As you command, Captain. Missile and Rail gun batteries online," Talyn said.

"Mr. Grant, what do we have on sensors?" Mori asked, turning to her tactical officer.

"A lot of motion, but all green, Skipper," Grant said, not looking up from his flickering console.

The immediate danger had passed, but Mori's stance remained alert. Space was vast, and today seemed ripe for surprises.

Another urgent ping on her holoscreen made her heart jump. The cruiser Atalanta had sent out a mayday during a possible Union attack before going silent. Worse, its transponder was now broadcasting from three different systems—classic Union hacking. Mori's gut tightened. Her Marines were on that ship. And Carson. She swallowed hard, pushing down the worry as her comms officer turned to her.

"Captain, Admiral's orders. Galatea is to leave orbit and steam to the jump point. The other ships in our group are spooling their engines."

"Thank you, Lieutenant. Helm, prepare to leave orbit and set a course, full speed."

"Aye, aye," the helm officer said, prepping for their new defensive position.

Mori stood as the Admiral's arrival was announced. Antonov looked almost bored as he strolled in.

"I see you received my message," Antonov said.

"Yes, sir. We should be at the entry point in under an hour."

"Good. What do you make of this, Captain?" Antonov settled into the XO's chair. "I have theories, but I'd like to hear your thoughts."

Caught off-guard, her mind still on Atalanta, Mori asked, "The boarding attempts, you mean?"

Antonov nodded.

She considered for a moment, her mind racing. "Honestly, I don't know. It could be a feint or a distraction." She paused, mulling over various scenarios. "They're hunting for something. Something big like the new FTL drives. We haven't upgraded the entire fleet yet, which they might not realize."

Antonov stroked his chin, nodding. "And if they get their hands on those drives, this war could drag on."

"Or put us on the defensive in Athenian space," Mori said, her mind now considering different scenarios. "And our shield tech, too. That's almost a given from what we learned after we caught the moles. Add the Imperial Nightguard ripping apart the plotters in Arcturus, and you will end up with desperate moves."

Antonov's face tightened in thought. "Navy Intel's been all over me about that plot. This stinks of a cornered rat's last gamble."

Galatea surged forward, afterburners kicking in. "So what's our play?" Mori asked.

"All ships in transit are jumping home. Fleet's on orange alert. I'm thinking it's time we hit back. An Atlas Missile down their throat at Mars Naval Yards might do it."

"What, no turning the other cheek?"

"Only to headbutt them. Hold on, getting a neural ping... Ah, good." He exhaled. "Atalanta is on her way here. They repelled the boarding party but suffered heavy damage. I'll forward you the message. No final casualty count yet, Anderson and Carson are still dealing with the aftermath."

Relief flooded Mori, but she kept her cool. "That's damn good news."

Antonov's mouth quirked up. "Sure is."

Chapter 32

Conference Room, CCV Galatea

Tau Ceti System

November 7, 2681

Carson slumped in his chair, surrounded by navy brass in Galatea's dim conference room. Flickering holoscreens cast eerie shadows, while squeaking chairs and tapping datapads punctuated the tense atmosphere.

Next to him, Anderson's anger was a smoldering ember, ready to catch fire. As survivors of the Union's surprise attack, they'd earned their seat at this table.

Major Lewis, from Navy Intelligence, always poised and professional, conducted the briefing. He had a knack for delivering bad news with a metaphorical spoonful of sugar—a really, really big spoon. "We responded to seven distress calls, all in uninhabited systems," Lewis said. "The destroyers Theseus and Heracles were destroyed, and the cruiser Antigone sustained heavy damage but escaped. The heavy cruiser Triton suffered a reactor malfunction during the attack and went down with all hands.

In a fatal miscalculation, one ambush backfired when the Union targeted what they thought was an isolated vessel, only to encounter Battle Group Sigma—a squadron of destroyers in tactical drills alongside an Arcturian Broadsword-class battleship. The Union ship, caught off guard, was destroyed, inflicting no damage on our forces. Next screen, please."

The room darkened as an image of the heavy cruiser Ajax filled the screen. In the corner, a photo of Carson's friend, Captain Yuri Dasayev, in full dress uniform against the Athenian flag.

Lewis continued, "Captain Dasayev kept transmitting until S3 commandos hit the bridge. He ordered evac, then detonated his Nyx missiles. He went down with the ship. A mining vessel in transit recovered the escape pods."

Carson snapped his pen in two, overwhelmed by thoughts of Yuri—who had a six-month-old baby and coached little league Breakball. The man who'd take a bullet for a stranger. A good man. A damn good man.

"Atalanta," Lewis said, "successfully repelled the attack, due to the presence of Marines from Echo Company en route to Alexandria. The cruiser sustained damage and reported twenty-six casualties among her crew and the Marines." He then shifted his focus to his datapad. "Union jump patterns point to bases in Eta Boötis, New Melbourne, and St. Albans."

Jorge Sanchez

"Those bases are part of the Union's Defense Research Agency, aren't they?" Mori asked. Carson wasn't surprised by her sharpness; even back at the Academy, she had a reputation for zeroing in on what mattered.

"Yes, Captain. St. Albans is the Union's main research and development center in the Orion Arm due to its abundant mineral-rich planets. Great question, and a good segue to our next screen."

As the following screen brightened the room, it displayed a detailed schematic of the Colonial FTL drive.

"SIGINT, alongside prisoners' testimony and our intelligence findings, suggests an attempt by the Union to steal our new FTL drive technology. The entire fleet is on threat-level one. We're bolstering the shipboard Marine complement on our fleets in the border systems. Eros, the destroyer they boarded, is a Selene-class ship and does not have the FTL upgrade. Minor stroke of luck in an otherwise heavy week for the Navy. We believe these attacks will escalate, and we expect additional losses."

The Lord General of Kliinat raised his hand. "I honor the sacrifices of my Klii brothers and sisters, but..." His voice trailed off as he drummed his fingers on the table. He shifted in his chair and leaned forward, hands steepled before him. "I am perplexed at our inaction. Why have we not shown the Union our resolve? Why does their aggression meet no equivalent response from us?"

His eyes bore into Admiral Antonov as if demanding answers.

Heat rose in Carsons's chest. "The Lord General's right. Your pretty presentation's all well and good, but I had to write to grieving families while the Union gets to shrug and try again. I've got three Marines in intensive care while we sit here 'analyzing' and debating." His frustration bulldozed his sense of decorum, and he couldn't care less. Writing condolence letters never got easier, but losing Marines to such a dirty trick? That stung extra hard.

Anderson slammed his hand on the table. "Damn straight. We should be jumping a fleet to Eridani or Miranda or one of those stupid bases and kicking their asses. Atalanta's ready. Just point us at 'em."

Lord Kaasam touched two fingers to his forehead and dipped his head to Carson and Anderson.

Antonov, his brow furrowed in concentration, nodded slowly. "I hear you, gentlemen. We can't base our strike on gut feelings alone — but it's time to act, not just play defense. We need to hit back with calculated force and to send a message: we will not stand idle. And hell," his voice dropped, "I want payback too. I lost friends on Heracles and Triton. And my nephew, the weapons officer on Eros, is now a POW."

He paused, then gestured for the Major to continue.

Carson crossed his arms, frustration bubbling over. He wanted to hit something, anything.

He caught Mori's eye, and she nodded. That simple gesture took the edge off. As she looked away, focusing back on the intel officer's grim rundown, Carson's shoulders loosened a bit.

"One of our assets tipped us about the operation's planning, code name TORCH. Thanks to our asset, we believe the order for this operation came from the Secretary-General." He paused, signaling the end of his briefing. "I've summarized our findings in the report I sent to your datapads. I'm at your disposal should you have further questions."

"Thank you, Major. I'm sure we'll be in touch," Antonov said.

The intelligence officer hesitated before adding, "There's one more issue—it's Command-Restricted, and we haven't completed vetting it yet." He glanced around, voice dropping. Carson had to lean in to catch it. "We have reports of unidentified ships attacking Union outposts. This might need further discussion."

Antonov stood. "Let's continue this in my quarters."

As everyone filed out, Mori hung back. "Skip, got a minute? Meet me out here in five?"

"Yes, Captain," Carson said, watching her walk off with that mix of authority and grace she always nailed. He had a hunch about what she wanted to chat about.

Anderson leaned in, eyebrow cocked. "Well, Skip, I'm torn. Bigger waste of time: this briefing or that video of the cat putting on a mask we watched in the dorm after finals? Gotta be this, right? I'm even more pissed now than when we started."

Carson managed a half-smile, but his mind was already racing. "You catch that bit about 'unidentified' ships hitting Union outposts?"

"Bits and pieces. But pirate attacks are up lately. Besides, it's the Union. Who cares?"

Carson chewed his lip, Lewis's offhand comment sticking more than he liked. "Yeah, I guess you're right. By the way, the cat was taking the mask off. The video was played in reverse."

"Oh... no wonder. Well, want to grab lunch? I'm going to take my frustrations out on a rib eye."

"Sure, but you're buying. Let me check in with the Captain first," Carson said.

"I'll save you a seat."

Carson hung by the conference room door, watching Mori wrap up with the other officers. When she motioned him over, they headed down the corridor, tension hanging between them.

Once they were out of earshot, Mori turned to face him. "Couple of things. First, I had a very awkward conversation with Adaara about that bar fight in Corinth. I don't care whose fault it is or who did what first; do not put me in that position again, understood?"

Carson straightened up. Facing enemy fire was one thing, but disappointing Captain Mori was quite another. "Yes, ma'am, understood."

"Good. Second... we haven't really talked since you got back. How're you holding up?" Her tone softened, easing the formality with genuine concern.

This shift caught Carson off guard. "Can I be honest, ma'am?" he asked.

"Of course."

He clenched his fist, frustration bubbling over. "I want to crack some skulls. Yeah, casualties happen in war, but Yuri and Ajax... it hits close to home. Most of my Academy classmates are gone now—Jenna, Marius, Sanjay, Benny... and now Yuri." His throat tightened. "I really want to punch the Union in the mouth, show 'em they can't frack with us. Uh, sorry, Captain."

A faint smirk tugged at the corner of Mori's mouth. "For what it's worth, I've been telling the Admiral the same thing. Fourth Fleet is back to full fighting strength, and if I had my way, we'd be jumping to Mars right now to blow their HQ to holy hell."

Carson smiled. "I bet you would, ma'am."

"Yeah, that's why I'm not in charge. But you're okay, Skip?"

Carson paused, wrestling with the truth. He nodded, almost buying it himself. "Yes, ma'am. Mission ready."

"I'm glad to hear that. And thank you for the thoughtful chocolates, by the way. Leander's is one of my favorites on Corinth."

"My pleasure, Captain. But it was a company effort. It's our way of saying thanks for everything you've done for us."

Mori's shoulders sagged a bit, her smile not quite reaching her eyes. "Oh... well, um, thank the company for me. And I have it on good authority that Adaara is very impressed. She's already bugging me to order a year's supply of chocolates from Athens. Tell Maalek he did very well, but he'll need to do even better next time."

"Will do, ma'am." Carson said.

"That's all, Skip. Carry on."

Carson saluted. "Yes, ma'am. Good afternoon."

***

Carson dropped into a chair across from Anderson in the bustling wardroom. The place hummed with mealtime chatter—small talk, laughs, and the clink of cutlery. Anderson was devouring a plate of steak and mashed potatoes, clearly enjoying his synthetic beef as much as the real deal. He swiped a chunk through gravy and popped it in his mouth as a steward approached Carson.

"Afternoon, Captain. Ready to order?" The steward asked, all crisp uniform and polite smile.

"Breakfast still on?" Carson asked, catching a whiff of fresh bread and crispy bacon from somewhere nearby.

The steward nodded. "All day, sir."

"The usual, then. Eggs, bacon, hash browns, a pint of Aegean beer."

"Coming right up, Captain," the steward said before zipping off.

When his beer arrived, Carson clinked glasses with Anderson. The Aegean lager was ice-cold and hoppy, with a sweet caramel finish—a solid number two in Carson's book. "So, how's your boat coming along?"

Anderson swallowed his mouthful. "Shipmaster says another week. Luckily, the space dock's done with Artemis. Otherwise, I'd be cooling my heels in Athens for three months waiting on a slot."

"You should ask him to paint flames on it while they're at it like some of the Dauntless jockeys do. More flames, more speed, right?" Carson raised an eyebrow. "Maybe ask Jammer for tips."

"Hell yeah. Do you know what would be cool? Shark teeth. Right on the bow," Anderson said.

"I would love to see you try to sneak that past Antonov."

Carson took a swig. "Guess I'm stuck with you."

"Likely for a while. Antonov told me Atalanta's been reassigned to Fourth Fleet." Anderson pointed his fork at Carson. "We should have made it official when Gianna was single. We would have been family. Stuck together, but forever."

"Yeah, right. Gianna has way too much taste to date a sailor. Besides, you and I are already family." He meant it. Anderson was as close to a brother as it got.

Anderson smiled, taking a pull from his beer. "So, what's next for you ground pounders?"

"We're supposed to take part in the assault on Luyten, but you heard the Admiral; that might change."

"I've never been to Luyten, but I hear it's nothing but ice and toxic air that could kill you in two breaths."

"Well, now I definitely want to visit. I'll bring my swimsuit."

They finished up quietly, Carson lost in thought. Pirates didn't have the juice to scratch a Union ship—so who, or what, was ballsy enough to try? The Arcturians, maybe, but only if their Emperor had lost his mind. Carson winced; a rogue Arcturian Navy was the last thing they needed.

His brooding was cut short as Maalek and Andaeer joined them. "Captain Anderson, a pleasure to see you again," Maalek said, formal as ever.

"You too, Maalek, Andaeer," Anderson nodded to both.

Carson caught the gloom hanging over the Klii Marines. "What's up, Andaeer?"

Andaeer's gaze dropped to the table. "I saw the updated casualty list from Ajax. My cousin Maateen is among the dead. He served as a midshipman. He wanted to command a warship someday. We were very close."

"I'm sorry," Carson said. He raised his glass. "To Maateen, to our honored dead."

They tapped their glasses on the table, then downed their beers.

"We will celebrate him properly tonight. You all must come and see how we toast Klii warriors. We will sing songs, wrestle, and play games of chance until dawn," Andaeer said.

Anderson's eyebrows shot up. "Are you kidding? That sounds amazing. I'm in. Skip?" He turned to Carson, who was miles away, staring at the bulkhead like it held answers. The feeling that something bigger was brewing gnawed at him until Anderson's nudge snapped him back.

"Skip, are you coming or what?"

"What? Oh, yeah, of course. I'd never miss it. You're coming, right, Maal?"

Maalek smiled. "Who do you think is bringing the alcohol?"

Chapter 33

Carson's Quarters, CCV Galatea

Tau Ceti System

November 9, 2681

Carson's head was a war zone. His heartbeat and the insistent buzz of his datapad were tag-teaming his brain, and the sliver of light under his door felt like a laser to the eyes. He groaned, smothering his face with a pillow in a futile attempt to block it all out.

His temples throbbed like they were caught in a vise. That third bottle of Klii' vodka' had clearly been a mistake. Hazy memories floated by—Gunny and Andaeer half-dragging him to his quarters, mumbling about heading back to the wake since it was about to really get going. They'd been considerate enough to yank off his boots and leave water by the bed. His parched throat was grateful, even if his aim was off—he toppled the glass and managed to douse the nightstand instead of his throat. Another groan, another face plant into the pillow.

The datapad kept up its relentless buzzing. Carson fumbled for it, squinting at the screen. An urgent message glared back: Admiral Antonov, conference room, fifteen minutes. Carson blinked, disbelief and vodka sloshing around his brain in equal measure. He dropped the pad back on the bed and used another pillow to cover his head.

That's it. I'm never drinking again. Ever.

Like most wakes, this one had started with stories, laughs, and tears for the fallen. It wasn't just Andaeer mourning his cousin from Ajax; half the ship was remembering someone from Ajax, Triton, Theseus, or Atalanta. What began as a small gathering had exploded into a ship-wide memorial bash. Even Captain Mori had shown up to pay respects, though she'd left before Maalek arrived with enough vodka to fuel a small rebellion. The XO had stuck around longer, maybe caught the first wrestling match. After that? Carson's memory was a blur of bad jokes and worse decisions.

As he wallowed in self-pity, his neural implant chimed with a call he couldn't dodge.

"Captain, priority call from Captain Anderson of Atalanta."

Carson mumbled into his pillow. "Tell him I'm busy."

"Captain Anderson, you're connected with Captain Carson," Eddie said, the traitor.

"Skip. Christ, I've been pinging you all morning. I had Eddie break past your do-not-disturb lock. Where the hell are you? Antonov's meeting is starting, everyone's here but you. Get your ass to the conference room, now."

"What meeting? The hell you talkin' about?" Carson asked, still half-convinced this was a vodka-induced nightmare.

"The meeting with Antonov. Move it," Anderson said.

The mention of Antonov hit Carson like a bucket of ice water. Those fifteen minutes now felt like a ticking bomb. He shot out of bed— spurred by the clarity that only impending doom provides—hangover clinging to him like a bad smell.

The following minutes were a whirlwind of motion. A frigid shower that felt like needles. ReGen Shots to clear the fog, stubbing his toe on a chair leg—swearing colorfully—downing painkillers, splattering eyedrops everywhere, all while the clock ticked down without mercy.

Carson skidded into the conference room with three minutes to spare, disheveled but presentable enough. He made a beeline for the coffee station.

"You're a lifesaver," he said to the attendant doling out liquid salvation in the form of caffeine. "Mind if I hug you?"

The attendant cracked a smile. "Figured a pick-me-up would be a good idea after last night's wake. Heard it got pretty lively."

Carson nodded, dumping a small mountain of sugar into his cup. "That's putting it mildly. I owe you one."

Lost in his mission to resurrect himself via caffeine, Carson was startled when he turned and bumped into the XO. The man looked like he'd been dragged backward through a bush— twice—and clutched his coffee as if it were the only thing keeping him vertical. His voice was pure gravel.

"Watch it, numbnuts. Oh, looky here, the Breakball star of

Alexandria. Pardon me, Captain," the XO said.

"Sorry, sir. I didn't see you there," Carson said, also stumbling over the words.

"You know, I lost a thousand creds on that Diamond Bowl disaster of yours. Maybe I should take it out of your pay."

Didn't anyone have anything better to do that day? That had been a disaster, sure, but for Thebes Polytechnic. Carson broke two school records that day. He shrugged it off.

"I had a lucky day. A couple of bounces broke my way."

The XO grunted, refilling his coffee without so much as a nod to the attendant. As he moved away, he threw over his shoulder, "See you around, twinkle toes."

"Good morning, XO," Carson said.

The attendant shot Carson a sympathetic look. "Officers like you make this job worth it, sir."

"Thanks. Save me some coffee, will ya? I plan on coming back for more."

"Don't worry, sir. We've got plenty."

Carson scanned the room, packed with officers from Galatea's and Artemis' carrier groups. Every seat was taken, giving the space the air of "big powwow" rather than a routine briefing. He spotted Anderson waving him over at the back. Jammer sat with him, looking like he'd been dragged out of a pub in the slums of Athens. Anderson seemed as chipper as if they'd just started their shore leave rather than coming off an all-nighter.

Carson weaved through the crowd, squinting against the too-bright lights, and collapsed into the seat between Jammer and Anderson. He rubbed his temples. "Kenny, how the hell are you even functioning? When I left, you were still going round for round with Sousa. Jammer here looks like he's gonna throw up."

Jammer clapped a hand over his mouth. "Don't say throw up out loud, or I might, which would be the third time this morning," he said.

Anderson grinned, his perkiness almost offensive to Carson's hangover. "I took a ReGen Shot last night—my own blend. I feel great. I don't know what you're complaining about."

"Good thing I didn't go to bed, or I'd have slept right through this," Jammer said.

Carson stirred his coffee. "You're telling me you pulled an all-nighter? How late did this thing go?"

Jammer stifled a yawn. "Well, didn't Andaeer say we had to stay till dawn? I haven't caught a wink."

"Anyone seen Gunny?" Carson asked. "Forgot to check if she made it back to her bunk."

"Yeah, bumped into her on my way here," Anderson said. "Andaeer mentioned they wanted to grab breakfast. I bet that's where she went. She looked stone-cold sober, too. That woman ain't natural."

"That's what I keep telling people," Carson said. He kneaded the back of his neck, still feeling last night's party. He glanced around the packed room. "So, what's this about, anyway? Half the fleet officers are here."

"Your guess is as good as mine," Anderson shrugged. "But

here comes the admiral."

Everyone snapped to attention as Admiral Antonov, flanked by Captains Mori and Biyombo, strode in and took the podium. "At ease. We have canceled the operation in Luyten."

A wave of surprise rippled through the room, officers trading confused looks.

"Okay, settle down," Antonov said, cutting through the chatter. "We've received intelligence that Eros is docked at the Union base in St. Albans, and we're going to get our people back."

The holoscreen behind him lit up, showing a detailed map of the St. Albans research base in the Bellatrix system. "Galatea and her carrier group will jump in close to disable the orbital defenses before we hit the ground. It won't be easy. There are at least six destroyers, a battleship, and a light carrier orbiting the planet."

The screen shifted to six boxy buildings arranged in a grid— standard prefab setup on terraformed worlds. "These are the secure facilities where the prisoners are held. Hell Divers will storm the compound and coordinate evac with Galatea," Antonov said, eyes sweeping the room.

Another image popped up, showing the system's hefty defenses. Antonov turned to Biyombo. "Artemis and her group will jump in at the system's natural entry point and neutralize those defenses. You'll be under heavy artillery the moment you arrive, Barry."

"Wouldn't want it any other way, sir," Biyombo said.

Antonov leaned in, gripping the podium. "This is a hot jump, people. All batteries hot, shields up. Your COs will brief you on the details after this. All leave's canceled till further notice. We're skids up in 72 hours." He paused, scanning the room. "Now, I'll turn this over to Captain Mori."

Mori stepped up, a flicker of surprise crossing her face after a quick word with Antonov. Behind the podium, she owned the room. "It's time we show the Union what happens when they tangle with the Colonial Navy. Let's get our people back and leave St. Albans a smoking crater. Galatea and Artemis are going to war, oorah!"

Her battle cry sparked a roar of approval that shook the room. Even after Mori, Biyombo, and Antonov cleared out, the energy hung in the air, buzzing through the crowd.

Jammer stood, turning to his friends. "Well, gents, I've got a date with the CAG in the ready room. Then I'm gonna sleep for about two days straight."

Anderson stood as well. "Hang on, Jammer." He dug in his pocket, tossing him a ReGen Shot. "Here, you'll need this. First one's on the house."

"Cheers. Catch you later," Jammer said, heading out.

Anderson looked lost in the shuffle. "I actually have no clue where I'm supposed to be."

Carson gestured toward a group of ship captains huddled together. "The ship Captains are talking over there. Go poke your head in."

"Why not. It's as good a plan as any," Anderson shrugged, weaving through the crowd.

Colonel Patel zeroed in on Carson as Anderson left. "Carson, a word," he said.

"Yes, sir."

"I want Echo leading the ground assault. I'll send you our intelligence on the building and personnel. I know Hell Divers will do the rescue and probably get all the credit, but this is prime intel-gathering territory. I want my best Marines on the job."

Carson blinked. He'd wanted payback? Well, here it was.

"Yes, sir. I'll put a plan together. Thank you," Carson said.

"Have something on my desk by morning. Solid work on Atalanta, by the way. And nice entrance." Patel clapped Carson's shoulder with a grin. "Just won twenty creds off the XO. He bet you'd sleep through this."

That really threw Carson off. The Colonel wasn't known for his sunny disposition and had a reputation for turning the screws on his officers. Carson knew, from experience, that the reputation was well-earned. He headed to the coffee dispenser, refilling his mug and grabbing one for Gunny. They had an op to plan, and they'd need all the caffeine they could get.

Chapter 34

Maalek bumped fists with each Marine boarding his Griffin shuttle, a ritual mirrored up and down the line as 2nd Battalion, 5th Marines prepped for the assault. Two shuttles over, Carson was tapping helmets with his squad. He caught Maalek's eye and flashed a thumbs-up, which Maalek returned.

The Galatea's shuttle bay was a whirlwind of preparations. Ordnance officers loaded ammo into rail guns while Marines piled into shuttles. Boots clanged on metal decks, mixing with the rhythmic groan of cranes arming the Griffins' air-to-surface batteries. It was like a deadly ballet, every move purposeful. Catapult officers in hi-vis yellow vests conducted the show, guiding loaded shuttles into launch tubes with practiced precision.

Pilots and navigators raced through their preflight checks, ensuring every detail was covered before diving into the fray. Across the bay, Dauntless fighters roared to life and launched, their engines drowning out everything else with a bone-deep rumble.

Maalek was last aboard his shuttle, masking his nerves with a grin. Launching into space was a hell of a lot scarier than any sim. Moments like these made him wonder how those Dauntless jockeys did this daily. He strapped in, feeling the harness bite into his armor, surrounded by the familiar sounds of Marines securing gear and locking battle rifles.

The ramp slammed shut with a bang that made Maalek jump. The deck thrummed as the shuttle prepped for launch. Red lights cast eerie shadows across waiting faces.

"Griffin seven-seven. We're third in line for launch. ETL three minutes," the pilot's voice crackled over the speakers.

Maalek swept his gaze across First Platoon. The human Marines wore expressions of confidence, but most of the Klii, himself included, couldn't hide their jitters. This was their first real combat jump, straight into the teeth of a Union stronghold.

Then Andaeer chimed in over a private channel, sounding almost cheerful. "This should be fun, old friend."

Maalek let out a dry chuckle. "That is not the word that comes to mind, Andaeer."

"Today, we strike at the invaders—what could be more fun?"

Maalek nodded, a rare spark of excitement lighting his

features. "I would be lying if I said I did not look forward to... what is it the humans say, a little payback?"

"Yes, they love that phrase," Andaeer's laughter filled the channel. "It took me a while to understand it, even though I am familiar with their vernacular. Did you know that eating and having your cake has nothing to do with real cakes?"

Maalek cracked a brief smile. "I did know that. Corporal Sousa told me."

"Yes, she has been very accommodating. She is a wonderful comrade and a better warrior." Andaeer chuckled, then paused as if considering his next words. "Which reminds me, are you familiar with colonial regulations on interspecies fraternization?"

Maalek shook his head. "Very much so. The penalties for such transgressions are rather severe. Death by airlock venting, I believe."

"Oh, that sounds fatal," Andaeer said.

"Indeed. Dare I ask what you are up to?" Maalek asked.

"Mild curiosity only, old friend."

"Yes, of course," Maalek said.

"Well, I will see you planetside, sir," Andaeer signed off, leaving Maalek alone with his thoughts and the shuttle's rumble.

Maalek caught himself tapping his foot, a nervous tic he thought he'd kicked back in his Scout days. The last thing he needed was his Marines thinking he was anxious —because they'd be right.

Back in Daalamas, stealth and surprise were his strengths. Hit them before they knew what hit them. Dropping straight into a hot zone from space was a different kind of challenge.

Maalek channeled that nervous energy. He flipped up his visor and stood up, going for the personal touch. Every eye locked on him.

"Status check," he said over the noise. "We are about to walk into the den of an angry beast. Let us make sure our claws are sharp."

The Marines snapped to it, checking ammo, running diagnostics, and syncing with BattleNet. Each move screamed 'seasoned warrior.'

As the shuttle thrummed with pre-launch prep, Maalek felt the squad's tension ratchet up, muscles coiling tight. A warning beep in his neural interface sang out—space jump, imminent.

The initial surge of acceleration twisted his stomach until the inertial dampeners kicked in to smooth the ride. His helmet muffled the engine's drone, creating an eerie bubble of calm. He might've thought they were still docked to Galatea if it weren't for the occasional jolt.

Maalek's hand found the makeshift bracelet in his pocket—gold scraps and twine cobbled together for Solee. As they cruised through the void, his mind drifted to his family, now as far off as stars in uncharted space. "Maybe today, I'll cross the Great Sea to see them again," he murmured. The thought steeled him, and he offered up a quick prayer.

"Thank you, ancestors, for your guidance. Thank you, Kaalahera, mistress of inscrutable depths, for lighting our path. Protect my Marines as you have protected me, and if I should trade my life for any of theirs, let it be so."

The loudspeaker crackled, snapping him back to reality. "Griffin seven-seven is about to enter atmo. Touchdown in ten." The Griffin bucked like an angry Vaal as they broke atmosphere and began their descent. Maalek clenched his jaw, half-expecting his teeth to rattle loose despite the dampeners' best efforts.

As they leveled out, Maalek tapped into BattleNet. A wave of relief hit him—all Griffins had made it planetside in one piece. His squadron was already lining up for a low approach, dancing around anti-aircraft fire. One Griffin took a hit from an air defense rocket, lurching sideways and nose-diving before its pilot wrestled it back into control. The craft steadied, staying airborne and keeping formation. Maalek made a note to recite a prayer of thanks to colonial shipbuilders.

The interior lights flashed green as they neared the base's southeast entrance. Maalek gave his rifle a final once-over and popped his harness. The shuttle's gentle sway above the LZ contrasted with the roar of battle outside— booming anti-aircraft guns and the sharp crack of Colonial Navy rifles trading fire with Union defenses. The door slid open, and Maalek led his Marines out, ready to dish out some long-overdue payback.

Chapter 35

Naval Defense Research Station, St. Albans

Bellatrix System

November 12, 2681

Chief Petty Officer Rollins slouched in his chair, feet up on the console, nursing a cup of instant coffee. He opened a new bag of mixed nuts, eyes glued to the Breakball match beaming in from Barcelona. He didn't have a dog in the fight since the Frankfurt Rhein bit the dust last week, taken out by the Winnipeg Tigers. He enjoyed the finesse of the North American teams, but the Europeans played hard and fast, and that always made their matches fun. The Tigers were up on the Barcelona Knights by two tries, but there was a lot of ball game left, and the Knights had shored up their back line.

The research station's command center was dead quiet, just how Rollins liked middle watch. No distractions from his games and comms flicks. The two scientists on duty with him were civvies working on drone programs, lost in their own worlds with headphones on. Probably watching vids or zoning out to the station's classical music channel. Neural implants had become the new craze back on Earth, but Rollins wasn't keen on tech messing with his brain. Not that it mattered — Navy regs forbid them anyway.

Only Spaceman Apprentice Meloni, a perky brunette fresh out of basic, seemed to give a damn about her job. She was scribbling notes on her datapad, logging sensor readings from system probes, and tracking the odd ship coming and going. New meat, taking things way too seriously.

Rollins glanced over, curiosity getting the better of him. "Meloni, you ever tell me how you ended up on this ice ball? What'd you do to piss off the brass?"

She popped out an earbud, flashing a half-smirk. "Come again?"

"Just wondering how someone like you gets stuck out here with us washouts?"

She shrugged. "Not much choice for slum rats like me, who enlisted as a way to get three squares; least not since the Asian drought. People flocked to the recruiting stations, and last I heard, they were not accepting volunteers anymore. It was either a destroyer patrolling the border near Eris or here. I heard the rumors about Eris. I'll take this backwater station any day."

Of course, he heard the rumors, too, but they were too awful to contemplate. Better to change the subject. "I didn't know you were a slum rat. What city?"

"Sacto."

Rollins grunted. "No kidding, you're from Sacto?" He tapped his chest. "Mega-building eight."

"Number four," she said, grin widening. "Looks like we're neighbors."

Small galaxy, Rollins thought. What were the odds of bumping into another slum rat from his hometown on this rock? He chuckled and returned to his game as Meloni popped her earbud back in.

She was right about St. Albans being a wasteland. Sure, it was close to the core planets, but this research station was it. No terraformed worlds, no fancy cruise liners dropping anchor, no five-star orbitals with their white sand beaches and casinos, not even any crazy wildlife for rich folks to hunt. Naval Defense Research Station Charlie was the only installation on the planet.

The battleship UNS Mumbai showing up with a colonial prize in tow was the most action they'd seen in months. They had to deal with extra marines prowling around, checking IDs and looking surly, but hey, at least it broke the monotony. A week after Mumbai docked, two more destroyers rolled in, plus two squadrons of Space Hornets and a squadron of Tornado Interceptors. For a hot second, Rollins wondered if their little outpost might be stepping up in the war. But nah, that was for the big boys like Eridani or Betelgeuse, the industrial powerhouses of the Union war machine. He doubted anyone in Athens could even point to St. Albans on a star chart. Hell, he wasn't sure anyone in the Union could.

As the third period wrapped up, Rollins figured he'd sneak in some actual work. He sifted through messages, updated the firmware on a probe circling Bellatrix, and jotted down readings from the drone vessels mining Saffron's moons. He tossed his empty nut bag, sipped his coffee, and stretched with a yawn, feet propped on the desk. Meloni's sudden shout sent Rollins into a flailing backpedal, his chair teetering on two legs before gravity won out.

"Sensor contacts! Multiple bogies at the jump point. Scratch that—six bandits. Sensors tagged 'em as CCV Artemis and her carrier group. We're under attack!"

Rollins scrambled back into his seat, heart pounding. "Double-check that, Meloni. The admiral will have our asses if you're wrong."

"I'm fracking right. Hit the damn alarm!"

She wasn't wrong. The sensor feed pulsed with Colonial signatures. Each new contact burned another hole in his certainty that this was just a drill. He slammed the alarm. "General quarters! General quarters! This is not a drill!"

Rollins glanced between Meloni and the other two scientists. They looked petrified. This wasn't part of their training, and he had no idea what the hell to do. They ran mining drones, programmed their firmware, and prototyped propulsion systems; they weren't trained to fight back against colonial warships for crying out loud.

One of the scientists, an older guy with hair dyed an unconvincing shade of brown, was hyperventilating. The other jumped up, frantic. "We gotta evac, get to the shuttles—"

His friend grabbed him. "We'll never clear atmo. We stay put."

Meloni's face went ghost-white as she turned to Rollins. "New contacts! Six, no, make that eight ships. Holy shit, they're right on top of us!"

The scientist lost it. "Oh my God, we're gonna die!"

Rollins checked the sensor screen again and felt his blood run cold. IFF had the new arrivals pegged as Galatea and her carrier group. Three cruisers, two dreadnoughts, two destroyers, and one strike carrier, all popping in just light seconds from the planet. Impossible. He repeated his message station-wide, voice cracking.

"Station under attack! General Quarters, battle stations!"

Then it hit him—what the hell was his battle station supposed to be? He decided under his desk would do just fine. Just fine, indeed.

***

Vice Admiral Mattias Almeida jolted awake to the blaring general quarters alarm. Five minutes later, he was dressed and sprinting towards the command center, shoving sailors and marines out of his path. Explosions rocked the base, the ceiling shuddering with each missile impact. He burst into the command center, collar askew, uniform hastily fastened. A massive blast wave knocked him off balance and he stumbled into a desk.

"Sitrep!" he yelled, once he'd regained his footing. "What the hell are you doing under that desk, Rollins? Grow a pair and tell me what the hell is going on!"

Meloni answered, her voice strained but steady. "Multiple contacts, sir. Colonials. Artemis and Galatea."

"How many?"

"Two full carrier groups. Fourteen ships."

Almeida's gut twisted. This wasn't a skirmish—it was annihilation. A message. His fingers tightened on the console edge. The Colonials hadn't come to fight—they'd come to erase. The Union had pushed too far with their dirty tricks—now, the Colonials were here to collect.

The older scientist kept repeating "this isn't happening" under his breath while the other pressed himself against the wall, mouth working silently. Almeida addressed Meloni. "Have the fighters scrambled? Put me through to the space station."

"Rio's launching her wing, but sir—the orbital station, it's gone. The first salvo took it out. Mumbai's gone too."

Red blips swarmed his defenses on the tactical map. They hadn't just underestimated the Colonials—they'd walked into a massacre of their own making.

"The destroyers?"

"Tacoma and Verapaz are engaging, but..." Rollins trailed off.

Those destroyers were on borrowed time, and they both knew it. Brave but doomed. Just like the rest of them.

His XO and a handful of officers scrambled in as another hit rocked the center. Lights flickered, then the backups kicked in, bathing everything in eerie red. Almeida white-knuckled the console. "Meloni, send out the distress signal. We need the Expeditionary Fleet here now."

"Third Fleet's closest, two jumps out. Mars isn't answering. We're jammed."

Almeida's heart sank. No cavalry coming. Just them against the full might of the Colonial fleet.

"Then we buy time," he said, jaw set. "Fire everything we've got. Give those destroyers some cover."

"We're down to three missile turrets, sir," Meloni said.

"I don't care. Keep firing."

The battle unfolded like a slow-motion disaster, one Almeida couldn't tear his eyes away from. Tacoma and Verapaz turned to scrap in minutes, their final salvos not even scratching the Colonial ships. His Tornados fought back, but they were gnats against the swarm of Dauntless fighters. Union ships and platforms winked out on the tactical screen one by one.

Rollins took a breath to settle his nerves. "Sir, Galatea just took out Rio."

Meloni chimed in, voice pained. "Admiral, sir."

"What now?"

"Exeter launched escape pods. A colonial destroyer's dropping to low orbit."

Another missile barrage shook the station. Almeida's grip tightened.

Meloni's voice cut through the noise, bringing the worst news yet. "Griffin shuttles inbound, sir. ETA five minutes. The Colonials have space superiority."

Twin impacts rocked the base. Lights died, and consoles flickered. The backup generators kept the room bathed in blood-red light.

Almeida watched the last fighter wink out on the tactical

display. This wasn't just a loss—it was obliteration. The station was falling, and he couldn't do a damn thing. But he wouldn't make it easy.

"Sir?" Meloni's voice cracked on the word.

These kids deserved better than this post, better than this end. But they'd held their stations, even Rollins. Even now.

"Protocol is clear." The words tasted like bile, but his voice stayed steady. "Initiate self-destruct. Burn it all. Every server, datapad, file—nothing leaves this base."

Minutes crawled as Almeida watched the Colonials dismantle the system. Probes, drones, mining rigs—all vanished. All their turrets gone. The carriers had stopped firing, but they didn't need to. This was beyond a one-sided ass-kicking. And they weren't done.

Twenty minutes had passed since the Griffins landed and Hell Divers stormed the secure lab, where they kept the prisoners.

Almeida checked his sidearm. Could he live with the shame of surrender? A minute later, as the command center doors blew   open,   he   got   his   answer.

Chapter 36

Naval Defense Research Station, St. Albans

Bellatrix System

November 12, 2681

The Griffin landed next to the base with a gentleness that contradicted the battle that had just unfolded in orbit. Carson often joked that Jones flew the shuttle like it owed her money, but her landings were top-notch.

Carson checked his M45 one last time as Second Platoon stacked up. The ramp dropped and they surged out, armor sensors adjusting to the darkness. Helmet lights carved paths through smoke rolling in from the burning anti-air battery. A colonial destroyer screamed overhead on a low-orbit run, its missiles turning another defense turret into molten slag.

Carson cranked his visor amplification to max. The Styxclass destroyer Nemesis hung above them like a storm cloud, its launch bays already disgorging Hell Divers in controlled free-fall. Their marker lights traced blue lines through the dark as they descended toward the prisoner block.

"Skip, this is Jones. We're skids off for air cover. Ring me up if you need an assist. Oorah."

"Roger that, Jones. See you on the way out."

Carson watched the Griffin bank away, Jones wasting no time to light up some poor Union sap who thought he could take down a Griffin with a standard-issue battle rifle.

Back on the ground, Carson focused on the job at hand. Williams and Rodriguez were rigging a shaped charge on the station's main airlock. The doors folded like wet cardboard, and two Marines pried them open in a heartbeat.

Akitani hit the console by the front doors as the squad filed in. "Place is locked down tight. Can't pop these doors from here," she said.

Carson didn't miss a beat. "Set up a detail to watch our six. Rodriguez, front and center. Blow these damn doors. Everyone else, switch your neurals to enhanced light mode when we breach."

"On it, sir." Gunny grabbed Andaeer, Williams, and Sousa, setting up a Hermes for rear cover.

The area seemed clear, but Carson felt naked. They needed to move, and fast. Any delay was an invite for a Union counter-punch.

"Gunny, sitrep?" He asked, trying to keep the edge out of his voice.

"Excellent, Sir. Not a peep. Just waiting for Rodriguez to remember which end of the charge goes boom so we can get this show on the road."

"Gunny, anyone overhearing us might think you don't like me," Rodriguez quipped.

"And they'd be right. Captain, permission to shoot Rodriguez," Gunny deadpanned, checking her rifle.

Carson paused, face serious for a beat. "Denied," he said.

"How about just in the leg?"

Carson made a show of mulling it over, tapping his visor. The banter helped take the edge off, and he knew it was his squad's way of dealing with pre-fight jitters. He'd play along—they'd snap into pro mode when the bullets started flying. "Alright, but just wing him."

Gunny flicked her safety. "Much obliged, sir. I'm set. If he's not done in twenty, he's losing a kneecap."

"Shoot him in the head," Williams chimed in. "Not like he uses it much anyway."

Rodriguez, finishing up the charges, flashed a grin. "Duck and cover!" he hollered, then hit the trigger.

The doors blew in with a teeth-rattling boom, shockwave rippling down the corridor, but not a speck of dust touched Carson's team. Maalek's voice crackled in Carson's neural as they prepped to breach.

"Echo actual, echo two-one," Maalek said.

"Go ahead, Maal, but make it quick. We're about to crack this nut."

"Dormitories secured, Skip. Moving prisoners to the shuttles."

"Any hiccups?" Carson asked, signaling his team to ready up.

"Nothing we could not handle. Most are as docile as a litter of Vaal calflings," Maalek said.

"Good work. Continue your intel sweep." Carson glanced at the time, aware of the tight schedule. "And do it with a quickness. Captain wants us back on the boat in two hours."

"Yes, Skip, understood. Echo two-one out."

Channel closed, Carson and his Marines pushed into the station, rifles up as they hit the main corridor. They met some resistance, but this was familiar territory—the fight they'd trained for.

They stumbled into what could've passed for an office lobby, complete with magazines, fake plants, and vending machines. Two Marines manning Dragonflies loaded with incendiaries opened up, pinning Carson's team. The whine of incoming rounds had them diving for cover.

Carson tucked behind a vending machine as the battle erupted. Heavy rounds turned chairs into kindling, sofas into ash, and electronics into thermite fireworks. A round pierced his cover, spraying metal and coolant. The coolant fogged his visor, leaving him blind. Pure instinct had him rolling as more rounds zipped overhead.

He'd had more close calls than he cared to count and wondered if he was burning through his lifetime supply of luck. It was only a little embarrassing when Rodriguez materialized to drag him behind a metal desk where Gunny was already set up. She leaned out, squeezing off controlled bursts from her M45. Carson tried to wipe his visor clean, only to smear it worse.

Just friggin' perfect.

He yanked off his helmet and opened a channel to Akitani. "Lieutenant, hug the left flank while we cover you. Take those guns out with extreme prejudice."

"Copy that, sir. Moving," Akitani said.

Gunny tossed him a rag as she reloaded. "Captain, I'd take it as a personal favor if you'd put that bucket back on. This should help."

"Cheers, Gunny," Carson grunted, wiping his visor. Not perfect, but it'd do. He slapped the helmet back on just in time to see heavy rounds shredding the air near their cover.

The Dragonfly fire had them plastered to cover. Each burst edged closer, eating through their protection inch by inch. Carson tracked the fire pattern—methodical, professional. These weren't green recruits. A plan formed, and he looped in the squad. "Listen up. Akitani's flanking left. Gunny, Rodriguez, and I'll lay down cover. Andaeer, Sousa, roll to that column by the magazine rack and hit 'em from the right. On three."

He snapped a quick look past the shredded desk. More Union Marines piling in, setting up interlocking fields of fire. Smart. But it meant they were committing to a single attack vector.

"One, two—" A burst of rounds sheared off the desk's corner. "Andaeer, try not to get shot this time—three!"

Gunny and Rodriguez's M45s roared to life. Akitani

broke cover in a burst of speed, but the Union gunners tracked fast—too fast. Heavy rounds stitched the wall behind her as she dove back. The air cracked with Mako detonations, concrete dust and cordite mixing into a choking haze. Then Maalek's voice cut through.

"Clear. Skip, are you okay?" Maalek asked.

Carson stepped out from behind the desk, taking in the carnage. Half a dozen Union Marines were down for the count. He found himself face-to-face with Maalek and First Platoon.

"Nice timing, Maal. Sweep done already?" Carson asked.

"There is not much there, Skip. They burned all documents and consoles, but we found two intact datapads. We heard the radio chatter and thought we should assist."

"Well, since you're here, we might as well storm the castle together."

***

Carson and his team hit the base's control center in no time. The doors were locked tight, as expected. "Clear the breach. Rodriguez, make it sing." Carson pressed against the wall, squad fanning out on both sides. The charges blew with a precision crack, and he keyed the command channel. Last thing he needed was to catch a bullet from some jumpy pencil pusher. "Weapons free on any armed response. Mark your targets."

"Sir," came the crisp response.

Marines flowed through the smoke. Two threats presented in the first three seconds: an officer yanking a Lassiter from his holster—center mass and head shot dropped him before his weapon cleared leather. Second officer's hand darted under his desk—another double-tap solved that problem. After that, nobody in the room so much as blinked.

Carson scanned the room. Most faces screamed terror. Two civvies were on their knees, hands over ears, shaking. Next to them was a young officer with her arms up as high as they could go, shoulders trembling. His eyes locked on the one officer with the spine to meet his gaze.

"I'm looking for Vice Admiral Almeida," Carson said to the room.

The officer lifted his chin. "That would be me."

"Sir, you're now a guest of the United Federated Colonies. Your sidearm, if you please," Carson said, hand out. Maalek and Williams kept their rifles trained on the admiral.

Almeida sighed, handing over his standard 9 mm Lassiter. Carson cleared it, popped the mag, and passed it to Williams. A nod to Gunny, and the Marines had the prisoners moving out.

Carson turned back to Almeida. "Now, sir, I need you to hit the evac alarm. We're gonna light this place up in under two hours, and we'd rather it be empty, but we're not doing a headcount. We have shuttles waiting and ready to take your people to our ships. It is my duty to inform you that everyone will be treated fairly and with dignity under the terms outlined in the treaties on interplanetary conflict. There are chaplains available for any of your people who need them."

Almeida paused, shoulders sagging. "Alright, Captain...?"

"Carson, sir."

"Thank you, Captain Carson. I guess I have no choice, then."

"No, sir."

Jorge Sanchez

Almeida's gaze drifted to his fallen officers, then back to Carson. His hand moved to the console with deliberate slowness. The base's sirens wailed to life, red emergency lights painting the corridors in blood. The automated evacuation sequence began its emotionless countdown.

The Admiral's fingers lingered on the console for a moment. Then he straightened, squaring his shoulders. "It's done. I surrender the base, Captain Carson."

Chapter 37

Naval Defense Research Station

St. Albans, Bellatrix System

November 12, 2681

Carson steered Admiral Almeida through the dim corridor. "This way, sir. My Marines will get you and your people to our shuttles."

"Thank you, Captain, for your offer of fair conduct, but what assurances can you provide that my people won't be mistreated?" Almeida'a gaze settled on Carson.

"Just my word, sir."

Almeida sized him up. "That'll do."

The Admiral's shoulders remained rigid as he walked out, chin high. Carson pulled Rodriguez and Williams aside. "Stick to Almeida and his officers like glue. Take the Griffin with them. Any trouble, double tap 'em. Clear?"

"Crystal, sir," they chorused.

"Take First and Second Squads with you."

They saluted and left. Trusting them to handle the brass, Carson turned back to the control center. Marines were trying to squeeze data from the consoles, but the Union eggheads had wiped them clean. Some paper files remained, which the Marines boxed up.

Carson scanned the room, not expecting much intel gold, but he'd let the spooks sort that out. He pulled out his datapad, recording console details, eyes catching the safety posters— loose lips really do sink ships.

A Marine approached with a datapad. "Captain, most consoles are fried, but we found a live one with a map. It shows an underground annex off the main network, tagged as a research lab. Might be worth checking out."

Carson nodded. They had time before the Galatea rendezvous—a research lab detour could pay off. "Good catch. Lieutenant Akitani, sweep this section. I'm taking First Platoon to the annex. Gunny, stay and back her up. Maalek, you're with me."

Akitani and Gunny shared a look. Gunny waved the Marines out.

"You heard the captain. We're hitting that annex—hustle up," she said, striding past Carson.

Before Carson could remind them who was in charge, Akitani placed a hand on his shoulder. "I've got this, Skip. We'll kill the lights on our way out."

***

Carson led First Platoon through the wrecked base, picking their way through rubble courtesy of the Fleet's bombardment. They moved under flickering emergency lights, dodging smoke and sparking wires. Every room they passed was deserted—consoles smashed or wiped clean. Carson had his team grab the least trashed units, hoping the techs could squeeze some data out.

They bumped into Charlie and Bravo companies herding prisoners to the shuttles. Most went quietly, but a few mouthy Union Marines got a sharp lesson in SHOCK baton etiquette.

Maalek pulled up the base map on his datapad and led the way. He stopped at a junction and tapped the screen a few times. "One moment, Skip. The map is not very clear past this point."

"Take your time, Maal. It's not like Galatea is going to redecorate the base with a couple of missiles in the next hour or anything," Carson said.

Maalek nodded, then after a beat, "I see. I found a path. Follow me."

They hit a dead-end corridor at a set of sturdy plasteel double doors, topped with a red light flashing with the evac alarm. A Marine wrestled with the keypad, trying to sweet-talk it open. He shook his head at Carson and Gunny. "No go, sir. Might need to knock louder."

Carson checked the time on his visor. They had a cushion, but not one he wanted to test against incoming missiles. He turned to Maalek.

"Does that map show if there's another way in?"

Maalek zoomed in on the map and rotated the datapad left and right. "It does not," he said.

"Alright, we're doing this the fun way," Carson said.

Gunny signaled to two Marines. "You two, snap to it. Captain wants a hole in this here door, and he wants it now."

"Gunny, I know this is weird, but I wish Rodriguez was here. That boy knows his way around plastic explosives like I know my way around Alexandrian pubs," Carson said.

"You're right, sir. It is weird."

Maalek laughed. "He is a very interesting warrior, one who hides his skill behind a curtain of foolhardiness."

"Yeah, he's a numbnuts, but he's our numb nuts," Gunny said, grabbing the detonator.

First Platoon backed up. Gunny eyeballed her squad, making sure everyone was clear.

"Here we go. Three, two, one," she counted, then hit it.

The boom echoed down the hall, leaving a smoke curtain. The door was still there when it cleared, just buckled with a twisted middle. Carson ran his hand over it.

"This is one good door. It may be armored plasteel. Now I really want to know what's in there. Let's try again, but put some more oomph into it. We don't get extra credit for returning to the boat with extra charges."

"Yes, sir," Gunny said.

The Marines packed the remaining charges into the gap to

crank up the explosive force. She stepped back to join Carson. "That's all the explosives we have, sir."

"What are you waiting for, then? Big bada boom," Carson said.

Gunny saluted. "Yes, sir."

The second blast ripped chunks from the ceiling and showered the Marines with debris. Carson approached the battered door, stepping over rubble and dusting off his armor. The door had folded further, but it still took four Marines grunting and sweating to pry it open.

As soon as the door creaked open, two machine gun turrets mounted on the ceiling sprang to life, spitting lead that cut down the four Marines at the door. Carson dove for cover. The rest of First Platoon scattered to either side of the corridor to escape the relentless gunfire. Carson's finger tightened on the trigger as he dove for cover—pinned down by gunfire twice in one day? Come on.

The turrets kept up their deadly rhythm, firing in controlled bursts. A quick glance confirmed the Marines in cover were still breathing. Maalek lobbed a Mako grenade into the room, but the turrets shrugged it off.

Carson caught his breath, tuning into the turrets' beat. He spotted a brief pause every ten seconds—magazine swap or cooling, maybe. An idea struck him. As soon as the guns went quiet, he rolled out, took a knee, and squeezed off a shot.

His first round pinged off the right turret's armor. He exhaled and aimed again, and this time, sparks flew. He held down the trigger, and within seconds, the turret went up in flames. Maalek and Gunny tag-teamed the other one, turning it into scrap metal.

Huh, that actually worked, he mused.

Carson got up, reloading his M45 with a satisfying click. Gunny gave him a thumbs-up.

"Top-notch shooting, sir," she said.

"Thanks, Gunny. Next base, we attack; remind me to load up on explosive rounds."

"Yes, sir."

Gunny typed a note on her datapad.

"Wait, you're seriously writing that down?" Carson asked.

"Of course. It's a good idea; I'm adding it to our SOP. Explosive rounds, stronger plastique, cheese crisps..."

Carson shook his head, leaving Gunny to her list-making. He turned back as First Platoon crept through the open doors. The medic tended to the four Marines who had tripped the turrets. Two were already KIA. One drifted in and out of consciousness, and the fourth clung to life despite new holes in his armor. Carson's hand lingered on the fallen Marine's shoulder plate before he turned toward the stairs, jaw set.

Maalek sidled up to him, weapon tracking down the shadowed stairs.

"What a treacherous trap we walked into, Skip."

Carson nodded, staring down the stairs.

"Yeah, real cozy. Let's take it slow. I've got a feeling this isn't their only surprise. I'll take point."

"You most definitely will not, Sir," Gunny said, stepping

beside Carson.

"Do I need to remind you of the chain of command, Gunnery Sergeant Reisman?"

Gunny smirked. "No, sir. It is the chain an officer might be beaten with if he doesn't follow the advice of his gunnery sergeant."

Carson cracked a grin. "Lead the way, Gunny."

"Aye, aye, sir." She waved two Marines forward, the squad splitting into two stacks on either side of the staircase. Despite Gunny's death glare, Carson slotted in behind the lead Marine on the left.

They crept down the stairs, tracking each shadow, each corner. The staircase curved into a long corridor, ending at another set of open blast doors. Side doors revealed ransacked offices, cleared out in a hurry. Carson poked his head into one on the left but found nothing. Gunny emerged from the right, waving a busted datapad.

"They Swiss-cheesed this one. The rest look even worse."

"Better be something good down there, after all this," Carson said, nodding towards the corridor's end.

Approaching the second set of doors, the Marines slowed, expecting another surprise. Point men tossed flash bangs in. Two heavy laser turrets on the far wall woke up, spitting fire down the hall. This time, though, the Marines were ready, already tucked into cover.

Carson and Maalek pressed against opposite sides of the doorway, ready to move.

"Maalek, let's see if we can go four for four," Carson said.

"Yes, sir," Maalek said, his grip tightening on his M45.

They burst from cover, aimed, and lit up the turrets.

Gunny peeked in. "Coast's clear, sir."

"Makes you wonder what other booby traps they've planted. Maybe killer rabbits," Carson said.

Maalek' head tilted. "What is a killer rabbit?" he asked, his hand drifting to his grenades.

"Never mind. Let's move," Carson said.

They stepped into what was clearly a prototyping lab. Rows of consoles, scattered science gear, circuit boards, servo motors, 3D printers, component racks, and test equipment everywhere. A central table sported a hand-soldered portable shield generator, a modified laser pistol, and a neural implant cloned from colonial tech. In one corner, sleek mechs stood silent, hooked up to a wall console.

Still, this isn't worth hiding behind machine gun turrets and impenetrable doors, Carson thought.

"What are the odds this place has a light switch? This enhanced light mode is giving me a headache," Carson said.

"I think the odds are very low," Maalek said.

Gunny knelt by something resembling a mini-fridge. "Maybe not. Sir, this is a backup generator. If I turn this key... bingo."

With a soft hum, the generator kicked in, flooding the room with light. Carson and the Marines winced, eyes screwed shut against the sudden glare.

"A heads-up next time, Gunny. Feels like getting eye-poked with a screwdriver. Jeez," Carson grumbled.

Once he killed the night vision and his eyes adjusted, Carson swept the room. "Okay, let's see what they have here that's worth guarding with laser turrets."

"Should we be on the lookout for these killer rabbits? They sound dangerous," Maalek asked, eyes darting around.

"You know, Maal, you're my favorite person," Carson said.

The Marines got back to it, rummaging through racks and drawers, setting aside anything that looked promising. Carson tossed another wiped datapad onto the growing pile. Wall consoles just blinked diagnostics at them.

Carson had two Marines haul two promising prototypes topside. Maalek, poking around behind a desk next to a terrarium, caught his attention.

"Skip, I think I have something."

"What've you got?"

"There is a datapad down there, but I cannot reach it." Maalek stretched, his arm wedged between the desk and the terrarium, straining for a few more inches.

"Wait...got it."

He yanked his arm free, datapad in hand. "It must have fallen in the gap. Perhaps it still works."

He thumbed the power button, and a green light blinked on, the screen lighting up. A login error popped up, and the antenna icon flashed as it searched for a network.

"Great find, Maal. Let's hope there's something on here besides games and pictures of food," Carson said, then addressed the rest of the platoon. "We're Oscar Mike in ten.

Grab any prototypes, anything exotic, and any technical docs. You know the drill."

A few minutes later, a Marine handed Carson a manila folder. "Captain, you might wanna see this. Found it boxed up on that shelf."

Carson spread the photos across a table. Grainy warship pics, but what caught his eye were two shots of what looked like honest-to-goodness aliens.

Well, well, well. Are these our Union boogeymen?

The figures were lean and bipedal, with triple-jointed legs like a dog's. Their helmeted faces looked avian and predatory, while their segmented silver armor came across as organic, with scale-like textures. The photos looked like screenshots ripped from a video.

"What in the... Gunny, take a look at this."

Gunny sidled up. "Huh, that's new. Another alien species? Is it one of the two we're keeping an eye on?"

"I doubt it. These look like space suits. See these two vertical lights? Might be sensors or cameras. The two species we know about are way less advanced—one just smelted their first iron spear, and the other figured out how to make semiconductors from silicon a year ago."

Gunny picked up a photo of a ship and rotated it. "This is some sort of carrier. I bet creds to donuts that these little dots are fighters. Weird-looking ships, though."

The ship did look bizarre, with bows sprouting tentacle-like protrusions that gave them an eerie appearance. Carson eyed the growing crowd of Marines that drifted closer to the table, necks craning. Time check—they were on the clock.

"All right, back to work. Let's do one more pass and then we blow this popsicle stand. Good score, Private." He stuffed the photos back in the folder and handed it over. "Stick this with the other docs. Nice work."

"Sir," the Private said, saluting before walking away.

The Marines were thorough—drawers, shelves, loose papers—but came up empty. After five minutes of turning the place inside out, Carson called it.

"Alright, let's pack it up and head topside."

As they filed out, Akitani pinged his neural. "Echo actual, Echo Two-One," she said.

"Echo Two-One, Echo actual. What's up, Lieutenant?" Carson said.

"We're all set here, Skip. I'm leading our haul to the shuttles."

"Have all the wounded been evacuated?"

"Yessir. Prisoners too. Everyone's en route back to the ship. Do you need us to wait?"

"Negative, we're shuttle-bound ourselves. I'll do a final sweep, but we should be wheels up in ten. Get going."

"Roger that, Echo actual. Akitani out."

Topside, only three shuttles were left; one was sealing its rear door, preparing to launch. They had found no stragglers or bonus intel, so they loaded their haul into a shuttle's side compartments and strapped in.

As they returned to Galatea, hanging out in the black,

Lieutenant Jones buzzed Carson's neural.

"Skip, that you bringing up the rear?"

"Yeah, I think we're the last ones out."

"Yeah, you are. Everyone else is already aboard. The fireworks are about to start. Tap into one of Galatea's feeds; you might catch the show."

"Good idea."

Carson pulled up a video feed from one of the ship's cameras. He blinked, then pulled the feed closer. Sure, the carriers were supposed to crater the base, cripple the Union's research... but this? His fingers stilled on the feed controls as the Atlas missiles carved bright lines across the black. Jones's voice came again, barely above a whisper: 'Holy shit.

Chapter 38

CIC, CCV Galatea

In Transit to Bellatrix System

November 12, 2681

Mori stood at Galatea's helm, heart racing as she awaited the final go-ahead for the FTL jump. Each mission brought that familiar pre-combat energy. Not fear—just the charge before the storm. She scanned the bridge, where her crew moved with the precision of seasoned pros.

"Captain, the board is green. We're clear for the FTL jump," the XO said.

That settled the butterflies. She gave the nod. "Execute."

The XO grabbed the mic. "General Quarters, General Quarters. All hands, battle stations. Set condition one throughout the ship. FTL Jump in three, two, one. Jump."

Jorge Sanchez

The GQ call was more traditional than necessary—Galatea had been locked and loaded for the past half hour—but it still lit a fire under everyone. As the FTL drive tore open a rift in spacetime, Mori braced for the familiar jolt. At least she wasn't alone—even battle-hardened veterans like her XO and Antonov felt that gut twist.

She zeroed in on St. Albans, a wasteland rich in precious metals and gases. Mining bots continued their work, oblivious to the approaching conflict. The tactical holoscreen displayed her targets—St. Albans, its orbiting space station, and the Union warships. Galatea and Artemis nailed their landing—right on the Union's doorstep.

Biyombo wasted no time. Artemis unleashed a barrage of missiles at the jump point defenses as soon as they arrived. As Carson would put it, mess with the Colonial Navy, expect a swift punch to the mouth.

"Talyn, weapons free, and target all surface-to-air defenses on that research base—I want our Griffins landing pretty and untouched," Mori said. "CAG, launch fighters."

"Yes, Captain," her officers said.

Xiphos and Corvus jumped in, their massive rail guns adding to the carnage. These spearhead-shaped monsters were the sledgehammers that cracked open fortresses. All business, no beauty—a perfect match for Mori's preferred approach.

The Dreadnoughts started swinging the moment they jumped in, hammering the dock with rail-gun fire. Explosions rocked the outer ring, sending flames and debris hurtling into space. The second salvo cut the orbital station's tether to the planet. The battleship UNS Mumbai, pushing off her berth to join the fight, caught a volley of rail-gun slugs. The impacts tore through Mumbai, ripping her apart from within. Then the Gorgon missiles struck, sealing her fate in a fiery blast. The explosion engulfed the Mumbai and two frigates that had spooled their engines, scattering fragments of ships into space.

Trading punches ship-to-ship was one thing, but destroying it while still docked seemed too much like murder. Well, war was war, no matter how you sliced it.

Mori gave the order: "Talyn, light up that carrier. Gorgon batteries first, then follow up with the Hades guns."

"Aye, Captain."

Union light carriers were anything but light when it came to firepower, packing a punch that rivaled strike carriers. They could also descend to low orbit, launching fighters that could dive into atmosphere—something the bulkier strike carriers couldn't do.

Grant's voice rose above the CIC chatter. "Skipper, we've got bogies. Incoming wing of Tornado interceptors and a flight of Broadside torpedoes from Rio de Janeiro."

"Keep the point-defense lasers hot in case they slip past the CAP. Talyn, how're we doing on softening up that station?" Mori asked.

"Unexpected interference deviated the Hydra missiles, Captain. Nyx interceptors would make a better choice—armored, faster, better AI."

"Make it so. Let me know when you have a firing solution."

"It is done, Captain. The batteries are primed," Talyn said.

Without missing a beat, she said, "Fire."

Sixteen Nyx missiles streaked out, leaving fiery trails in their wake. Three SAM batteries on the research base ate direct hits, while near misses knocked two more offline.

Galatea's assault turned the base's shuttle dock into a scrapyard. A squadron of Dart shuttles became twisted metal strewn across the devastated landscape.

"Captain, station defenses are down to less than ten percent. We're clear for the ground assault," Grant said, his fingers dancing across the tactical display to highlight the crippled defenses.

Mori turned to the CAG. "Launch the Griffins."

Galatea shuddered as her point defenses took out two incoming torpedoes from Rio de Janeiro. The shields held, but the whole ship felt the punch.

"Are the Hades guns ready for another round?" Mori asked, turning to Talyn.

"Capacitors at 95 percent, Captain."

"Full salvo on that carrier."

"As you command, full salvo," Talyn said, setting his sights on the carrier.

Moments later, Galatea's rail guns tore through the carrier's weakened shields, ripping massive holes in her hull. Air, fire, and debris vented from the wounds. Mori didn't let up, ordering a brutal follow-up of Gorgon and Hydra missiles. The onslaught left the carrier a floating wreck, though by some miracle, Rio de Janeiro was still in one piece. But her number was up.

The XO didn't look up from his holoscreen. "The carrier's

launching escape pods."

"Be ready to recover survivors," Mori said.

"Why? Let the bastards tumble for a bit."

She shook her head, firm. "No, launch the rescue shuttles, STAT."

The XO turned to face the bridge officer in charge of flight operations. "Have the rescue birds on standby."

"Yes, sir. Search-and-rescue Griffins standing by," the officer said from his station.

The XO's lack of pushback surprised Mori. She shot him a quick look; maybe she'd filed down another rough edge. Only a few hundred more to go, she thought, turning back into BattleNet.

Two destroyers escorting Rio de Janeiro closed in on Galatea and launched a volley of Taipan missiles. Mori tracked their progress on her holoscreen.

What the hell are they thinking? The two small ships were like gnats trying to take down a bear. They had guts, she'd give them that. Two Taipans slipped through Galatea's defenses, taking out a laser turret and a shield generator. Talyn didn't waste time, swinging the Gorgon batteries around to target the gutsy destroyers.

Battered but not backing down, the two warships kept coming, trailing debris as their hulls vented atmosphere. Guts indeed. Their captains knew their ships were doomed, yet they pressed their attack. They deserved a toast and a salute. Instead, Galatea's Hades guns tore into them.

Chapter 39

Saber Leader Dauntless two-two-one

Bellatrix System

November 11, 2681

Jammer rocketed out of the launch tube and straight into a hornet's nest of Union fighters. The space around Galatea lit up with the first exchange of fire. No time to think; just react. His Vulcans blazed, their roar vibrating through his ship. His squad mates launched one by one, each diving headfirst into the fray.

He wrenched his Dauntless into a sharp dive, trying to break away from the Tornadoes on his tail. These bastards had three Stingers each—one under each wing and one in the nose—spitting walls of depleted uranium. Fast too. Jammer hadn't been able to shake 'em since they jumped him. His shields flared as they struggled to hold back the incoming fire. Some rounds punched through, tearing apart his nose cone and knocking out both a long-range sensor and a reaction thruster. Around him, his squad was knee-deep in their own battles. Two Bit was dancing with a relentless Hornet missile barrage. He was on his own.

"Two Bit, I could really use a hand here!" His voice cracked on her call sign.

Jammer jerked the stick left, maxing out starboard thrusters, sending his Dauntless into a wild spin. The g-forces crushed him against his harness, straps biting into his shoulders. Stinger rounds riddled his starboard wing, each impact a bone-jarring thud.

"I've got problems of my own, Jammer. This bastard's all over me," came Two Bit's strained answer.

His rear camera showed the Tornado guns still hot on his six. Alarms screamed as console lights flickered. Then, his neural link crackled.

"Jammer, Lunchbox here. I've got you, babe."

Lunchbox barreled toward him on a collision course. Just as Jammer yanked left, she opened up with her Vulcans. One Tornado disintegrated under the hail of bullets, erupting into a shower of flaming debris.

"Splash one," Lunchbox said, cool as ice.

The second Tornado juked hard to dodge Lunchbox's barrage, giving Jammer his chance. He yanked the stick, pulling a Crazy Ivan, his Dauntless turning 180 degrees. The fighter strained to its limits, inertial dampeners screaming, alarms blaring. G-forces pinned Jammer to his seat, but his bird held together. The fighter flew backward for a heartbeat, then the engines roared back to life. Jammer patted the console.

"I knew you had it in you, baby. Now it's our turn."

His console beeped. Missile lock on the Tornado.

"Jammer, Fox Two. Second Fox Two."

Two missiles streaked out, homing in on the Tornado. The enemy fighter broke left, spewing chaff, but the Ballistas weren't fooled. The pilot punched out a second before his ship became a fireball. The shockwave rattled Jammer's Dauntless, but he kept his focus, gunning for Two Bit, afterburners maxed.

"Two Bit, Jammer. Hang tight; I'm coming."

"Move your ass! Port engine's down, can't accelerate. Shields are gone!" Static crackled.

"Two Bit, punch out!" His orders dissolved into a plea. "Now!"

Jammer pushed it, bringing the Hornet into his sights, but he was too late. The Hornet's rounds shredded Two Bit's naked hull.

"Jammer, I'm hit! I'm bleeding. Shit, I have to—"

The Hornet fired again, and Two Bit's ship vanished in a flash. She never had a chance. Two Bit was his wingman, his best friend—the one who'd slip into his quarters on those endless nights when the void pressed too close. His targeting reticle drifted over the Hornet. He stopped shaking only when he locked on.

"Jammer, Fox Two." His voice was mechanical, detached. "Second Fox Two. Fox One. Second Fox One."

"Jammer, Lunchbox, what the hell are you doing?"

"I'm getting this asshole, that's what. Fox three."

Jammer's first missiles found home, and the Hornet exploded. The Phalanx anti-radiation missile, almost an afterthought, arrived to find nothing but debris. Jammer triggered its self-destruct, obliterating what was left. He locked away the sorrow in a box of grief already overflowing with sad memories. There would be time to mourn her later, because they still had a battle to fight.

"Saber Squadron, Saber Leader. Resume combat air patrol, double-time."

The squadron regrouped on Galatea's starboard, facing off against four stubborn Hornets that wouldn't quit. Thanks to Galatea, their carrier was space dust, leaving them nowhere to land. Jammer got it. Roles reversed, he'd be doing the same damn thing.

Galatea had thrown her entire space wing into the mix. With all fighters and interceptors in play, the fight was over quick. Jammer didn't even need to fire his last missile. VF-20 and VF-21 tore apart the Hornets. A Union ejection beacon lit his tactical display. His hand hovered over the marking protocol—training ingrained to the point of muscle memory. For three seconds, he watched it drift. Then muscle memory won. Even enemies didn't deserve to suffocate alone in the black.

The CAG's voice crackled in his neural. "All pilots, we have space superiority. Beginning search and rescue. VF-20 and VF-21, remain in FORCAP. Everyone else, come on home."

Jammer lined up behind his squadron, approaching Galatea. As squad leader, he was first out and last in. Two Bit's death weighed on him, turning his usual landing excitement into dread. Today was supposed to be a celebration—his hundredth shipboard landing. But Two Bit wouldn't be there, helmet tucked under her arm and a smile that lit up the deck. He doubted he could keep it together in debrief.

He'd miss how she punched his arm when she was happy and hugged him tight when she was sad. He'd miss what an obnoxious brat she was. Tears welled up, but Galatea's hail gave him a lifeline.

"Saber Leader, Dauntless two-two-one, you're on final approach. Starboard deck, checkers green. Call the ball.

Jammer swallowed hard, forcing the lump in his throat down. "Two-two-one, Saber Leader Dauntless. I have the ball. Fuel at one point five."

"Saber Leader, Dauntless two-two-one, copy. You're cleared to land. Welcome home, Jammer."

He guided his bird onto the starboard deck, letting the AI take over when the tractor beam locked on. The elevator dropped him to the hangar. Once the airlock cycled, he popped the canopy and climbed down. He handed off his helmet, fumbling with his collar seal until his fingers steadied. The Rust Devils were waiting: Beaker, Lunchbox, Alphabet, Packrat, Snowball, and Half Pint. They closed ranks around him without a word. Their usual post-flight chatter died somewhere between the deck and ready room.

A rescue Griffin pilot jogged up. "Jammer, hold up."

"Hey, Bouncer."

Bouncer ran a hand through his auburn hair. "We, uh, we found her. Beacon kicked in when she tried to punch out. She's back there. Thought you'd want to know."

Jammer nodded once, not trusting his voice.

Bouncer pressed Two Bit's tags into his palm. "Figure she'd want you to have these."

Jammer's fingers closed around the warm metal. He made it two steps toward Two Bit's body bag before his legs gave out.

Chapter 40

CIC, CCV Galatea

St. Albans, Bellatrix System

November 12, 2681

The bridge was bathed in dim, bluish light, throwing long shadows against the bulkheads. Only the hum of equipment, distant alarms, and occasional sensor pings broke the silence. Mori stood, arms crossed. The air turned thick, almost suffocating, as if her next decision was sucking the oxygen from the room.

She turned to her XO. "All escape pods accounted for?"

"Yes, Captain. We've picked up all the pods and even snagged a couple of fighter jockeys who punched out—ours and theirs."

"ETA on the Griffins?" Mori asked. "They're fifteen minutes late."

He swiped through his holoscreen. "About ten minutes out. Carson's bird's almost at the port deck."

"And the crew from Eros?" she asked.

"All present and accounted for. Doc's giving them the once-over—word is they're all smiles," the XO said.

"That's good. Then we have time for another sweep. Let's make sure we haven't missed anyone—on the planet's surface, too," she said.

"Yes, Captain."

Mori scanned the tactical display, then turned to the CAG. "Bring our fighters home."

"Aye, aye."

For ten minutes, reports flooded in from flight ops and tactical. Mori soaked it all in, her ears picking out the important bits from the chaos of frantic typing and hushed chatter. Every report came back the same—no signs of life detected.

She turned to Grant, her face stone. "Rerun the scan, Mr. Grant."

Grant swiveled in his chair with a soft creak of synthetic leather. He glanced at the XO before turning back to his console. "Just did, Skipper. It's negative."

"That was an order, Lieutenant. Run. It. Again."

Under Mori's steel gaze, Grant's eyes darted between her and the XO, his fingers hovering over the console. "Yes, Skipper," he said, getting to work.

Mori's gaze drifted toward the viewport and the expanse of

space. Past battles replayed in her mind—all those lives lost under her command, and now she held millions more in her hands. The Atlas missiles could obliterate everything. She had to be certain. Absolutely certain.

She pulled up the system map on her console, fingers dancing over the holographic display. She zoomed in and out, checking and rechecking the positions of the scattered escape pods near the jump point—soon to be collected by Artemis and well out of danger.

The holo emitted a faint hum as she traced vessel paths and final positions. With all of Galatea's fighters home and the last Griffin lining up for the port landing bay, the stage was set. The carriers had reduced every facility in the system to smoking wrecks and space junk. Time to send the Earth Union a message they couldn't ignore.

Mori turned back to her tactical officer. "Mr. Grant, scans?"

"Still negative, Skipper," Grant said.

This was it. Mori pulled two red envelopes from her jacket, each bearing the Athenian Senate's official seal. Her hand was steady as she passed one to the XO, but her mind raced. The XO tore his open, glanced inside, and then looked up at her, unblinking. They both knew what these orders meant.

She was back on the Destroyer Kairos, a fresh-faced weapons officer, her finger on the trigger for the first time. That first enemy engagement had never left her. Those experiences had driven home a crucial lesson: leadership meant making the tough calls and living with them. Today, that lesson was staring her in the face.

Mori slapped the plastic card from her envelope on the

console and opened a public channel. "Eddie, authenticate orders."

"Orders authenticated and confirmed, Captain."

The card held the Atlas missile launch codes, authorized by the Chancellor, the Secretary of the Navy, and the president of the Athenian Senate.

"Talyn, arm two Atlas missiles, tubes one and two," Mori said. She nodded to her XO. "Your hand, if you please." On the bridge, only the hum of equipment broke the silence.

Talyn swiveled, nodded, then snapped back to his station, crests flaring. "As you command, Captain." His fingers danced over the console with an urgency that filled the quiet bridge. Officers glanced at each other, then back to their consoles.

"Atlas missiles are armed, Captain," Talyn said.

Mori and the XO pressed their palms on the scanners. Biometrics verified, compartments popped open to reveal glowing red buttons. Mori pressed hers without hesitation.

Eddie's voice came over the speakers: "Captain Tomoe Mori, authenticate." She stated her code clearly: "Bravo-November." Her button flashed green.

The XO's eyebrows shot up. "We're really doing this?"

Mori locked eyes with him. "Any reservations, XO?"

He paused, then slammed his hand on the scanner. "Screw 'em."

"Captain Norman Carrigan. Authenticate," Eddie prompted.

"Kilo-Romeo." The XO's button lit green.

Talyn then said, adhering to the strict protocol: "Captain, codes authenticated. Missiles are armed and ready. Permission to remove safeties."

"Remove all safeties," Mori said.

"Safeties removed."

Mori checked BattleNet one last time—Eddie had plotted the missile trajectory. Today, she was about to unleash Atlas missiles—so costly and complex that only a handful existed. Each carried an antimatter warhead powerful enough to knock a planet off its orbit, leading to its destruction as gravitational forces ripped it apart. As the Captain of Galatea, she was about to issue an order that could end millions, if not billions, of lives in an instant. The mantle of command was heavy, but she'd trained for this moment. She'd chosen this path.

"Launch missiles," she said.

"Launching missiles, Captain," Talyn said.

Two doors on Galatea's superstructure slid open, and moments later, two Atlas missiles streaked toward the planet. Mori watched the holoscreens. She would witness what she had ordered. When the smoke cleared and Galatea's cameras captured the aftermath, she gave the order to jump.

Chapter 41

Rue Philippe-Plantamour, Geneva

Earth

November 14, 2681

Stevens stepped out under Geneva's brooding sky, the somber clouds mirroring his mood. A chill bit at him as he approached the waiting car. His driver, already on duty, opened the door with a crisp snap.

"Morning, Admiral. Coffee's ready inside," the driver said, his breath visible in the cool air.

Stevens nodded with a slight smile. "Morning, Sergeant. Thank you."

He settled in and reached for the newspaper. Though he valued the ritual of thumbing through actual paper, today's headlines offered little comfort—food shortages, flu outbreaks, and protests over rising costs. He skimmed an editorial criticizing the ongoing war with The Colonies—public sentiment was shifting, fueled by their recent defeat at Tau Ceti. Protests were brewing across major cities over a laundry list of discontent. He set the paper down with a sigh and took a small sip of coffee—the warmth and bittersweet flavor provided a brief distraction.

He gazed out the back window as they made their way to the headquarters of the Union government. Traffic choked Geneva's streets at ground level and in the skyways that crisscrossed the city, weaving around skyscrapers like an intricate plasteel web. And that was nothing compared to the labyrinths in megacities like Phoenix, Shenzhen, or Dresden.

He patted his briefcase, containing reports of their failed covert ops, relentless Hasha advances, and the destruction of their prized research station. The situation was dire. The Colonial Navy had obliterated St. Albans with the same effort one might use to flick a crumb off a table. Reports showed rapid destabilization of the planet's orbit—in two weeks, it would be cosmic debris. With options depleted and time running out, the Union—and humanity itself—teetered on the brink.

The thought of falling on a literal sword had crossed his mind, but a bold idea struck him. If he couldn't persuade McIntire and Kaneda to retreat from Athenian space, why not lead the charge at Cancri himself? Desperate, sure, but suddenly appealing. It would be better than shoving casualty reports under the metaphorical rug. Why the hell not? Nothing tied him to Earth anymore, and the thought gave him a sense of purpose.

The car stopped, and the driver glanced back. "We've arrived,

Admiral. Shall I wait for you?"

Stevens straightened his jacket, smoothing back his now silver-streaked hair. "No need, Sergeant. Take the rest of the day."

"Thank you, sir," the driver said, tipping his cap.

Why not, indeed.

Stevens stepped out into the unfolding day, his resolve to take action lifting a weight from his shoulders. Childhood memories from Toronto washed over him. He could almost see himself as a boy, waving at the star-bound transports with his father. How times change.

"Welcome, sir. May I take your briefcase?" His aide said as the door closed behind him.

"Not necessary. Has the meeting started?"

"Yes, sir. Kicked off ten minutes ago. The Secretary got the briefing and didn't want to wait."

A light drizzle fell, gentle droplets kissing his face. Stevens savored it—perhaps his last on Earth—and marched into the building. He bypassed the queue at the entrance and strode down the corridor. His aide hurried to catch up, thrusting out a folder.

"Sir, the numbers you asked for."

"How do they look?" Stevens asked, unable to hide his dread.

The aide's face was grim. "Better see for yourself, sir."

Stevens exhaled. "That bad, huh?"

"Yes, sir. Do you want to look at them now or after your

meeting?"

He didn't care if he arrived late to what he realized might be his last meeting with the Secretary-General. Liam could bloody well wait—or not. Stevens took the folder and flipped through it. The documents blurred as he scanned, despair settling in his gut like a stone. The losses were staggering—eight carriers, fourteen battleships, seven cruisers, eleven frigates, twenty destroyers—not to mention tens of thousands of lives. They'd kept the Hasha war under wraps, but with numbers like these, a leak was inevitable. And this didn't even touch on their losses at the hands of the Colonial Fleet. Their chickens were coming home to roost, riding Hasha and Colonial warships. Heart heavy, he stuffed the folder into his briefcase.

Before stepping into the elevator, Stevens turned to his aide. "Get a transport ready to Cologne Spaceport in thirty minutes. Tell Captain DiMarco on Repulse she's leaving Union space in forty-eight hours, and to prep my cabin. Do whatever it takes."

The aide, tablet in hand, snapped to attention. "Understood, sir."

As Stevens held the elevator door, he fixed his aide with a steady gaze. "You've been a good lad, Billy. Thanks for everything. God bless."

Billy hesitated, mouth opening, but Stevens let the door slide shut, cutting off any reply. The elevator's climb to the top floor was interminable, each second stretched by his desire to leave and the dread of the coming meeting.

As soon as the doors opened, Stevens walked straight into a tempest. Liam McIntire, secretary-general of the Earth Union, was storming back and forth across the room. His arms were flailing, and he was mid-rant, his voice booming through the spacious office. "No, no, no! How did this happen? How did you all manage to turn this into such a colossal disaster? One failure after another! Anyone care to explain?"

Stevens took a seat next to General Kaneda, who remained impassive. McIntire's meltdown sent heat flooding Stevens' face, a throbbing vein on his forehead betraying his rising anger.

Behind McIntire's desk, Lake Geneva stretched out, its surface choppy from a southerly wind that made the ships at anchor pitch and roll. Stevens caught sight of the distant snow-capped mountains, heard the gentle patter of drizzle on the window, and for just a moment, felt a fleeting sense of peace.

McIntire paused, one hand on the window frame above his head. His earlier fury evaporated as he surveyed the room. His next words were tinged with resignation. "How the hell did we lose St. Albans? How did two colonial carrier groups turn the system into a junkyard and take hundreds of prisoners right under our noses?"

Kaneda shifted in his seat. "They snuck one by us, but let's not kid ourselves and give them too much credit. St. Albans was an important research lab, but it had light defenses. If they'd hit Eridani or Ross, we'd have sent them packing back to Athens in pieces. It's a setback, but we're ready to execute Plan Orange and hit the Hasha with the might of the Union Navy."

Stevens turned to Kaneda, struggling to reconcile this with the mentor he knew—top of his class, celebrated hero of the Second War of Unification. "What Antonov did to that research station, they could do to Eridani with one more carrier group,"

Stevens said. "And what if they decide to hit us with that same weapon they used to split a planet like a walnut? I've said it a million times — we need to sue for peace and throw everything we have at the Hasha, every single ship. The only way to do that is by pulling our fleets from the border systems."

"Are you prepared to face a tribunal if we make peace with Athens and they find all the skeletons?" Kaneda asked.

"I'll do whatever it takes to ensure the survival of Earth," Stevens said. That sense of purpose stiffened his spine.

Kaneda waved a dismissive hand. "Oh, get off the cross, Tom."

"What happens when this Hasha counterattack goes south? Or when Antonov realizes he's got us by the short hairs and jumps a fleet to Sol?" Stevens pressed.

Kaneda shrugged, sipping his tea with infuriating calm. "The attack won't fail. And if he grows a pair and jumps a fleet here, our defenses will turn it to scrap."

Stevens leaned back, sizing up Kaneda. No point arguing if Kaneda and McIntire wouldn't even entertain a doubt. Self-preservation was one thing, but blind faith? He shook his head, a tired smile tugging at his lips. Never attribute to malice what can be explained by stupidity. "You really believe that, don't you?"

McIntire sauntered back to his desk and lit a cigar with exaggerated flair, an assistant scurrying to provide a light. Stevens half-wanted to stuff the cigar down McIntire's throat.

"General Kaneda, what odds do you give Plan Orange?" McIntire asked.

"Of success? One hundred percent. Not a single simulation has shown us losing this battle. Not one," Kaneda said. Each word carried a weight of confidence that Stevens couldn't help but notice—misguided, dangerous confidence.

"Very well, send the order to execute with all haste."

Stevens let out a derisive snort. "All the simulations assume the shield modulation will hold. Remove that variable, and our odds of success drop to thirteen percent."

Kaneda shifted, clearly uncomfortable, but his eyes never left McIntire. "The shield modulation works. We've tested it ad nauseam against the Hasha weapons' frequency range."

Stevens' frustration simmered, but he wasn't ready to give up. He jabbed a finger their way. "What happens if they change their frequency?"

Kaneda scoffed. "They won't. They haven't changed tactics once. If there's one thing we can predict about the Hasha, it's their consistency. The upgrade's already been deployed."

Stevens shook his head, disbelief etched in his face. "You have lost your minds, both of you."

Kaneda met Stevens' eyes. "Have I? The Third Expeditionary Fleet, Sixth Fleet, and Fifth Fleet are ready to jump to Cancri and reinforce the Combined Fleet."

Stevens' frustration boiled over as the futility of their plan hit home. "It's not enough. Cancri's our last frontier system; we lose that, we lose it all. This is our chance to strike, our last chance. The simulations show better than fifty-fifty odds when we add the First, Second, and Fourth Fleets, plus Sol Fleet and the First and Second Expeditionary Fleets."

Kaneda leaned forward, his voice rising. "You want to leave us defenseless against Athens now that we have the means to beat these Hasha sons of bitches. I think it's you who's lost his goddamn mind."

McIntire's lips curled into a sneer, his eyes cold. "If you've lost your nerve, Tom, get out of the way. I'll take your resignation right now and give your post to someone with some stones."

Goddamn it, why won't they listen.

Stevens had enough. He rose to his feet. "I'm done here. You two do whatever the hell you want." With that, he turned to leave.

As Stevens walked away, McIntire's words chased him, dripping with anger. "Where the hell do you think you're going, Tom?"

Stevens didn't bother looking back. "I'm heading to Cologne to catch a shuttle to Repulse. I won't ask our people to die while I sit here, banging my head against a wall, trying to talk sense into you two. I'll join Sixth Fleet and help however I can. Hell, I'll run ammo to the Stinger guns if that's what it takes."

Behind him, McIntire's threat hung in the air. "If you walk out that door, I'll make you regret it."

Stevens slammed the door on his way out. It felt like an enormous boulder had been rolled off his chest. For a moment, he considered going public with the impossible situation they faced, why so many sailors came home in bags or not at all. But to what end? It wouldn't help them in the coming fight. It might even make things worse. They'd painted themselves into a corner, and the only way out was to punch through the wall.

When did he lose his way? When did he give in to temptation, to the trappings of power? He'd betrayed the ideals that made him join the Navy in the first place. No worldly gains—money, women, luxuries—were worth losing his family. None of them were worth losing his convictions.

He couldn't change the past, but he still had control over his own destiny. And by God, he knew how to fight a warship.

Chapter 42

Tau Ceti System

November 22, 2681

Mori sank into the chair in Antonov's office on Galatea's top deck. The subtle scent of polished wood mixed with fresh flowers from a nearby vase painted a picture of calm that couldn't have been further from reality. Major Lewis sat across from her, his words fading into the ship's constant hum. Antonov perched beside Lewis, concern etched on his face, mirroring the XO's unease.

The intel from the Union base sprawled across her lap, heavy as lead, squeezing the air from her lungs. Memories of that devastating day on the colony ship came flooding back, her heart pounding. The room seemed to shrink, the air thickening around her. She clutched the photograph from the day

Valorous Hope was lost—the day everything changed—her fingers digging into the intelligence report. Lewis's voice became white noise as she zeroed in on the damning evidence in the photos Carson's team had recovered, the ships she'd seen that day.

A fiery surge of betrayal raced through her veins. She shot up from her seat and hurled the papers across the desk at Major Lewis.

"You knew—all of you!" Her voice rose to a shout as she locked eyes with Lewis. "Get off my ship now, or I swear I'll toss you out myself!" She turned her gaze on Antonov. Her mentor, her trusted advisor, had lied to her? She fought to keep her composure.

Caught off guard, Lewis's eyes darted between Mori and Antonov, his fingers drumming a nervous rhythm on the table's edge. Antonov sighed—the man always sighed before delivering bad news, a tell she'd picked up on early. Across the table, Lewis looked like he was praying for the deck to swallow him whole.

"Captain, please, sit down," he said, attempting to soothe the storm.

Mori ignored him and keyed her comm. "Eddie, send in the Marines. Tell them to escort Major Lewis off my ship—however they see fit."

Antonov stood, urgency clear in his voice. "Captain, don't do something you'll regret."

"This is my ship," Mori said, standing her ground. The door swung open, and two Marines took up positions by the entrance, backing their Captain.

Antonov slumped back, fatigue etched on his face as he pinched the bridge of his nose. "Please sit, Captain. I'll tell you everything I know."

Mori paused, anger simmering. She weighed his words, then jerked her head toward the door. "Wait outside. And keep it shut."

The Marines snapped a salute and filed out. Silence fell. Mori sat, tense, as her XO nodded encouragement.

Antonov's shoulders sagged as he collected his thoughts, the lines on his face seeming to deepen. "They are called Hasha. We knew about them before the attack that killed your parents. We know they've been in a war with the Union and that we might be their next target. We first learned about them when we studied the crash site in Arcturus during the First Contact War. I couldn't tell you earlier—it was a decision far above my pay grade."

The XO's snort was brief, but Mori could almost hear the sarcasm dripping. "Way to pass the buck, Admiral."

Mori's response was cold, each word clipped with simmering anger. "Does Biyombo know?"

Antonov shook his head. "No. Very few outside of this room do."

Mori closed her eyes, fighting back frustrated tears. He didn't know. She opened her eyes, fixing Lewis with a steely gaze. "Start talking, now. I'm not in the mood for secrets or half-truths. And trust me, you don't want to test my patience."

Lewis squirmed, clearly uncomfortable. "We've got incomplete, mostly speculative info at this point. This was meant as a heads-up, not a full briefing."

The XO leaned in. "The Captain just gave you an order. I suggest you follow it."

Antonov nodded. "Go ahead, Major."

Lewis rubbed his chin. "Captain, what we know about the Hasha could fit on a single sheet of paper. Their societal structure is ironclad—no dissent, no deviation. It's a straitjacket that might give us an edge. They outmatch the Union military and pose a significant threat to us." His eyes shifted between Mori's intense gaze and his datapad as he spoke.

Mori's patience wore thin. "Fleet strength?"

Lewis hesitated. "Nothing concrete, but based on SIGINT and the images we've gathered, we estimate they have engaged the Union with ten capital ships, similar to our Theia-class strike carriers, double the number of battleships, and triple the number of cruisers, destroyers, and troop transports."

Mori bristled. "I meant total fleet strength."

Lewis cleared his throat. "It's difficult to say, Captain. Vice Admiral Almeida has thus far been uncooperative, and we think what he knows about the Hasha can fill up a room. We're still working on cracking him. Figuratively, of course."

The XO, ever practical, chimed in. "Give me ten minutes with him. During the First War of Independence, Union spooks could make a guy sing with a toothpick. I say we return the favor."

"That's not how we do things in Athens," Lewis said.

The XO shrugged. "Shame. You let me know if you change

your mind."

Mori kept her eyes locked on Lewis. "What else? I need more than that."

Lewis shifted again. "There's not much else, Captain. Their biology favors right-handed amino acids, and they breathe sulfur dioxide. They've already terraformed the systems they've conquered, which appears to be their top priority. We estimate that civilian casualties total twenty to thirty million so far."

Setting her datapad aside, Mori turned to Antonov. "We need more data. We can sling a probe around the Orion Arm to jump it into one of the captured systems and listen in. The sooner, the better. And we've got to share this with the rest of the fleet. No more of this need-to-know crap. Our people need to understand exactly what kind of storm's brewing."

The XO nodded in approval. "Damn right. If we ever tangle with these goddamn Hasha, we need to start sharpening the knives."

"What if this sparks a panic back home?" Lewis asked, worry creasing his brow.

Mori's gaze snapped back to him. "We've fought the Union to a standstill twice, won and kept our independence twice, and we're about to hand them their asses a third time. We've weathered it all, and we've done it together. This won't be any different."

Lewis nodded, point taken.

"Captain Mori," Antonov said, "I want you to be the lead on this. Work with Major Lewis on a tight report we can share with the fleet and our sister branches in the colonies."

Mori paused, her feelings toward Antonov a jumble—she couldn't forgive him, not yet, but he was her commanding officer. She pushed her personal grievances aside, responding with professional crispness. "Yes, sir. We also need to share this information with Prime Adaara."

"I'll need approval from the Chancellor, but consider it done. Move forward as though it's fait accompli. Let's get to work."

Chapter 43

Admiral's Quarters, UNS Repulse

Dorado System

December 1, 2681

Admiral Stevens limped down Repulse's corridors, each step adding to his already aching body. Twenty-six hours straight, and his bed was calling. But in war, rest was a luxury they couldn't afford. ReGen Shots and DermaGel were running low, saved for sailors who really needed them—not an old sea dog too stubborn to admit a limp might slow him down. He couldn't justify tapping into those dwindling supplies. In a few days, it might not matter anyway.

The ship was alive with repairs, sparks flying and metal clanging as the crew worked to exhaustion to keep her space-borne. Stevens paused to boost the morale of two sailors—they were almost through the worst, he told them. Across the way, a team lugged ammo to the Stinger turrets, exhaustion etched on their faces. No rest for the weary, not with the Hasha breathing down their necks.

After the debacle at Cancri, retreat became their only option. Twelve days of dodging enemy attacks had reduced the once mighty Union fleet to a smattering of battered ships. They were bound for Mira now, but even that felt like jumping into the proverbial fire.

Leading the Hasha straight to Earth's doorstep was a nightmare Stevens couldn't stomach, not with Sol Fleet still intact. Better to gamble on the fringes than risk it all. He'd made his stand with what was left of the Navy, and for a moment, it looked like they might actually stop them. But as always, the Hasha adapted, outmaneuvering them at every turn.

Now, only shield modulations—a power-draining desperate trick—stood between them and oblivion. Repulse limped forward, patched just enough to keep her in the fight.

Stevens entered his quarters, making his first stop at the liquor cabinet. A shot of bourbon burned down his throat, then another. It didn't make the casualty list any easier to swallow. Two thousand souls in three days. Cold stats on paper, but each one a life cut short. The doorbell chimed. On the monitor, Koothrapali stood outside. A week ago, she was a Lieutenant JG; now, she was engineering officer.

"One moment, please," he said into the monitor. He splashed water on his face and ran his fingers through his damp hair, trying to pull himself together. The mirror showed a tired, worn-out man, heavy bags under eyes that had lost their spark. Back at his desk, he hit the intercom.

Jorge Sanchez

"Come in, Miss Koothrapali," Stevens said.

The door hissed open. Koothrapali entered, balancing a tray of coffee and sandwiches. She paused at the doorway, her eyes darting around the room more than necessary. It was subtle, but Stevens caught it.

"Something on your mind, Miss Koothrapali?" Stevens asked.

"Just double-checking, Admiral," she said with a quick smile.

Stevens returned the smile. He took the tray, set it on his desk, and poured two cups of coffee, the dark liquid promising a brief reprieve. "Have a seat, join me for a minute," he said.

As he handed Koothrapali her coffee, he caught her eyes darting to the corners of the room, then to his personal datapad lying askew on the desk. Once settled, Stevens noticed how her gaze kept sweeping over his desk items—a family photo, a model ship, scattered papers. Each glance seemed casual, almost instinctive, like she was just taking in the scenery.

Rubbing the bridge of his nose—his go-to stress tell—he asked, "How're things holding up out there?"

Koothrapali took the coffee, her fingers brushing his. "It's rough, sir. We're scraping the bottom of the barrel for ammo and fuel; casualties are piling up. But we'll keep swinging. We know what's on the line." Her eyes drifted again, lingering on the model ship before snapping back to her coffee.

She smiled, glancing at the ship once more. "It's beautiful, sir. A reminder of why we fight, maybe?"

Her smile didn't quite reach her eyes, Stevens noted. "Exactly. Keeps the past close, reminds us what we've been through and what we're fighting for," he said, settling into his chair. "You and the crew are going above and beyond. Makes an old sailor proud."

"We all have our parts to play, sir," she said.

He motioned to the chair opposite. "Sit down, Miss Koothrapali, take a break. You've earned it."

Koothrapali's uniform told the day's story—stains, creases, and the unmistakable aroma of sweat mixed with fresh coffee. She hesitated, exhaustion flashing across her face. After a moment's pause, she nodded and sat.

"Thanks, sir," she said, sinking into the chair.

She bit into a sandwich, her expression blissful. "Can't remember the last time I ate something this good."

He chuckled, taking a bite himself; even a BLT felt like a gourmet meal. He washed it down with coffee. "Reminds me of when our FTL drive blew during the Second War of Unification and we got stuck in deep space. We ate our last crackers and started on the mission paperwork. After we got picked up, I swore off mac and cheese forever after gorging on the rescue ship. But those first bites of real food felt like a feast."

She smiled. A comfortable silence fell, broken only by satisfied chewing and the clink of cups on saucers. Stevens welcomed the break from their daily run for survival. He knew they might not be running much longer.

"You didn't really eat paper, did you, sir?" Koothrapali asked, curiosity cutting through her fatigue.

"Sure did," Stevens said, grinning. "Nothing puts life in perspective like munching on your ship's maintenance logs." He paused. "Miss Koothrapali, might I ask you something a bit...

unconventional?"

"Sir?"

"Do you ever wonder if we're the bad guys?" he asked, leaning forward to refill her coffee.

She hesitated, her brow knitting as if weighing her words. "I... I'm not sure how to answer that, sir."

"With honesty. Whatever you say stays here."

She bit her bottom lip, her gaze drifting. "Sometimes, it does feel like we're on the wrong side of history. I mean, the Colonies hit us first at Tau Ceti, but we started the whole mess. And then there are rumors we might've poked the Hasha first." She set her cup down, looking uneasy. "I should probably check on the port Taipan batteries, sir. I've taken up too much of your time. Anything else?" Her words trailed off, and she looked away, discomfort written all over her face.

Stevens motioned for her to stay seated. "No, stay a moment. If it feels like we're on the wrong side, it's because maybe we are. I bear a lot of that responsibility. I should've stepped up sooner, done something... anything. Because of my hesitations, too many good people have paid the price. It might be too late for me to fix this, but I'm going to try. I'm the villain here, not you, not any of our sailors. If we get through this, I promise things will change."

She looked at him, uncertainty clouding her eyes. "You think we'll make it?"

"Of course. There's hope yet," Stevens said. The lie slipped out too easily. He'd gotten used to the bitter taste of half-truths, but seeing that flicker of hope in her eyes, he felt a twinge of guilt.

Koothrapali nodded slowly, her face settling into acceptance. "We all gotta do what it takes to survive. Mars taught me that." Her back straightened, a subtle move that Stevens thought spoke volumes about her inner strength. "Thanks, Admiral. I'll make sure those batteries are ready, just in case. By your leave, sir."

"Carry on, Lieutenant Koothrapali."

"Good evening, sir," she said with a crisp salute before heading out.

Stevens gave her a final nod, her footsteps fading into lonely echoes. Alone again, he mulled over his mountain of mistakes piled up like so much space junk. Time was running out, but not gone—every second counted, and he'd be damned if he'd waste another.

Maybe a little shut-eye wouldn't hurt.

He set a glass of water on his nightstand and flopped onto his bunk, ready to surrender to exhaustion. Just as he was about to kick off his boots, the doorbell cut through the quiet. His gut clenched.

More bad news? If they've caught up again, this might be it, he thought.

He sighed and trudged to his holoscreen. Koothrapali stood outside, ramrod straight, her eyes darting to the side. "Yes, Miss Koothrapali?"

"Uh, sorry to bother you, sir. Left my datapad on your desk."

"Hang on." He returned to his desk, spotted the datapad, and grabbed it.

He swung the door open, datapad in hand. In a blur, another sailor barreled past Koothrapali. Stevens caught a flash of a knife as the sailor lunged, burying the blade in his gut. Pain exploded through him, sharp and brutal. He clamped down on the sailor's wrist, fighting to keep the blade from twisting.

"Get him, Terry! Kill the bastard, and let's get the hell out of here," Koothrapali shouted.

Stevens' gut screamed with every breath, his hands slick with blood. Despite the pain, decades of combat training took over. He seized Terry's wrist and wrenched it, exploiting the younger man's momentum. Terry yelped in surprise as Stevens shoved, sending him sprawling over a chair. Stevens' vision swam, but adrenaline surged through his system, dulling the pain just enough to keep him in the fight.

Koothrapali pounced, blade slicing through the air. Stevens lifted his arm, the knife carving a fiery path from elbow to wrist. He grunted, using the motion to step inside her guard.

He stumbled back, buying time. Koothrapali and her accomplice were impassive, faces set in stone.

"Nothing personal, Admiral. Just business," Koothrapali said, cold as space. "I'll make it quick."

Stevens coughed, tasting iron. "Koothrapali... why?"

She lunged again, but Stevens was ready. Muscle memory kicked in as he sidestepped, grabbing her wrist and twisting. The joint lock bent her arm back, her scream piercing as the knife clattered to the deck.

"My arm!" she wailed.

He didn't hesitate, driving his knee into her face. Blood

sprayed as she crumpled.

Shudders rippled through the bulkheads. Stevens had been aboard enough ships in his lifetime to recognize the telltale vibrations of a Union warship firing her guns. An alarm blared.

DiMarco's voice cut through the din of alarms over the loudspeaker. "Action Stations. Inbound hostile warships. The Hasha have caught up to us."

Stevens staggered, the knife wound blazing.

They're here ... I need to get to the bridge ... I need to—

Before he could finish the thought, Terry lunged for another strike. The blade sank deep into his left shoulder, a rush of air escaping his lungs as pain lanced through him. "Die already," Terry hissed, pressing the knife deeper.

Stevens knew he couldn't match the younger man's strength. Instead, he used Terry's forward momentum, sweeping his legs and sending him crashing to the deck. The move cost him, pain flaring through his wounds.

The alarm jolted him back. Koothrapali was out cold. Stevens spared her a glance, uniform soaked red, vision blurring. He saw Terry struggling to his feet, knife in hand. Stevens knew he couldn't last much longer. He had to end this now.

As Terry charged, Stevens sidestepped at the last moment. He grabbed Terry's knife arm, twisting it behind his back. Using the last of his strength, he slammed Terry face-first into the bulkhead. The younger man's head connected with a sickening thud, and he slumped to the ground.

"Now it's personal," Stevens said, his breath in ragged gasps.

He stumbled to his desk, the world spinning. With trembling

hands, he activated a script he'd prepared—a final contingency. Confirmation flashed on his holoscreen: Done. Data packets raced across the cosmos, carrying all he knew about the Hasha and their atrocities to every media outlet on Earth.

"Chew on that, Liam, you son of a bitch," he mumbled.

The room tilted. Stevens opened a channel to the bridge. "Captain DiMarco... it's Tom," he rasped.

DiMarco's voice came fast. "Admiral, you okay? I need you up here. The Hasha found us." A pause. "Tom? You there?"

"Execute... execute Hail Mary." Stevens gasped, words fading as his legs gave out. He hit the deck, cold steel against his cheek. Alarms faded to a distant buzz. His breathing slowed, heartbeat sluggish in the growing quiet. He tried to move, to think, to... what was it again? He struggled for air as warmth spread beneath him—his lifeblood pooling out. His thoughts flickered, dim and far away, as the lights faded. He let his eyes close, surrendering to the encroaching dark.

Chapter 44

Deck Six, CCV Galatea

Kliinat, Tau Ceti System

December 6, 2681

Carson feinted left around Andaeer, then pivoted right, blasting past a Klii Marine. He batted away grasping hands that tried to snag his waist. Ten yards. Twenty. Thirty. He passed the ball to Maalek on his right with a quick flick.

Maalek caught it cleanly, charging forward in a tight line. Blocked by Akitani, he lobbed it back to Carson. Williams, Rodriguez, and Sousa converged, cutting him off thirty yards from the goal. Carson kicked it into high gear. Rodriguez lunged—Carson executed a textbook strong-arm, shoving him aside as he slipped by.

Shoulder lowered, he barreled into Williams, sending her

tumbling. He skidded to a stop, dodged a diving Sousa, leaped over her sprawling form, and hurled a bullet straight into the net. Gunny's whistle blew, signaling the try and halftime.

Williams sat up, massaging her shoulder with a wry grin. "So that's how you earned the name 'Skip'." She took Carson's offered hand and stood.

"You squared up, left yourself flat-footed," Carson advised. "Stay on your toes, cut me off at an angle, keep shuffling. You'll get me next time."

"Thanks. I'll try," Williams nodded. Her gaze drifted to three Klii passing the ball back and forth. "Didn't think they'd pick it up so fast. They're pretty good."

"Those slender fingers help. They're nimble too, even with their long legs."

"I bet it won't be long before we see the first Klii in the pros," Williams said, catching her breath.

"Yeah, that would be pretty cool." Carson made a break signal with his hands and jogged to the water table, where Marines hydrated, swapping stories of less sweaty times. His knee ached, as if it was considering retirement. Gunny joined him, wiping sweat from her shaved head.

"Excellent run, sir," she said. "That knee giving you trouble again?"

"It's not too bad, but I'll ice it anyway," Carson said, twisting off the bottle cap. "It's been a fun scrimmage. I'm glad we skipped the obstacle course today."

Rodriguez stumbled over, dousing his head with water, steam rising from his heated skin. Nearby, Williams accepted the towel Carson tossed her with a grin.

"That why you never went pro?" Rodriguez asked, glancing at the ice pack. "Haven't been stiff-armed that hard since the Titans tryouts."

"No, that happened later, during my first deployment. I had offers before the academy, but since my great-great-grandfather fought in the first war of independence, every Carson has served in the Navy. I'm just keeping up the family tradition." He shrugged. "Maybe once this war is over." A part of him knew he was more likely to leave the Marines under a flag than in retirement. It was the sobering reality of his chosen career, but he wanted to stay positive for his troops. Was he being pessimistic? Yes, but he'd like to think of it as pragmatic.

Williams dropped to the ground with a sigh, dragging the towel across her sweaty brow. She leaned closer, lowering her voice. "What if this war never ends, Skip? What about these Hasha everyone's whispering about?" Her eyes darted around as if ensuring no one else was in earshot. Carson recognized that look—he'd seen it more often lately, as whispered conversations about the Hasha replaced the usual pre-meal chatter in the mess.

Navy intelligence had revealed the Hasha weeks ago, sparking panic across the colonies. Carson had watched Kliinat's citizens start stockpiling supplies, boarding up windows—familiar preparations from the last time aliens darkened their skies. His Marines picked up on that tension, carried it in their shoulders during training. He'd grappled with the same doubts. Peace had seemed within reach until intel about the Hasha landed on his desk, turning certainty to smoke. But dwelling on it wouldn't help his Marines today. "We handle today's war today,

Williams. Tomorrow's war can wait. But stay prepared."

"Aren't you worried?" Rodriguez asked, frowning. "Scuttlebutt says the Union hasn't downed a single Hasha ship."

"Sure, I'm worried," Carson said, forcing a casual expression to mask his unease. "But it's that edge of fear that keeps us sharp. When the time comes to face them in battle, I'll be in the front with you guys, running the colors."

Gunny clapped his shoulder hard enough to register on seismographs. "I don't doubt it, sir." She turned to Rodriguez. "As far as I can tell, they don't seem to be bulletproof, and I intend to put that theory to the test. Oorah."

Akitani sauntered up, water bottle in hand. "Count me in." It was exactly the kind of bravado Carson had come to expect from his officers—half swagger, half steel, all Marine. "Tell you what, Gunny. You pop one before me, I'll ink your mug right here," she said, tapping her bicep.

"That'd be the third such tattoo of yours truly," Gunny said.

Akitani flicked a brow upward. "You're kidding."

"I wish I was, Ma'am."

Rodriguez rolled up his right sleeve to reveal a tattoo of Gunny armed and ready. "We were playing pyramid, and I was out of creds," he said.

"It wasn't a cakewalk for me either; I had to hold that pose for an hour," Gunny said.

Laughter started to bubble up just as the General Quarters alarm rang, transforming relaxed athletes back into Marines between one heartbeat and the next. Carson watched easy smiles harden into game faces he knew too well.

The XO's voice boomed over the loudspeakers: "General Quarters, General Quarters, this is not a drill. Enemy ships in sight, repeat, enemy ships in sight."

Carson's water bottle hit the deck as he bolted for the armory. His body switched from scrimmage mode to combat ready before his brain caught up, muscle memory erasing his knee's protests. Another day, another fight—at least they were warmed up. The thunder of boots on metal followed close behind. Time to put Gunny's theory to the test.

Chapter 45

Captain's Quarters, CCV Galatea

Tau Ceti System

December 6, 2681

Mori lounged at her desk, flicking through holograms of Sophia and a new puppy, stealing a moment from the grind of paperwork. But her quiet was shattered by a sharp ping from her console: high-priority message incoming.

She swiped open a notice from Navy Intelligence. Earlier reports from their assets on Earth had hinted at trouble, but this update painted a nightmare: planet-wide riots, government in shambles, Union fleets MIA, and the revelation of the existence of the Hasha. The message ended with an ominous directive: "Colonial Fleet at Condition One." What the hell is going on? she wondered.

The ear-splitting General Quarters alarm cut her thoughts short. Mori jolted in her chair, adrenaline spiking as the racket echoed through her cabin. "On my way," she said into the comm.

Mori bolted from her cabin, banking right for the express elevator to the CIC. As she stepped in, the lift's hum filled the space.

Why does everything go to hell when I'm not on the bridge? She thought.

After an eternity, the elevator doors hissed open, revealing the CIC's buzzing hub of activity. Officers and crew scrambled to their posts against a backdrop of beeping sensors and clattering keyboards.

Mori spotted the XO at his console, doing his best to scare the bejesus out of the crew. She swept her gaze across the bridge, raising her voice to be heard over the noise. "What do we have, XO?"

"Sensor contacts at the jump point—Union ships, twenty and counting. It's ballsy, gotta give 'em that," the XO said.

"Get the alert fighters up. Talyn, find me a target," Mori said.

The XO turned to flight ops. "Get those birds in the air, now!"

She turned to the helmsman, whose eyes ping-ponged between flashing displays. "Helm, how soon before we push off?"

"Thirty minutes, Captain. Dock's a madhouse."

No, not good enough. "Make it fifteen. We leave with whoever's aboard. XO, spread the word."

"Aye, Captain," the XO said, already turning to relay the new orders.

He grabbed the mic and broadcast across the ship with an urgency tinted by colorful metaphors. Mori winced at his choice of words but let it slide. If it got her crew moving faster, so be it.

Daniels swiveled, face tight as she addressed Mori. "Ma'am, we're receiving a transmission from UNS Repulse. It's on an open Q-channel... they're signaling a mayday. Artemis and Cassiopeia are asking for orders."

Before Mori could respond, Grant barreled to his station, bumping past over a startled ensign. Winded, he blurted, "The ships have struck their colors."

Mori's brow furrowed. What the hell? Giving up without a shot fired?

The XO grunted, breaking the hanging silence. "What kind of crummy trick is this? They really think we're gonna fall for that?" His stern gaze then fell on Grant, who looked like he'd slept in his uniform. "Mr. Grant, clean yourself up. This is the bridge of the bloody flagship, not some backwater scrapper."

Grant smoothed his jacket, nodding, "Yes, sir."

Mori tapped her console, face neutral as she juggled possibilities. "Keep the ship at condition one, XO. Talyn, prepare a firing solution for the Hades guns."

Crummy trick or a genuine plea for help? The email about the mess on Earth nagged at her—what in God's name is going on?

A Marine guard snapped to attention, announcing the

Admiral's arrival. "Admiral on deck!"

Antonov strode in, motioning to comms. "Get them on screen. Tell the fleet to hold position."

Daniels' fingers flew over her console. "Aye, sir. UNS Repulse, this is CCV Galatea. Switch to Q-channel One-Niner-Four-Bravo-Zulu. Video transmission. Acknowledge."

A crackling response followed. "Colonial Carrier CCV Galatea, this is Union Battleship UNS Repulse. Switching to One-Niner-Four-Bravo-Zulu."

Mori leaned forward, her interest piqued. "Put it on the main holoscreen," she ordered.

"Yes, ma'am. Repulse, you're live with Admiral Vasily Antonov and Captain Tomoe Mori."

The holoscreen flickered to life, revealing the distorted image of a disheveled captain. Mori noted the tremble in the woman's voice as she rushed through her message. "Admiral Antonov, I'm Stephanie DiMarco, Captain of UNS Repulse, flagship of the Combined Fleet. I am requesting terms of surrender. We have many wounded, and... we need your help."

A low murmur rippled through the bridge crew.

The XO snapped from his console, "Quiet on the bridge." He gave Mori a side glance. "Nuts. I say we find out how they like our Hades."

Mori studied the holoscreen, taking in DiMarco's worn-out look and her crew's rough shape. Their scorched uniforms and visible injuries spoke of hard fights. Maybe this wasn't a con job after all. What could push a Union fleet to surrender?

"Captain DiMarco," Mori said, eyes narrowing as she

weighed her words, "your last trick cost us a lot of good people. I'd love nothing more than to cut this call and load every single one of my missile batteries."

DiMarco nodded, glancing off-screen. "Fair enough, Captain. Please stand by to receive a data packet. It's something you need to see."

The XO jumped in, "Daniels, isolate that on a virtual console. The last thing we need is a Union virus messing with our systems."

"Aye, sir."

Antonov's brow furrowed. "Captain DiMarco, you're the ranking officer now? What happened to Admiral Dietrich?" He asked.

"Admiral Dietrich is dead. Admiral Stevens was the ranking officer, but we lost him a few days ago. I guess, for now, I'm it, sir."

As this was happening, Mori received a discreet ping from Talyn. She stepped aside, keeping her voice low. "Maintain that firing solution, but hold fire."

"As you command, Captain."

This might be an emergency, but she'd be damned if she took any chances with her ship or her people.

Antonov sliced through the unfolding tension. "What's this all about, Captain DiMarco?"

"I hoped I could tell you that in person," DiMarco said.

***

Mori, Antonov, the XO, and a detail of Marines lined up in

the hangar, an immense steel cave bathed in the harsh glow of fluorescent lights. The place smelled like a mechanic's dream— oil, fuel, and cold metal.

The air grew tense as the elevator lowered the Dart shuttle carrying DiMarco. The thump of its landing echoed through the hangar, and with a sharp hiss, its doors slid open. DiMarco stepped out, flanked by her own Marine guard. Their arrival had been covered every step of the way—a squadron of Dauntless fighters had escorted the shuttle to Galatea, relieving a squad of Space Hornets that kept formation until the shuttle lined up for approach. During this time, Antonov had corralled the Union fleet to orbit Qaamat, fenced in by Cassiopeia's carrier group.

The Colonial Marines snapped their rifles, echoing the Union Marines' posture. It was a tense standoff until DiMarco gave a curt wave, signaling her people to relax. Mori gave a subtle nod, and her Marines eased up, still alert but less twitchy. Half the Marines were Klii—a nice touch, Mori thought. She caught Carson's eye; this had his fingerprints all over it. No wonder.

DiMarco marched down the shuttle ramp and saluted Galatea with due formality before facing Mori. "Permission to come aboard," she said, following protocol.

"Granted, Captain DiMarco. I'm Captain Tomoe Mori. Welcome to Galatea," Mori said, keeping it civil. Diplomacy first—hostility could wait.

The handshake was crisp and professional. The XO, however, couldn't hide his distaste, wiping his hand on his uniform as if to clean away the contamination of touching a Union officer. Antonov's handshake mirrored DiMarco's—all military courtesy, devoid of warmth.

"May my executive officer join us?" DiMarco asked.

Mori was firm. "No. And your Marines stay here, too." This was her ship, her rules.

DiMarco's face tightened, but she nodded, accepting the terms. "Understood."

Echo Company's Marines led them through the corridors as the crew's curious eyes peeked from every corner. Mori whispered to her XO, "Next time someone tries to rubberneck, they're cleaning the head with a toothbrush."

The XO, his expression steely and determined, noted names on his datapad, his eyes narrowing, nostrils flaring.

DiMarco took in the ship as they walked, her eyes sweeping over the scene. The soft lighting highlighted the pristine bulkheads, while the ship's systems emitted a steady hum. At the Admiral's office, she turned to Mori.

"She's a beautiful ship, Captain."

Few captains were immune to compliments about their ship, and Mori sure wasn't, but she wouldn't let DiMarco get in *that* easily. "Thank you. She is," she said, keeping her replies professional.

"Is she your first command?" DiMarco asked, attempting to pierce Mori's professional armor with friendly curiosity.

"Third," Mori said, keeping her guard up.

"Repulse is my fourth. I love them all, but you never forget your first command, right?"

"That's what I hear," Mori said with a polite but

noncommittal smile.

Nice try.

Mori then ushered DiMarco into the Admiral's office, a space dominated by the cool glow of holographic displays and the steady hum of data feeds. The aroma of warm tea and fresh pastries softened the atmosphere.

DiMarco blew across her steaming tea before taking a careful sip. Mori poured herself a cup, letting the herbal scent ease the tension that mounted since the Union fleet's unexpected arrival. Behind DiMarco, the Marine guards remained vigilant, their hands close to their M45s. Truce or not, Mori wasn't taking unnecessary risks.

"Captain DiMarco, let's get to the point," Antonov said, pleasantries over.

"I presume you have some intelligence on the Hasha?" DiMarco ventured, phrasing it as a casual observation.

Antonov exchanged a glance with Mori, then nodded. "Go ahead, Captain."

The probe they sent to Cancri, information their assets on Earth pieced together, and the reluctant cooperation of Admiral Almeida filled in some blanks.

"We know they're a vast empire, that you preemptively struck their terraforming operations, that there's a large number of missing Union fleets, and that they have powerful energy-based weapons. Perhaps you could elaborate on the details."

"I see you're well informed," DiMarco said.

"You have spies, we have spies; it is what it is," Mori said. Whether or not she felt sorry for DiMarco, the Union remained an enemy of the Colonies, and dropping that tidbit gave Mori a little joy. She'd hated them far too long to pass up an opportunity to twist the knife, even a little.

DiMarco nodded, her expression hardening. "We learned of their punching power the hard way when they jumped one of their battle groups after our first strike. They've been pushing into our space ever since, wiping out every battle group we've sent to counterattack. It wasn't until we adjusted our shield frequencies that we saw any real success, but even that was too little, too late."

The Union built good ships: fast, strong, and well-armed. Sure, Galatea had come out on top recently, but if the Hasha were wiping out fleets wholesale, they might be a more formidable enemy than Mori had imagined. That familiar knot of dread and resolve tightened in her stomach.

DiMarco met Mori's gaze, exhaustion etched on her face. "We rallied all available ships at Betelgeuse, hoping to make a stand. It turned into a catastrophe. What you see here," she swept her hand in a vague arc, "is what's left of the Union Navy."

Mori's eyes widened. "You're telling me this is what's left of the entire fleet?" Despite her reservations about DiMarco, she couldn't help but feel a twinge of respect. Leaping into enemy territory, waving a white flag—it wasn't just desperate, it was the last flicker in a dying candle. Observing DiMarco's charred uniform and the weariness in her eyes, Mori's heart softened, just a notch.

Captain DiMarco stared into her mug, pausing before she spoke. "There are a few stragglers out there—frigates, destroyers, battleships—but essentially, yes. Sol Fleet is holding for now. The remnants of First and Second Fleets are jumping back to Earth to bolster our defenses. I've sent a distress call to any ships in range, directing them here. We've had replies, but some are damaged, others may not arrive at all."

"Why here, Captain? Why this system?" Antonov asked, leaning forward.

DiMarco met his questioning stare. "They've been tracking our FTL jumps since the retreat, and we lose more ships each time they catch up to us. We had nowhere else to go. Medical supplies are critical, and we haven't had the chance to repair damage."

The XO leaned back in his chair and shook his head. "So, you decided to bring this turd and drop it on our front step? You could have jumped home instead of screwing us. Guess you'll get the last laugh after all."

Mori shot a quick glance at the XO, who echoed her own concerns. She bit her bottom lip as the implications of DiMarco's arrival sunk in: the Hasha would track the Union fleet to Kliinat.

DiMarco held the XO's gaze. "There are fifty billion souls in Sol, twenty billion on Earth alone. You don't know what it would mean to jump home—or maybe you do. And after us, where do you think the Hasha will head next? You've got months, maybe less."

The XO scoffed. "That gives us time to prepare, doesn't it?"

DiMarco leaned forward. "We understood the risks of coming here," she said. "But please, hear me out. If we combine our forces, we stand a chance. We've paid in blood for the lessons we've learned—lessons that could prevent you from suffering the same fate."

The XO snorted a laugh. "So you want us to fight these Hasha for you. That's fracking rich, lady."

Captain DiMarco sipped her tea, turning to Mori. "People who wanted to keep the Hasha conflict under wraps murdered Admiral Stevens in his own cabin, on my ship," she said. She placed her cup on the saucer with a soft clink, her fingers lingering on the handle for a moment. "Before he died, Stevens broadcast an intel packet to Sol, making our war with the Hasha public. Earth's a mess, and now we're on our own. I don't know what happens next, but I have one last round in the magazine, and I'm using it."

The XO pointed an accusatory finger at DiMarco. "You have some stones. You're asking us to forget three wars and hundreds of thousands of deaths. Screw you; that's what I say." He turned to Antonov. "Tell them not to let the door hit their asses on the way out. We can take care of the Hasha ourselves."

DiMarco's patience broke; she slammed her fist down, the thud echoing through the quiet room. The Marine guards tensed, their rifles inching higher. "I'm not asking for shit. If you decide I'm full of crap, I'll take our ships back to Earth, and we'll defend our home. But when we lose, and we will, it will be your turn."

Mori's eyes narrowed, considering. DiMarco knew her fleet lacked the fuel to reach Earth, but she was making a desperate gamble. Maybe there was no other choice.

"You need to decide if you're going to hold onto old grudges and let billions die, or accept this olive branch and join us against a greater threat," DiMarco pressed. "Look, I'm not a politician. I don't know what'll become of this war. Mine not to reason why, mine but to do and die. All I know is we're facing humanity's extinction. By our estimates, the Hasha will be here in less than seventy-two hours. If we can't stop them here, there won't be an Earth to return to," DiMarco said.

Mori noticed Antonov's intent gaze on DiMarco. "Explain their military capabilities, their tactics," he said.

DiMarco nodded, leaning forward, "Their EMP weapon makes our ships go dark, then they fire an energy beam that slices through tritanium as if it was paper—our people started calling it the Scythe. Their fighters are agile and hard to pin down but not invincible. It's that damn EMP that's been kicking our asses. Was kicking our asses. Two weeks ago, we cracked it."

DiMarco took a bite of biscuit, brushing crumbs from her uniform before sipping her tea.

"We gathered forty-eight ships at Cancri," she said. "We adjusted our shield modulation to counter their EMP, and it worked. We unleashed everything we had. Their shields are tough and familiar, but we broke through. Took down two battlecruisers and several destroyers, even damaged a Dreadnought's engine. But then—they hit us again, changed the EMP frequency, and our ships went dark. Just like that. Admiral Stevens ordered a retreat when the battle line collapsed."

Mori's frown deepened, her eyes narrowing on DiMarco. "You're not exactly painting a rosy picture here. What makes you think we'd fare any better than you did?"

DiMarco leaned in. "It's your shields. They have a familiar

ring because you adapted the tech from that wreck in Arcturus to upgrade your ships. We've been trying to crack that nut for years." She caught Mori's scowl and offered a shrug. "You have your spies; we have ours; it is what it is."

Mori bristled, not thrilled about having her words tossed back at her, but let it go. She leaned back, the ship's soft hum filling the silence. "Then we can take our chances, let the Hasha do the heavy lifting for us, and take you off the board."

DiMarco nodded, her expression sincere. "True. I'm betting on the fact that you won't stand by and watch humanity die. I won't blow smoke up your ass. You hate us, and feelings are mutual on our side, too. I'm hoping, more than you could ever imagine, that this is where we turn the page and bury three hundred years of hatred to face our common enemy. And don't be too confident that shields alone will win the day. We're wounded, yes, but we're ready to fight."

Antonov's chair creaked as he stood. "Give us a moment, Captain. We'll ask the mess to prepare something more substantial."

Mori noticed DiMarco's shoulders sag slightly. "Thank you, Admiral," DiMarco said. "And if it's not too much trouble, my Marines have had it rougher than me. They could use a hot meal."

"Of course. And your arm—should we have a medic look at it?" Antonov asked.

"No need for a full exam, but I wouldn't turn down a DermaGel patch or a ReGen Shot."

"I'll see to it," Mori assured.

Outside, Mori ordered meals for their unexpected guests and requested first aid from MedBay. The XO stopped and faced Mori, disbelief in his eyes. "Tell me we're not really considering this."

Mori crossed her arms, tapping her chin as she weighed their options. "DiMarco isn't just gambling here. She knew what she was doing, bringing her fleet here. It was a calculated risk. We can't abandon the system; it'll leave Kliinat exposed."

The XO cast his eyes upward. "Which means we have to stay and fight. Remind me never to play poker with that woman."

Antonov lowered his head and tugged at his right earlobe. "This has Steven's fingerprints all over it. That man was as cunning as they came."

Mori wondered about Antonov's history with Admiral Stevens. He sounded almost nostalgic. She, however, harbored no such sentiment.

"Captain," Antonov said, facing Mori. "Once this is settled, brief Prime Adaara. Put Kliinat on high alert."

"Admiral, Adaara will go supernova when I tell her we're considering a truce with the Union fleet," Mori confessed. "She's a warrior; she wants complete and total victory, and she won't be satisfied with anything but their abject humiliation. They have long memories in Kliinat."

Antonov gave her a sympathetic look. "I'm sure it'll be a complicated conversation, but I know you'll handle it."

Mori sighed. An order was an order, no matter how uncomfortable. "Yes, sir."

"XO, find me every ship that can get here in two days. Every single one. If DiMarco's right, we need to prepare the system's defense," Antonov said.

"Yes, sir."

Back inside, they faced DiMarco, who sat rigid in her chair, mid-bite, lowering her sandwich as her eyes darted between Antonov and the XO, awaiting their verdict. Antonov laid out the terms. "Captain, here are the terms of surrender: your fleet is now under the custody of the Colonial Navy. I will grant you and your ships parole to address this common threat. If we're all still here after this, you will be turned over to Navy Intelligence, and your ships will either be scuttled or towed to Athens. Is that clear?"

A deep flush spread across DiMarco's cheeks as she set her sandwich down with a decisive clatter. "I have no choice, do I?"

"No, you do not," Antonov said.

DiMarco swallowed hard. "Then I accept the terms of surrender."

"Good." Antonov picked up a sandwich. "Let's figure out how to beat these Hasha."

Chapter 46

Council of 64 Headquarters, Kliinat

Tau Ceti System

December 9, 2681

Carson stood next to the broad boulevard ringing the Citadel, once the bustling council headquarters of Naadan. Now a ghost town, its boarded-up shops and locked shutters sketched a somber picture. The eerie quiet only deepened his unease. Where had everyone gone? Did they evacuate or flee into the city's labyrinthine tunnels to escape the looming storm? Probably for the best—no civilians around to catch stray bullets or, worse, get caught in mortar fire.

Beyond the desolate streets, Naadan's hills bristled with Aether missile batteries and Cerberus mortars that Carson had requisitioned from the fleet for the imminent showdown. These were the big guns, the kind you didn't bring out unless things were about to get real ugly, real fast. He counted on them to hold off the Hasha's warships and troop transports that rumor had it were itching to pay a visit.

In contrast to the silent streets, the Citadel's courtyard was a hive of activity. Klii soldiers and Colonial Marines moved with purpose, stacking sandbags in a rhythm that echoed across the yard. Hermes machine guns peeked out from gaps in the fences, mortars claiming spots on rooftops and corners.

Time was not on their side, and Carson felt every second. Kliinat might have weathered invasions before, but this time, it had an ally in the fight: Athens would stand shoulder-to-shoulder with them.

Colonial crews had stripped every ship of arms and ammo. Griffin shuttles buzzed back and forth, ferrying supplies and providing air support. Centaur Tanks, Apollo mobile artillery, and Trident IFVs now ringed the city, a steel wall showcasing Colonial Navy muscle.

Even the Union fleet had chipped in with Hammerhead tanks and Mamba missile batteries, which was a miracle given their recent shellacking. But with every battleship needed at the front and no room for orbital strikes, the ground forces were on their own. This time, the Marines and Scouts alone would face whatever the Hasha threw at them. No pressure, just the fate of a planet hanging in the balance.

In a twist of irony, hundreds of Union POWs, paroled by Antonov mere days ago, stood shoulder to shoulder with former enemies. They were dug in at Daalamas' council HQ, smack dab in the city's heart. Trust wasn't exactly flowing—many Klii, Maalek included, could not mask their distrust, if not outright disdain, for their new allies. But then, Carson figured being wiped out by the Hasha was a decidedly worse option. For their part, the Union Marines, having learned of the destruction of so many colonies, were very motivated.

At first, Adaara had received the idea of a truce with the Union fleet about as well as a cat would a cold bath. Union troops on Kliinat soil? Over her dead body—considering they'd brought the Hasha nightmare to their doorstep. But somehow, Captain Mori had changed her mind. Maybe it was those harrowing videos of terraformed planets, or that chilling audio from Cancri of colonists gasping their last breaths. When Carson first heard that recording, his gut reaction was to walk out; instead, he stayed, steeling himself against the creeping dread. He needed to understand the kind of devil they were up against.

A low-flying shuttle roared overhead, afterburners lighting up the sky. It arced back toward the fleet, followed by a couple more, their silhouettes shrinking to dots against the vast, cloudless expanse. Carson's thoughts drifted to his friends in the fleet—while the ground forces prepped for the storm, the fleet would first feel the Hasha's wrath. The earlier briefing had hammered home the urgency: Callisto and her carrier group, along with the dreadnoughts Ulysses and Ares, were burning through space from Alexandria to Kliinat, racing to make it in time. A probe from Mira, a jump away, had clocked the Hasha's rapid advance toward their system.

Carson took a long drink from his canteen. The cool water offered a brief escape, easing his anxiety as the battle loomed. He twisted the cap back on and headed to the central sandbag pile in the courtyard.

That's where he ran into Maalek, Andaeer, Williams, and Gunny—each wearing expressions carved from the same block of granite as his own. As he reached for a sandbag, he found himself face to face with Adaara, decked out in Scout fatigues. No one around batted an eye at the sight of their leader in combat gear.

Carson stared as Adaara hoisted a sandbag onto her shoulder, surprised to see her there. "Your Primeship, I didn't expect to see you here. Shouldn't you be inside, in the keep?"

Adaara shot him a wry smile. "Not if I have a say in it. Alas, my advisors insist on tucking me away in a bunker, shall the worst come to pass."

"We can't afford to lose you in battle—another rifle won't make a difference," Carson said.

"Will it not? I led raids against the Union base near Neskfaat. I have twenty kills to my name and can handle a rifle better than most Scouts," Adaara countered, her posture firm, her gaze unwavering.

Not for the first time, he was reminded that Kliinat was in capable hands. He glanced around at the bustling activity. "How come no one's come looking for you?"

"Oh, they tried. But I slipped away and donned this uniform. They haven't spotted me yet," Adaara said, mischief dancing in her eyes.

Carson couldn't help but respect her cunning. "Well... I am sorry," Carson said.

"For what?"

"For this." Carson put his bag down and keyed his comm for

Maalek. "Maal, turn around and look at me. On your right. No, your other right. Yeah, that's me waving. Adaara is here with me. I need you to come escort her back to the keep. Post a Marine guard and tell them they will not leave her side. Copy?"

Adaara clenched her fists. After a moment, she relaxed, a faint smile curling at the corner of her mouth. "Well done, Captain, but I will be back. You shall see."

Carson smiled. "Not this time."

Maalek arrived and stood before Adaara, his expression one of exasperated surprise. "Kaalahera save us. What are you doing out here?"

"You, too, Maalek? Should I hide away as you, all of you, spill your blood for our planet?"

"Come, let us discuss this inside," Maalek said.

Adaara hesitated, then followed him, her shoulders tense. She cast one last glance at Carson. "I will see you soon, Captain."

Carson kept an eye on her until she vanished into the building, then grabbed his sandbag and got back to work.

Chapter 47

Council of 64 Headquarters, Kliinat

Tau Ceti System

December 9, 2681

Maalek and Adaara's footsteps echoed through the Citadel's deserted halls. Once a hub of political activity, now it felt more like a tomb preparing for its last stand. Dim light filtered through boarded windows, casting long shadows across their path.

The silence wasn't absolute. Distant sounds filtered through—hurried footsteps, hushed voices, gear being prepped. Some council members had retreated to the tunnels with civilians, but a determined group remained topside. Maalek taught them the basics on M45s that morning and assigned them supporting roles. They weren't seasoned soldiers, but they'd defend their ground if necessary. It was a sobering thought: if the fight reached them, the battle was likely already lost, but Maalek admired their resolve to fight.

They passed a deactivated laser scanner, its usual hum replaced by unsettling quiet. It made Maalek uneasy, thinking of the guards who should be manning it, now reinforcing the outer defenses. A pair of Marine squads clattered past, equipped for battle and headed for the roof.

In a fleeting moment of calm, Adaara's fingers found Maalek's. They shared a look, drawing strength from each other. The air changed as they approached the makeshift hospital—yesterday's cafeteria. Sharp antiseptic mingled with clean linen while medics and Corpsmen prepared for the inevitable casualties.

Maalek squeezed Adaara's hand. "This will be a heavy day," he murmured, voice echoing off cold stone.

Adaara met his eyes, steel in her gaze. "Yes, I expect it will be. Yet we will stand fast, no matter how dire."

As they descended the spiral staircase, every step brought a subtle drop in temperature, and the chill of the underground air mingled with a faint dampness from the stone walls.

Outside a secure room, Maalek paused, eyeing Adaara. "Do you intend to escape again?" he asked.

Adaara's answer was quiet but resolute. "Of course. Would you have me do nothing?"

"Yes."

"No, I will not sit inside this velvet cage while my people endure another invasion. Even our colonial allies are concerned about these Hasha. When I talked to Captain Mori, she sounded... uneasy. I do not have to tell you what a bad omen that is. This is a time of darkness, and we must all stand against it."

Kliinat legends spoke of celestial beings heralding an age of destruction and rebirth. Some had mistaken Union soldiers for these harbingers. Now, with the Hasha threat, old fears resurfaced. Maalek wasn't one for prophecies, but these new enemies gave him pause. Still, he masked his doubts.

"When we beat back this invasion, we'll rebuild. For that, we need you," he said, trying to reassure her.

Adaara's jaw clenched. "Why must you be so obtuse? We need you, too, but you will stand by the gates with dagger in hand, yet I am supposed to hide like a nesting Kaava."

A ghost of a smile broke Maalek's stern expression. "I am dispensable. You are not."

Her response stirred a gentle, swirling warmth in his chest. "You are not dispensable to me."

Maalek looked away, emotions warring within him. Memories of his family, his driving force, pulled at his heart. It had been simple before her: fight, free his people, die with honor. But she'd changed everything, opening a path he couldn't ignore.

Adaara's touch on his cheek snapped him back. She stepped closer, eyes searching his. "I want a future for our people. I want a future for us, together."

"And if it is not in the scrolls?"

"The scrolls would not be so cruel to separate us now, after everything we have endured," Adaara said with captivating confidence. "Amunkeera watches over us. I pray to her every night. She would be a poor Goddess of Love and Family if she did not cast her protection over her most devout follower."

Maalek glanced at the nearby Marines, who suddenly found anything else fascinating. "I would like to believe that. And yet, here we are, facing the destruction of our people a second time. The Daia abandoned us once before."

Adaara shook her head. "You cannot believe that. They would not leave their children helpless in the face of such an enemy. No, this is a test, one we cannot fail. It is no coincidence that the Colonies arrived when we needed them most. The Daia's finger on the scales tipped them in our favor."

Maalek paused, pushing aside his doubts. "You sound so certain that I would be a fool not to believe it. But you are right. I should not let doubt cloud my thoughts. Now, no more delays. Please, go inside."

Adaara's smile held a challenge as she released his hands, fingertips lingering on his cheek. "You know I will be back."

Maalek's lips quirked. "We'll see."

Adaara entered the safe room with a resolute nod. Maalek secured the door, then turned to his Marines.

"You are not to move from this post, no matter what."

"Yes, sir," they said in unison.

Outside, the deep thuds of missile batteries shattered the silence. Maalek's neural interface flashed the dreaded alert. Gripping his rifle, he raced up the stairs. The Hasha had arrived, and with them, a battle that would determine the fate of   Kliinat.

Chapter 48

Captain's Quarters, CCV Galatea

Tau Ceti System

December 9, 2681

Mori slumped into her chair, head throbbing from a sleepless night. The holoscreen's glow painted her face in soft shadows. She sipped her third or maybe fourth cup of lukewarm coffee, no longer registering the bitterness. Time played tricks on her—too fast when she needed it slow, too slow when she wanted it fast. She rechecked the time—five minutes since the last time she'd looked.

Her cabin felt like a prison cell. She paced from desk to couch and back, restlessness gnawing at her. The Hasha were coming. When, not if. Mori still had one ace up her sleeve thanks to her exhaustive planning, although anticipation buzzed under her skin like an angry hornet.

To hell with this. She bolted for the CIC, craving its familiar embrace.

The bridge's unusual quiet hit her as she entered, contrasting with the storm brewing outside. The Marine at the hatch snapped to.

"Captain on deck!"

"As you were," Mori said, taking her place. "I have the deck."

Galatea's heartbeat—scrubbers humming, grav generators purring—wrapped around her like an old, worn blanket.

Talyn approached, his crests adorned once more. "Captain, may I speak?"

She cocked an eyebrow. "What's on your mind, Talyn?"

Talyn drew his dagger, held it blade up, and bowed. "Your command, my blade. By steel and blood, my life is your Legatar. I stand with you until final breath is drawn." He straightened, locking eyes with her.

Mori was not very familiar with Arcturian customs, but she recognized the Blade of Loyalty. Talyn would indeed stay by her side, bound by blood and steel, to whatever end. Unsure how to respond, she borrowed a page from the High Daimar. "You honor me, Sentar. Would that you had been born an Athenian, to stand as kin, shoulder to shoulder." Every word rang true. Talyn's crests rippled, a ghost of a smile flickering across his face as he returned to his post.

The XO sidled up beside her. "What the heck was that?"

"The Blade of Loyalty. If I go down with the ship, so will Talyn. Wild horses couldn't drag him away."

The XO shook his head slowly. "Crazy Arcturians." He eyed her. "Well, I'm guessing you couldn't stay away either," he said.

"No. I hate waiting. Might as well do it here."

"Same. I'm on a coffee run. Want one?"

"Please," Mori nodded.

Mori glanced at him as he walked away. He was being nice, and that didn't happen often. Of course, the coming battle against an enemy they'd never faced had everyone jittery. Perhaps that's how he dealt with nerves.

Mori scanned the formation on her screen. Ships hung in a delicate ballet above the planet — four carrier groups and two dreadnoughts leading the charge, their lines bolstered by Union vessels. The AI model updated in real-time, showing the slow dance of the fleet. But not all the dancers were in top form. Six Union ships had been turned to scrap, and two more limped along on patch jobs. A ragtag group of latecomers—a light carrier, two destroyers, and a cruiser—hung back in support.

Outgunned and under the gun, they were as ready as they'd ever be. A cosmic David facing an unknown Goliath. DiMarco's promises about upgraded shields played on repeat in Mori's head. A thin thread of hope, but it was all they had as they stared into the maw of the coming storm.

Mori accepted the coffee with a nod. "Thanks."

"Black, one sugar," the XO said.

She sipped, savoring the warmth. Somehow, the brew always tasted better on the bridge. Interesting that he remembered her preference.

The XO leaned on the console, nodding at the Union ships

on the holo. "I'm not gonna lie. It's gonna be weird fighting alongside those squids. Just thinking about it grinds my gears."

Mori's lips quirked. "Yeah, it'll be... interesting. But DiMarco seems motivated."

"I know I gave her a hard time, but she got her ships ready for battle four days after getting the jam beat out of them. That deserves at least an attaboy."

"I won't tell her if you don't," Mori said.

"Deal."

They lapsed into comfortable silence, watching readouts crawl across their screens. Seconds stretched into an eternity.

"Any word on Callisto and the other dreadnoughts?" he asked after a moment.

"Still transiting through Fenris. The radiation's playing hell with their systems. I doubt they'll make it in time. Looks like it's just us," she said.

The XO's voice carried a quiet resolve. "The fewer the number, the greater share of honor."

"And when this is over, we will strip our sleeves and show our scars."

And there'll be plenty of those to go around, she thought.

The bridge holoscreen flared to life, bathing everything in an eerie blue glow. The Hasha fleet materialized against the backdrop of deep space, ending their long wait. Mori's butterflies vanished, replaced by crystalline focus.

Grant's voice cut the silence. "Sensor contacts. Incoming fleet at the jump point. Marking as unknown."

The XO snapped, "Mr. Grant, did you forget how to do your job? How many contacts? Speed and bearing?"

"Sorry, sir. Seventy-two ships, zero-eight-nine by zero-four-three, port bow. ETA to Kliinat: four hours, thirty-six minutes."

Mori tapped her console, bringing up the intelligence report DiMarco had sent earlier. As the data scrolled by, she matched the sensor readings to the known Hasha ship classes. "Looks like we've got the whole menagerie," she said, her voice tight. "Nine Reaper-class capital ships, twenty-two Revenant battleships, eighteen Havoc cruisers, twenty-three Draugr destroyers, and... an unknown number of Banshee fighters."

The XO leaned in, studying the display. "DiMarco's intel was spot on. They really brought everything they had."

"And then some," Mori said, her eyes scanning the holographic fleet. "Let's hope our surprises are as effective as we planned."

She fired off a laser relay to Qaamat, Kliinat's moon. Hundreds of Devastator bombers, Dauntless fighters, and Vindicator interceptors waited in powered-down silence. The message read: "Enemy sighted. Stand by for orders. Remain under radio silence."

"Captain, Repulse confirms signatures match Hasha warships," Daniels said.

Mori slammed the General Quarters alarm. Galatea's sirens wailed as she shifted to war footing. Mori's lingering childhood fear—helpless days adrift in a lifeboat—morphed into steely resolve. She wasn't just any captain now. She commanded a Colonial Strike Carrier, ready to rain hell on her true enemy.

The holo showed eighty-four Hasha ships knifing toward Kliinat. One lagged near the jump point, as if hesitant.

"Skipper, intercept ETA down to seventy-six minutes. They're accelerating," Grant said.

"Helm, break orbit. Set intercept course," Mori said.

"Breaking orbit, intercept course set, aye."

Grant's fingers flew over his console. "Skipper, Hasha still accelerating. ETA now forty-four minutes."

The XO leaned in, frowning. "Hell. DiMarco told us they're fast."

"We'll cut them off, but they'll overshoot if they don't slow soon," Mori said, eyes locked on tactical.

"Hopefully, right to Earth," the XO said under his breath.

The Colonial Fleet tightened formation beyond Kliinat's moon, each ship taking its place in the defensive wall. Mori watched as the Hasha fleet finally began to decelerate, crawling into missile range. She pinged the moon, checking on their hidden assets. Still dark. Perfect.

Every second stretched out as the two fleets crept closer. The hum of systems and the distant chatter on comms filled the silence, but the real weight was in the waiting. For what felt like an eternity, nothing happened—just the slow, deliberate closing of space.

Grant finally broke it. "Power spike from the Reapers. Marked on BattleNet." He stiffened, double-checking. "Eddie confirms. It's the EMP signature."

"Brace for impact. We're about to find out if this will be a quick fight, or a good fight," Mori said. They were staring down the barrel with nowhere to run. She held her breath.

Darkness engulfed the bridge. A pulse thrummed through the grav generators, making Mori stumble. Holoscreens scrambled, ship systems stuttered, then steadied. As lights flickered back to life, Mori shook off the disorientation and tapped her console, which frustratingly rebooted.

"Engineering, report," she snapped into the comm.

The reply from engineering was immediate. "We're okay, Captain. The shields took the brunt, but we're down to eighty-two percent capacity."

Better than she'd dared hope, but had the others made it? Mori's eyes flicked across the holographic display of BattleNet, her gaze tracing the shifting icons that marked the fleet's status. A Colonial cruiser and two Union destroyers had gone dark. Someone—probably Antonov—had already scrambled destroyers to cover the wounded ships.

"Captain, we have entered the weapon's envelope," Talyn said.

Adrenaline surged through Mori. Years of loss, doubt, and sleepless nights crystallized into pure clarity. She clenched her fists, eyes blazing. "Fire everything we've got."

The Colonial Fleet unleashed hell. Missile batteries thundered to life with unrelenting Gorgon, Hydra, and Nyx missiles. Union ships launched Broadside, Scimitar, and Taipan missiles. The Colonial Strike Carriers led the assault, and Mori aimed to drive the spear deep into the enemy's heart.

"Talyn, lock Hades guns. Fire as soon as you've got a

solution," Mori said.

"As you command, Captain. Ten percent away from target acquisition," Talyn said.

Grant stiffened. "Skipper, incoming missile wave. Two thousand strong. Impact in two minutes."

The number and speed blindsided Mori. Two thousand? And faster than theirs? No way to dodge this punch, but Galatea was no helpless target. She'd face this storm head-on.

"Less than sixty seconds to impact," Grant updated.

Mori swiped sweat from her brow—battle heat, not fear. Her gaze swept the bridge, meeting determined eyes. They were forged in fire, Galatea their stalwart shield.

She leaned in, palm pressed to cool metal. "Don't let me down... not today," she said to the ship that had seen her through countless battles.

Grant locked eyes with Mori. "Ten seconds," he said.

"Brace for impact," Mori said, knuckles white on the console. The bridge's cacophony faded to white noise as she zeroed in on the incoming threat.

Missiles slammed into the fleet. BattleNet lit up, displaying the Hasha onslaught. The dreadnoughts shrugged it off with their heavy armor, but the smaller ships weren't so lucky. Three destroyers and two frigates took heavy hits, left limping. Union ships in the rear weathered it better.

Each impact rattled Galatea, jolting Mori to her core. Alarms screamed as holoscreens flickered with damage reports. Forward shields held, but a few missiles had slipped through her layered defenses, carving into Galatea's armor. Mori dispatched repair teams with quick-hardening plasteel to patch the wounds. Still, Galatea stood firm.

That's my girl, Mori thought, a flicker of pride burning in her chest.

Her eyes bored into the holoscreen, willing their missiles on. "Come on," she muttered. Seconds crawled by. The missiles streaked across the screen, then impact. But as the smoke cleared, she gripped the console tighter. The Hasha kept coming, unfazed.

"Mr. Grant, did we score any kills?" she asked, tension coiling in her gut.

"Negative, skipper," Grant said grim-faced. "Multiple impacts, but their numbers are unchanged."

The Hasha took one right in the jaw and didn't even flinch. She wondered what it would take to kill the bastards.

"Keep firing until I say otherwise," she said to Talyn. The battle was far from over, and Galatea was not yet done fighting.

A fresh salvo screamed towards the Hasha as the Colonial fleet maneuvered. This wasn't just trading blows but a calculated effort to grind the enemy down.

In the rear, CCV Perseus and her escorts bolstered the line with the Union remnants, ready to swat down any Hasha landing craft. Up front, Galatea and Artemis drove into the Hasha's heart while Cassiopeia's group climbed high, angling for a top-down strike.

"Captain, another power spike. Shit—it's gone. They're arming the energy beam," Grant said, professionalism be damned.

Mori's voice thundered across the bridge. "Break, break, break!" Each heartbeat as she waited turned into an eternity.

Space fractured as blinding beams lashed out from the Reaper-class ships. One ferocious beam sheared through the battleship UNS São Paulo, severing her bow and bisecting the light carrier Bucharest, turning both into infernos of spiraling flames and debris.

One beam tore through the colonial heavy cruiser Achilles, slicing off her starboard engine nacelles. Out of control, she slammed into a nearby destroyer. Both vanished in a colossal fireball.

A third strike gutted the Union cruiser Gothenburg, slicing open her hull. Atmosphere vented into space as the ship began her slow-motion demise, marked by a gruesome bloom of fire. A fourth beam cleaved the colonial destroyer Hector in two. The reactor detonated in a blinding inferno that sent shockwaves tearing through space. The explosion pummeled the nearby battleship UNS Valiant. She buckled under a hail of shrapnel, crippled and out of the fight. The surrounding ships were pummeled by the storm of shrapnel.

Mori's breath hitched as escape pods scattered across BattleNet—the shields had done jack against the energy beams. But fear didn't freeze her—it galvanized her.

"Talyn, keep hammering with the Hades guns. Minimum cycle time," she said.

"As you command, Captain," Talyn said.

Galatea and her sister ships unleashed a furious railgun salvo. The starboard Hades guns of Galatea labored under the strain, cycling at intervals to prevent a meltdown. The payoff came when a Revenant-class battleship, pummeled by Galatea, Artemis, and Cassiopeia's combined fury, crumpled and imploded.

Mori's fist pumped. "Take that," she muttered. It had taken the combined firepower of three carriers to bring down one ship—that wasn't lost on her—but by God, the Hasha weren't invincible. If only her rail guns were back online.

"What's the status of my starboard guns?" she asked.

"Online in less than a minute, Captain," Talyn said.

BattleNet flared as the Hasha slowed their approach to Kliinat. The Colonial Fleet seized the moment, unleashing a synchronized railgun barrage. Revenant battleships erupted into flames—three in rapid succession. Smaller Havoc and Draugr-class ships limped away, mauled.

The fleet held their missiles, knowing the Hasha's robust defenses. Instead, they traded furious railgun salvos, like the naval battles of old.

The XO pointed to a fresh development on the BattleNet display. "Looks like DiMarco grew tired of waiting."

Mori watched as Repulse slid into formation with the colonial carriers. DiMarco's rail guns shredded two Hasha destroyers, then, in concert with Artemis, they focused fire on a Reaper. As the capital ship disintegrated, Banshee fighters spilled from its dying hull.

The XO exhaled a long breath. "About time we took down one of their heavy hitters. I was beginning to worry. We need to keep those guns firing."

"That is precisely my plan, XO," Mori said.

Daniels spun around. "Captain, incoming transmission. It's the Hasha."

"They're not surrendering, are they?" Mori said. "Main screen. Now."

"This should be good," the XO said, leaning in.

The holoscreen flickered to life, revealing the alien bridge. Pulsating tendrils cast an eerie glow behind three Hasha figures. Their elongated claws and silver armor with glowing blue visors radiated cold menace. Energy rippled across their bridge, adding to the otherworldly effect.

The Hasha's voice, distorted and amplified by the ship's speakers, filled the CIC. "Surrender, human fleet. We claim this system for the Hasha Hierarchy. You have twenty seconds to comply."

Mori's jaw clenched. Who did these bastards think they were? No one asked her to surrender her ship. No one.

"What's even the point of that? Tell them to go frack themselves and cut off the transmission," the XO said.

"Open a channel," Mori said. "Send this. Verbatim: Go frack yourself."

"With pleasure, Captain," Daniels said, flashing a grin.

Grant leaned forward. "Skipper, another missile wave incoming at 300 klicks per second. Enemy fighters launched too. ETA three minutes for the fighters."

Mori's mind raced. Those missiles were faster than—

The thought shattered as Galatea reeled under a barrage of impacts. Explosions tore through the ship, hurling crew like rag dolls. Lights died, leaving only blood-red emergency lighting. Inertial dampeners failed, stomachs lurching as gravity shifted. Grant's face met his console with a sickening crunch. Daniels lay still, blood pooling under her head.

Mori's own meeting with the deck was far from gentle. She pushed up with a grunt, her right shoulder screaming in protest.

She gritted her teeth against the pain. One thought dominated: Get up. Fight my ship.

The bridge was chaotic, filled with groans and cries. She forced herself upright, agony be damned. Her eyes locked on Grant's still form, his dark curls matted with blood. The kid who'd stayed up three nights straight reprogramming the tactical simulations just to prove a point, always with that crooked grin—

The XO rushed to her side, steadying her. "Captain, are you okay?" he asked.

"I'm fine," she said, tearing her gaze from Grant's body. Fine was light-years away, but the battle raged on.

As practical as ever, the XO assessed Mori's injury with clinical detachment. "Dislocated shoulder. I can pop it back now, or you can limp to MedBay."

"Do it here," Mori said, bracing herself against the console, breath coming in quick gasps.

"Lean forward, let your arm hang. This'll hurt like hell," the XO warned.

Mori complied. In one swift motion, the XO grabbed her wrist and—

White-hot agony exploded through her shoulder. A raw cry tore from her lips as the joint slammed back into place. "Son of a—!"

The XO wasted no time, snatching a ReGen Shot from the emergency kit on the wall and slamming it into the corrected joint. "This will dull the pain, but it'll take time to repair any tendon damage."

"Thanks," Mori said, feeling the edge fade. She keyed her neural link. "Orderlies and fresh crew to the bridge, now."

She surveyed the carnage, heart sinking. Talyn knelt by Grant, gently closing his sightless eyes. The two had grown close—she'd caught them playing chess in the mess hall countless times. More than that: Grant had been the first to really welcome Talyn, to treat him as more than just "the alien officer." He'd dragged Talyn to movie nights, insisted on celebrating both Human and Arcturian holidays together.

The young tactical officer had shown such promise. More than that—he'd been part of her family, like all of them were. She'd write to Grant's mother about her son's courage, about the friend who grieved him in an alien tongue. But not now. Now, she had to keep the rest of her crew alive. Blood smeared the deck as medics scrambled, the ship still shuddering under fire.

The XO took over tactical as the bridge swarmed with techs and medics evacuating casualties. "It's a mess, but I've got it," he said, fingers flying over the displays. "Not too different from Axios—that's where I cut my teeth."

Mori straightened. "XO, tell me we still have a fleet."

"Three destroyers are offline, one Union battleship is gone, and the cruiser Thalia is a burning wreck," the XO said. "Most ships report some kind of damage or another. Without the Vulcans, it would have been much worse."

"Captain," the engineering officer said through her comm. "The inertial dampeners are shot, running at half strength. We've got injuries in the aft decks. It's ugly back there."

Mori's gut twisted with each report. Galatea was reeling, like a boxer on rubber legs.

As if on cue, the XO announced the arrival of the Hasha swarm fighters—ominous spheres studded with spikes. "And here come the Banshees."

Galatea's defenses sprang into action, spitting fire at the agile fighters. But the AI targeting systems struggled against their agility, scoring only sporadic hits. Mori gripped the console, knuckles white, as she watched the display.

Thwarted by colonial shields, two Banshees broke formation. They slammed into the cruiser UNS Nairobi, embedding themselves before detonating. The impact was devastating, vomiting crew and debris into space as the cruiser began a slow, sickening spin.

Silence choked the CIC until the XO spoke. "The Nairobi's gyros are shot. If they don't correct that spin, she's going to tear herself apart. Seen it before on Nilus—we were scraping bodies off the deck for days."

Mori winced, not just from the grim image but also from a stab of pain in her shoulder. She zoomed in on the stricken Nairobi. "They need to launch those escape pods now."

As Galatea's Vulcan turrets blazed, another colonial

destroyer fell to a trio of Banshees. "There goes Electra. Pods are launching," the XO said.

Mori's frown deepened as she assessed their predicament. The Hasha's kamikaze tactics were brutally effective—disturbingly so. But as Union reserve fighters scrambled, a tiny ember of hope flickered in her chest.

The XO, noting the same development, turned to her. "That's guts, right there. They know they don't have a cat's chance in hell, and still they launch. That takes stones."

"They launched sooner than we'd hoped, but they'll draw the fighters away from the fleet. We need to make sure their sacrifice is not in vain." Mori turned to the new comms officer. "Comms, send the fighters a message: 'Good hunting. Godspeed.'"

"Aye, Captain."

"Talyn, give our pilots some cover. Get a message to the carrier group to focus on those Banshees," Mori said.

"Acknowledged. Eddie recalibrated the laser turrets—we have a lock. Vulcan guns are online with new parameters," Talyn said.

Galatea's rail guns tore apart two Draugr destroyers even while under missile fire. Colonial point-defenses had struggled against the nimble fighters, but after the AI recalibrated, Argus laser turrets and Vulcans swatted them from space. Banshees carved through Hornets and Tornadoes, but the pilots' forced them to break their attack runs wide. Still, two more ships died in the onslaught—Hesperus and Yorktown, vanishing in silent explosions that lit up tactical like new stars.

The XO rubbed his scalp. "Power surge from the Hasha. They're charging that damn beam weapon again."

Alarms blared as trajectory predictions flashed across screens. "Hard to port! All power to thrusters!" Mori said as Galatea rolled and veered, sliding past the beam that would've sliced her in two.

The fleet scattered in frantic evasion as the second wave of deadly energy lanced through space. Once-orderly formations dissolved into chaos. Beams that had found easy marks now seared past, leaving trails of ionized gas glowing in the void.

Then, disaster struck. A beam sliced Artemis from starboard bow to port quarter. Debris erupted into space as the ship's engines detonated in a massive explosion that flung Artemis out of the battle line and ripped her apart.

Mori leaped up, harness clattering to the deck. No, not like this...

The comms officer's voice broke through the stunned silence. "Captain, Artemis is launching escape pods. The bridge... Captain Biyombo and the crew, they're gone."

Barry Biyombo. Her mentor. Second father. Gone. Mori stared at the tactical display where Artemis had been. "We'll get them for this."

"Bastards," the XO growled, slamming his fist on the console.

Mori's hands stilled on the console, drawing a slow breath. Mourning would have to wait. She straightened, then turned back to tactical. The Hasha were past Qaamat. Good. "XO, confirm the enemy fleet's speed and bearing."

"Zero-eight-nine by zero-four-three, starboard bow, just past

Qaamat." The XO snorted. "They've left their asses hanging out. Our ground AA in Kliinat's engaged. Hasha have touched down in Naadan."

Naadan, where Skip and the two-five held the line. Give 'em hell, Skip.

"Engineering, she said into her comm. Get those dampeners stabilized. Do whatever it takes."

"On it, Captain."

"CAG, send the command. Execute Foxtail," Mori said.

"Yes, ma'am."

Mori squared her shoulders, eyes hard as steel. "Helm, flank speed."

Chapter 49

Council of 64 Headquarters, Kliinat

Tau Ceti System

December 9, 2681

Carson huddled behind a crumbling brick wall, bullets whizzing past close enough to make him question his life choices. Again. He was getting real tired of having philosophical debates with incoming fire. Dust and stone chips flew as rounds chewed the cover to pieces. In under an hour, Hasha hand-held mass drivers had downed two hundred Marines. Those coil guns came as a nasty surprise—the kind that punched through Marine armor like it was made of tissue paper. New gear requisition forms were definitely in someone's future, assuming anyone was left to file them.

The Hasha dropped from their transports in waves, their armor glinting as they twisted mid-fall to land in perfect fighting stances. No parachutes, no jump jets—just gravity-defying drops that shouldn't have been possible. The courtyard transformed into a killing field of broken concrete and spent casings, where cover lasted only until the next mass driver round found it. Despite their bulky, segmented armor, the Hasha moved with a sort of horrifying grace. Their silvery suits and faceless helmets gave them an otherworldly dread and added a heavy dose of "nightmare" to their appearance.

The Aether AA batteries had given them a hearty welcome, and knocked down several transports. That's when the troopers decided to just jump from the damned things.

As Hasha after Hasha thudded down, the Marines learned one thing fast: they might be gravity-proof, but they weren't lead-proof. Carson discovered Hasha blood was green, acidic, and a hell of an addition to his day. Klii scouts with thermal knives carved a gory path from Citadel to gates, finding a sweet spot in Hasha air hoses. One quick slice, down they went.

After retaking the Citadel—barely—the Marines were boxed in. If the Hasha decided to redecorate from orbit, it was game over. Carson swapped mags on his M45, feeling a round singe his shoulder plate. Fifth "too close" today. How many of those did he have left?

The battle teetered on the edge of disaster as Hasha waves hammered the wall of defenders, who clung to their ground with little more than stubbornness. Cerberus mortars lit up the sky, their plasma shells casting weird shadows as they arced down to meet the drones. Each explosion painted the courtyard in strobing blues and oranges. The last Centaur tank mowed down a Hasha platoon before a tripod-mounted mass-driver tore it to shreds. Carson had pulled every trick he knew. Now, it was down to guts and grit.

Beside him, Williams kept a running tally. "That's forty-three. Ooh, forty-four."

Carson grinned despite the knot in his gut. "Nobody likes a show-off, Williams."

"It's not showing off if it's—"

The crack of a high-velocity round cut her off. It slammed into her chest plate with a sickening thud. Carson's heart stopped as she staggered back, blood spraying across her visor.

He lunged for her, hands shaking as he ripped away the shattered armor. It was bad. Real bad. Blood soaked her uniform, spreading fast. His fingers slipped on a ReGen Shot; he jammed it in with more desperation than skill.

"Stay with me, Williams," Carson said, trying to keep his hands steady as he activated his comm. "Corpsman, to my position, STAT!"

Williams' eyes locked onto his. Through blood and pain, she managed a ghost of a smile. "Forty-five... I think," she whispered, each word no more than a breath.

"Hang on, Lizzy. Help's coming." Carson ripped her shirt open. She nodded weakly, breaths shallow, as he pressed down on the wound. The battle raged, but his world narrowed to the Marine bleeding out in front of him. He slapped on a DermaGel patch, praying it would hold.

As the medics arrived, Carson stood up, stepping back to let them work. His throat tightened as they loaded her onto a stretcher. Rodriguez appeared beside him, face ashen.

"This wasn't supposed to happen, not to her," he said, more

to himself. "She always talked about going back to that lake, you know?"

Carson nodded, jaw clenched. "I know." He balled his fists, her blood alien against his armor. "But it's not over yet, Frankie." As the medics prepped to move, Carson unclipped Williams' dog tag. He handed it to Rodriguez. "Keep it safe for her."

Rodriguez clutched the tag, nodding.

"Now," Carson said, steel in his voice, "let's give those medics some breathing room."

"Yes, sir," Rodriguez said, chambering a round.

Back at the wall, Carson unleashed a fierce burst of automatic fire. Two Hasha dropped in quick succession. His rifle made its point: definitely not bulletproof. He caught another in his sights and fired. The shot missed armor but nicked the air hose. The trooper spun, frantic to seal the leak. Panic, it turned out, was a universal language. Carson, fluent in it, put two more rounds in the bastard before ducking back to cover.

Carson reloaded, taking stock of their dwindling supplies. Armor-piercing rounds—their only real bite against Hasha armor—were running low, with most Marines down to their last magazine or two. Yet the enemy kept coming, unfazed by their losses.

He surveyed the hellscape before him. Fallen bodies and brutal combat as far as the eye could see. The Hasha advance was relentless, using their own dead as stepping stones in their crazed push to break through.

Marines pressed against the defensive wall, using blast craters and fallen chunks of concrete as makeshift gun rests for their M45s. The air echoed with the sharper notes of Mako grenades and the steady pop of Spartan Arms handguns. The Hasha countered with coil guns and plasma grenades, supported by the ominous shadows of their landing ships. Aether batteries and ballsy Griffin pilots fought tooth and nail to keep more troops from dropping in.

A young Klii Marine from Third Platoon crumpled beside Carson. Without thinking, he grabbed the kid and hauled him behind a fortified wall. The slug was buried in the Marine's shoulder—nasty, but not fatal.

Carson sent another plea for medical help into his comm. "Need a medic front gate, left side. Ping my position."

The medics answered, though not with the cavalry charge he'd hoped for. "Patch him up with ReGen Shots and hold tight, Captain. We're underwater here but will send someone when we can."

Biting back a cascade of choice words, Carson bit out a terse, "Copy that." He looked down at the wounded Marine. "You hear that, Corporal? Just a little scratch. You'll be bragging about this in the mess by next week."

The Klii Marine grinned through the pain. "Appreciated, Sir. But I think we have different ideas about what counts as 'little'."

"Don't worry," Carson promised, jabbing in the ReGen Shot. "You'll be back to dodging bullets in no time."

Medics were stretched thin everywhere, trying to patch up wounds that defied description. Those mass driver slugs weren't just lethal; they were catastrophic, making "exit wound" an understatement.

This bloodbath surpassed even the bloody days of Kliinat's liberation. Carson's own unit was in tatters. Lieutenant Akitani was out cold in the med bay, one arm lighter. A Klii Marine had gone out with a bang, literally, taking a cluster of Hasha down with a grenade clutched to his chest during the first chaotic moments of battle.

Gunny, sporting a head wound that was doing its best to claim her left eye, manned a Hermes that never stopped firing. Head wrapped in whatever wasn't already blood-soaked, she mowed down any Hasha that dared get close.

The Marines kept fighting despite mounting casualties and dwindling odds. Shouts for ammo, backup, and medics pierced the clamor. And the battle was far from over.

Carson's eyes snapped skyward. A flurry of missiles from the Aether batteries drew lines of fire across the clouds. Two heavy Hasha transports, loaded with reinforcements, pressed forward. Three Griffins swooped in, their gun barrels roaring. One Griffin burst into flames under a Hasha missile, while another danced away and returned fire. Still, the Hasha advance continued.

Suddenly, a brilliant orange streak—a Nyx missile—screamed down from orbit. It vaporized one transport in a ground-shaking blast. A second Nyx took out the last ship, but not before it dumped its payload. Hundreds more Hasha troopers began their descent.

Carson nodded, watching them disappear to safety. He checked his sidearm—old reliable might see some action today. Back in position, he tallied his ammo. Two mags left for the M45. Not ideal. He switched to single-shot, found a sniper's perch on a crate, and zeroed in. The Hasha were so close that he started aiming for the blue lights on their helmets. Inhale, aim, exhale, squeeze.

A shrill whistle ended in a crash as a Hasha drone slammed into his cover. Carson flew into the sandbags. His neural interface scattered his vision into double images. Each heartbeat sent lightning through his skull, and the taste of copper filled his mouth. He shook it off just in time to see another Marine take his spot—and catch a slug to the head.

Oh, c'mon, not again, he thought. A high-pitched whine filled his ears, the taste of blood sharp on his tongue. Carson's legs argued with his brain about which way was up, the ringing in his ears making both sides lose the debate. That's when Rodriguez and a ragged Klii lieutenant dropped beside him.

"How you holding up, Skip? Can you stand? How many fingers?" Rodriguez asked, holding up a hand.

"Shut up and help me up," Carson said, catching his breath.

Rodriguez grabbed one arm, Maalek the other, hauling him to his feet with a joint effort.

Carson brushed off his armor and was about to reassess the front line when an unnatural quiet fell over the battlefield, sinking his heart. He spun around to see every Marine staring, dumbfounded, at their silent, dead weapons. They tapped and prodded in vain. The Aether batteries went silent. A Griffin spiraled earthward in the distance. Even the Hasha's relentless mass drivers had stilled, their drones dropping like stones.

And then, the clincher—Carson tapped his visor, frowning as the tactical overlay flickered and died.

"Well, that's not good," Carson muttered. The sudden silence hit like a physical blow, making his ears ring. After hours of gunfire and explosions, hearing his own breathing was somehow worse than the combat noise. He picked his way to the fortified wall, boots crunching on spent cartridges and broken concrete. From his perch, Carson surveyed the battlefield's sudden paralysis. Both sides stood watching each other, weapons raised but silent, as if neither could quite believe the fight had just... stopped. Hasha soldiers across the way stood hesitant, their alien voices carrying in the quiet. Once crackling blue, their portable shields sputtered and died, leaving them as exposed as everyone else.

Who the hell turned off the lights? He wondered.

Maalek sidled up next to him. "They are pulling back, and we share the same predicament. Do you know what is going on?"

Carson let out a sigh as he wrestled with his rifle, the mechanism jammed, refusing to cycle a round. "Not a damn clue." He scanned his Marines, their armor scarred and streaked with battle's grime. Some used the lull to gulp warm water from dusty canteens, hands shaking from adrenaline crash. Others slid down walls, leaving smears on concrete as they tried to catch their breath. They tapped dead triggers and cycled empty chambers, their high-tech rifles reduced to expensive clubs. The ammo counter displays flickered once and died.

"Perfect time for a care package from the fleet," Rodriguez quipped. "Maybe toss in some fresh Marines while they're at it."

"My neural's flickering. Maybe it's just a glitch," Carson said, hoping for some miracle.

Maalek grimaced. "If the Hasha attack us now, ammo or not, it would be a very short fight. I doubt we would last but a few minutes."

Gunny joined their huddle, reeking of nitric oxide. Her tank top clung to her under chest armor—sleeveless, for some godforsaken reason. She adjusted her bloodied head bandage, hefting the Hermes. "You guys doing a powwow without me?" she said, grunting as she adjusted the machine gun to a comfortable position.

Rodriguez turned toward her. "Just talking 'bout the direness of this here situation."

"We're not getting out of this one alive, are we?" she asked.

"Well, I might," Rodriguez squeaked. He flipped up his visor and scratched his nose. "You know, we could just charge them. Take 'em by surprise while they're befuddled."

Gunny rolled her eyes. "Your helmet's on too tight, Rodriguez."

Maalek's hand found Gunny's shoulder. "Is it such a terrible idea, Gunny? Our numbers are dwindling; theirs are growing. We are low on ammunition and mortars. Our wounded crowd the halls, and the fleet cannot resupply us. My neural is also rebooting, and our weapons may soon work again. We must seize this sliver of opportunity the Goddess has granted us. It is time to ride into the jaws of death and meet the enemy head-on."

Carson remained silent, mulling it over. They never tried a frontal assault because they were too busy dodging bullets, not charging into them. But what if the Hasha couldn't handle a surprise? No higher command to call for advice—Colonel Patel was gone, and the command chain with him.

Screw it.

He looked around at his makeshift council of war. Carson had little faith in divine intervention, but as last stands went, this was a hell of a time for the gods to show their hand.

"Maybe it's time to do something unexpected. If our guns come back online, and theirs don't..." He met Maalek's eyes. "Boldly we shall ride, and well."

Gunny dropped the Hermes and slung her M45. "Right beside you, sir."

Carson nodded. "Pass the word, Gunny; we're gonna form up and let these Hasha know they picked a fight with the wrong Marines."

Maalek put a hand on Carson's shoulder. "There's something I must do first," he said. Carson looked at him with a puzzled expression.

Stepping into the courtyard's center, Maalek raised his fist. All eyes turned to him. "My name is Maalek ur Aal ur Jheet vas Daalamas. Today, I cross the Great Sea to take my place at the great council fire." He clicked his thermal bayonet into place, then drew a semicircle in the dirt.

Andaeer launched himself over the sandbags in a single fluid motion, thermal blade already glowing in his grip. "My name is Andaeer ur Ihm ur Haan vas Daalamas. Today, I cross the Great Sea to join the great council fire."

The other Klii Marines joined in, each drawing semicircles before them. Carson watched the Klii Marines draw their circles with reverence. Something about their calm acceptance, their unity in the face of death, made him stand straighter, grip his weapon tighter.

"These," Maalek said as he rejoined Carson, "are the words of our forebears. It means we are ready to face death, and we ask them to hold our places for the feast of fallen warriors."

"And the circle?"

"For the choosers of the slain, to collect our souls."

Marines traded glances, the kind that passed between people who'd already seen too many friends die today. Carson clasped Maalek's hand, then pulled him into a fierce embrace.

If this is to be our end, then we shall make sure it's worthy of remembrance, he mused.

Carson's mouth was dry as sand, but his voice came out steady. Command voice. The kind that didn't betray how his stomach was doing acrobatics. "I am Matthew Carson, son of Samuel Carson, son of Alexandria. Today, I cross the Great Sea to take my place on the great council fire." He etched a circle in the dirt.

"Two-Five, retreat?" he called.

"Hell," came the unified reply.

"Retreat!?" Carson bellowed.

"HELL!" The Marines roared.

"Marines, fix bayonets!"

Blades clicked into place across the compound.

"Form lines, form lines!" Gunny shouted.

They lined up at the gates, Klii warriors raising rifles with fierce cheers. Carson strode to the front, the weight of command feeling oddly right. Maalek on his left, Gunny on his right. Rodriguez, Sousa, Andaeer, and Echo Company stood behind.

Carson met Maalek's eyes. "Half a league, half a league onward."

"Into the mouth of Hell, my friend," Maalek said.

Carson raised his arm. "Charge!"

Their boots thundered as they crashed into the Hasha lines.

Chapter 50

Jammer sat in his Dauntless' darkened cockpit, the void outside a vacuum of sound compared to Galatea's usual bustling launch tubes. The silence was thick—he could hear every breath, every heartbeat, even the odd creak of the ship settling. His fighter was in stealth mode, radio silent. Only the passive scanner and shortwave receivers were on, but they'd been dead for the past four hours. Engines were cold, but he knew they'd roar to life in five if needed. He wasn't sweating that. Yet.

Scanning the darkness, he picked out Galatea's space wing. Twenty-four squadrons parked beside him, hiding on Kliinat's moon, Qaamat. 192 ships, including forty-eight Devastator bombers and twenty-four Vindicator interceptors, all coiled like predators ready to pounce. Artemis, Cassiopeia, and Perseus' wings flanked them. Hundreds of fighters packed tight enough to reach out and touch, all launching in near-darkness. He'd seen the Air Boss's launch plan three times, but the gaps between ships still looked impossibly small on the display. His thoughts drifted to the planet below, where Griffins provided close air support to the Marines and Klii scouts preparing for a ground assault. The intel on Hasha spaceborne fighters was solid, but they had next to nothing on their ground troops. His fingers drummed against the nav screen showing Carson's landing zone—another friend he might not see again.

Jammer fished out a picture of Two Bit from his pocket. Taken on Corinth, the morning after the Rock Bottom brawl, she looked happy, carefree. Her hair was in a ponytail, and she wore her favorite Ramjets shirt. He ran a thumb over Two Bit's grinning face, her captured laughter making the cockpit feel a little less empty. He tucked it into a console seam next to his sister's. Two Bit would've loved this plan but not the wait—she'd probably have broken radio silence by now.

He glanced starboard at his new wingman—Racetrack, a nugget fresh from Athens. The kid was a natural, but he didn't like how green she was. With Hasha fighters in the mix, he needed someone he could trust when everything went to hell. Maybe he was overthinking it. He'd seen her scores and done a few runs with her; she was good, and they needed every pilot they could get in a Dauntless.

His finger hovered over Lunchbox's shortwave frequency, but thought better of it. The silence pressed in, broken only by his own breathing and the occasional creak of his helmet against the headrest. His neural feed was tuned to a Titan dock channel, showing the fleet orbiting in the distance. The Colonial carriers loomed massive against the stars, their war-grey hulls catching flecks of distant sunlight. Even from here, their gun batteries bristled with promise of retribution. The Hasha had picked a fight with the wrong humans, and they were about to learn that the hard way.

A red blip popped up on his scanner, then two, then three. Each heartbeat thudded against his ribs as red dots multiplied across his scanner, the rhythmic pulse drowning out even the hum of his cockpit systems. A series of clicks crackled over the shortwave, pilots acknowledging the incoming threat. The muscles across his shoulders unwound as he returned the signal. His next breath came easier, steadier, as the familiar call-and-response of combat communications grounded him. His screen blinked with a new text: Enemy sighted. Stand by for orders. Remain under radio silence. The Hasha had arrived. Jammer leaned back, taking a deep breath. His fingers tapped an irregular rhythm on the control stick, pausing only to recheck his weapons systems for the third time in as many minutes. Any moment now—the call would come.

Jammer tracked the battle through the passive scanners and shortwave receiver. When the EMP weapon failed to breach colonial shields, he couldn't help but pump his fist. But the Hasha gained ground soon after, and without fighters, the carriers were vulnerable against the smaller Banshees. He could only guess at the power of the weapon slicing through ships like paper. If they didn't move soon, there might not be a carrier left to return to. Then again, he had a plan for that.

His mind drifted not to fear of the end but to the importance of his mission. As one of the top pilots, he was one of the few who could get close to the Hasha capital ship.

It had been an easy call, not about glory or survival, but about making a difference. His friends' lives hadn't been lost in vain, and his wouldn't be either. This mission could save countless others from the same fate.

The loss of Artemis came close to breaking radio silence as her pilots funneled their shock, acceptance, and seething fury into the text chat. Jammer's fingers drummed the console, minutes stretching into forever as he waited for the lift-off order. A bead of sweat trickled down his temple, mixing with the cool cockpit air. He almost laughed—here he was, the pilot chosen to thread through a capital ship's defenses with a payload that could vaporize them both, and his leg wouldn't stop bouncing with impatience. He didn't have long to wait. The message he'd been expecting popped up.

Execute Foxtail.

The random fidgeting of his hands ceased as he wrapped them around the controls, grip firm but not white-knuckled. Each breath came slower, deeper. Jammer tightened his harness straps, each pull grounding him deeper into the moment. As he fired up his fighter, the familiar sound of the Dauntless waking wrapped around him, as comforting as a warm blanket on a cold night. The tension bled from his shoulders as the Dauntless' systems came online one by one, their familiar startup sequence as reassuring as a well-worn flight suit. He patted the console where his special payload's status glowed green. If this was his last dance in a Dauntless, at least it would be one hell of a finale. Around him, canopies lit up and engines flared as colonial fighters sprang to life. They took off in pairs, a well-rehearsed dance, forming into squadrons. His neural pinged when his turn came.

"Saber Leader Dauntless two-two-one. Go."

He responded with a radio squawk. Using the reaction control system, he lifted off the moon and guided his fighter out of Qaamat's weak orbit. His body tensed for Galatea's familiar catapult kick, but found only the gentle push of Qaamat's weak gravity. No rattling teeth, no straining metal—just a quiet drift into the black.

Once spaceborne, he goosed the throttle and formed up behind VF-20. His squad mates fell in line. They pulled away from the moon at a steady clip, melding into a massive attack formation as Devastators, Dauntless, and Vindicators from the Colonial Fleet flexed their muscles. Artemis' pilots, in particular, had a score to settle and were out for blood. By the battle order, Artemis' birds led the charge, set to hit the Hasha first.

Seven hundred forty fighters and bombers flipped on their scanners, going active. Immediate pings bounced back from Hasha ships, but Colonial fighters locked onto targets, too. The air boss's message crackled in every pilot's ear.

"Tango! Tango! Tango!"

Jammer shoved the throttle to max, his Dauntless leaping toward the Hasha fleet. Reaper One, his prey, blinked on his console. His hands moved through the weapon arming sequence without hesitation, muscle memory taking over as Reaper One grew larger in his sights—he had a special gift for that son of a bitch. All he had to do was survive a gauntlet of cannon fire, laser turrets, and Banshees. He spared a glance at

Two Bit's picture.

One hundred thousand kilometers out.

The Dauntless slammed him back as refined tritium flooded the afterburners, rocketing him forward. His throttle stick vibrated, the force pressing him into the seat as he sprinted through space. Thrusters of fighters and bombers ahead lit up the murky darkness, casting brief halos. His radio crackled with his squad mates' excited chatter.

"Let's go!"

"We're gonna get those assholes for Artemis."

"Weapons hot; it's showtime!"

Fifty thousand kilometers.

His scanner highlighted a squad of Banshees vectoring to intercept. The Banshees hung back in perfect defensive positions, protecting their capital ships even as they launched their main assault. Someone in their command knew exactly what they were doing. All of Saber Squadron flew ahead, forming a protective shield. He was the linchpin in this attack, the fighter they couldn't afford to lose. He watched his squadron take another hit meant for him, their shields flaring orange against the void. Their comm chatter remained steady, professional—making it worse.

Twenty-five thousand kilometers.

He flicked the missile select switch, arming his payload. The missile outline lit up on his holoscreen. Systems green across the board.

Ten thousand kilometers.

The first Hasha anti-ship missiles hit their formation, taking out dozens of fighters in a fiery blaze. The Colonial formation tightened around the gaps where their squad mates had been, maintaining spacing and speed as if they'd drilled for this exact moment. His console beeped a warning—missile lock. He threw his Dauntless into a spin and popped countermeasures. The missile flew past, recalibrated, and locked on again. These Hasha ship killers were smaller and nimbler than Colonial Ballistas or Union Taipans. Just as the missile closed in, Lunchbox swung her fighter between him and the threat. It locked onto her and exploded, tearing her fighter apart.

She ejected, her voice crackling through his comm. "Not today, babe. We got you."

"Thank you, Lunchbox. You saved my ass," Jammer said.

"Don't forget to come pick me up on the way out."

"You got it."

One thousand kilometers.

Light blips flickered in the distance—explosions from missile hits and dying ships. Debris from shattered fighters pinged off his canopy as capital ships traded fire around him, their massive weapons turning space into a killing field. The command came—weapons free. He cleared his guns with a short, satisfying burst—just in case. Colonial pilots delivered a wall of missiles, their synchronized launch trails painting vengeful streaks across space. Devastator bombers, shielded by Dauntless squads, paired up and launched Helios hull busters at the capital ships. Explosions tore through multiple Hasha vessels.

One hundred kilometers.

Almost there. His console beeped, signaling a lock on the capital ship.

"This one's for you, Two Bit."

He kept a tight bead on his target. A salvo of chain shot from Reaper One flashed past him. He dove and twisted right, but the rounds struck Alphabet instead. The Dauntless disintegrated in a fiery bloom. He couldn't see if Alphabet had ejected.

"Alphabet, Saber Leader. What's your status?" Jammer said into the comm.

Alphabet's voice was harried. "Saber Leader, Alphabet. Yeah, that was pucker time, but I punched out. Give 'em hell."

"Roger that."

A pair of Banshees locked onto him. Racetrack and Packrat swooped in, engaging them and drawing them off. The Banshees were fast—too damn fast. The Dauntless pilots struggled to keep them in their sights, their missile targeting systems struggling to lock. Snowball and Bouncer teamed up on a Banshee and, with the wider field of fire from two fighters, nailed the bastard. They wasted no time passing that tactic to the other pilots.

Ten kilometers.

Go time. The capital ship loomed ahead, point defense turrets tracking colonial fighters. Blue lights rippled along its grotesque, lumpy hull. A tangle of long cables trailed beneath it like tendrils. Sensors, antennas—who cared. It was one ugly mother. He decelerated, making sure he wouldn't overshoot, and then the AI matched his target's speed. His stomach flipped as the inertial dampeners fought the sudden momentum loss and his reverse thrusters screamed in protest.

One kilometer.

Point defense rounds hammered his fighter, but he didn't flinch. His shield flared with bright orange sparks but held firm. They'd need to do better than that to take down a Dauntless.

He clicked the safeties off and said his challenge code. Eddie authenticated from Galatea. His launch light went green. Showtime.

"Jammer, Fox Zero."

He fired his single missile. Jamming the stick left, he punched the afterburners. Behind him, his squad mates launched a salvo of Phalanx ARMs as insurance. He shot a message back to Galatea.

The Hasha point defenses were too close to engage, and his squad mates kept them busy. A blinding flash engulfed the capital ship as the antimatter missile tore through its core, setting off a chain reaction that shattered the vessel from within. The blast sent shockwaves through space, ripping the ship apart in a burst of energy. Jammer's Dauntless jolted, the impact slamming him against his harness.

The fighter convulsed, rattling Jammer in the cockpit as it spiraled out of control. Alarms blared, lights flickered, and for a moment, all he saw was a chaotic blur. He wrestled with the stick, knuckles white, fighting to regain control. With quick thinking, he stuffed the pictures back in his pocket. Maybe not today, after all.

One wing sheared off, the canopy ripped away, and smoke billowed from his console. His port engine rattled loose, the whole fighter shaking itself apart. He punched out. Floating in space, he watched chunks of Reaper One rain past him like deadly meteors, each piece of wreckage confirming what the explosion had promised. Mission accomplished.

Chapter 51

CIC, CCV Galatea

Tau Ceti System

December 9, 2681

Mori stared at the BattleNet display. Each blip was a fighter, a life, all banking on her plan. Next to her, the comms officer's finger hovered over a button, tension written all over her.

"Ma'am, message from Saber Leader, Dauntless two-two-one: 'Committed Executed Sortie.'"

"Send the command, Ensign," Mori said. She counted down in her head: three, two, one...

The bridge lights flickered, Galatea's steady hum replaced by fading beeps and static. The holoscreens distorted, and then everything snapped back to normal. Five seconds of heart-stopping tech terror. Mori's eyes locked on BattleNet. One

Hasha capital ship blip vanished.

The XO, as expressive as a brick most days, jumped from his chair, punching the air. "My God... they did it. Splash one capital ship, Captain. I take back every crummy thing I've said about fighter jockeys."

The XO celebrating? That was new.

After she'd given the Foxtail code, hundreds of fighters had launched from Qaamat, engines roaring in sync. Their job: hit the Hasha from behind and escort a gutsy Dauntless pilot who'd volunteered for a suicide run—flying within spitting distance of a Reaper capital ship to deliver a very personal package, an Atlas missile armed with an antimatter warhead. BattleNet lit up as dozens of dots blinked out under Hasha fire. Yet, they flew on.

After meeting with DiMarco, Mori had cooked up a plan. She and Eddie had pulled an all-nighter refining their model, culminating in a pitch to Antonov: an Atlas missile with a payload Eddie had tuned to a hair, designed to disrupt the enemy's shield harmonics on detonation. If it worked, the Hasha fleet would be sitting ducks. And if that failed to crack their shields, the antimatter warhead was her way of, as Anderson put it, blowing some shit up. Of course, there was a catch — their fighters and ships risked losing shields and facing total blackouts. But Mori had an ace up her sleeve—adjusting the fleet's shield harmonics to the millisecond. The wild card was whatever effect the blast might have on the planet below.

Mori spun her ring. One second. Two seconds. Three—

The XO swiveled in his chair, a grin tugging at his mouth. "Captain, I'm not reading shield signatures from the Hasha fleet."

A second later, a command flashed bright and urgent on her holoscreen: "Execute Star Shatter."

Let's see how the Hasha like our missiles now.

"Talyn, train the Gorgon and Hydra batteries on the capital ships. Give them hell," she said.

The Colonial Fleet's missile batteries roared as one. Space around the Hasha carriers erupted in a blaze of fire and metal, transforming formidable vessels into expanding clouds of debris. The Union fleet unleashed their own fury, firing volleys of Taipan missiles and Broadside torpedoes that hammered the defenseless Hasha ships. Within minutes, the once-threatening enemy fleet became a scattered junkyard. Yet, the surviving Hasha ships fought back with the desperation of cornered beasts.

Just as the bridge crew started to breathe easier, the XO's sharp call snapped everyone back to attention. "Captain, we've got six Banshees making a beeline for us. Those buggers aim to slam into us and pull their little suicide stunt."

Six Banshees, six chances to tear Galatea apart. "Talyn, concentrate point defenses on those ships." This battle was still hers to win, and Galatea wasn't going down without a fight.

"Yes, Captain. They target the weaker shields aft. Our fighters remain at some distance for effective defense," Talyn said.

"Divert power to the aft shields and drop mines," Mori said to the XO. Metal and fire twisted through space around Galatea as Mori tracked each threat on her console. A Tornado intercepted one of the Hasha fighters—the irony wasn't lost on her. Galatea's Vulcan turrets put on a show, shredding three Banshees in an impressive display of firepower. A Nyx missile hit another, turning it into space dust. Yet, one pesky fighter dodged death, weaving through the magnetic mines, dancing past Nyx missiles, and shrugging off a laser turret blast before kamikaze crashing into Galatea's upper starboard engine nacelle.

Alarms wailed through the CIC, and the grav generators glitched, tossing everyone off balance —not quite a full inertial dampener failure, but still not anyone's idea of a smooth ride.

The stoic XO rattled off the damage report like he was reading a grocery list. "Engine two's toast. Shields at sixty percent, grav generators holding. Fires along the power grid, but contained. Decks twenty-one to twenty-six locked down."

The bridge thrummed with alarms, and the damaged engine sent shivers through the bulkheads—a not-so-subtle reminder of their brush with disaster.

Then, the engineering officer's voice crackled through, words quick and breathless. "Captain, I've shut off engine one. I'm getting some oscillations in the containment field; if that goes, we all go. Engine three's unstable, but I think she'll hold."

Four engines down to two. Her ship was crippled, and they were far from finished. She tapped a rhythm on her thigh. "Comms, tell the fleet we're taking up rear guard." She gripped the console, head bowing as the setback stung.

"Yes, Captain."

Mori was Relegated to rear guard while her fleet fought on. The acrid smoke from burnt circuits stung her nose—Galatea's pain made physical.

What was left of the Hasha forces wouldn't quit, trading shots up to their fiery end. Surrender didn't seem to be in their playbook, and they hadn't gotten so much as a peep asking for terms. They'd fight to the last. Well, so would she. If the Hasha thought they would cower the Colonial Navy, they'd be wrong—dead wrong.

The mysterious ship still lingered near the jump point, unbothered by the battle. It hadn't budged, even when the Reapers and Revenants went down. Studying, learning—just like she would do. But sending ships to chase it now would be a waste of resources. She tapped the enigmatic dot on her screen, but the signature came up blank, question marks dancing like an annoying riddle. What's your game, you little bugger?

Her focus snapped back to BattleNet, where the displays showed the frenetic dance of war in crisp, unforgiving detail. The Banshees raced to their targets like hornets defending their nest while the thrum of Galatea's point defenses reverberated through the ship, sending vibrations straight into Mori's spine.

The Hasha's attacks, once precise, had gone wild and desperate. Icarus, Argeus, and Shenyang went down—three ships and their crews, gone in moments. But the tide was turning. A Space Hornet pilot's gutsy dive saved Atalanta from a critical hit, flipping the script on the Hasha. The Dauntless and Vindicators swooping back in tipped the scales further, proving again that while speed killed, raw firepower had a charm all its own.

As they tightened their grip on the dwindling Hasha forces, Mori knew it wouldn't be long before they cracked.

"Board's lighting up with new contacts," the XO cut in, his

voice sharp over the bridge's buzz. "Ten light seconds out from Kliinat, bearing three seven seven by two six four, starboard bow. It's Callisto and her group."

"Thanks, XO," she said with a curt nod. Well, that clinched it. The Hasha were finished—between their fleet and Callisto's carrier group, this trap would snap shut like a steel jaw. The Antonov two-step, she'd dubbed it.

Antonov entered the CIC, waving off the usual formalities. "Good work, everyone, but the battle's not over yet; don't bother with me," he said, striding over to Mori. "Well, Captain, I'd say your plan worked. Well done."

Too many good people had died executing her plan for any real celebration. "Yes, sir, thank you. Credit to the pilots, though. They're the ones that executed. They flew right into the jaws of the beast and threw a grenade down its throat."

Antonov's next words clouded their brief celebration. "That's why they're Navy pilots. I just wish I had better news from the ground. Our forces in Naadan are running low on everything—ammo, men. We can't reach anyone on comms or backup radios."

Skip and her marines were down there. Had been down there for hours with no word. Mori forced her attention back to protocol. "Yes, sir. I've been following the battle. If these damn Hasha surrendered, we could throw support their way without risking a catastrophe from orbital strikes."

Antonov locked eyes with her. "There is one thing we can do involving Captain DiMarco and her people. I like it much more now that Callisto's carrier group is here."

Finally, a way to reach the ground forces. Mori leaned in as

Antonov laid out his plan.

"Comms, get me a line to Repulse, STAT," she said.

Chapter 52

Outside the Citadel, Kliinat

Tau Ceti System

December 9, 2681

Carson's bayonet plunged into the enemy with a sickening squelch, the thermal blade slicing through alien flesh with gruesome ease. He fired twice, the bullets following the blade and dropping the Hasha trooper into the dirt. As he sucked in a harsh breath filled with the sharp scents of smoke and sweat, he kneeled and aimed at an unsuspecting Hasha rounding the corner. His bullets punched a neat pattern into the trooper's helmet light.

"That one's for you, Williams," he said.

Whirling around, Carson's focus narrowed to the chaotic battlefield. His blood mingled with someone else's on his armor—probably not a good sign, but at least the lack of burning sensation meant it wasn't Hasha acid eating through to skin. The constant crack of Colonial rifles mixed with thundering frag grenades until Carson's helmet just gave up trying to filter it all. At least the Hasha were getting the worse end of the acoustics.

Marines dashed past him, their boots thundering on the broken pavement. Some faltered, others fell, yet the line pressed forward, driving back the Hasha with relentless fury. Carson rushed to a fallen Marine, but it was too late; her neural was dark. He snatched the Marine's half-empty magazine—no sense in letting it go to waste.

His heart hammered against his ribs as he charged down the cobblestone street, feeling jolts through his exhausted legs with each impact of his boots. Despite their initial surprise and the momentum of his Marines steamrolling the Hasha front line, each advance came at a cost. He'd lost track of Gunny and Andaeer in the opening melee, and Maalek had vanished moments later.

A few steps away, a Klii Marine grappled with a Hasha, who brandished a crackling energy mace. Time slowed as the Hasha lifted its crackling mace, the Marine's armor already smoking where the weapon had grazed it. Without hesitation, Carson fired his M45, peppering the Hasha's flank. The Marine didn't waste the chance, leaping up to thrust her bayonet deep into the Hasha's gut. Green blood sizzled on her armor as the alien fell.

Carson hauled the Marine to her feet. "Still with us?"

"Yes, sir. Just a flesh wound." The Marine nodded, wincing. "I owe you one."

"I'll start a tab. Stick with me." Carson turned, leading the way.

They maneuvered through the streets, treating the urban landscape as an obstacle course—diving for cover, vaulting over debris. Carson's handgun clicked empty, and he tossed it aside with a frustrated grunt. Around another corner, the buzz of Hasha weaponry filled the air, backed by the rumble of something big on tracks. Calls for retreat clashed with his forward momentum.

Gunny and Rodriguez appeared, sprinting around the corner and straight toward Carson.

"Gunny, Rodriguez! I've been looking all over for you," Carson shouted, waving them over.

Gasping, Rodriguez bent over, hands on his knees. "Skip, we need cover. They're advancing with tanks and a shit ton of infantry."

Other Marines raced past, some supporting their wounded comrades. Gunny checked her weapon, her expression tense. "I'm out. Sir, we need to fall back to the Citadel," she said, The scene behind Gunny looked like someone had taken their offensive and put it in a blender set to 'Charlie Foxtrot.'

Carson's advance had devolved into a scramble for survival, reduced to 'run like hell' in under a minute. He'd seen better-organized bar fights back on Corinth. They had to retreat. "Okay, open a channel and tell everyone to pull back. Maybe we can buy time for the fleet to send help." Carson forced his voice into something resembling calm, the kind of tone you'd use to convince yourself the ship wasn't actually on fire.

"I can't, sir. My neural's glitching. It keeps rebooting," Gunny said, smacking her helmet with the heel of her hand. "Stupid thing."

Carson's focus shifted as a squad of Hasha charged their position. He yanked Gunny to the ground as bullets whizzed overhead. Their bullets found gaps in Hasha armor, each hit marked by sprays of green acid that ate into the pavement. Mid-battle, a familiar voice called his name.

"Captain Carson! Over here!"

Carson looked up to see Adaara waving from behind a makeshift barrier, Drakon sniper rifle in hand. Maalek and Andaeer were firing into enemy lines with precise shots. Carson, Gunny, Rodriguez, and their squad scrambled to join them behind the barrier, gulping recycled air through filters clogged with concrete dust and gun smoke.

Gunny took a long swig from her water pack and then eyed Carson. "Those bastards regrouped, sir. We're about to have company—lots of it."

Carson weighed their options. Retreating to the compound was risky, but holding their ground could bog down the Hasha advance. "We must hold this position. This is our line," he decided. "Gunny, organize our defenses."

"Yes, sir. And here they come," Gunny said.

Carson peered over the barricade. Two armored carriers, shaped like starfish, approached, flanked by infantry. The carriers' turrets spun with a menacing whir.

Their barrier took the hits in chunks, each impact sending concrete shrapnel singing past Carson's helmet. It wasn't going to last another minute under this kind of fire, and Carson had run out of fallback positions. Maalek passed him a battle rifle with a knowing look. "I hope you remember how to use this."

Carson managed a tight smile. "Let's find out."

His first shot rang out, aimed at one of the advancing armored personnel carriers. It might as well have been a pebble for all the good it did. A second shot followed, just as ineffective. Around him, the music of battle died down to a desperate finale as the Marines' ammunition ran dry. Each Klii battle rifle fell silent with depressing finality, marking their ammunition status better than any tactical display could.

Then, as if on cue, the Hasha surged forward. Their mass drivers spun up, a deep hum signaling imminent death. A few went down, tagged by the last desperate rounds from the Marines' dwindling supplies, but it wasn't enough. The Hasha pressed on like an unstoppable tide.

"Gunny, fall back. To the Citadel, double-time!" The order rasped out of his throat like he'd been gargling concrete dust, which, given the day's events, wasn't far from the truth. It was retreat or be overrun. "Damn it."

"On it, sir," Gunny snapped back. She turned to the troops, arm slashing through the air. "Everyone, fall back to the compound, now!"

In the middle of their scramble, Carson's neural spat out a burst of static-filled hope. "... On the way... hang tight... we're... ETA two..." He blinked, processing the fragmented lifeline.

"Gunny, are you getting this?" He said, voice almost lost in the noise.

"Nothing but a garbled mess, sir," she said, shouting over the din and lobbing her final grenade over the barrier in a farewell salute. "If we get out of this, I want two minutes alone in a room with the idiot who designed these neurals."

A high-pitched whistle sliced through the battlefield's uproar—sharp and distinctive, like atmosphere giving way to something moving way too fast. Carson's head snapped up. He'd heard that sound before, chilling Marine blood on a dozen battlefields. The Hasha were about to learn what that whistle meant.

Maalek went still, his usual warrior's confidence replaced by something Carson had never seen in his friend's eyes before. "No, it cannot be."

As the figures came into focus through his visor Carson almost laughed. The gods hadn't just shown their hand—they'd flipped the whole damn table. "Bloody hell."

The whistling intensified as a squad of meteoric forms accelerated to the ground. The first figure slammed down between their makeshift defenses and the advancing Hasha—towering at seven feet and wielding a Stinger gun like some ancient goddess of war. She wore the unmistakable, gleaming white and blue armor of Union Archangels. Another Archangel landed with a ground-shaking thud, then another, their thrusters scorching the earth.

As they swept the battlefield, the Archangels unleashed a storm of depleted uranium, their rotary guns a blur. One stumbled under a direct hit but recovered with surprising grace. More whistles, more landings; the sky was raining Archangels.

Carson blinked hard, wondering if that knock to the head was making him hallucinate. But no—those were real

Archangels turning the Hasha advance into a highlight reel of destruction. All those times he'd watched Union propaganda vids of their elite shock troops hadn't done justice to the real thing. Three Archangel Coursers—their *heavy* infantry—hit the Hasha flank, Crusader plasma cannons carving through enemy ranks like divine wrath.

Carson turned as Gunny tugged his arm, pointing up. "Holy shit," he breathed.

A second barrage of streaks tore across the sky. Rockets rained hellfire on one APC after another, transforming them into twisted metal and catching squads of Hasha infantry in the blaze. On the other Hasha flank, Hell Divers landed with all the subtlety of an anvil, their red and black armor etched with the scars of countless battles. Emblazoned on their chests were white symbols of their companies—skulls, dragons, flaming swords, claws. They unleashed devastation, their arm-mounted cluster munitions scything rows of enemy soldiers.

Hell Diver Daemons joined in, landing among the Archangels. Their Vulcan guns spun up, shock-absorber limbs bracing as they mowed down Hasha ranks. The Citadel became a fortress ringed by fire, with more Archangels and Hell Divers streaking in and heavy guns hammering out destruction.

A ragged cheer echoed through Naadan's streets—the sound of Marines who'd just watched certain death transform into certain victory—as Tornado interceptors and Dauntless fighters roared overhead. Their rockets and rotary guns tore into Hasha landing ships and ground forces.

A Hell Diver flanked by two towering Archangels approached Carson. The Hell Diver, sporting Master Sergeant stripes, snapped a crisp salute. "Captain Carson. It was time we repaid you for helping us out of that jam in Kaarja. The Hell Divers have a long memory."

Carson clasped the Master Sergeant's hand, his arm heavy with fatigue but his grip firm. The world still felt slightly unreal—like someone had switched scripts in the middle of their last stand. "Perfect timing, Master Sergeant. Drinks are on me when we hit Corinth."

Gunny joined them, smirking. "Well, well, well, Master Sergeant Cooper. Looks like they'll let anyone be a Hell Diver nowadays. It's damn good to see you."

"Hey, Gunny. Hope you don't mind the interruption," Cooper said with a grin.

Gunny's curiosity piqued. "Callisto wasn't due for another twelve hours. How the hell did you pull this off? We thought the fleet was too busy to pay mind to us ground pounders."

"Captain Kalani lit a fire under the afterburners and jumped us ahead of schedule. We hitched a ride with the Archangels on a Union light carrier that beat the Hasha fleet here. Our boats are mopping up what's left upstairs, so here we are," Cooper said. He then turned to Carson. "Sir, we'll take it from here. More help's on the way, plus supplies. You take your team back to the Citadel; we'll handle cleanup."

Carson wanted to laugh or cry, maybe both. He'd been in more scraps than he could count and dodged more bullets than seemed fair, but he never felt as close to his last breath as today. "That sounds like a great plan, Master Sergeant," he said.

"Thank you, sir. By the way, that charge? Ballsy as hell. Oorah."

Chapter 53

Adaara's Palace, Kliinat

Tau Ceti System

January 10, 2682

Maalek woke before sunrise, just like in his days in the Free Army, and now in the Colonial Navy. Instead of jumping out of bed, his body urged him to linger on the cozy sleeping mat. Adaara's gentle breathing next to him almost lulled him back to sleep. He'd hoped for a lazy morning, but his internal clock had other ideas.

Last night, Adaara had thrown a fancy dinner party for the Council of 64 Ministers and Colonial big shots. For Maalek, more soldier than socialite, playing her plus-one among the political crowd felt strange, but he stood tall beside her. His military bearing softened around her natural grace, like a warrior's shield finding unexpected harmony with a diplomat's silk. In those moments, the stares from others reminded him how far they'd both come from their separate paths. Everyone wanted time with her, so they'd cooked up a system of secret signals to rescue her from long-winded conversations. By night's end, Maalek had mastered the art of whisking her from group to group. She'd play along, pretending to be annoyed: "Oh, Maalek, must we go? The General and I are having such a lovely chat."

He would respond in mock seriousness, "Indeed, Your Primeship, but you promised Minister Gael you would listen to his education proposal."

During one of these escapes, Adaara steered him to a quiet garden for a quick break. They settled on an old bench under a massive tree, its gnarly roots hinting at years of stories. Soft torchlights cast a warm glow, making everything feel cozy and private. Her faithful guards kept watch, never straying too far. Those ten minutes in the garden were pure bliss.

Maalek ran his fingers through Adaara's short hair, then pressed a kiss to her forehead. Careful not to wake her, he rolled off the mat and tiptoed away. The wooden floor stayed quiet, letting him reach the balcony without a creak. He eased open the double doors, letting the fresh morning air in. Behind him, Adaara mumbled something unintelligible, pulled the blanket over her head, and drifted off again.

On the balcony, Maalek let the cool breeze tug at his white sleeping gown. He leaned on the fancy gold railing, taking in the view. Adaara's summer place, perched on a hill, looked out over Neskfaat's tallest mountain. Its snow-capped peak stood out against the lilac meadows below. To the west, a short walk from the house was Lake Eetza, often packed during Pincer Fish season. If not for the war, the lake would already buzz with eager fishermen and boats. Everyone knew dawn was prime time for hauling in the abundant catch. Every glimpse of Kliinat's lilac meadows and snow-capped peaks reminded him what they'd fought for—not just survival, but the right to wake up to this view, to build something worth defending.

Wildlife calls grew louder as the fog lifted, showing off the world in all its glory. The first sunbeams hit the lake's surface, oblivious to the warships hanging in orbit thousands of kilometers up. In a few days, Maalek would join that fleet. He wrestled with how to tell Adaara—the weight of his uniform hanging in the corner pulled at him even as Adaara's sleeping form anchored him to this moment, this peace he'd have to leave behind again.

So much had changed for Maalek and his people. For three years, he'd dreamed of reuniting with his family and hugging his daughters when he reached the shores of the Great Sea. But the Goddess Amunkeera had other plans, tying his fate to Adaara's. The Goddess' wisdom had surprised him—showing him how love could feel both familiar and entirely new, like discovering a different melody in a well-known prayer. He still loved Sanya, but he knew she'd approve of his new companion.

Each step closer to Adaara felt like a step away from Sanya's memory, until he learned his heart could hold both—past love and present hope, like two stars sharing the same sky. But as time passed and things settled, he grew sure they could build a life together—one dedicated to leading their people to a brighter future.

He lingered longer than usual at the balcony, Sanya's name catching in his throat even as Adaara's presence warmed the room behind him, but deep down, he knew his family would welcome him when it was time to join them.

Maalek shut the doors, headed back in, and made for the basin. He splashed cool water on his face, washing away the cobwebs, then scrubbed his hands and feet, enjoying the refreshing feel as he dried off.

He walked to the corner where Adaara had set up an altar for the Daia. Twelve small statues formed a circle on a rustic wooden table. In the middle, a stone bowl held clear water. Maalek unrolled a prayer mat, laid it out, and knelt.

He dipped his fingers in the bowl, sprinkled water on each statue to purify them, and then did the same to himself. He recited names of fallen comrades, friends, and neighbors. When he got to his wife and daughters, he slowed down, each name heavier than the last. Head bowed, eyes closed, he asked for forgiveness. "Kaalahera, mistress of inscrutable depths, wash the sins of this humble servant on the crisp waters of the never-ending falls. I ask forgiveness for the lives I took, for the lives I could not save. I ask forgiveness for the lives that I must yet take."

Maalek turned, surprised to see Adaara kneeling silently beside him. She took the water bowl, sprinkling him as she prayed. "Amunkeera, mistress of love and understanding, this man's heart remains untainted yet troubled by memories of past deeds. Guide him toward the shores where hearths never grow cold, where the memories of loved ones never fade." Their eyes met over the prayer bowl, and her touch on his cheek spoke what words couldn't—that she understood the warrior's path wasn't just duty, but part of who he was, just as leadership was part of her. "I know the weight you carry, and I will share the burden with you." Her lips curved in that knowing smile he'd come to recognize. "And since I have many spies, I know you will rejoin the fleet when Galatea returns."

Maalek's shoulders relaxed—the tension he'd been carrying since receiving his orders melted away, like morning fog under Kliinat's sun. "I didn't know how to tell you," he said.

"I am no youngling, Maalek. Speak what needs to be spoken. Each day without you will be like a moonless night, but I understand this is the path you must tread."

"Will you wait for me?" he asked.

"For as long as it takes."

Maalek smiled. "Then I shall swiftly vanquish our enemies."

"You had better come back to me alive. Because if you do not, I will kill you myself," Adaara said, a smile flickering across her face.

Maalek grinned. "I will find a place in the rear to keep myself safe."

A glimmer danced in Adaara's eyes. "I know you will not."

His smile widened. "No, I will not."

"And I love you the more for it. When do you depart?" she asked.

"In three days."

"We have time, then, to relish this respite," Adaara said. "I have yet to treat you to my famous grilled Pincer Fish. Let us venture to the lake tonight and indulge in some fishing."

"I would love that," Maalek said.

"First, let us freshen up with a shower, and then we will join Lord General Graal and his wife for breakfast," Adaara said.

"Ah, well, this is rather awkward. You see, I... um... must report to base today. Last-minute orders. Please convey my regards to the Lord General."

Adaara kissed his cheek. "I see Captain Carson's influence has rubbed off on you. Come, the sooner we start, the sooner we will be done, and we can enjoy these next few days in peace."

She headed for the washroom, letting her gown fall. Maalek's eyes followed her, then he got up and joined her.

Each morning prayer now held different names, different hopes. The warrior's path remained, but now it led back to Adaara's gardens instead of the shores of the Great Sea. He lost old friends, made new ones. He found himself checking the sky more often these days, not just for threats but to count the days until he could return to this place, to her quiet breathing in the morning light. Adaara was his anchor now, holding him steady in the storm. Even after two invasions, his people hadn't broken. The hardship had only made them tougher, more determined.

Maalek breathed in the morning air as the sun crept over the horizon. They had allies now, good ones. The odds were still stacked against them, but when had that stopped the Klii? As long as one of them was left standing, the fight would go on.

Maalek squinted at the sky, where the faintest stars were still visible. Somewhere out there, the Hasha threat loomed. But he was ready. Whatever came next, he'd face it head-on, under these   shattered   stars   they   all   called   home.

Epilogue

Tier Two, Corinth Station

Athenian Space

January 13, 2682

Carson indulged in the universal pastime of coffee drinking at Café Lupin on bustling Corinth Station—a place that swung between cozy and cramped, depending on who you asked. The air was filled with the scent of roasted coffee beans and the promise of pastries so fresh, rumor had it the flour still dreamt of breezes on the wheat fields of Platea. A sugar cube met its end in his cappuccino, adding just the right touch of sweetness to his drink.

With the practiced motion of a seasoned pro, he tapped the spoon against the cup's rim, shaking off excess foam, before placing it on the table. He paused for a moment before taking that very important first sip.

Glancing at the time, Carson realized he still had a few precious hours before he needed to board the ship bound for

Alexandria. The well-deserved two-week liberty allowed him to spend time with his family and enjoy the comforts of home, even if only for a short while. His mom and sister still held out hope he'd discover a sudden passion for accounting or maybe space station administration—anything that involved fewer explosions. But they'd gotten better at hiding their winces when he told stories over dinner. Sure, the Colonies and the Union might not be at each other's throats anymore, but a far more treacherous enemy lurked in the depths of space.

He leaned back, people-watching. Corinth Station buzzed with tourists and travelers, each with a story. Sailors and Marines strolled by, medals on their uniforms telling tales of bravery, stupidity, or sometimes both. But they all knew the steep price of "peace." The war might be over, but its ghost still hung around.

Well, one war is over, he mused.

Once the Hasha fleet had been defeated in the battle over Kliinat, Earth's new government had extended an olive branch to the Colonies. Everyone knew it was really a cry for help. Athens answered by sending their best to Sol—the carriers Perseus and Callisto. On the surface, they were there to boost Earth's defenses against the Hasha, but Carson figured it was also a "keep your friends close, enemies closer" kind of deal.

After the Colonial carriers proved their mettle in Kliinat, he doubted anyone on Earth would be foolish enough to pick a fight with them. A lot of bitterness remained between the two sides, but the relationship between Earth and the Colonies had improved from "Begrudging" to "Tentatively Not Trying to Kill Each Other." The return of the Lyra system back to Athens was a significant gesture, a sign that maybe this time, they could have lasting peace. Lyra had been a sore point since the First War of Independence, and Athens had wanted it back ever since. With Lyra's citizens ready to vote, their overwhelming support would soon make rejoining the Colonies a reality.

The Second Battle of Kliinat had kicked things into high gear, with Kliinat on track to become colony number twenty-three by year's end. Carson got a taste of what peace might look like during a week at Adaara's place for the celebration. But that future had to wait; first, they needed to sort out new alliances, new possibilities, and getting Klii citizens into Colonial forces.

Anderson and Atalanta, now part of a joint fleet stationed at Eridani, prepared for the assault on Cancri. Even the most ardent anti-Union politicians in the Athenian Senate were outraged at the sheer scale of the destruction the Hasha brought when they redecorated Eridani: three million lives lost, and the system turned into a desolate wasteland that would take generations to restore. The bill for the Colonies to join forces with the Union passed without a single "no." Carson figured his battalion would be in on the ground assault, though he hadn't gotten official orders yet. Maybe Captain Mori had asked to meet him at Café Lupin to tell him in person?

As Carson contemplated the upcoming battle, his gaze landed on young Marines. Their unmistakable air of invincibility and confidence marked them as fresh graduates from boot camp. He couldn't help but feel a pang of familiarity—he'd been in their boots once, full of bravado and a whole lot of dumb.

The faces of friends he'd lost drifted through his mind— Drystaan, Muller, Ortega. He'd gotten good at writing condolence letters, but that wasn't the kind of skill he'd ever wanted to perfect. He'd been to all their memorials, and even stood at Muller's family plot in Platea. His heart ached, but there was a silver lining; Williams had somehow pulled through. She was in for a long recovery back on Persephone, but her spirit was unbroken. Word was, she was driving the hospital staff crazy.

His mind drifted to Jammer, who'd been MIA for hours after punching out of his Dauntless. Space had almost claimed him, but fate had other plans. Carson joked that even space didn't want him. Rescue teams found him just this side of unconsciousness, but alive and mouthy as ever. He was back running Galatea's CAP in a week with a shiny new Navy Cross pinned on his chest.

The buzz of his tablet snapped Carson back. He thumbed it open to find a message from Lieutenant Akitani. Each swipe through Akitani's photos loosened something in his chest. That familiar cocky grin of hers, that spark in her eyes—some things even Hasha rounds couldn't change.

First shot: Akitani flexing her new cybernetic arm. Second: her crushing an iron kettlebell with said arm. It made him wonder if being a bit more machine and a bit less bullet magnet might not be such a bad idea.

Mori's approach in civvies brought him back to reality. There she was, commanding attention, her presence drawing eyes in a way that had nothing to do with her rank. Carson stood, saluting more out of habit than need. He tried to keep his voice regulation-crisp, but something softer slipped through anyway, like it always did with her.

Mori took her seat, greeting him with a casual wave. "Hey,

Skip. Been here long?" she said.

Carson paused, choosing his words. "Yes and no. I've been relaxing, watching people come and go. It's been... nice."

She nodded. "I enjoy it too. I was headed to change into uniform. Galatea departs this afternoon, and I didn't want to keep you waiting. Sorry, I'm late."

Her apology wasn't needed, but he appreciated it. "It's not a problem, ma'am."

Mori's gaze shifted to his empty cup. "Ready for a refill?"

"Sure."

She flagged down a server, flashed a V-sign for two more coffees, then turned back to Carson. "Heard you extended past your OBLISERV. It couldn't have been an easy decision. I wanted to catch up before we redeploy—I'm glad you're staying," she said.

If there was ever a time to seize the moment, this was it. The Navy had stringent rules about fraternization and severe penalties for transgressions. He would never violate those rules or put his Captain in a moral hazard, but he had to know.

"Is that the only reason you're glad, Captain?" The question hung in the air, each passing second feeling heavier than the one before.

Mori tilted her head, eyes locked on him. The server dropped off two coffees with a subtle smile, leaving some sugar packets behind. As Mori sipped her coffee, she kept her eyes on Carson, not dodging his question. A tiny trickle of regret hit him, but he couldn't un-ring that bell.

"It's not. But that's all I'm saying." She looked away, and was that a sigh? "That's all I can say."

His chest tightened with contradictory sensations: the lift of possibility and the weight of regulations he'd sworn to uphold. Neither of them would—could—do anything about it.

"I understand. I just... needed to know. I won't bring it up again, Captain." He kept his voice light despite the weight on his chest.

"Thank you," she said. The silence felt like those endless seconds between seeing incoming fire and hearing the impact— charged with anticipation and just a touch of fear. After a beat, she asked. "And you, Matt... do you feel the same way?"

For once, he didn't hesitate, nor did the words tumble out of his mouth to form an anxiety salad—which was basically his trademark. "Yes," he said. That simple, unspoken-till-now word lifted that boulder off his chest, leaving behind something lighter, something that felt a lot like peace. And now he couldn't un-ring that bell either. "It's a torch I don't mind carrying. It's strange, but I'd miss it if it wasn't there."

Her smile lit up her face in a way that made him forget, just for a moment, about rank insignias and chain of command. "It's not strange at all. One day, when I'm no longer a Navy officer and you're not a Marine Captain, we'll have coffee again, or dinner, and we'll have all the time in the world to talk about everything we can't right now," she said, her eyes softening as she tucked a stray hair back.

Carson had no delusions. Mori would be off commanding fleets and tying the knot with some hero out of a Navy poster, while he had a date with a bullet with his name on it.

But then, something shifted in his chest, like the first ray of sunrise breaking through storm clouds. Maybe that bullet wasn't as inevitable as he'd always thought. Sitting here with her, sharing truths they'd both kept under lock and key, made him wonder what other impossible moments were waiting their turn. His heart did that thing it usually reserved for incoming fire, but this time it wasn't about dodging bullets. The future suddenly felt as vast and unpredictable as space itself.

His smile started in his eyes before reaching his lips, the kind of real smile he'd almost forgotten how to make.. "I know the perfect place, too. It has spectacular views of Athens, and the coffee is pretty good. It's my favorite spot to watch people come and go," he said.

"It's a date." Mori set her coffee down. "So, any plans while you're in Alexandria?" she asked.

"I promised Gianna I'd take her and the kids fishing at Dad's old spot. She loves it there," Carson said.

Mori pulled a strand of hair behind her ear and reached across the table to touch his hand. "Tell me all about it over lunch. I have a couple of hours to spare."